51
Weeks

51
Weeks

Julia Myerscough

Matador
9 Priory Business Park,
Wistow Road, Kibworth Beauchamp,
Leicestershire. LE8 0RX
Tel: 0116 279 2299
Email: books@troubador.co.uk
Web: www.troubador.co.uk/matador
Twitter: @matadorbooks

ISBN 978 1788032 957

British Library Cataloguing in Publication Data.
A catalogue record for this book is available from the British Library.

Printed and Bound in the UK by 4Edge Limited.
Typeset in 11pt Minion Pro by Troubador Publishing Ltd, Leicester, UK

Matador is an imprint of Troubador Publishing Ltd

*For those who believed in me and inspired me
to write this story.*

I recently learned that we have fifty thousand thoughts a day. Just think: a fleeting thought that you or I might have at any point in a twenty-four-hour period has the potential to change our lives, transform the lives of others or affect the future.

So, if enough people tell you that something *you* think is a really good idea is a seriously *bad* one, should you listen to the sceptics and let your good idea pass you by? If Dyson had listened to his critics and given up on his idea for a bagless vacuum cleaner, my life would be much less rewarding and meaningful (watching the amount of dust being sucked up from my lounge carpet is just the best...). However, I digress.

We were on our family holiday when I had *my* good idea. You know, that much-longed-for yet often overrated event during our so-called summer? The occasion that the average person spends eleven months dreaming and romanticising over? Well, my husband Geoff, an incredibly busy accountant who simply can't stomach the thought of being away from his desk for more than a week at a time, agreed for us to go away to the Isle of Wight for six nights in early September to mark the end of his fiftieth birthday celebrations.

Reclining in a deckchair, a glass of wine in my hand and the sun beating down on my face, I was half-listening to him chuntering on about how wonderful his fiftieth celebrations had been when an innocuous question kick-started my thought process.

"It's not long until your fiftieth, Amy. What are you thinking of doing?"

Those few words unlocked something within me. Of course, I'd been aware of the approaching landmark birthday for years, but right at that moment, something about the thought of turning fifty put me distinctly on edge, and I started to think about it – *really* think about it. I stared fixedly at the sea, tears pricking my eyes, no longer aware of anyone or anything around me. Subconsciously, I could hear chatter, laughter and screams, yet they made no impression. I shut my eyes, inhaled deeply and absorbed the salty sea air into my lungs as I sought clarity and focus. My breathing slowed. I became still and chewed on my finger with frustration.

This milestone means something to me; it means much more than a piss-up that I'll have to organise. I want more than that. I want… what exactly do I want? I don't know.

And it was on the way home from that holiday, when we took our daughters, Pippa and Evie (fifteen and ten years old respectively) to the Sir Frank Whittle Jet Heritage Centre, that it all became clear.

A riveting short film describing Sir Frank's life and achievements is playing. Emotion wells up inside me. "What a man," I whisper to Evie, wiping my eyes. "He let his imagination run free, took on a challenge, came up against brick walls – but he had a go. Inventing the jet engine changed lives around the world." It is my eureka moment.

"Mr Whittle, you have *inspired* me," I say aloud. Somebody to my right tuts disapprovingly. *I know what to do,* I scream internally. *Oh my God – I think I've just had an epiphany.* The room is suddenly unbearably hot. Muttering something to Geoff about runny noses and tissues, I somehow make it to the foyer. *I must experiment and experience,* I think to myself, pacing up and down. My thought process and my pacing synchronise and quicken. *Yes,* I hiss under my breath. *I will challenge myself and get to know myself better. It's time to break out of my comfort zone and try out new things – stuff I secretly dream of doing but never believe I can or should. When I am old, I must be able to shout* "Je ne regrette rien!"

Five minutes later, my family find me running wildly around the car park outside the entrance to the Heritage Centre. "Mum!

Mum! What's wrong with you?" shouts Pippa. "Have you gone *mad?* Stop it, you're *embarrassing me.*" She turns and runs back inside the building. I stop. The initial adrenaline rush has passed. I lean against a bench, my lungs burning, and tear off my fleece jacket. As I regain my composure and cool down, I exhale so sharply that Evie and Geoff are concerned.

"Mum?" Evie hugs me.

"Oh yes, sweetie," I reply calmly, hugging her back and smiling broadly. "I am absolutely fine." And, for the first time in a very long time, I have uttered the absolute truth. I am fine.

9.00 p.m.

We have been home three hours. Geoff is somewhere on his laptop and I have the joyous post-holiday task of sorting piles of dirty clothing into organised molehills. I must get a wash on, and fast. It's getting late, I have work tomorrow and I need some 'me time' before bed. I toil frenetically to clear the mess around me. There's no time to lose. I simply *have* to harness this energy bubbling inside me. I laugh to myself. Goodness, if I were connected to the national grid right now, I'd be able to light up the whole of our town.

By ten o'clock, Evie is in bed, Pippa is still unpacking (and will be for weeks to come) and Geoff is totally engrossed in a TV programme about Ancient Rome. Good. I won't be missed. Time to start work. I sneak upstairs, throw on my PJs, jump into bed, snuggle down and prepare to brainstorm onto my laptop. Now then. I chew on my finger as I try to concentrate. *Think, Amy. What is this about? Things to do when I'm fifty? Things to do before I'm fifty? Fifty Shades of Fifty? Ha ha! A bucket list for the fifty-year-old?* Fine if I was planning my funeral, which I am not. I need inspiration. Sod it, I need wine.

Geoff catches me scuttling back upstairs with my second large glass of Pinot Grigio and fires a stern laser-beam look in my direction. We've made a pact to be alcohol-free during the week, and I have now broken it. What he doesn't know, however, is that having a drink in my hand helps my creativity. At work, I always have a cup of something (non-alcoholic, of course) close by. Without a drink, I feel bereft.

Two glasses of wine later, my mental block clears when I Google 'Things to do before you are 50' and 'Bucket lists for the over-50s'. I think I've got it. I am going to take on a number of challenges and adventures, falling into four categories:

Face my Fears.
Self-Improvement.
Good Deeds.
Bad Stuff.

I lie back and smile to myself. I am on my way.

"Do you know?" I remark to Geoff over dinner a fortnight later. "It's interesting how many people have tried to put me off doing this. They look at me as if I'm off my head. D'you secretly think that too? Geoff, are you listening?"

Geoff is busy checking out the bran cake I bake exclusively for him every weekend.

"Mmm. This effort looks interesting. Fig and apple? I don't think you're mad." He pokes the cake with his index finger. "It's a sensible project, Amy. We both know the value of continuous self-improvement and personal development, don't we? We have personal development plans at work, so why not have one at home too? How many challenge ideas did you say you have?"

"Six. I'm not good at this sort of thing. Do you have any ideas?"

"Ask around and try the web."

"Can you think of any challenges, Geoff?"

"Encourage Pippa to put her crap away instead of leaving it here," he says, pointing to her school bag and shoes that are lying under the kitchen table.

"That's not quite what I meant."

"Leave your list with me, Amy. I'll have a think."

I take Geoff's advice and bravely hijack my work colleagues in meetings, corridors and even the toilets. I slowly but surely develop an eclectic range of challenge ideas. The list becomes my best friend and goes everywhere with me. "I can't stop looking at it," I say to Pippa, holding it to my chest. "It's like it's my new baby."

"That's just stupid, Mum," she replies curtly. "Get a grip."

But I can't 'get a grip', and every time I steal a look at my beloved list, I am filled with excitement, trepidation and resolve.

3.00 a.m.
I wake up in a cold sweat. I have had another brilliant idea. I sit up in bed as slowly and carefully as I can so as not to disturb Geoff, attempt to pull open my bedside cabinet drawer in the darkness, and delve around for paper and a pen. I am not quiet enough. He hears me scrabbling about.

"*Amy*, what *are* you doing?" I hear him tearing open a strip of tablets and swallowing one with water. "Won't get my seven hours now," he mutters, "I'll have a bad head." I don't speak. I have done enough damage for tonight but I simply cannot let this idea go. I *have* to write it down – right now. I slip out of bed, go downstairs and turn on the kitchen light, blinking at the sudden brightness. I hunt out my laptop, sit at the kitchen table and tap furiously.

"My final task will be to write a book, magazine article or blog describing the challenges and adventures I experience. It will motivate and inspire all those reaching fifty and beyond. I will provide invaluable information and guidance to the discerning reader contemplating a similar journey." I smile to myself. I like that.

Adriano's Restaurant. Friday, 8.00 p.m.
'The Girls' are a band of sisters united by our families and a love of wine, spa days, coffee and gossip. We've known each other for years and get together on the final Friday of every month.

Our catchphrase is: 'Never forget the six degrees of separation'. In our small North Cumbrian town, instead of six degrees of separation, however, it is only two or three – and we know *never* to divulge any information outside our perfectly formed ring of friendship that may be considered of 'value' to others. For example, three years ago, Geoff hired a decorator. Within a day, I learned that he knew Evie's swimming teacher, whose son dated my boss. And *everybody* knew about *that* scandal. The number of secrets we share is incalculable. Our objective is to never become the subject of mindless tittle-tattle ourselves, thank you very much.

After the usual cathartic dump about work, partners, children, school and all the other important stuff we need to get off our chests since we last met – oh, and after the consumption of a bottle or two of Pinot Grigio, conversation turns to the list. With bated breath, I unveil my 'good idea', present my long list of potential challenges and ask my dear friends – Bea, Claire and Cate – for their honest opinion. To my delight, they really like the idea.

"Oooh – I never knew you had such a dark side, pet. It's bloody brilliant. Can we join in with some of them?" enthuses Bea.

I take a sip of wine and consider Bea's request. Oh, I'd love The Girls to share my year with me; we'd have so much fun. However, deep down I know that this is something I must do on my own.

"Right," I say. "I've just made a decision. I'd like you three to decide on my challenges. These," I say, waving my list in the air, "are suggestions only. Perhaps you've other ideas? What I do will be entirely up to you. My final challenge will be to write a book or whatever about my experiences, but you can choose the rest. Write them down on these slips of paper. Decide which category they fall into, fold them up so they can't be read and put them into this bowl. Don't, under *any* circumstance, tell me anything about them. Okay?"

"You can rely on us to give you something to remember," smiles Bea. "Lots of – what's that last category again? Ah yes, *Bad Stuff*."

"Hmmm, that concerns me slightly," I chuckle. "I'll be back in a few minutes."

Twenty minutes later, we count up the number of slips in the bowl. "Blimey, we have fifty challenges," I say in surprise. "Plus the one I've already decided on, of course." We look at each other in silence and then it all falls into place.

"Well," says Claire, "it's obvious, isn't it? That means there's one challenge a week for your fiftieth year and a week off for Christmas."

Sorted.

January

Randomly picking out:

FUNDRAISE FOR A GOOD CAUSE

as the first of the challenges had felt like the perfect opportunity to throw an impromptu party and welcome the start of my fiftieth year – my Year of Adventure and Self-Discovery – and to launch the list and nail challenge one. I have decided that the money raised will go to our local branch of Age UK, an apt choice considering that, all too soon, I'll be a fully fledged member of the 'third age'.

The party has been in full swing for a couple of hours. The list, now entitled '51 Weeks, 51 Challenges', is proudly displayed on the wall, and a huge 'Good luck, Amy' banner swings across the windows. A donations bucket is rapidly filling with loose change and the bar is doing a roaring trade. The raffle tickets have sold well at £1 a strip, with the winner – my boss (of all people) – having the honour of pulling the second week's challenge from the now officially named 'Bowl of Chance and Opportunity', which has pride of place on the kitchen table.

I stand amongst my guests, chewing absentmindedly on my finger and staring intently at the fifty folded slips of paper sitting in the bowl. I take a mental photo of the scene before me: the familiar – my family, my friends and my neighbours, and the unfamiliar – the Bowl of Chance and Opportunity. I pick it up.

1

A frisson of panic runs down my spine. *Oh, my Lord*, I think. *It's nearly time to plunge into the unknown.* Although I am super-excited, for some inexplicable reason I cannot shake a feeling of dread. I'm pretty sure that many of the challenges will test me in ways I can barely imagine. I turn to Bea for a confidence boost. "Why am I scared, Bea? I badly want to do this but I have absolutely no idea what's coming next. What if I don't like it?" I trail off.

"What you're feeling is completely normal, pet," laughs Bea, hugging me close. "Why are you so down? It's going to be an exciting year for you, and if you really don't think it's working, you can always drop out. No one will mind. It's just a bit of fun, really, isn't it? Something to spice up our boring and predictable old lives?" She takes my hand and drops her voice. "Although, pet, I hope you don't bail," she says seriously, her hazel eyes flicking around the room before settling back on me. "I think you might regret it if you do. There's a lot of interesting adventures waiting for you in that bowl. You're going to have the time of your life and learn a lot – as long as you want to. Your grandma will be proud." Her tone lightens. "Hey, it's your fiftieth year!" Snatching up the bottle of Pinot Grigio from the table, she tops up our glasses. "Stop gnawing on your finger," she giggles. "Get this down you, turn up the music… and let's boogie."

Midnight.
I have drunk rather more than my limit of three alcoholic drinks and have seamlessly progressed into the 'I don't care how much I consume because I feel really good, and it tastes nice' phase.

Geoff makes his obligatory 'good luck' speech and proudly announces that the evening has raised a whopping £200. He stands on the kitchen table, praises me for my courage and ingenuity, kisses me on the cheek and wishes me lots of luck. Everybody cheers and Pippa takes snaps for posterity on her mobile – her permanent appendage. I hear somebody whisper,

"Let's hope Geoff doesn't regret the chaos that this might cause," and I snigger uncontrollably. I'm so damn nervous, yet I just can't wait to get started and find out what this year will bring.

I straighten my glasses and watch in a drunken haze as my boss is ceremoniously presented with the Bowl of Chance and Opportunity by Evie, who fiddles nervously with the toggle on her yellow hoodie. In slow motion, he pulls out the second challenge. It is:

GET A SET OF HD BROWS.

Week Two. Friday.
What the hell are HD brows, exactly? All I know is that every time I suffer an eyebrow wax, Harmony, my beautician, remarks on my beautifully shaped brows and says that they would *so* benefit from the HD experience. Pippa looks over my shoulder and takes a photo of the challenge in my hand. "Mum, you are going to look *great* with HDs," she snorts. "Do you realise that your and my credibility will be zero if you get them done? *No one* your age should have them."

That, of course, is not the point, so I ignore her and pluck up the courage to casually ask what the 'HD' stands for. She looks at me incredulously and yells, "You know, like HD TV – high-definition."

"Oh. Thanks," I stammer. *Ah-ha*, I think. *Now I know. High-definition means higher resolution, which means bigger and bolder... on my face?* I experience a vivid flashback to a Christmas party where I simply could not take my eyes off the number of clown-like, thick black eyebrows staring back at me. Oh God, oh no.

It is late evening, and Geoff and I are in bed. I casually mention to him that I am going to visually enhance my eyebrows. I like the sound of this definition; it exudes sophistication.

"What's that, then?" he murmurs from behind his iPad, his eyes still on the screen. "Does it cost?" I don't think he is really listening. I poke him. I am worked up with excitement and I want to share this moment with him.

"Hey, are you listening? This is my first real challenge."

He hasn't a clue what I'm going on about. I still don't either, but I don't want to seem uneducated, so I authoritatively explain. "Thicker and darker eyebrows are on trend, and..." In one long breath, I shoot out a definition that I memorised earlier from a fantastic article I found in my lunch break on Browbabes.com.

I exhale and wait for his reaction. Nil. However, I am prepared for this. I take another deep breath and fire out what I consider to be a simply awesome reason for having the brows: "HDs emphasise your eyes, frame your face and make you appear rested, as if you have been on holiday". Ta-dah. I breathe out again. There is a pause. Geoff lays down his iPad and rubs his tired grey eyes that so remind me of Pippa's. Then he fastens them on me.

"Why *on Earth* do you want to look like a clown, Amy?" he yawns. "I've seen those brows on the girls at work." He notices the time. "Ha. 11.20." He takes his customary drink of water and turns out the light without waiting for me to close my book. We lie in the darkness in an embrace and I feel him drift off to sleep.

Saturday, 10.00 a.m.
How to get the best HD brows ever? I sit at the kitchen table imagining the admiring looks and comments I will receive. However, I'm not totally convinced. The Clown Brows tag just won't go away and I have got major butterflies.

What is it that I fear about this challenge? I ask myself, taking a bite of fruit scone. *I'll ring Cate for advice and reassurance. She has a monthly facial, so she might know. And she is sensible, placid and pragmatic.* I finish my scone and make the call.

"Hi, Ames – how's things?"

"Will getting the HDs be a bit like a trip to the hairdressers, Cate?" I ask. "You know, kinda like when I was in my late teens and experimenting with my hairstyle and colour? I'd go in with an idea of what I'd like and I'd always take one of those hair mags along so that we could discuss it first. Is the HD experience like that?"

"I've never had it done myself, but last time I tried a new hairdresser for a cut and colour, I ended up in tears 'cos the 'warm brown' turned out almost black and made me look like a washed-out witch. Luckily, it was semi-permanent, so it faded after a few dozen washes," she laughs.

My finger automatically moves to my mouth and I begin to chew rhythmically. "How can I best minimise the risk of a total disaster?"

"Go to someone you know and trust – like Harmony, perhaps – and remember that they will eventually fade," Cate chortles.

I spend the entire afternoon scrutinising copies of *Now* and *Heat* magazines, rating celebrities and their brows and assembling a collage of 'Best Brows' that I will take with me to the beautician's on the appointed day.

"When are you going, Mum?" asks Pippa, casting her eye over my efforts.

"I'll call Harmony at the salon on Monday, but I have until Friday to complete this challenge, so there's plenty of time," I smile.

"Just let me know the day so that I can warn all my friends," is her catty reply. "Why don't you just forget about this one and move onto the next? Who'll know and who'll care? Is it really that important to do them all? You're too old and you're going to look terrible. I hope all your other challenges aren't as inappropriate."

I pick up the Bowl of Chance and Opportunity, and as I stir the contents with my finger, a swirling fireball of determination surges through me.

"What will be will be," I say brightly. "*I* care and I *will* complete all fifty-one challenges, whatever it takes. Nobody is going to persuade me otherwise. This is my first real test, so please accept it and be happy for me."

This is non-negotiable. Don't give in to her, I say to myself. Inside, I'm whimpering. There are another forty-nine 'tests' to go; one to work through every seven days. This one seems bad enough. What is to come? What have I done?

I find an article on the internet entitled 'Avoid Scouse Brows', print it out and put it in my bag. Now I feel slightly better. I have absolute evidence of the look I definitely don't want. What can go wrong?

Monday afternoon.
The proud owner of two dark facial slugs attempts to slink seductively down the road, trying to catch her reflection in every shop window she passes. I deliberately outstare people to check out their reaction. I think that they are grinning appreciatively but it's not easy to tell. I don't half feel self-conscious. This just feels so *wrong*. I speed-walk to the car park to find a decent mirror.

It is only when I'm back in my car that I am able to fully appreciate the full HD effect, and I don't like what I see – not one little bit. My eyebrows have been tinted, waxed and plucked, and they look as if they have been stencilled onto my forehead with black marker pen. They are *dark*. This isn't just high-definition – it's high-intensity. I look seriously scary. How can I go home or – even worse – go anywhere else looking like this? I need to think – and fast. I grab my mobile. I know who to call in a crisis.

"Bea, I have the brows," I wail.

"Do you look rested, as if you have been on holiday, then, pet?"

"No. I'm supporting two leeches and it looks as if I've been the victim of a Stag night prank. I don't feel at all in touch with the youth of today, I just feel bloody stupid. The phrase 'mutton dressed as lamb' springs to mind. What can I do?" I squeak. I hear frantic tapping from Bea's end. A number of options race through my head. I could wear a very stretchy hat pulled down low over my forehead, or shave them off and pencil them back on…

"It says here that the tint is semi-permanent and will gradually wear off with water," she says.

I am reminded of what Cate told me about her hair colour fiasco. "So, should I do that, then?"

"I think so," replies Bea. "Send me a selfie, pet, and let me assess you." I do as she asks and wait for the inevitable reaction. "Ha ha, pet – start scrubbing."

9.00 p.m.

"I hope my challenges aren't all like this one," I mutter into my bathroom mirror as I bathe my eyebrows in shampoo. "I can't believe it was given to me as a warning against future fashion faux pas?" And then, all of a sudden, I get it. "It's important to keep in touch with the youth of today because it'll keep me young in mind, body and spirit," I say aloud to my reflection. I pause. "And," I almost shout at myself, "I recognise the importance of remaining connected to my children as they grow up. If I do, I'll have a better chance of being able to support them through the ups and downs of life. I must find better ways of keeping the communication channels open, mind. Getting a set of HD slugs will never help me to do that. Lesson learned."

Week Four. Friday, 6.30 p.m.

Pippa draws my next challenge, reads it to herself and mutters something under her breath. "This is as bad as the last one. Good luck, Mum. You're going to need it," is all she can say before bursting into hysterical laughter and tuning back into her mobile. I hold out my hand for the slip of paper. It says:

MOSH IN A MOSHPIT.

"Great." I smile at her wanly. The phone rings before either of us can say any more. Ah, it's Grandma. Grandma is eighty-six, is hard of hearing and peppers her sentences with Yiddish.

"Amy! What are you up to? I'm going *meshuggeneh* that you haven't called."

"Well, Grandma, I'm going to be busy next weekend. I'm going moshing."

"What, *bubelah*? You're going to be a moshling?"

"No," I shout down the phone, "Not a moshling, I am going *moshing*."

"Why didn't you say? Just remember to keep your mouth shut and wear a hat."

I hold the phone away from my ear. *That's a strange comment to make. I think she's finally going loopy.* I let her finish and say goodbye. I need to calm down and think rationally. What shall I do?

8.00 p.m.
Pippa lets Bea into the house and leads her to the lounge, where I am lying outstretched on the floor, eyes closed, attempting to listen to a relaxing CD while Evie wafts a bottle of lavender essential oil under my nose. It's not working.

"Amy, pet," she says, sitting by my side and stroking my hair. "Stop stressing about a dancing challenge. At least it's more exciting than that creating your family tree one from last week." She delves into her bag. "Here, have a glass of Pinot Grigio and a breadstick."

Geoff pokes his head around the door. "Still panicking about the mosh? You get to go to a gig. What's not to like? I'm watching a highly informative programme about stress where a woman has developed a real talent for achieving instant relaxation by orgasming through word association. Every time

8

she says or thinks 'balloon', boom! Learn how to do that, Amy. That'll sort you out when you're crowd-surfing. Try 'scone' – you love those." Geoff winks vivaciously and closes the door behind him. *What*? Bea and I look at each other. I can't think of anything worse. I would be a wreck if every time I said or thought of the word 'scone', I lost control. I love scones too much.

11.25 p.m.
Geoff is on his e-reader (as usual) when I flop into bed beside him, ready to apologise for my tardiness. However, tonight, he doesn't appear at all bothered that it is past his usual 'go to sleep' time. He has *other* ideas. Ever since we married, he's only ever wanted sex on a weekend before eleven, something that I've never questioned and been happy to accommodate. My attention is alerted to the significant fact he is using his official 'I am ready for date night' voice and his breathing is laboured.

He's as handsome as hell when we're in bed, I think to myself, as he pulls me towards him and wraps his arms around my waist. I bury my nose in his hair, run my hands over his six-pack and drink in the heady, alluring scent of his expensive aftershave that I love so much. When he's horny, he makes me feel so special. I'm so lucky to have him in my life.

Sunday.
It's time to consider moshing and I have lots of questions. What is a mosh pit and how exactly do you mosh? I think it's similar to pogoing. I had a go at that, aged fourteen, at a school disco, when punk was 'in'. What about crowd-surfing? Is it like being on a travellator at the airport? What is the probability of serious injury (bad) or groping action (not so bad)? How do you dismount from the human travellator? I turn to Facebook to find a moshing expert. Distracted by Evie, I type *If you know*

anything about moshlings, please private message me, and press Send without *checking*.

By midday, ten replies to my moshling request are sitting in my inbox. I message each of them back, thanking them for their time, and start again. "If you know anything about 'moshing', please message me." Send.

That afternoon, I discover that Claire's son, Ewan (aged seventeen), has 'stellar pit experience' and is a *huge* fan of Slit Killer. He thinks that my challenge will be great 'mum education' and has invited me to a gig with his mates. He's assured me they will help me to achieve my challenge, and, very importantly, take care of me should any mishap arise. The way he describes a typical mosh sounds alright. I love dancing, so perhaps I have misjudged the situation. I leave the arrangements in his capable hands.

Claire sends me an email. I open the attachment. It's an article entitled 'Essentials for Moshing Virgins' – and there are pictures. Ha. This really is mental, I think as I read, but at least I now know exactly what a mosh pit is. I wonder if everyone has been just *a little* economical with the truth, though. Moshing is *extreme* pogoing – violent, body-slamming, aggression-releasing dancing. The thought of being doused in the sweat, saliva or blood of complete strangers and possibly catching something unpleasant doesn't quite appeal. If I read any more about this, I know I won't go, and I will fail the challenge. I want to cry. I sit in front of my bedroom mirror and use self-talk to try and take control.

I can do this and it will be fun. Lots of women mosh. People of all ages go to gigs and dance, and I am capable of joining them, I declare with passion. I smile at my reflection, repeating my mantra twice more. And then I reason with myself. *If it was that dangerous, it would have been banned by now, wouldn't it? Yes, it would. And remember how my parents used to react when I went anywhere? I used to think they were past it, over-*

protective and unable to relate to me. And what did I do as a result? I pause. *They tried to stop me living my life and live theirs instead.* That's why I did what I did. "I won't be old, boring and out of touch like they were," I say aloud. "I mustn't lose my children."

Have you forgotten your other challenges already? scolds my inner voice. *You said you wanted to remain youthful in body, mind and spirit.*

Yes, I did – and I do, I reply.

A text pings into my inbox from Ewan:

All set for Thurs.
Pick you up 6pm.
No dresses or heels
and def no handbag.

Mosh Night. Thursday, 6.00 p.m.

Sandwiched between Ewan and his mates in the back of Claire's people carrier, I try to mentally prepare myself for what is to come. Claire is the designated driver and has decided to come along to the gig to record the event on her phone as a 'memento'.

I am wearing what I consider to be suitable clothing: a bright red long-sleeved top, leggings and pumps. I reason that if I wear red, it is more likely that my protectors will be able to see where I am at all times and keep me safe. I've tied back my shoulder-length hair, but I have had to keep my glasses on as I have run out of contact lenses. This concerns me slightly, for if I lose them, I will be as blind as a bat. Then again, I reason, this might work in my favour, as I won't be able to make out all the mayhem going on around me. The lads are knocking back cans of cider and there is a lot of seventeen-year-old banter about women, music and – er – women. I sit quietly between them, eyes closed, focused on controlling my breathing.

I have decided to remain stone-cold sober. After browsing some hard-core images of moshing late last night, I am concerned that if I drink *any* alcohol at all, there is a distinct danger of me throwing up over the crowd as I surf along or weeing in sheer terror.

Claire, on the other hand, is simply buzzing with excitement. "I can't wait to see you up there, Ames." She catches my eye through the rear-view mirror and smiles supportively. "You must let me know what it feels like. I wish I had the guts to do it but Bob won't let me. He's so boring – unlike your Geoff. Never wants me to try new things. Bloody old before his time. He hit forty and turned into his father overnight. Now all he's interested in is golf, gardening and our annual holiday to the Canaries *and always* to the same flipping apartment. We keep telling him that his lack of adventure is killing off his brain cells but he won't listen, ha ha."

"Ummm," I murmur, deep in concentration, feeling ever so slightly light-headed.

We arrive at the venue and hurry towards the entrance. I notice an old man selling plastic rain ponchos. "Doesn't look like it's going to rain tonight," I remark, looking up at the clear sky. "There's not a cloud to be seen."

"Oh no, love, it's gonna piss it down," he replies. Claire buys a poncho.

Inside, it's dark, sweaty and loud. The din from the warm-up act is overwhelming. Claire disappears to the balcony to get ready to video my challenge, leaving me alone with the guys. Ewan signals to me to follow him and leads us to the front of the stage. I'm trying to appear cool, when really I'm terrified.

The warm-up band leaves the stage, and the Slit Killer crew starts to prepare. The room begins to fill. The temperature is rising, the buzz is getting louder and I am becoming more nervous. There's a bit of jostling, and a guy to my left stands on my foot. I poke him, and he turns to glare at me. Perhaps I shouldn't have done that, I think, as I see the HATE tattoo on his forehead. "Do you mind?" I bellow.

"Fuck off, grandma," he mouths, but before I can retort, the hall is plunged into darkness, the music starts, the room explodes and the elbowing begins. The HATE tattoo guy throws a bottle of liquid over me, and without thinking, I jump on his foot –HARD.

Smack.

Nothingness.

Next thing I know, I am being offered a cup of sweet tea by the St John's Ambulance crew. Claire is beside me, frantically checking her phone. Tears are spilling down her cheeks, and she can hardly speak for laughing.

"Bloody hell, Ames," she splutters. "It's only been twenty minutes and we've had two thousand hits on YouTube. We're going viral. You're a celeb. Here." She shows me the recording and I watch in silence.

Apparently, I was smacked in the head and knocked out. A steward automatically triggered a health and safety announcement, the band was told to stop playing, the lights came on and I was passed over the crowd – backwards – towards the exit. I see that as I am crowd-surfed out of the venue, unconscious, the entire crowd is booing. I also notice that as I float along on a sea of hands, there seems to be a lot of water flying around. "Did the fire sprinklers activate automatically?" I enquire innocently. Claire erupts again.

"No, you daft cow. That's the pints of piss they're throwing at you. Should have bought a poncho."

Fortunately, I can see that my mouth was shut.

Back home, I have scrubbed myself raw, yet I'm convinced I still reek of urine. I'm also sporting a shiny black eye. Geoff is mega-impressed. It transpires that the editor-in-chief from *the* revered rock music magazine is desperate to speak with me, and that Geoff has already given them some 'cracking fodder' for a feature (to be entitled *Silver Surfers*) and has negotiated a 'decent' fee.

I retire to my safe, cosy bed, just thankful it's over. I have tried a new experience. I didn't like it, but I did it. Lesson two. Move with the times. Don't stagnate. Vegetate, and you deteriorate.

Week Five. Friday, 4.30 p.m.

Today, I am at the hairdressers – not because I need a haircut, but because I want to research the next challenge carefully. Becca, my gorgeous hairdresser, is a woman of the world. Her knowledge of life is extensive and I love to tap into it. Every time I visit, she has wondrous new tales to tell about herself, her family or her customers. I could sit for hours being entertained by her anecdotes: the teenage years of angst, the time she went inter-railing and slummed her way around Asia, relationship traumas... I always leave her salon feeling I have learned something. It certainly justifies the £70 I pay her. If anyone can help me with this challenge, she can. I show Becca the challenge slip. It reads:

BECOME A SEX CHAT LINE OPERATOR. YOUR CALL MUST BE FROM A STRANGER.

She snips her scissors in the air with relish. "Now then," she says with purpose. "How long have you been complaining that you're lacking motivation at work? This is just *perfect*. It's everything you need from a job, and it pays well too." She goes off to make me an Americano, and I consider what she has just said. I would like a change of career. Don't get me wrong; my job is fine. But perhaps it's time for something different. *Well,* I say inwardly to my reflection in the mirror, *that is exactly what this year is about, isn't it? Exploration and having fun?*

Becca returns and picks up her hairbrush. "Let me tell you why this career would be ideal for you." She brushes my hair

14

and continues: "Flexible working hours. You can work from home. No office politics. You'll meet a variety of customers. Your services will be valued. High job satisfaction all round." Becca puts down her hairbrush and we stare at each other in the mirror. She *may have a point.*

Saturday afternoon.
I am alone in the house. Pippa and Evie are doing their homework, and Geoff has retired to his Man Cave. It's time to research. I set to work and Google 'Sex chat operators'. Wow, there are pages of this. It's actually quite technical. I begin by scrolling rapidly through several websites for ideas and decide that a good place to start will be to read the Frequently Asked Questions.

"How's it going?"

"Take a look, Geoff. I've just discovered that I can call myself an Adult Chat Line Operator – sounds more professional, don't you think?" I giggle. "I need to feel the part, if you know what I mean." We explode into laughter. "I never realised that there were so many services on offer these days," I sigh. "It's all a bit confusing."

Sunday, midnight.
My research into the world of Adult Chat Line Operators is almost complete. I have spent a fruitful day rereading the first part of *Fifty Shades of Grey* over a box of Maltesers, and I am now avidly watching the free ten minutes of *Television Sexy,* one of the many porn channels that I am entitled to access as a valued customer of the nation's largest satellite TV provider.

The two female presenters are reclining topless on sofas and chatting to the viewers. I wonder if they are cold. Perhaps being topless helps them to get into role. How will I get into role? Should I go topless or get naked? I make a note of my thoughts on my laptop.

The next evening, Becca and I meet in town. I need advice on how to advertise my services. Somehow, I have to entertain a stranger. This is good, because – whatever happens – we will never know each other. However, this is also not good, because I actually have to find someone to ring me.

"Back in the day, we made calls from phone boxes, and the walls of the booths were papered with 'business cards' advertising this sort of thing," I explain. "Nowadays, though, I think the only way to advertise my services is through the local paper or leafleting around town, which sounds decidedly dodgy." Becca looks thoughtful, leans forward and carefully explains exactly what to do.

Tuesday evening.
I have joined Nookie For You, an agency of repute which lists many testimonials from satisfied customers. They have confirmed that I have the necessary qualifications (in that I am over eighteen, I have a corded landline telephone, and I am comfortable with sexuality and sexual situations). Other reasons for selecting this agency are that it's free to join and, best of all, I will receive a complimentary training course with certificate of competency to boot. Wow! I can add this to my CV.

To complete my Adult Chat Line Operator training, I take half a day off work on Wednesday afternoon and dial into a two-hour webinar. I am soon in conference with four other trainees and Marie, our trainer, deciding on our 'user names'. Marie explains that exotic first names always go down well, and as we all know that France is renowned for its laissez-faire attitude towards sex, I have chosen Françoise for mine.

The training session ends with Marie informing us about our 'assessment of competence'. Tomorrow, we will each receive a 'mystery shopper' type of call from one of their valued customers, who will provide constructive feedback on our performance. As requested, I book my call for between half past ten in the morning and midday, and I email the office to inform them that I will be working from home. Well, I *will* be working from home – just slightly different work than they expect.

Thursday, 8.30 a.m.
Once my daughters have been dispatched to school, I am able to focus on today's competence assessment. I can tell I'm nervous because I'm manically cleaning: dusting, mopping, polishing… I must stop this and prepare myself, I think. I need to get into role and feel the 'three Cs' I learned about in the webinar: confidence, calmness and being coquettish (cleaning wasn't mentioned). I force myself to relax by indulging in one of my guilty pleasures – watching an episode of *Snog, Marry, Avoid* on iPlayer. That always cheers me up.

10.00 a.m.
My workstation is plastered with multi-coloured sticky notes. 'Listen', 'Never Divulge Personal Information', 'Be Open', 'Empathy', 'Sexy Voice', 'Breathe', 'Detach', 'Enjoy', they say. A helpful A3 flow chart is taped to the wall to remind me of the standard call structure, the process and the various courses of action that I may choose to take, depending on the situation. As my trainer suggested, I have assembled a selection of helpful 'aids for success', namely a detailed thesaurus of 'useful' images and adjectives for sex words/acts to help my (and definitely their) 'creative juices' flow, a pot of squelchy stuff, a fly swatter to make slapping noises, a jug of water… I realise I have forgotten my vacuum cleaner and rush off to get it.

10.25 a.m.
Somebody is at the front door. "Oh, go away," I yell angrily. It's a parcel for Geoff. I grab it and slam the door in the postie's face. "I am not being interrupted again," I growl. "This is too important."

11.20 a.m.
I have succumbed to a glass of Pinot Grigio and two paracetamol to settle my nerves and am now feeling strangely calm. I sit in silence, chewing my finger, watching the clock and waiting…

11.35 a.m.
The phone rings. I answer on the third ring, as instructed, my hands trembling as I take a deep breath and say hello. I hope my voice isn't shaking. *Remember the three Cs*, I think. My client replies. He sounds fairly young. I open my mouth to ask him how he is feeling today (the opening question we were told to use in the webinar) but before I can begin, he speaks. His opening line floors me.

"I love chicken. Do you have any?"

What? I glance at the flow chart: *If the client asks a closed question, reply yes or no.* I gamble.

"Yes," I breathe sexily and cross my fingers. It's the right response – phew.

"Good," he breathes back down the line. "Do you have chicken breasts?" I smile to myself; ah, now I know where this is heading.

"Oh, yes," I purr.

"How big are your chicken breasts, then…?" And off we go.

Ten minutes later, I'm vigorously vacuuming the skirting boards. My, they are dirty. Moreover, the conversation with my client is getting rather dirty too. I am really getting into this sex chat. I lie on my back on the carpet, the hoover hose sucking up cobwebs, talking to my client as I work. The hum of the vacuum is doing its job exceedingly well. My customer believes it's a vibrator (how mad can you get?) and I can tell that he's having an exceedingly good experience by the way he's responding to my questions.

The conversation has progressed from chicken breasts

to chicken legs to chicken thighs, and I am now describing a "delicious coq au vin" to "fill a small hole". This is right up my street. I adore chicken, so it's easy to wax lyrical about its merits, and cooking is a passion of mine. I sit on the floor, the phone glued to my ear, surrounded by cookery books, trying to second guess where this is going. Perhaps I could turn the subject to 'Coq Monsieur' instead of 'Croque Monsieur'? It is quite difficult to hear my client at times, mind you. It sounds like it's starting to rain where he is. I look out of the window to check on the weather...

Another five minutes has passed and I am still vacuuming – having moved on to the window sills – and the chat is going strong. I'm sure it's not raining where he is. If I listen carefully I can hear running water, and I think that he's taking a shower. I can hear him soaping himself and some rather strange slapping sounds. The 'rain' at his end stops suddenly and a second later I hear a click as he puts down the phone receiver. For a minute, I'm confused, and then I realise what has happened. That's it – job done.

Later that evening, I receive my feedback from Nookie For You. I scan it in total amazement. I've passed with flying colours. My certificate of competence is attached and Marie, my trainer, has included a personal note:

> *Our client thought you were a natural, and we would be delighted to offer you a position within our company should you so wish.*

I beam with pride.

6.00 p.m.
My certificate of competence is framed and takes centre stage on the kitchen table. Geoff can't see what all the fuss is about. He thinks any female can do what I just did and is unable to

appreciate the range of skills that I've discovered. What he does acknowledge, however, is that what I've learned could be of benefit to *him*.

"You'll have to try out some of this on me, Amy," he says, "and I'll take the *greatest pleasure* in assessing you." He reads through the list of competencies that I have been assessed against. "I'd quite like to test out your 'oral' communication skills first." He looks at me slyly and winks.

Bloody men, I think. *So transparent.*

Adriano's Restaurant. 8.00 p.m.
The Girls take me out for a celebratory drink at Adriano's – any excuse – and I recount the past month's challenges in great detail, finishing with a blow-by-blow account of my amazing day today. The Girls listen, transfixed. I raise my dark glasses to reveal a black eye that has now turned a wonderful shade of greeny yellow, Claire plays back the YouTube video from my moshing challenge which is greeted with hoots of laughter, and there is rapturous applause when I admit to hating the HDs.

"Well done, Ames," applauds Cate. "I never thought you would actually go through with some of those challenges. Have you learned anything from them?"

"Oh yes," I reply emphatically. "I've learned quite a lot and I am *loving* my life at the moment." I pause and look around the table at my friends. "The best thing of all," I say carefully, "is that every day, I wake up excited, energised and invigorated and I think… no, I hope, that at the end of it all, I'll be a better person." I pass around my framed certificate and feedback sheet courtesy of Nookie For You. Everyone is mega-impressed with the comments.

"You scored such high marks," exclaims Bea. "I'm proud of you, pet, especially the ten out of ten for 'use of imagination, creative problem-solving, customer focus *and* interpersonal sensitivity'". She reads on. "Not sure why you received a nine for 'drive for results' though? Did your client think you were rushing a bit? My Spanish ex-boyfriend once told me that 'discreet stops make for speedier journeys'," she quips.

"Yeah, perhaps I shouldn't have stretched it out so much," I laugh. "I did wonder if I was gabbling on a bit – especially about the coq au vin. Tell you what, though – it was an empowering experience. Nobody was standing over me telling me what to do. I used my brain, felt strong and in control and not only that – being able to take full advantage of a man was invigorating. This challenge has given me much food for thought."

February

Week One. Monday, 7.00 a.m.

Evie has been up all night with a hacking cough, and as a dutiful, loving parent, I have been looking after her. Geoff is sleeping soundly in our bed. Not surprisingly, Evie and I are not in the best of moods. She sits slumped at the kitchen table, coughing sporadically, and I am by her side, nursing a super-sized mug of coffee. I take her temperature – it's slightly raised. I attempt to cheer her up.

"You pick the challenge that I forgot to choose on Friday." I rub her arm affectionately. A bleary-eyed Evie dunks her hand into the Bowl of Chance and Opportunity, pulls out a challenge and puts it on the table face down. "Wouldn't you like to read it out, darling?" I coax. She looks at me as if I am a bad smell and has a coughing fit. "Ah yes," I reply. "That's a bit of a problem, so I shall read it out to you. Pass it here. Thanks." I read to her that today, I have to:

TELL THE TRUTH ALL DAY.

"… And the challenge starts right now."

I want to make light of the situation, but I can't. *Bugger*, I think to myself. This could signal the start of a very difficult day.

7.45 a.m.

Geoff surfaces. I watch, detached, as he strolls into the kitchen and begins his breakfast routine, from which he never deviates.

Without a word to anyone, he prepares his usual bowl of designer muesli, plonks himself at the kitchen table, opens his e-reader and buries himself in the *Financial Times*. I can't help it. I grunt in disapproval. He looks up. "Anything wrong?" Now usually, I swallow any words of resentment swarming in my head like wasps around an open bottle of fizzy pop and focus on other, more pressing, matters until my top has been firmly screwed back on and I feel calmer. Today, though, is different. It is Tell the Truth Day, so I do – no holds barred.

"We have been up all night... without *any* sleep... I have made two packed lunches and three breakfasts, washed up, hung out the washing, got myself ready for work, checked school bags and uniform are correctly organised..." I am very aware that my voice is getting louder. "And I am now about to chase Pippa out of the door, minus appendage, to catch the school bus on time and try to blag an appointment at the doctor's this morning for Evie." I continue at full throttle. "You, on the other hand, have slept peacefully through the night in our bed, come downstairs at a time convenient to you and made your breakfast, yet you are somehow oblivious to what is going on around you. Have a lovely breakfast now, won't you."

As I storm out of the kitchen, I realise that I have actually never openly expressed what I feel about Geoff's complete lack of involvement or concern with our morning routine. I often allude to needing help, but it's ignored. There's always something better or more important that comes along, and so I carry on regardless because I have to and because I can't be bothered to rock the boat. I reach the top of the stairs and overhear Geoff's indignant comment to Evie. "Your mother *is* tetchy this morning. Does she have PMT?" and he laughs.

8.00 a.m.
Pippa has precisely seven minutes to eat her breakfast, brush her teeth, find her coat and shoes and leave the house or she

will miss the school bus. "Mum?" she asks, teary-eyed. "Am I spotty?" Oh no. I don't need this. Usually, with less than seven minutes to go, I will do and say *anything* to ensure she leaves on time. Today, of course, I cannot.

"Yes, darling," I am forced to reply. I stop. I want to say more, but if I do… I try to change the subject. "Put your mobile away. You can survive without your appendage until you get on the school bus."

"Can you *see* the zits, Mum?"

I consider my response. Her nose, chin and forehead are covered with raised, inflamed red papules. What can I say? I glance at the kitchen clock… four minutes to go. I have to get her out of the house. "We'll talk about this once you have put your shoes on and your mobile is safe in your bag," I say icily. Pippa dutifully acquiesces and I am about to heave a sigh of relief when she throws a killer dart in my direction.

"I'm not going until you say how bad they are." She folds her arms in defiance and glares at me.

I have to answer her truthfully, and so I guide her towards the door, muttering "Your face looks like a pepperoni pizza. I'll book you a facial. Bye." And with that, I push her out of the house, lock the door and run upstairs to ring the GP. *With any luck, she'll have forgotten all about it by tonight*, I cringe as I go, *If not, I'm in for a fun evening… not.*

The doctor's surgery is always a hive of activity. I like it here, as you can bet you'll meet somebody you know, and it is one of the few places where you can chat in relative peace without the worry that you need to be somewhere else or you have to move the car because your Pay and Display ticket is about to expire. Evie is dozing on my shoulder, and I take the opportunity to indulge in one of my favourite activities – watching people and imagining what their lives are like. I take in today's clientele, and my gaze falls on a young man, probably in his thirties, sitting opposite and engrossed in a novel. He is of medium build, about five feet ten, possibly Spanish or Greek, and he hasn't made a scrap of effort with his appearance. He's wearing a paint-splattered navy hoodie, an un-ironed Quo t-shirt that was once white but must have been put in the wash with something dark and has now turned an unfortunate shade of grey and a pair of baggy jeans that could really do with putting into quarantine. His short, straight and very dark hair looks as if it hasn't had a hair brush taken to it in a while.

My analysis of him continues. *Bet he hasn't got a girlfriend looking like that*, I imagine. *If he were taken in hand, I reckon he'd be quite good-looking. Dressed in one of Geoff's designer navy blue suits and silk ties, he'd be hot. I wonder why he is such a scruff? That t-shirt has certainly seen better days. Builder or decorator? Mind you, his hands look quite soft. There's a small scar on the back of his left one, but I can't see any signs of hard manual labour. No dirty fingernails either, but they're bitten to the quick. He might be shy... He might have a girlfriend or wife who isn't bothered about his appearance. Brave woman*, I smile to myself. I look for a wedding band. There isn't one. *Then again*, I muse, *many men, especially tradesmen, don't wear wedding rings these days for health and safety reasons.* I note a tattoo on his left arm. *Yicht – hate them, though*, I say to myself. I sneak another look at him, catch his eye and take a sharp intake of breath. *Oh, you have the most gorgeous eyes. If I were younger...* I feel a bit embarrassed by my rather scruffy appearance today and find myself surreptitiously taking my lip gloss and mirror out of my bag...

"Mum, why are you putting on lipstick in the doctors?" asks Evie suspiciously.

"Well..." Oh no – I have to tell the TRUTH. "It helps mummies to look, well, more attractive and feel better about themselves... and my lips are dry."

The man takes a tattered copy of Cressida Cowell's *How to Train Your Dragon* and a black plastic bottle from a carrier bag.

Evie sits up and stares pointedly at him. "Mum?" she says loudly. "Why is that man reading a children's book?"

"I really don't know, sweetie." I reply. "Perhaps he likes it." I want her to shut up.

"But he's old," she says more loudly. Before I can answer her, she turns to him and says directly, "Aren't you a bit old to read that?" I am about to quieten her down when the man looks up and asks if she has read the book. Evie replies that she likes it a lot and before I know it, she and he are deep in conversation about the qualities of the book versus the film. She asks if she can go and sit next to him.

"Of course," I reply. *Oh my*, I think to myself, *he is hot, in a scruffy sort of way. Well done, darling – you've given me a great excuse to legitimately ogle him.* For the next ten minutes or so, I look on as the pair conduct a highly animated conversation. *God, he really is lovely. Not many men would be able to engage a ten-year-old like he can. I wonder what he does for a living? He could be a teacher? No, he can't be. They'd never let him teach children looking like that.* I decide to ask him – as it's Tell the Truth Day – and I inconveniently butt into their conversation.

"What do you do for a living?" I smile.

"I'm an engineer," he replies, taking a swig from the black plastic bottle.

"Ah, that explains why you are a bit well... um... unkempt." I cringe inside as he looks surprised. "You should teach. You've got a lovely way about you, and you are doing a fantastic job engaging my daughter. I haven't seen her this chatty in ages."

"Mum has to tell the truth all day today," Evie kindly explains. "She's doing different challenges every week." She looks at me out of the corner of her eye. "She's not normally like this. In fact, she never talks like this."

"Why are you doing challenges?" he asks. And I find myself staring into a pair of incredibly alluring blue eyes.

I tell him as briefly as I can about my Year of Adventure and

Self-Discovery, as that way I don't have to be too truthful – but I let on that my fifty-first challenge is to write about what I do and what I learn, which will hopefully inspire others. His vibrating mobile interrupts our conversation. He puts his book and bottle away and gets up to go.

"Mum's waiting. I'd better be quick or she'll flip," he chuckles. He thinks for a minute and picks up a pen lying on a nearby table. "Take my number," he says, scribbling something on the back of a receipt he finds in his back pocket. "Give me a call. I have contacts and I think you're awesome for doing this. It's a fascinating project." He passes the receipt to Evie. "That's for your gorgeous mum," he winks. My heart skips a beat and I blush. *Oh no!* I think to myself as I find myself accepting his offer.

Back in the car, I compose myself and add his mobile number to the contacts list in my phone. He hasn't left his name. "What shall I call him, Evie? I can't leave a blank contact in my phone alongside his number. I'll forget who it is."

"Well, he is a man, and we don't know his name – so call him Him?" she replies gaily. And that is what I do.

8.00 p.m.
Lying in the bath and indulging in a small glass of Pinot Grigio, I reflect on my day. What have I learned about Telling the Truth? Well, Catherine of Siena, you cool fourteenth-century saint, I now completely understand what you meant when you said 'Proclaim the truth and do not be silent through fear'. I told Geoff exactly what I thought of him this morning, which I wouldn't normally do. Perhaps I should speak up more often? Then again, what if people don't like it? Should it matter if they don't? I know of a few women who have a bit of a reputation for being vocal, and I don't much like what Geoff says about them.

I take a sip of wine. I have also learned that telling the truth is an art. Sometimes you have to be totally upfront. On the other hand, perhaps it's kinder not to always say it as it is. Should I be advising Pippa and Evie to tell the truth no matter what? I ponder. It's an interesting question, and I'm not sure what the answer is.

I take another sip of wine and think on. In fact, sometimes we do not lie out of malice – we lie to protect. It's an act of kindness. I think back to this morning when I couldn't lie to Pippa about her spotty face. On any other day, I would have lied through love for her – to protect her self-esteem – and I wouldn't have felt bad about it. But would she have appreciated the lie? Would she have preferred that I tell the truth instead?

I take a third sip of wine and remember something totally unexpected that has resulted from my challenge. Today, something occurred that I never, ever dreamed would happen to me after too many years of marriage. Today, without warning, I met a man to whom I felt an attraction. No, today I met a man who really fascinated me. Deep inside, I know that for some unfathomable reason, I'd like to meet him again. I lie back in the comforting warm water, stretch, sigh and smile. And this year, I will. I am going to meet him again and find out why he fascinates me so much. Why not?

9.00 p.m.

I bump into Geoff. Wish I hadn't. He is waving a credit card bill around and he has some questions for me that have to be answered RIGHT NOW. I shudder as I notice that he has switched to his Professional Voice. "Amy, we need to talk. What is this £39.99 payment for and what else have you been buying in Bromley's?"

It's tricky concentrating on what he's saying because I am totally focused on his Pointy Finger, as we call it. It was Pippa who drew my attention to this habit of his. I'd never really noticed it before, but she is right. Whenever Geoff is in a particular frame of mind, he stabs around with his index finger. In fact, I think that one day, the Pointy Finger will mutate into a weapon of torture that I've nicknamed the Lightsaber Finger. *The world will rue the day that happens.*

I hate conflict of any kind and stand soberly in front of him, waiting for the ranting and pointing and steam that's pouring from his ears to fizzle out. He finishes. Now, on any other day, I would manipulate the truth, *just a little,* to justify my purchases, smooth the waters and get out as quickly as I can. However, today isn't over yet, and I have to tell the truth. So I do. I take heed of Catherine of Siena's advice again and freely admit to what I have spent and why. Geoff leans back in his chair, hands clasped behind his head, and listens. I finish and wait for the fallout, chewing nervously on my finger. "Thank you, Amy." He smiles and files the bill, and his tone changes. "Fancy watching a DVD?"

"Yeah, great – I'll get the wine." *Yippee! It's over.* I sigh happily and scurry off before he can say any more.

As we settle down in the lounge, I am struck by three thoughts. *Firstly, why do I allow Geoff to talk to me as he does, and secondly, why do I put up with the Pointy Finger? During the conversation we've just had, it felt as if he was my boss, the accuser, and that I had committed some dreadful misdemeanour. I know he has to be a strong communicator, but he's not at work now. And thirdly, I know sod all about our family finances. I'm sure I used to know more. I must get back up to speed again.* I make a note on my laptop.

My mobile is bleeping. I rummage for it in my cavernous handbag and glance at the message. It's from a friend asking if I can forward our next-door neighbour's contact details as a matter of urgency. I search for the 'Hillman' number to forward, and as I do so, I see Him listed directly below. I stare at the phone for some time and am struck by the urge to thank him for suggesting that he might be able to help with my fifty-first challenge. *Yes,* I think. *That would be a nice thing to do. I think he would appreciate it.* I would. I compose a short, friendly text, keep it light and press Send. He now knows my name.

Week Two. Friday, 9.00 p.m.

Claire, Bea and I have just finished a trial 'kill ourselves through keep-fit so we can have wine without guilt' class. Hot, sweaty and smugly virtuous, we sneak to our local for an obligatory celebratory tipple and catch-up. Finding a quiet spot in the corner by the fireplace, Bea pours the Pinot Grigio while I initiate an animated discussion about the previous week's 'being truthful' challenge. I describe my assertive moment with Geoff that morning and the incident with the credit card. "I'd never quite noticed how rude he can be, and this morning he ridiculed me in front of the children. Bea, what's wrong?"

"Listen up, pet. Are you a woman of the twenty-first century or a nineteen-fifties housewife? You do so much for your family and you're a fantastic role model to your daughters. Do you want them to learn that a woman should simply put up with that sort of crap from a bloke? He humiliated you with his words and his bloody Pointy Finger and you sat back and took it."

"Calm down, Bea," Claire cuts in. "I've known Geoff longer than the lot of you. In fact, I introduced Amy to him, and I can tell you that it's just the way he is. He's forthright and holds traditional values, and a bit of 'bad boy' lurks beneath his executive exterior – but he's always been the same, and you've done alright by him, haven't you, Amy? He's the main breadwinner, for goodness sakes, and, well, maybe he was tactless when he challenged you about your spending habits. But thinking about what happened that morning, I would say that he was preoccupied and getting himself into gear for a busy day in the office. You read too much into it. And as for the credit card incident, he was probably worried about balancing the books. You said yourself: you're out of touch with your family finances. You have a charmed life, Amy, and I'd give my right arm for a bit of that."

"You're talking complete garbage," interjects Bea. "Amy, you're not passive at work or with us, but when you're at home, you change. Deal with it this year, and break out of the cycle. Telling the truth all day forced you to say what you really think. Write down what happens every week and think about it, pet."

I remember to pull out this week's challenge on Saturday morning and laugh aloud with relief. "Listen to this," I remark. I read that I am to:

BE A GOOD NEIGHBOUR AND HOUSE-SIT.

Pippa unplugs from her phone and looks at me shrewdly. "Did you pull out that challenge on purpose?"

"No, I didn't," I reply truthfully. It's amazing that I really am looking after Chris and Mel's house, garden and pets next Monday until Wednesday evening. The forecast is for snow, and they really do not want to return home to frozen pipes or a slippery path.

Chris and Mel are two eccentric ladies in their sixties. We're not sure if they are gay, and (as I keep reminding Geoff) it really is of no consequence. However, the men in the village consider the very idea that they possibly could be lesbians to be of the utmost importance. After a few beers, several have been seen loitering with intent outside their house. Bea once caught Geoff peering through their kitchen window in the hope of witnessing some 'lesbian action', which didn't go down well. In my opinion, their sexuality is their affair, and I refuse to discuss it.

Later that afternoon, I pop round to Chris and Mel's, and they explain my list of duties:

- *Water all house plants.*
- *Clear garden of leaves, twigs, general windfall items, each day.*
- *Feed and water Snack and Attack the guinea pigs.*

- *Food kept in the garage in large plastic container.*
- *Walk Rusty the Labrador twice a day. Feed and water.*
- *Salt driveway and path – rock-salt in sack at rear of garage to the left.*
- *Leave post on kitchen table.*
- *Bins out Tuesday evening.*
- *Clear the lawn of snow – blower in garage.*

"That all looks fine," I say.

"Before you go, Amy dear, we'd better introduce you to our pets," says Chris. *Ah yes, the pets.* Now, one thing that Chris and Mel don't know about me is that I am not overly keen on animals. However, I am prepared to try and bond with their beloved animals for the sake of neighbourly love and this challenge, and I have a sneaky plan to involve my daughters with their care if necessary. They lead me into their large garden to meet Rusty, a bouncy Labrador, and Snack and Attack, the guinea pigs, who are snoozing in their palatial two-storey cage. The cage is a bit smelly.

"All you have to do is provide our babies with clean food and water, cuddle them and sing to them every day. It's good for their karma," smiles Chris.

"I have to hold them and *what*?" I ask incredulously. "Um, how long should I sing for, exactly?"

"Ten minutes is usually enough," replies Chris. "Here, hold Snack for me." She passes a wriggling white ball of fur across to me and I take him reluctantly.

"Will he wee on me?" I ask nervously. Since my moshing experience back in January, I have developed an aversion to urine anywhere near me and even the smell of it causes me to retch. Chris laughs. "Perhaps, but don't worry. Wee washes away."

Chris and Mel sing their repertoire of guinea pig special hits to me so that I know what I have to do. I so want to laugh at the sight of two elderly ladies singing to rodents that I have to dig my fingernails into the palm of my hand and bite the inside of my cheeks to keep myself in check.

Sunday, 4.00 a.m.
I lie on my back in the darkness, listening to the steady rhythm of Geoff's breathing as he sleeps. All is still except for my brain that is whizzing away like an electric mixer on full speed. I can't stop re-running clips of my and Evie's chance meeting with Him and especially the part of the conversation when he gave me his number and called me gorgeous…

Bea has a point. I must record everything that happens to me over this year because otherwise I will forget it. I can't afford to let any part of my journey pass me by. If I do, then there will be no writing to inspire others – no fifty-first challenge. I turn onto my side. *And I will record exactly how I feel, what I have learned, the changes I might like to make and what should remain the same.* I continue. *I will start tomorrow.*

At midday, Geoff finds me sitting on my bed, madly tapping on my laptop. I have been working on my diary entries all morning, and I am so absorbed that I have completely forgotten about lunch. "Amy?" I do not hear him. He taps me lightly on my shoulder and I jump. "How about a quick bite to eat and a family walk? It's a beautiful day and I don't want to waste it."

Nooo. Please not today, I growl to myself. I don't want to be interrupted, I don't want lunch and I certainly don't want to go on a family walk, even if the sun is shining. I only want to write and think. "Do we have to?"

"Come on, Amy," Geoff groans. "I really could do with the exercise, and it would do you good too. What about if we have a quick something and go out for a couple of hours, and then you can come back and do whatever you want." Uh-oh! Warning bells are sounding in my head. He sounds like he is going into one of his huffs that manifest when I don't want to do something that he wants. Then I make an error. I do what I always do when we have this sort of conversation. I give in.

"Ok," I say slowly, "*However,* I am not going on a long walk and I must be back for four as the girls have swimming at six and they need a decent tea. Do you hear me? Four at the latest." I smile, but the smile doesn't meet my eyes. My eyes are hot pokers branding my words onto his brain.

Geoff smiles back. "Great," he says lightly. "You put the soup on, butter some of that seeded loaf you picked up yesterday and get the girls ready. Say we leave in half an hour?" And, grinning broadly, he struts purposefully into the study and closes the door behind him. I hear the rustling of maps. For a split second, I make to get up and demand that if he *so* wants to go on a damn family walk that he can bloody well help make the soup, butter some bread and chivvy the girls along. It's so damn obvious that they won't want to go – they never want to go on walks these days – and now *I'll have to* cajole and bribe them to come along, simply to placate him. But I don't.

If I don't do this, I voice to myself, *life will be intolerable for the rest of the afternoon and perhaps into the evening too, and Geoff might even ground Pippa and Evie which will mean no swimming and more anguish.* So, to maintain the status quo, I reluctantly do as I am asked – but I make a note in my diary of everything that has just transpired. This is one area in my life that is going to change, I write in bold. Definitely.

4.45 p.m.
We return from our 'short' walk. As predicted, the girls are absolutely furious that their dad has made them negotiate several hills, and I am livid that we didn't get back at the time I specifically requested. We are grumpy and plastered in mud, and Evie's prized yellow hoodie is sopping wet.

"But why, Dad?" whines Pippa. "You know we hate hilly walks, and that last one was really steep and slippery."

"It's good for you to get some exercise," replies Geoff coolly, pulling off his walking boots.

"Why make us walk up a really steep and dangerous hill when you know that we don't like it?" she complains. "There are lots of FLATTER walks that we could have gone on." She stops mid-sentence, stands tall and declares in a very clear voice: "I know why you did it. It's because *you* wanted to go out and because *you* wanted some hard exercise – so *you* decided that we would climb that hill. You'd planned it all along." She storms off, and I silently applaud her. This happens all too often. Today, she has come out and said something that has been bugging me for a long time. But perhaps I should have said it, not her? *All this might not matter to you but what about us? It mattered to us,* I write.

Monday morning.
Geoff will be away with his work until Friday evening. As he leaves, he gives me a friendly reminder that it's going to be cold and snowy and to remember to grit the path and driveway well. "It'll all be just fine," I reassure him. "I have a week off work and no time constraints to worry about as the schools are shut until Thursday. If anything, it'll keep me fit." I walk round to Chris and Mel's house and begin my duties.

11.30 a.m.
I begin to realise just how huge their garden actually is, and I am already starting to loathe it. Having salted their ample driveway, cleared the paths of twigs and general garden detritus, watered the house plants and fed the animals, I am ready to curl up and cry. Frazzled and aching from head to toe, I crawl back home and lie down on the sofa with the curtains closed.

It's six in the evening, and I've been back at Chris and Mel's since half past four. I've bribed Evie to play with Rusty in the back garden for an extra three pounds pocket money as I simply don't have the energy to walk him properly. They'll never know, I think guiltily. The weather forecast has been updated. It's going to freeze first, then the snow will arrive just before breakfast time.

6.30 p.m.
Hell – I have forgotten to feed, water and sing to the guinea pigs. I shout across to Evie and we hack it round to the utility room where I check their water and dump three carrots and a lump of hay inside their cage as instructed. "Are they dead?" I whisper, peering inside the cage. I feel faint.

"No, Mum – I can see them hiding," replies Evie, pointing to their tunnel. I open the cage, pass Snack to Evie and bribe her to sing with me for another pound. "Perhaps we could give them a treat to say sorry?" she suggests.

"Good idea. I'll find some tasty veg in the fridge when I lock up," I reply.

I return shortly afterwards with half an iceberg lettuce and feed a few leaves through the cage bars. "That'll cheer you up, guys," I say, and we go back home.

I wake at half past three on Tuesday morning worrying about my house-sitting duties. I am not coping very well. I can hear a storm outside and peek through the bedroom curtains. It's blowing a gale and hail-stoning. I can just make out the end of Chris and Mel's driveway, and my heart sinks. Damn, this is all I need. I mentally run through the list of family activities planned for Tuesday and Wednesday: *dentist, Brownie run…* Now, *that's* an idea…

Wednesday, 10.30 a.m.
Ten excited Brownies, a Young Leader and their Brown Owl rock up to Chris and Mel's. Some have arrived on foot and some by toboggan. Others have hitched a lift with Brown Owl in her battered four-by-four. All are kitted out in a wonderful array of

hats, scarves, gloves and boots. They have each brought a spade or shovel along as requested. "Girls, we should be extremely grateful to Mrs Richards for allowing us to come here to get our Community Service Badge," says Brown Owl. "Now, Mrs Richards, what needs to be done?" We divvy up the tasks – snow blasting and shovelling, dog-feeding, de-icing, bins, post-sorting and warm-drink-making because it is perishingly cold and we don't want the Brownies to become hypothermic.

Two Brownies, accompanied by the Young Leader, are permitted to walk Rusty around the village with strict instructions to return by one o'clock. Brown Owl hands them high-visibility jackets to wear, and the Young Leader is put in charge of a mobile phone to be used in case of emergency. We watch everybody run off to their designated tasks, and work begins. At first, Brown Owl and I keep a tight eye on proceedings. As time goes by, however, we relax a little. Well, quite a lot. Everyone is busy and having fun. "How about a cup of tea?" I suggest. We tramp into the kitchen and pop the kettle on.

11.00 a.m.
Brown Owl receives a call on the emergency mobile. She listens in silence. Her expression says it all. "Amy," she says carefully. "The girls have lost Rusty." I go to find the dog. I feel sick. I spot the Brownies and Young Leader by the postbox. They are all crying and apologising. Rusty is nowhere to be seen. I feel even more sick.

A passer-by clad in full ski gear and carrying a snowboard over his shoulder informs us that a stray Labrador has been spotted up the road near the shop. He is found. We discover him leaping about, as happy as can be. Rusty sees me and barks, as if to say: *This is great!*

Back at Chris and Mel's, I search out the Brownies tasked with clearing the lawn. One is using the blower to cover the others in snow. A snowball fight is happening dangerously close to the extension cable and, as I go to warn them, there is a loud POP. The machine cuts out.

1.00 p.m.
Ten shivering Brownies, a tearful Young Leader, a relieved Brown Owl and a very stressed me are singing and eating chocolate by the guinea pigs' cage. I am desperately trying to work out how I can explain away the broken blower and why Rusty has sore paws from getting too cold. One of the Brownies holding Attack yells and drops him. "Mrs Richards – he's got diarrhoea…" I ring the vet.

9.00 p.m.
When Grandma calls at nine, I'm so wound up that I vent my feelings about everything that's happened this week. However, by the time I come off the phone to her, I feel so much better. Talking to somebody I love and admire has helped me realise that this challenge has been unexpectedly enlightening. *Grandma said that I'm a people-pleaser and have allowed myself to take on too much. I did find it hard to say no, I type on my laptop. Do I let people take advantage of me? Is my kindness and generosity used by others for their own personal gain?* I close up my laptop, pensive.

Week Three. Friday, 6.00 a.m.

It's Evie's eleventh birthday and, as in many families, there are customs and traditions that we follow religiously. I personally ensure our family upholds these momentous events every year because I *so* want our children to have fond memories of this extra-special time in their lives. I have valiantly tried to involve Geoff in the birthday preparations over the years, but I have had to accept that he just doesn't get it. His friends don't get it either – I have asked them. Perhaps they just don't want to get it? In fact, if I think about it, Geoff doesn't get all the preparation that goes into making Christmas and his birthday special either. He thinks all the wonderful meals, presents, treats etc. appear as if by magic. *Wonder what he'd say if one year I went on strike?* I muse. *Wonder what he'd do if I put him in charge of Christmas or a birthday?* "No way," I mutter. "We'd have a bloody awful time." I leave him sleeping and sneak downstairs to get to work on 'The Cake'.

When I was a child, birthday cakes were nothing like today's masterpieces. My mum bought a jam Victoria Sandwich from the supermarket and stuck in a few candles, and I was supposed to be grateful. Today, however, the pinnacle of the event is the *unveiling* of The Cake. This year, Evie has requested a home-baked Pokémon-style creation. Thankfully, the cake is a standard round ten-inch iced sponge, but with an iced Poké ball on top. The sponges were baked in advance and frozen, and now they are defrosted. I only have the icing and decoration to do. I've just finished when Geoff marches into the kitchen, ignores the spectacle before him, grunts and embarks on his usual morning breakfast routine. My stressometer rises three notches and I start to chew on my finger. I cough and point at the cake. There is a pregnant pause.

"Yes, Amy. I know that this is the day she was born and supposedly made our lives complete," he retorts. "I'll see her later. I couldn't sleep last night – I've been away with work and I need time to recover. You know I can't function properly without rest."

"But you are coming to her party?"

"Oh no, Ames, it's really not my thing."

"You've never been to any of her parties… You said that you would."

"Amy," he sighs. "I never signed up to doing kids' things when I agreed to have them, and I don't see why my presence at a snotty kids' party is that important. She'll be too busy hanging out with her friends, and to be frank, it's not a worthwhile use of my time."

"But…"

"Stop it, Amy," he interjects. "We'd save a fortune if you didn't spoil her like this. I bet she wouldn't give two hoots if you got rid of all this sentimental crap like balloons and banners and fancy cakes… It's all a marketing ploy aimed at women like you. And by God, it works, doesn't it? Just look at this stuff. Don't try and involve me, because I DON'T want to be a part of it."

"I do… I know… but…"

"It's a day, Amy. It's one more fucking day and tomorrow is another fucking day… it's a day that says you're one year older, that's all."

Before I can say another word, he leaves the house and I hear his car pulling out of the drive. *Is this what happens in other families?* I wonder sadly. *Are my expectations too high? He does work hard and we want for nothing.* A surge of white hot anger takes me by surprise and I am scared by its intensity. "I don't do this for me – I do it for HER," I scream at the goldfish. "If you didn't get a carrot cake baked by *me* or presents bought by *me* or some sort of celebration organised by *me* for your birthday, *you* would be the first to complain." I try to calm down. "I'm not going to let this ruin today," I mutter as I grab my bag and leg it out of the house. "I must remember to write this up."

9.00 p.m.
Basking in the afterglow of another successful party, I reward myself with a celebratory glass of Pinot Grigio and pick my next challenge:

TRY A TWENTY-FIRST CENTURY ANTI-AGEING TECHNIQUE.

Although knee-deep in wrapping paper and plastic packaging, I immediately ring my sister. Jess is the only person I know who has openly admitted to regular Botox, and she often suggests that I treat myself to 'a jab'. She and I are different –

so different that we've actually questioned if we share the same parents. Scatty and opinionated, Jess is on a constant diet, pours her svelte body into figure-hugging outfits and totters around in killer heels whatever the occasion. Furthermore, she and Stanley, her partner of sixteen years, are extremely open-minded about certain 'activities' that make me cringe in horror.

I wonder if she is a secret swinger. I know that she has a fancy-dress box filled with whips and stuff (it's under the bed in her spare room) and that Stanley, a traffic warden, is the proud owner of a pair of silver lamé hot pants. I saw them drying on the line once, and Jess admitted that they were his. I haven't had the courage to ask her about any unorthodox sexual tendencies, though, and I'm not sure I really want to know. She'd probably try to persuade me to join in.

I examine a recent picture of her on my phone. Geoff asks what I'm doing. I show him the image. "What do you think? Jess is fifty-three and looks quite youthful for her age," I say. *Especially considering the number of sleepless nights she's had trying to knock sense into her wayward seventeen-year-old son. When Adam Anthony was excluded for fighting in school, I didn't know what they'd do. Then again, I suppose it was inevitable that he'd suffer for being named after the eighties pop star. It was very generous of Geoff to agree to pay for his private schooling.*

"She's got a great rack on her. I'd give her one," Geoff sniggers.

"Oh, go away," I laugh. "She probably paid for them and, for your information, she'd never look twice at you." He guffaws loudly as I dial her number.

"You *know* what I think, Ames. Get filled and you'll never look back. My lower jaw non-surgical lift took years off me," she proclaims. "Stanley's hair transplants – to cover his widow's peak – cost thousands, but he looks awesome. Adam Anthony had to forgo a school trip to Mexico because I used the money Geoff sent – sorry – but the op helped Stan get promoted over those younger guys. He's a Team Leader now," she preens.

"Geoff sent what?"

"Hell – do it!" she screeches down the line, ignoring my question. "You'll feel confident and desirable. Don't you want to feel hot when you hit the town – and I don't mean hot as in flush. People won't ever talk openly about having fillers, but they indulge on the sly. Most women would do it if they had the money. Stay young in mind, body, face and spirit for as long as you can and have lots of sex. That's my motto."

I analyse myself critically in my hand mirror. *It's true that we label based on what we see,* I think. *If I see a wrinkled face, I think 'out of touch' and 'past it'. I wonder what people think when they look at me. Do I look old? Make-up helps me to feel good about myself. If I looked 'fresher' on the outside, would I feel different on the inside? When I was called gorgeous by Him, I felt amazing. Nobody's called me that for years.*

Just thinking about it makes me melt inside, and I realise that I desperately want to see Him and come across as a vibrant, sexy and amazing mum again. For some reason, it is very important to find out what he thinks of me. *This is bloody stupid,* I say to myself sternly. I try to push my thoughts out of my mind, but they won't go away that easily and even as I kiss Geoff goodnight, my subconscious is troubled.

On Saturday, I bump into Bea in town. She asks how my challenge is going. "My sister is adamant that I should get filled. Would you ever go there, Bea?"

A mischievous look crosses her face. "I've been having fillers for years now, pet. It's not really something you shout about, but it's changed my life," she grins. "It's two hundred and fifty quid well-spent. I'd forfeit sex to pay for it; that's how good it makes me feel about myself."

"You are a dark horse," I laugh. "Good for you. I love that you don't give a damn what others think and you live your life as you choose. I'm learning that I'm too concerned about what others think of me at times. Do you think I've any deep wrinkles?" I ask.

She studies my face. "There's one between your eyebrows. Apart from that, you look good to me." I take note of what she's said about my one deep wrinkle.

Monday, 11.15 a.m.
I can't believe that I have agreed to be filled – today. I'm not a spontaneous person, but I am so excited at the prospect of getting rid of that wrinkle in my forehead, and Dr Jane is so knowledgeable, that I have booked an appointment for later this afternoon. *Sod the cost*, I reason. *I'll stick it on my secret credit card.* I text The Girls and tell them my plans.

When I arrive at the clinic, Cate and Claire are there, waiting for me. I look at my friends in astonishment. Cate smiles back at me sheepishly. "Well, Ames, Claire and I have always secretly wanted to do this, so we decided to share this challenge with you," she grins, nervously. "I'm going first though. I have a fear of needles." And she is sick in the waste paper bin next to her.

My deep wrinkle has been plumped out and a tiny bit of filler injected around my mouth. It didn't really hurt, but it does feel sore. Dr Jane hands me a mirror, and I stare at the instantaneous results in wonder. I look the same, yet different. I feel *wonderful*. "You're totally refreshed," confirms Dr Jane, "and no one will ever know your secret unless you tell them."

Pumped with adrenaline (and filler), we simply have to celebrate. So we glam up and go out for a drink to toast the fact that we have faced our fears of going under the 'knife', that we feel fantastic and that Cate overcame her fear of needles.

11.00 p.m.
Geoff and I are in bed. He's on his e-reader. I'm examining my face in a mirror. "Amy," he says irritably. "Stop staring at yourself."

"Just admiring my wrinkles."

"You're middle-aged – of course you have wrinkles. You just

have to learn to live with them like I have to live with my dodgy knee. It's called 'getting older.'" He turns back to his e-reader.

"I'm not ready to be old," I announce. "I don't feel old inside, and I don't want to appear old on the outside."

"Can't help getting older, love. Embrace it. You are as old as you feel. Come over here," he laughs, "let me have a good feel and I'll estimate your age. Jess and Stanley don't let age stop them from enjoying life, eh, Ames? I hear that they're in great demand on the swinging circuit." He turns back to his reading. I ignore his comments. I don't want to know about Jess and Stanley's perversions. I stare at my smooth forehead and smile inwardly. I am *glad* I have had the filler and the courage to do it. I am only sad that I don't feel I can tell Geoff. I don't think he'd ever understand.

Thoughts of Him jump back into my head. How old did he think I was? I want Him to call me gorgeous and awesome again. Why hasn't he replied to my text? I sent it over a week ago now. I drift off to sleep feeling quite sad.

Week Four. Friday, 7.30 a.m.
At breakfast, I'm deep in thought about the grand adventure I'm on and my fate. *Will this year change anything for us?* I wonder. *Will my challenges simply come and go, leaving us all in exactly the same place as we are now?* I want *different* but I can't quite define what *different* is yet, let alone how to make *different* happen. My thoughts are rudely interrupted by Evie telling Geoff about meeting Him at the doctors' recently.

"Have you texted *Him*, Mum?" she giggles.

"Why not? If he can help you make some money out of it, that's good enough for me," Geoff sniffs.

"You don't mind?" I say, feeling quite odd.

"It's not as if he's after a quickie with you, Amy – unless he's got an Oedipus complex, that is." He smooths down his hair, rubs a smudge from his Tissot watch and leaves for work, chuckling. I resist the urge to say something extremely rude to him as the children are in the room and I cannot give any hint as to what I felt – no, feel. I shiver. My chance meeting with Him is etched on my brain. However hard I've tried, I'm still thinking about it – every... single... minute of it – and especially those amazing blue eyes...

If Geoff had the slightest inkling, it would put an end to the chance of communicating with Him again. He'd get such a kick out of it and play on it for evermore at my expense. Life would become intolerable. No, Geoff must never know how I feel about Him, I decide as I check my emails and open one from school that's promoting a fundraising coffee morning:

> From: Josie Jamieson, PTA Chair
> To: All Parents and Carers, Daisy Hill Academy
> Subject: Charity Coffee Morning – School
> Fundraising Event
>
> Dear Parents and Carers,
>
> As you are aware, we need to raise as much money as we can to improve the outdoor play area for our children to enjoy.
> I know that we have many excellent bakers in our school community, and so the PTA have organised a community Coffee, Cake and Chat morning on Thursday 25th February in the School Hall between 09.30 and 11.30.
> We desperately need your support, so please let me know if you are able to volunteer to bake some goodies. ☺
> Come on, ladies and gents. I know we can do it. If I can, with four children under the age of twelve, a six-bedroomed house to clean and a full-time job, so can you. And you know you can't resist my home-baked scrumptious triple-choc-chip-dipped brownies served with whipped cream and sprinkles.

Hope you're tempted. If you need any advice or guidance about baking, please do get in touch with me through school. I have several diplomas in cake and biscuit baking, working with chocolate and sugar paste. I would be *absolutely delighted* to share my expertise with you.

Thanks a bunch.

Josie Jamieson (Mrs)

School Governor (Daisy Hill Academy)

"You are not going to make me feel inadequate today, Josie Jamieson," I say aloud, slamming an email back, thanking her profusely for her communication and confirming that I will be attending her damn annoying coffee and cake event. I add that I will bring cake, although I do not say what. *That'll get her*, I fume. *She'll find it bloody irritating that she doesn't know exactly what I am bringing, and there is no way that I'm letting on. Stew woman, stew.*

During my coffee break, I reflect on my reaction to Josie's email. There aren't many people I really do not like, and I try to get on with most. I consider myself to be somebody who tries not to judge others, whatever they may do. But Josie Jamieson is difficult to warm to in the loosest sense. Not only is she the chair of the PTA, she is one of our School Foundation Governors – so I cannot avoid her. The worst thing about her (which is truly nauseating) is that she pretends to be the perfect wife and mother, despite her terribly 'hard' life.

What she doesn't let on, however, is that her husband earns squillions as a lawyer in London, that she virtually lives at a health and fitness club an hour's drive away, that she has a cleaner, a part-time nanny and a gardener, and that sometimes she even hires a personal chef. *Bet that chef made her bloody triple chocolate brownies* I think, returning to my desk.

Adriano's Restaurant. 8 p.m.

Tonight, it's Abba theme night at Adriano's. The restaurant is packed to the rafters with Abba-esque memorabilia. The tables have been named after Abba's greatest hits, gold and silver chocolate coins are scattered across the tables in place of table confetti, and huge blow-up posters of Bjorn, Benny, Agnetha and Anni-Frid adorn the walls. The lights are turned down low, and a glitter-ball twinkles above. The entire Abba back catalogue is being played at volume and everybody is singing along.

As is the custom, we take it in turns to relate the trials and tribulations of the past twenty-eight days or so. It comes to my turn. "Girls," I say. "Have you read the latest missive from 'alpha mum'?" They all know exactly who I'm referring to.

"Yes," replies Cate resignedly. "What is that woman on?"

"She's being her usual parasitic self. You know, we really do need to get one up on her," says Bea wistfully. "and stop her using us to take all the glory for herself."

"Now, that would be fun. But how?" I reply. "We always feel inadequate around her."

As I munch my way through a bowl of mini prawns smothered in luminous pink cocktail sauce, my thoughts turn to my next challenge. "Oh, I haven't told you what's in store for me this week, have I?" I exclaim. I read it out to them. My challenge is to:

LEARN A SKILL TO IMPRESS.

"What are you going to learn, and who will you impress then, Ames?" asks Claire.

"Exactly," I shrug. As our plates are cleared, we go round the table, brainstorming. Bea speaks first.

"Circus and magic tricks," she announces. "I once met a woman whose husband bought her an 'Adult Tricks Experience' for her birthday, where she learned the art of inserting ping pong balls into her Jemima and pinging them out, one by one, in a controlled manner – into a soup bowl of all things."

"That would certainly impress Geoff, and it'd be great practice for improving my pelvic floor. However, I'm not sure I'd like to spend a happy day with some pervy trainer helping me to… Sorry, your idea is *rejected*."

"Sign up for that TEFL course you saw advertised recently, Ames. You've always wanted to do that. Then, once you're qualified to teach English as a foreign language, you could always go abroad as a missionary?"

"That's impractical, Claire," interjects Cate. "Amy has a week in which to complete this challenge, and she'd never do it."

"It *is* a lovely idea, though," I smile. "That is definitely a skill I'd like to have under my belt, but you are right – it doesn't quite fit within the challenge rules. So what do you think I should do, Cate?"

"Oh, something practical, of course! Learn to knit or crochet… or try felting, perhaps?" Cate suggests. "You could start up your own business selling online or at local craft fairs."

"No," exclaims Bea, "that's just too boring. Amy is supposed to be spending this year having fun and exploring herself…" She stops mid-flow, and we explode into hysterics.

"So, it's back to the ping pong ball challenge, is it then?" giggles Cate. We sit in silence, contemplating the problem.

"Got it!" Bea explodes, almost knocking her drink over with excitement. She is positively beaming. "I know exactly who you can impress and how."

"Go on, then," I reply, and we lean forward to listen to her idea.

"Why don't you *show* that Mrs Alpha Parasite – bake a Mary Berry style show-stopper cake for the Coffee, Cake and Chat morning? That'll steal her thunder. She'll probably hate you forever, but it'll be worth it."

"Bea, that's genius!" I exclaim.

We bat the idea about while the main course of Duck à l'Orange is served. However, it is only when the retro sweet trolley arrives, groaning with ten different types of dessert, that the challenge is finally decided.

"I am going to wheel in a sweet trolley just like this one," I proudly announce, sweeping my hand grandly in the direction of the trolley. "*And* it will be laden with at least ten Mary Berry and Paul Hollywood style cakes and biscuits that I will learn to bake all by myself," I declare. "Not one cake will come from the supermarket." The Girls love it. They all clap and cheer, and we toast the challenge with glasses of Mateus Rosé.

Later that evening, we successfully press-gang Aidan and Mario, the chefs and owners of Adriano's, to sit with us and talk cake and biscuit baking. "It is very important that they look amaaaazing and taste absolutely fantastic," I slur drunkenly. "They have to be up to Mary and Paul's standards, which means that they must be perfect. No soggy bottoms."

Aidan thinks that it will be pretty easy for me to learn some basic skills, as I do bake a bit. He kindly offers to give me a few lessons *and* he allows me to use all the gadgets in the restaurant kitchen. This is brilliant, as I do not own such things as a super-duper mixing machine, a chiller or a deep fat fryer. We agree to start our teach-ins on Monday evening, and I promise that tomorrow afternoon I will email him a list of sweet treats that I might like to learn how to bake.

Saturday afternoon.

My friends are assembled in my lounge, nursing dreadful hangovers and downing bucketfuls of herbal tea. We occupy ourselves watching random episodes of The Great British Bake Off. Geoff, the self-proclaimed cake connoisseur, has decided that he should be fully involved in this challenge to ensure I learn to bake some healthy fruit-based treats he can enjoy. "You'll need an eff-off show-stopper four-tiered gateau," adds Claire, taking a sip of her tea.

"And something for the children. Chocolatey, cookies, pastries... and what about something exotic?" throws in Cate. She is watching the iPlayer. "Ooh, look at this," she exclaims. We gather round the TV, rewind the clip, and watch it again.

"I do like the sound of that Lincolnshire Plum Braid," I say. "It's packed full of fruit and Marsala wine. That'd look fab on the trolley, but is it okay to use alcohol for a school do?"

"Why not? I think you should add alcohol to everything," Bea chuckles. "It'd make for a fun morning."

Pippa and Evie are dispatched to the kitchen to find my cookery books, which they ceremoniously dump on the coffee table. "How shall we go about this?" asks Cate, staring in horror at the pile.

I turn to Pippa. "What do you think, sweetie?"

"Well, Mum. I think each of us should suggest something we'd really like to eat ourselves, and then we can vote on it. That's how we make decisions when we have cake-baking nights at Rangers. What about a Valentine's theme?"

"Good idea," I say. Twenty minutes later, we have nailed it:

Cakes and Bakes – Valentine's Theme
Doughnuts injected with a swirl of jam and custard.
Medley of mini-scones: cheese, fruit and plain.
Choc-dipped fruit kebabs.
Smartie cookies.
Show-stopper: Heart-shape tiered Victoria sponge-cake
topped with strawberries and blueberries.
Flapjacks – date and plain.
Toffee apple crumble traybake.

"Three more to find," announces Pippa. We settle on gluten-free cupcakes, shortbread and a dried fruit tea loaf. Pippa emails the list to Aidan and Mario.

Sunday, 7.00 p.m.
Mario and Aidan teach me how to use the deep fat fryer. I have never made doughnuts before, and so this is where we have decided to start. Two hours and thirty-six attempts later, I am

ready to collapse – but I have finally mastered the skill, and they taste good. "One down, nine to go," I yawn as we clean up the mess. The men just laugh. "See you tomorrow. Don't forget to wipe the jam off your nose before you go."

On Wednesday evening, I invite my friends and Geoff to Adriano's to applaud the results of my labour. In the freezer sit all the finished cakes and bakes – bar the show-stopper. I have been advised to bake the sponges at half past six tomorrow morning to ensure they are at their very best. I also have biscuit decorating to do and chocolate-dipped fruit kebabs to prepare, but Mario and Aidan have assured me that they won't take long. The sweet trolley has been polished and sits ready, gleaming. Claire loads the trolley into her people carrier with strict instructions to deliver it to school for quarter past nine in the morning. I will transport the cakes and bakes and meet her in the school car park. We are set.

Thursday morning.
Everything has defrosted. The biscuits are iced. Two square sponges are cooling, and I am cutting up strawberries for the show-stopper cake. I cut the sponges in half. *Hmmm... they look dry*, I think to myself. *Have I overbaked them?* I taste a tiny piece of sponge. "Yep, too dry," I say aloud. "They need something to moisten them."

I go into panic mode and pace the kitchen, searching for inspiration; my Star Baker status in danger. And then I see an unopened bottle of sherry sitting on the shelf. Without a second thought, I stab skewer holes in the sponges, drizzle a good half-bottle of the sherry over them, layer the cake with cream, decorate it with fresh berries and take a good slug of sherry myself – for medicinal purposes.

10.00 a.m.
I make my grand entrance, casually wheel the trolley up to Josie

Jamieson and present my contribution. She looks aghast, then quickly recovers. "Mrs Richards…" she simpers. "Amazeballs." She recovers her composure and tries to stick the knife in. "I *do* hope they taste as good as they look, my dear."

"It's my pleasure, Josie," I reply, refusing to rise to her provocation. "Your email really did *tempt* me and fortunately, I had a little time on my hands." Trying not to laugh, I disappear into the crowd to find The Girls, who are anxiously waiting for me.

Towards the end of the event, we purposely wander past the sweet trolley to see what has been eaten and what is left. "Hey," remarks Cate. "The show-stopper has all gone." On cue, Josie Jamieson appears at my side and gives me a big bear hug. She hiccups and appears to lose her balance slightly.

"Mrisses Richarrrds," she slurs. "I have to tell you that…" She hiccups again and puts her hand to her mouth. "That Berry Merry cake, that very, no, that Merry Berry cake ish the mosht *wunnerful* cake ahhv ever teshted." And with that, she turns abruptly and staggers across the room towards the headteacher.

It is at that moment that I, along with everyone in the school hall, observe her skirt hem neatly tucked into a black lacy thong, exposing a peachy and toned buttock complete with a Daisy Hill Academy coat of arms tattoo. She slithers onto a nearby chair, shuts her eyes and appears to go to sleep. My hands fly to my mouth. *Oh, my Lord. How embarrassing. Is she drunk on my cake?*

"Who'd have thought Mrs Prim-and-Proper Jamieson would have a good old tramp-stamp on her arse?" giggles Bea. "Such dedication to the school. I didn't expect that the 'Merry Berry cake' would cause such an uproar." And we all fall about laughing.

March

Week Two. Friday.

I have to tell someone about what happened to me at the doctor's recently, and I've decided to confide in Claire. She and I have been close for years, and she knows me well. In fact, she's the most moral person I know. She's always been trustworthy, and I'm sure that she will give sound, unbiased advice.

However, something tells me that I mustn't give too much away. I feel guilty that what I'm experiencing is fundamentally wrong, even though it feels so right. Have I done anything wrong? I don't think so, but I don't know for sure.

I'm so keyed up that I can't face a scone today (and I adore the blueberry ones at Tea and Tranquility). Claire tries to tempt me. "No scone? I don't believe last week's Advanced Driver course challenge was that bad, Ames? So, what's up? Anything exciting?" Her eyes sparkle.

I take a sip of my comforting Americano and, trying to act indifferent, describe how Evie and I met Him. It's easy – oh, so easy. I could wax lyrical all day, but I curb my enthusiasm and keep the conversation light and tight. "I know nothing about him, not even his name." I force a laugh. "He's years younger than me; he's not even my type. You know I don't do men who make zero effort with their appearance, and he's got tattoos for Pete's sake – yet for some reason, I just can't get him out of my head."

I continue in the same light, airy vein and animatedly describe how he offered to help with my fifty-first challenge. "He says he has contacts, Claire. They'd be useful. I haven't a clue about writing, and he seems knowledgeable and keen to help." I shrug my shoulders nonchalantly. "What do you think? Should I bite the bullet and text him again?"

Claire bites into her chocolate brownie and I chew on my finger, anxious to hear what she might say. She looks me squarely in the eye. "Text him. Meet in a public place – a coffee shop perhaps, but a quieter one. Have your conversation. Treat it as a business meeting; that way you'll be able to control your emotions. No one will judge you. Just because he turns you on doesn't mean you have to avoid him. Listen," she blushes. "Nobody knows this, but I really fancy Steve Steele – my daughter's physics teacher. Parents' evenings are bliss, 'cos I get to stare into his eyes for all of ten minutes. Don't get me wrong, Ames – I don't go to parents' evenings with the aim of seducing him. God would strike me down." She laughs out loud and blushes again. "Doesn't stop me thinking about it, though."

"Does Bob know?" I ask incredulously. "I couldn't tell Geoff. You know what he's like. I know you love Geoff's schoolboy humour…"

"Oh no, I'd never let on," she replies. "Mr S is one of my two top-secret man fantasies. My faith keeps me on the straight and narrow these days. As for you, well, there's nothing to tell, is there? Hey, is that the Bowl of Chance and Opportunity in your bag? May I?"

"Go on, then," I say. "Make it a good one."

Claire mixes the papers around and makes her choice:

HEALTHY BODY, HEALTHY MIND – RENOUNCE YOUR GUILTY PLEASURES.

"Bugger. That's me in a bad mood for the next seven days. No tea, no coffee, no wine or crisps – and worst of all, no scones. How will I cope?" I complain.

"Look on the bright side, Amy," smiles Claire. "At least you'll really savour your glass of wine next Friday night."

Thank God for small mercies.

We leave the coffee house in companionable silence. I feel so much better. It's as if a partial weight has been lifted from my shoulders. Perhaps I'm not going mad after all.

Back home, I go online to investigate juicing and healthy eating and decide to buy an Italian brand of super-high-speed blender. It sounds highly sophisticated and will look fab in my kitchen. Unsurprisingly, Geoff is supportive of me spending his money on this gadget. As he reads about the associated health benefits, he becomes visibly excited and praises the person who set this challenge.

"Pay for next-day delivery, Amy," he says. "The sooner you start, the sooner we'll see the benefits. I trust that this isn't a one-week wonder, though? You kid yourself you're fatter because you've given birth twice and it's supposedly natural to gain a few pounds when you're older, but I don't believe it. I expect to see some return from my investment."

I wholeheartedly disagree with his viewpoint, but to keep the peace and the blender, I humour him. It's not worth starting an argument. The children are upstairs and the last thing Pippa needs is to overhear Geoff's warped opinions about women and their weight. She's embarrassed enough about her body as it is.

10.00 p.m.

Geoff has an early start tomorrow and has gone to bed. I'm trying to ignore an extreme craving for wine by composing my new improved text to Him. Without a drink in my hand, it's extremely hard to do, and it takes several attempts before I'm satisfied. What I'm dying to write is the following:

DAMN YOU!
REPLY AS SOON AS YOU READ THIS

WHICH MEANS RIGHT THIS MINUTE
AND SAY YES.
I AM SITTING HERE WAITING.
MY PHONE IS GLUED TO MY SIDE.
I AM DYING WITH ANTICIPATION.
PLEASE DO NOT MAKE ME WAIT,
PLEASE DO NOT IGNORE IT OR SAY NO.

What I come up with, however, is slightly more restrained:

Hi.
We met at the surgery recently.
I'm the lady doing fifty-one
challenges this year and want to
write about them.

I read that back. It sounds professional, friendly and not
pushy. I carry on.

I'd really appreciate your advice.

I like that too. Now for the most important bit.

Please let me know if you are happy to help asap.

I only hope he takes note of that last line. It's so important
that there is some sort of closure. *Don't leave me hanging – it'll be
pure torture,* I think as I add a smiley face to lighten my message
before pressing Send.

Saturday.
I am in a foul mood. I woke with a throbbing headache, and I
know that today is going to be difficult as I can't eat or drink my
favourite things *and* he has not replied to my text.

Claire rings. "Have you done it?"

"I texted him last night, and since I woke up I've been checking non-stop for a reply. I've even taken to talking to my phone – begging it for a sign."

Claire laughs. "My advice is to keep busy and remain positive. Blokes aren't like us when communicating – you know that. He'll get in touch when *he's* ready. He won't have a clue that you're an emotional wreck waiting for his reply. He might stay silent for a few days 'cos that's how men are, but do *not*, under any circumstance, text him again."

"You're right, Claire," I say, resolute. I have much better things to do than waste time and energy on him."

"And if he doesn't reply, then you're probably better off without him anyway, hon," she concludes. "I'm sure you can find somebody else to help you with your fifty-first challenge."

That afternoon, Evie and I assemble my new Italian super-expensive high-speed blender. Pippa's plugged into her mobile as usual, refusing to participate. "Come and see!" I yell across to her enthusiastically. "This recipe booklet looks really interesting. It's for *bambini e adolescenti* too and will help your acne."

She casts a disdainful look in my direction. "Could've spent the money on a phone upgrade for me," she huffs, and stomps from the room.

"Ignore the behaviour," I breathe, and occupy myself with attempting to translate the instructions.

Evie examines a colour image of a smiling, slim, radiant-looking woman holding a luminous green drink in her right hand. She stares at me sceptically. "Mum, there is no way I am drinking *that*," she says, pointing to the image. "It looks like snot."

Later that afternoon, I persuade Pippa and Evie to accompany me to the supermarket, where we purchase at speed everything I need to achieve my challenge, as advised in the *manuali de buone pratiche*. I have promised to take them to the six o' clock showing of *How to Train Your Dragon II* at the cinema if they help me. My trolley-full costs triple my usual weekly shop, but I console myself with the fact that for once it's full of healthy stuff, so Geoff cannot complain.

We arrive at the cinema with minutes to spare before the film begins. I'm boiling hot, but I daren't take off my fleece for fear of revealing hidden healthy treats. As we inch forward towards Screen 3, I scour the queue to try and see why it's moving so damn slowly and freeze.

It's Him – with a friend – and they are about to walk past me right… now. I hold my breath and my stomach in and try not to catch his eye, but he recognises me. Our eyes lock, and then he is gone.

Sunday, 11.00 a.m.

I surface late, having spent a couple of lazy hours absorbing *Heat* and *OK* magazines over my healthy breakfast pulverised drink. I'm ecstatic that I have already had four of my recommended daily fruit and vegetable portions – and it's not even midday. I lie in bed, enjoying my freedom. I so love it when Geoff is away, as I can indulge in all the guilty pleasures he finds so shallow.

Before the children, Geoff and I would spend many a Sunday morning together in bed, nurturing our relationship. I have fond memories of us downing boxes of chocolates, listening to CDs and watching TV. Twenty-odd years down the line and two children later, this is a dim and distant memory. Nowadays, regardless of what day it is, he springs out of bed at seven. By half past eight (on a weekend) he has made me feel guilty enough to crawl out of bed, and by half past ten he is in full flow doing 'stuff of value' while I have been somehow press-ganged into whipping up pancakes for breakfast, baking Geoff's weekly pie and fruit loaf, tidying the house, chivvying our daughters to get up and doing other 'obligatory' household chores.

I know that reading in bed and connecting with his wife on a Sunday morning is no longer on Geoff's radar. In fact, it saddens me that this aspect of our lives has somehow been lost. *I don't think we'll ever get that back again, though, however much I might like to,* I reflect. *Things have changed.*

I keep myself from thinking about Him and the absence of a text (even though he definitely recognised me yesterday) by cooking a roast dinner – a wonderful childhood tradition that never happens in our house when Geoff is around.

Pippa sees my efforts and kisses me lovingly. "Yummy! Why don't we do this more often? Is it because Dad doesn't like wasting the day eating and chilling?"

A wave of nostalgia washes over me. She's right. He used to, once – but nowadays, the only time he'll happily indulge in a hearty roast dinner is on Christmas Day. I grab my laptop and add comments to my diary entry about food, diet and weight.

By ten in the evening, my home is an oasis of calm. Evie's tucked up in bed and Pippa, who is supposedly doing her homework, is chained to her mobile. We have had a lovely day, chatting, laughing and playing board games. I haven't felt so relaxed on a Sunday for ages. I flop onto the sofa, ready to indulge in past episodes of *Don't Tell the Bride* once I've typed up my diary entry. I can't quite believe how easy it's been to eat healthily. I have missed caffeine, wine and crisps, and my head is still sore – but I have survived. I feel most positive about the rest of this week, but I'm not so sure I want to keep it up for much longer, whatever Geoff says or thinks. The novelty of blending fruit and veg is wearing off a bit, and there's a part of me that's angry and wants to spite him and his sexist opinions. *I'll tell him I've lent it to someone,* I think. *That'll keep him quiet.*

My mobile bleeps with a message. *Ah, telepathy, Geoff,* I smile, flicking on the TV. *I suppose that's from you. I'll pick it up later.*

Monday, 10.00 a.m.
What with Pippa missing the school bus and my remembering at

a quarter to nine that I had a blood test booked for nine o'clock, I haven't had time to look at Geoff's text. The unread message is not from Geoff at all.

> Sorry not been in touch.
> Keen to meet, babe.
> You decide when and where.

I ring Claire, my hands trembling. "What do you think?"

"His text sounds friendly enough, and he's keen to help you. It's up to you now. Just remember what I said about meeting in a public place, and dress appropriately." She giggles in a most inappropriate manner. "No Bea-style low-cut tops or push-up bras."

"It's not a date. I'm not going there with any intention of shagging him. He has no sense of style, he has tats and I am much too old for him. There is absolutely no way that anything is going to happen, is there Claire?"

"Not when you put it like that, Ames," she jokes. "Wait until Friday before you reply. Then go for it. Find out what you need to know, stare into his beautiful blue eyes and get him out of your system. You are allowed to have a coffee with him, you know. You're *not* betraying Geoff. Keep procrastinating, and you'll overthink the situation and drive yourself mad. You'll imagine things that aren't real and, believe me, you don't want to go down that road. I've been there. Take it from me – it's not worth it."

Week Three

Friday.

My lunch break usually consists of a quick whizz round the local supermarket. Today, I have to be extra-speedy because at long last it's Friday and I'm desperate to reply to his text. It's sod's law that only two tills are open. The queue is long and I am *impatient.* I wait in line, fists clenched in sheer frustration as I inch towards the cashier.

"Hiya. Cash or card?"

"Card." *Be quick, be quick, be quick,* I mutter inaudibly. I simultaneously pack my purchases and punch in my PIN. I have exactly ten minutes left to text and get back to my desk which is just enough time.

I've spent ages mentally creating my message, and once back in the office car park, I type:

> How about next Friday afternoon at 3pm?
> Do you know The House café?
> It should be quieter there at that time
> so we can talk.
> If any problems, text me. Amy.

Hopefully, he will turn up.

3.30 p.m.
Work over. Next stop: Daisy Hill Academy.
This week's challenge is to:

INSPIRE THE NEXT GENERATION.

I must organise it this afternoon.

I press the intercom and wait to enter. Hands thrust deep inside my pockets, I steel myself to smile at 'Dragon' Deacon, the School Administrator.

Mrs Deacon acquired this rather unfortunate nickname because, sadly, she is a fire-breathing, scaly creature who has held the same position at Daisy Hill Academy for nigh on thirty years. A formidable woman, arrogant, with an inflated sense of self-importance, she has complete contempt for whoever crosses her path – which unfortunately, we *all* have to do because her office is right by the school entrance and we cannot avoid her.

As an avid people-watcher, I have noticed something most intriguing about Mrs Deacon that few others have spotted. Only *women* trigger such derision from her. Men, whatever their age, elicit a totally different response, and today I am fortunate enough to see her in action. "Good morning," I smile. "Is it possible to have a quick word with the headteacher, please?"

"Wait here," she replies icily.

The intercom buzzes. It's a delivery man. Hooray. Let the extreme flirting begin. I watch astounded as Dragon Deacon simpers, preens and flutters her eyelids at him. I text Bea:

Mrs Dragon is doing her stuff...

The reply is instant:

NOOOO.
Has the stroking begun?

On cue, Dragon Deacon casts her eyes briefly downward, and the blatant 'come on' begins. She smiles at him in an overtly sexual manner, fans herself under the pretence that she's feeling flushed, s-l-o-w-l-y unbuttons her sensible black cotton cardigan to reveal a figure-hugging blood-red t-shirt and deliberately makes as if to brush imaginary fluff from her upper body; her hands gliding rhythmically from her shoulders, around her neck and across her ample bosom. The delivery man, (in his late fifties, I'd say) slides just a tiny bit closer to her, colour flooding his face as he realises her intentions, his eyes fixated on her heaving breasts.

I cough deliberately, unable to stomach any more of this schmoozing. Mrs Deacon comes to with a start. Her head snaps round as she remembers that I am there. "Ah, Mrs Richards," she says coolly, "Class Three." I thank her most profusely for her time and scuttle away.

Daisy Hill Academy. Tuesday, 3.15 p.m.

"Mrs Richards. So pleased that you can help us out," says the headteacher, pumping my hand enthusiastically. "If you would be so kind as to follow me? No running please, Kerri... I'll introduce you to Tamicka, our after-school club leader... Sorry about the noise... Year Five, stand in line quietly please, we have a visitor... Ah, here's Tamicka."

4.00 p.m.

Fifteen hyperactive 'dogs' wolf down toast and jam. Tamicka is the 'chief dog', and she sits on a throne of sorts, wearing a decorated paper crown.

"Tamicka," I whisper. "Why are you all woofing?"

"We're communicating in canine," she replies. "Tomorrow, we're elephants or meerkats. We'll vote on it later." She turns to the children. "Mrs Richards is helping us out today. Shouldn't she be a dog too?"

The children kindly nominate me to be 'dog mother', in charge of a rabble of naughty puppies. I spend the whole time disciplining them and putting them in the naughty kennel. They absolutely love it. I absolutely hate it. I thank Tamicka, take two headache pills and resolve *never* to do this again. I go to find the headteacher.

Wednesday morning.

Now, this is more like it. Assisting Year Six with French is right up my street. Mr Kniver, the class teacher, welcomes me warmly and admits that his French language skills aren't that great. "I'm sure my pronunciation is a bit off, Mrs Richards," he says. "Perhaps you could help me there?"

Oooh. Yes.

I observe his attempts to engage the class. His pronunciation isn't 'off' – it's appalling. Within minutes, three children are being 'spoken to', a group of boys are making paper darts and the rest of the children look thoroughly bored. I stifle a yawn.

In the staff room, we review what happened. Dare I tell him that his lesson was totally uninspiring? He hands me a steaming mug of tea and rubs his eyes. "That didn't go too well, did it?" He looks quite upset.

"Well…"

"Be honest, Amy."

So, I tell him straight, and we make a plan.

Thursday, 11.00 a.m.

Before the lesson begins, I rearrange the classroom. *Nowhere to hide today, mes enfants, I mean war. Oui, c'est la guerre,* I smile to myself.

We learn numbers to sixty using an excellent action song that Pippa found on the web last night. *Everyone* is attentive. *Nobody* misbehaves. "Was that ok?" I ask nervously, at the end of the lesson. "I was concerned that I might be asking too much of them."

"No, Amy," he replies, smiling. "You're doing great. See you tomorrow."

Tomorrow… I pale.

"Anything wrong?"

"No… It's just that I've just remembered an important appointment… tomorrow. Bye, then."

Oh, my Lord.

Tomorrow.

I'm seeing Him.

Week Four. Friday, 2.30 p.m.

It's almost time to meet Him. I luxuriate in a lavender-scented bubbly bath, trying hard to de-stress and practising for The

Moment We Say Hello. Fortunately, I was so busy in school this morning that I had no time to think about what I'm about to do. Leaving the kids was surprisingly emotional. The class came a long way in such a short time, and I thoroughly enjoyed the experience. I'd volunteer in school more regularly if life were different…

My mobile vibrates with a text message. Sighing, I climb out of the bath, dry myself off and pick up my phone.

> Sorry, something important's come up.
> Next Friday, same time?
> I'll be there. Promise.

Bugger.

7.30 p.m.
Geoff grills me at length about my volunteering challenge.

"I've always thought that teaching would be a suitable career for you once the children were older, Amy. It'd fit in around their school hours, and you'll earn decent dosh. It's time for you to drop that little job you have and find something more appropriate."

"What do you mean, 'more appropriate'? I like my job. It's important to me. It fits in around the children's needs and it's not *little*," I reply.

"Pfft! You know what I'm saying. It's not exactly stretching, is it? The kids are less trouble now, and you're only working part time. You've far too much free time for coffee mornings with non-entities and superfluous shopping trips these days."

"I work full time. I work really hard. A lot of my work here is unpaid, but it's still work. And who are these non-entities, Geoff?"

"It's not work, Amy. It's nothing like the high-powered sales position you held when we first met. I allowed you to indulge yourself because I understood that being at home with the children was important to you. It clearly stated in our marriage agreement – point number nine, as I recall – that the wife, namely you, would take on the primary role of child-rearer and housewife until the children were of an age. It's what you signed up for when you said you wanted marriage and kids with me, and you're very good at it. However, this challenge of substance has identified to me that it's high time you gave up watching daytime TV and some of the other stuff you've been doing. Set yourself an objective to get your brain back and have a *real* career."

He looks at his watch. "I'm gonna be late for the Chartered Accountancy dinner. Fasten my bow tie for me?" He takes a cursory glance around the kitchen. "This house is a bit of a tip, isn't it? While I'm out do you think you could file that pile of your crap over there and tell Evie to put her fleece away? Oh, and remind the kids that if they don't tidy their pigsties by tomorrow, it'll all be going to the tip. Now then." He fastens his dinner jacket, admires his reflection in the bedroom mirror and smiles. "I'm ready for action. How about curry for tea tomorrow night? We've not had one for ages. Quite fancy a Rogan Josh – with wholegrain rice, of course. See you later – bye."

I hear his car reversing out of the drive. That 'crap' he's referred to is *his* paperwork relating to a lads' golfing short break next spring that *he's* organising. I am *so* incensed at what he's said and at his attitude, I shred the lot.

The phone rings. It's Grandma. Given my mood, I'm reluctant to chat and decide to cut our usual conversation short, telling her that I'm going out for a meal and asking if I can ring her back tomorrow.

"What, *bubelah*?" Grandma sounds very excited. "You're going out with Seal? That song *Kiss From a Rose* makes me cry every time your mother plays it."

How on Earth does she know that song? I snigger to myself. She's so cool. "No, Grandma," I yell down the line. "I am eating out with my friends. You remember Claire?"

"The one who introduced you to Geoffrey? Don't trust her. She's trouble. Liked his jokes too much."

"You're confusing her with Jess's ex, Grandma. Listen, gotta go. I'll call you back tomorrow. Bye."

Adriano's Restaurant. 9 p.m.
I arrive late at Adriano's to find Bea and Cate acting out the scene that I witnessed between Dragon Deacon and the delivery man last week. There's a lot of hilarious embellishment and my mood softens. I feel my phone vibrating in my pocket. *If it's a message from Geoff telling me to do anything else, I'm switching it off,* I think grimly. I glance at the text and do a double-take. It's from Him again. Claire registers the look of surprise and pleasure on my face. "Is that who I think it is?"

"Yep," I reply curtly, opening the message, prepared for another let down. It reads:

Feel bad about today, honest!
Defo see you Friday? Xx

My eyes widen and I suddenly feel quite warm. "Claire," I say, my eyes bright as I stare at the kisses at the end of his text. "Pour me a large wine, will you?"

11.45 p.m.
Geoff is sitting up watching reruns of QI when I sway drunkenly into the lounge. "Good time?" he asks absentmindedly, his eyes firmly fixed on Stephen Fry.

"Yesh, I had a very good time thank you very mush. You waiting up for me? You *never* do that. What did you think? That I'd run away from you and you'd lose your cake baker? Ha ha ha." I flop down on the sofa next to him, attempt to remove my shoes and overbalance, landing in a heap on the carpet. "I sink I am drunk. I had sush a good night, sush a funny night, because…"

"Shush, you're pissed," he cuts in. "I'm waiting up because I can't find my bloody golfing break info and I thought you'd know where it is. You sounded happy in the kitchen, singing away," he adds.

"Yesh, I like singing when I'm happy or sad and tonight I am very, very happy. Because I'm happee…" I sing. "Pharrell Williams. Shee what I jussh did, I sang Pharrell's song… because I'm happee," I cackle. Geoff's eyes remain fixed on QI. "Shhure you don't want to hear about my evening, kind sir?" I slur, stroking his arm. "Ish it date night?" I kiss his cheek and take his hand. "Shtop watching QI and come wish me," I whisper. "You will find your golfing stuff tomorrow."

Saturday, 10.00 a.m.
My mouth. My head. I can't think straight. The dehydration and nausea is overpowering. Oh, my Lord. What happened to me? I can't quite remember why I got completely blitzed.

Geoff comes into the bedroom, sees I am awake and throws open the curtains. He is in an exceptionally good humour. "Good morning, wifey. Here you go, dearest darling," he says, handing me a cup of tea, some headache tablets and a banana.

Dearest darling? I think, stupefied. *Where did that term of endearment spring from? He hasn't called me that in years. I know we had sex last night, so I'd expect him to be nicer towards me… but this?*

"You stay there and I'll sort out the children – you deserve it." He kisses my forehead and gives me a cheeky grin. "Hope we have more nights like last night, Amy. I haven't seen you so amorous in ages. If you keep that up, I'll happily ditch my other women. Still looking for my golfing info." He winks and goes.

I cower under the duvet as it all comes flooding back. I know why I was so passionate last night, why I completely let go. It's all because of that text. He sent me *kisses*. Oh shit. I can't believe how damn crazy it made me feel. I haven't felt so excited in years.

I've never lusted after anyone else since I met Geoff. What is going on? It's so wrong. Then I remember Claire's words, which makes me feel just a bit better. I'm not doing anything bad. I'm not cheating. I didn't do anything wrong. If a bit of secret lusting spices up our sex life and does this to Geoff, that's gotta be good, hasn't it? I'm overcome by a wave of nausea and try to sleep.

Lunchtime.

"Were you drunk last night?" accuses Evie.

"Of course she was," snaps back Pippa. "Didn't you hear her caterwauling when she crashed her way in at midnight?"

I open my eyes. *I don't remember that.* "I was singing? What was I singing, exactly?" I ask, curious.

"Something about 'pushing it'. Couldn't really tell as you were slurring a lot. You were well gone."

"Ummm. It happens sometimes." I murmur. *What was I singing?* I Google '*Push It*' and the girl group Salt-n-Pepa magically appears at the top of the search engine. *Oh no! I was singing about sex.* I can't help but laugh. I sit there propped up in bed and I laugh so hard that I double over. *I was singing about... NO!* I can't believe it. *Amy Richards, this has got to stop – right now,* I reprimand myself, throwing the laptop aside and going to find Evie, who has my next challenge ready.

We go round to our neighbours' house for Saturday evening drinks. Talk eventually turns to my next challenge.

"Amy is supposed to be going to Blackpool Pleasure Beach to:

RIDE A BIG ONE.

"... You know, that *huge* rollercoaster," crows Geoff. "You successfully rode a big one last night, and now this," he winks. "Not sure if you'll be so 'happeee' at the end of this ride, though," he chortles, leering at me. My eyes narrow and my gaze hardens. He knows full well that I have a fear of heights. It's just mean.

Sunday, 11.00 a.m.
The doorbell rings. It's Mel.

"Amy, I couldn't help but notice how unhappy you looked last night when we were told about your next challenge. Are you afraid of rollercoasters?" I decide it's time to admit my phobia.

"I'm scared of heights. When we visited the Eiffel Tower in Paris a couple of years ago, I stayed at the bottom. It's a bit pathetic, isn't it?"

"Not really," Mel smiles. "We all have our issues. How about seeing a hypnotherapist? This one helped me stop smoking a while back." She hands me a business card for 'Rachel Mighton'.

Geoff returns from work on Tuesday evening, elated at having bought us *Pleasure Beach* passes for Thursday night. Evie and Pippa are ecstatic, while – not surprisingly – I am less amused. "The *pleasure* is all mine," he laughs.

"You're only doing this because you want to see my pain and suffering," I reply, slamming the dishwasher shut.

"No. Face your fear and you'll be fine with being at high altitude. Then, I can book us on a walking holiday in Austria next spring. I think that once you have ridden The Big One, you'll be fine with cable cars and mountains. We'll have a healthy holiday, and while I am there I can…"

And he's off, animatedly describing what *he* thinks, what *he* will do and what *we* will do when we all go on this wonderful family break. My laptop gets the brunt of my frustration. I call Rachel Mighton.

Thursday, 7.00 p.m.
I feel resentful and angry. Thanks to Rachel, I'm no longer anxious about the rollercoaster ride. However, I simply cannot forget what Geoff said about the Austrian walking holiday, and

I really don't want to see his smug face watching me. I realise something about the challenge, and while my family are riding *The Grand National*, I slip away. "Ha ha," I scream as I race along the track on a bobsled-type ride based on being in the Alps. "I am riding A Big One in the Alps. It's not as high as *The* Big One, but it's higher than anything I would ever have managed before." I buy the photo to show as evidence, feeling vindicated.

April

Daisy Hill Academy is hosting its annual fayre today, and (as usual) it's us long-suffering parents who've been press-ganged into helping out. Evie's been trying to encourage Geoff to come along. Unsurprisingly, he has much more important things to do than help the school raise funds for musical instruments, and he's still sulking about how I 'disobeyed' him in Blackpool.

"You girls enjoy this sort of thing, and I'd just get under your feet," he says, wheedling his way out of it. "Tell you what, I'll pop in later. Okay?" He picks up his clubs and goes, leaving me to console a desolate child. I consider chasing after him, but I don't. He won't change his mind. Golf always takes priority and always will.

Down at the fayre, there's a buzz of activity. Bea, Claire and I are in charge of the book stall. "I don't understand why Geoff is so against helping out at school fundraising events, Claire. He knows full well the financial pressure that school is under, and Evie would kill for her dad to be here – but golf is always more important. Sometimes, I don't get him at all."

"I reckon he's a bit insecure because he has a fear of not being in control," she replies. "Anyway, do you really want him here, getting under your feet? I've happily left mine at home doing whatever men do. It's more fun without the added stress of having to manage them. If Bob were here, he'd be forever asking what he should do, not doing it well and whingeing that he's bored. I'd have to keep patting him on the head and filling him up with tea and cake. You agree, don't you, Bea?"

"Nice to hear you're talking sense for once, pet. When I got married, I was given a very good piece of advice from my aunt: keep their stomachs full and their balls empty. Then they're happy and you get a quiet life, which means that you can do whatever you like without retribution. Just think about how loving and caring they become the morning after sex the night before. It's all bollocks, really."

"I agree about the benefits of the 'wifely duty,'" I groan, thinking back to my drunken night of passion. "Geoff did say that he might pop in later – for healthy cake, naturally."

"He never changes," smiles Claire. "It'll be nice to catch up with him. Let me know when he arrives."

By late afternoon, the fayre draws to a close and the various raffles are drawn. Geoff has finally materialised and is busy scoffing copious amounts of carrot cake (it's now half price) and chatting animatedly with Claire, leaving me to box up the unsold books.

Josie Jamieson, the chair of the PTA, announces that it's time for me to pick the winning raffle ticket for the person who is going to draw my next challenge. I take the Bowl of Chance and Opportunity up to the stage. "Ticket number fifty-four," calls out Josie Jamieson with aplomb.

"That's mine." A dull-eyed woman, her right shoulder spattered in baby sick, drags two whining toddlers onto the stage. "What you're doing is inspirational. I hope you find fulfilment. And when you do, let me know what to do to wangle it," she mutters under her breath as she unfolds the slip of paper. "Your next challenge is a good deed." My challenge is to:

TREAT A HOMELESS PERSON.

Sunday, 11.00 a.m.

Today is an official 'family bonding day', and we are out visiting a local castle and gardens. This is usually deemed a successful outing, as the obligatory walk that Geoff demands is a relatively short stroll, with no major hills to negotiate and plenty to see. If anyone does have a strop and walk off, they can't go too far and get lost. The other great thing about this day out is that there is always a lovely tea room to try, which means a guaranteed scone fix. What could be better?

It's a typical dank Cumbrian day, and I'm trying to make the best of it. Pippa is lost in the music on her mobile, as usual. Evie's in a strop because she's had to come out minus her yellow hoodie (it's in the wash). This leaves Geoff and me to make pleasant conversation. "You're quiet," he says. "Feeling guilty about your insubordination at Blackpool, or is it menopausal moodiness, Amy?"

"I have a slight headache."

That is a lie. I don't have a headache, I'm definitely not menopausal, and I certainly don't feel bad at having refused to do what he wanted me to at Blackpool. But I am in a total head-spin about something else. *Do I meet Him? Should I meet Him? Perhaps say no?* I chant rhythmically in my head, keeping time with my footsteps.

Despite my best efforts to rationalise the situation, I feel guilty about meeting Him because, deep down, I am very aware of the possible implications. Can I do as Claire suggests and treat it as an oh-so-innocent professional appointment? I am so mixed up that I could scream. We continue with our walk and I think on.

"How am I going to *find* a homeless person, let alone befriend one and take them out for a treat?" I complain bitterly to Geoff over dinner. "It sounds a bit, well, condescending and creepy."

His reply shocks me. "Why the fuck are you wasting your

time on them? They got themselves into a mess, and they should get themselves out of it. Parasites."

I say nothing. There's no point.

Google gives me a hard time when I search 'How to help the homeless'. There's tons of information about making financial donations, which isn't what I need to do. "None of this is relevant," I sigh. "I'll try something else." I look up 'Help homeless in my area'. Bingo. I scan the list hungrily. According to the sites, I could contact the church or a voluntary organisation in town and get involved that way. *That doesn't sound too difficult*, I think. I open another tab listing local soup kitchens and locate our local branch of a charity for the homeless. I cheer up considerably, note down the number and go to bed feeling positive.

Tuesday, 4.00 p.m.

My challenge doesn't specify how to 'treat' a homeless person. What sort of treat should I provide? I don't want to be condescending or give them something useless. My treat must be… what? Valuable? Unique? Useful? I group-message my friends:

If I were to treat you, what would you like?
Please be realistic.

Half an hour later, the results are in. I skip through the suggestions: a good book, restaurant meals, trip in a Limo, spa pamper… I stare into space. *How about giving myself – my time? That would be useful and valuable and unique and definitely something that money can't buy.* I need a second opinion.

Pippa is in her bedroom, knee-deep in homework. I take her a bowl of chocolate to (hopefully) improve her mood and get her interested in my task. "Brain food, Pips."

"Hey, Mum," she replies, snatching the bowl out of my hand and turning back to her work. I perch on the end of her bed.

"Help me out here. If I were to treat you, what would you like from me – apart from chocolates," I smile.

"I don't need to be treated," she says indignantly. "I don't have a problem, and I'm not ill."

"No, silly," I say, amused. "Treat as in spoil – not treat as in cure or make better. If I were to give you a special *treat*, what would it be?"

She sucks on a chocolate. "What I'd really like," she says quietly, "is for us to hang out like we did when you made Sunday dinner. I really enjoyed that."

My instincts are correct. The greatest gift that I can give someone is my time – time to listen, to sit with somebody and then, maybe, offer more if I possibly can. I note on my laptop the profound comment that Pippa's just made. I need to find more time to chill out with my daughters.

That night I contact a local church and offer to serve food in their community café on Thursday evening.

Thursday, 6.00 p.m.
May, the person in charge, has been most welcoming, and has informed me that I will be serving portions of shepherd's pie. She's allocated me a buddy called Pete. May reliably informs me that Pete is a seasoned volunteer with a great sense of humour, and that he likes the ladies.

The minute I meet Pete, I just know that we are going to get on. He gets down on one knee, takes my hand and bursts into song, albeit very badly, to the tune of *Daisy Daisy*. "Amy, baby, give me your answer do. I'm Pete an' crazy, oh to be working with you." He stands up again. "Welcome to this place of kindness and service, Amy. Behold your gallant knight, who will protect you from the marauding masses about to descend upon us."

"Wow, what a welcome!" I laugh. "Tell me what I have to do. I don't know how to behave, and I'm a bit nervous. These 'marauding masses' can't be that bad, can they?"

Pete is in his forties but looks at least ten years older. He must've had a tough life; he's wearing what was once an expensive white cotton shirt that's now badly stained with a fraying collar, his hair is lank and his face is leathery. As Pete articulately describes my duties, my eyes are drawn to his delicate hands. Although we've only just met, I inexplicably feel completely at ease with him. He reminds me of my dad.

Pete gives sound, honest advice. "Remember that homeless people are just like you or me. When they come up to you, they might meet your eye and smile or want to talk. Some will thank you as you serve them. Others might be tired, depressed or hungry and will simply want their food served quickly. Just be yourself, Amy baby," he grins. "I can tell that you have a good heart."

Service begins. I observe Pete cracking jokes as he works. However, I can tell that it's a front. Although he's a great laugh, there's sadness behind his smile.

The time flies by, and I realise that I'm having a ball. Even collecting dirty crockery and cutlery and wiping down the tables is enjoyable. As I work, I reflect on my achievements so far. I have successfully made twelve people smile and seven laugh at my jokes. Three have looked at me as if I am mad, and I am now clearing a table while having a wonderful conversation with a lady called Julie and her teenage daughter Bianca about how best to deal with cyber-bullying through social media.

I notice Pete watching me. "I'm not slacking as I chat, you know," I call over, not quite sure if I'm breaking any rule.

"Take five, Amy baby. Here's a cuppa. Now, look around you and tell me what you see?"

I do as instructed and observe thirty homeless people eating in silence or staring into space. "Pete? Isn't there anything for these people to do once they have finished their meals? Some of them look, well... bored."

"Interesting. What could we do about it, babes?"

I think for a minute and whisper in Pete's ear. We approach May, and I make a couple of calls. An hour later, thirty homeless people are no longer bored. Becca, my hairdresser, is offering free haircuts. Harmony, my beautician, and two of her team are performing head rubs and doing mini-manicures. Claire's giving lessons about using social media, and Bea's supervising raucous games of bingo and cheat. There is a buzz in the room. I see Pete and May chatting and laughing. I feel good.

By half past nine, everyone, apart from the staff, has gone. "Do you know why I really came here today?" I ask Pete, chewing nervously on my finger.

"Not really, Amy baby," he yawns. "Why are you here?"

I open up to him about nearly everything: my epiphany, my year of self-discovery and adventure and this week's challenge – including how troubled I am by Geoff's prejudicial attitude.

Pete listens intently, and as I finish, he hugs me. "You cheered many people up tonight, and you gave me and May lots of ideas for improving our service here. Come back again and perhaps bring your husband along – maybe we'll be able to change his mind about us."

"I'm beginning to think that Geoff could learn a lot from this year of mine, and I *definitely* plan to come back a lot more in the future." I look him squarely in the eye. "It's been good for me."

It's gone midnight when I write up my diary entry on my laptop. I think of Pete. Lovely, kind-yet-sad Pete. *I want to keep in touch,* I type. *You have a story to tell. I've learned that I'd like to volunteer more regularly once this year is over and be more giving, although I doubt that Geoff will be too chuffed. How can I open his mind to the possibility? If I sell him the benefits, he won't refuse me, will he? Perhaps we could volunteer together?* I yawn and stretch. I don't expect Geoff to be waiting up for me or to be interested in my experience. No, I can clearly hear that he's in bed, fast asleep and snoring like a train.

Week Two. Friday, 2.15 p.m.

The day has finally arrived, and I am waiting for Him at the café we agreed on. I have purposely arrived early: firstly, because I have been wearing out my kitchen carpet pacing to and fro like a border-patrolling sentry; secondly, to ensure I secure a table in the *right location*; and thirdly, because I need to control myself. I cannot let him see that I am unbelievably, incredibly, ri*dicu*lously nervous.

Unfortunately, the café is busier than I would have liked for a Friday afternoon in April. There appears to be a parent and toddler group meeting at one end of the room and a raucous coach party of pensioners taking tea and cake at the other.

The rhythmic ticking of a clock on the wall to my right is grating on my nerves. With every tick, my blood pressure rises; the passing seconds feel like an eternity. I try to immerse myself in the latest copy of *OK* magazine. However, instead of madly enthusing over the latest fashions, baby arrivals and celebrity events as usual, I aimlessly flick through its glossy pages, willing Him to arrive and for our business meeting to be over. The door to the café opens and I automatically look up to see who it is.

2.22 p.m.
Café door opens… I look up… No, not Him.

2.23 p.m.
Café door opens… Still not Him.

2.24 p.m.
Café door opens… Bloody hell, it's Josie Jamieson. What is she doing here? He is going to arrive at *any moment* and Mrs Gossip will see us together. What shall I do? I need advice right now. Claire's at home. I'll call her.

"Claire, in approximately six minutes I will be with Him, and Josie Jamieson's just swanned in," I whisper, panic-stricken.

"Should I casually rock up to her, explain that I'm about to have a business meeting and walk away, or should I ignore her presence and wait to see what the fallout is? She'll put two and two together and make five – you know – that I am on *une mission secrète*, having *un fling,*" I say in my worst French accent.

"Say nothing and wait and see what she does," Claire giggles. "That would be really fun. But ultimately, it's up to you." I glance up the clock and my stomach flips. Four minutes before He arrives. I can't ignore Josie. I'm damned whatever I do, so I stride purposefully over to her.

"Afternoon, Mrs Richards. You're looking smart. On your own?"

I fire out a totally unplanned response. "Oh, I'm just about to have a fli… a *business* meeting with *a work colleague,*" I stress emphatically, pointing to my briefcase. "So, I'd better get back to my table as he'll be here in a minute. Just thought I'd say hello… and let you know… so… see you soon!" I glance up at the clock again.

"Well, enjoy." She looks at me strangely and, thankfully, she pays for a drink to take out and leaves.

2.33 p.m.
The door opens. I look up. No.

50 seconds later.
The door opens. I look up. No.

2.35 p.m.
The door opens. I look up. Yes.

Now then, Amy. Into role. Be friendly, smile and use positive body language. Think business meeting, think 'book' and 'advice' and 'guidance'. Do not think 'CCC'. A throwback rogue thought from my challenge as a Sex Chat Line Operator crosses my mind. *Think 'professional', 'awesome author'… and… Action.*

"Hi," he smiles. "Let me get you a drink. It's on me."

I watch as he goes to place our order and relax, just a tiny bit. I check him out. Scruffy t-shirt, oil-stained jeans, trainers, unbrushed hair, tattoo… Yep. No change. Yicht. I send Claire a quick text:

He's as scruffy as ever.
Think I'm over it.

He returns with our drinks; tea for me and a beer for him.

Our table is square with four chairs placed around it. He opts for the chair directly opposite me and places his drink, a notepad, a set of keys and a pen in a straight line in the centre of the table between us. I mirror him, placing my drink, large pad and mobile in a line directly in front of me, between us. Next, he repositions the condiments, menu and napkin holder and places them behind his drink, notepad, keys and pen in a second straight line. The battlefield is drawn. Two lines of infantry are in position, protecting their officers. I speak first.

"Thank you for coming here today. Jeez, I sound like I'm at work about to make a presentation," I blush.

He laughs easily. "How are you, Amy? I'm sorry; I only have an hour so we'd better crack on." His blue, blue eyes stare into mine…

Fifty minutes later we are still enthusiastically discussing challenge number fifty-one. He's so easy to talk to, and I'm making loads of notes. There's laughter and it's all very comfortable. The café door opens and closes constantly, but I don't look up, not once. Blimey, he really does know what he's talking about, I muse as I scribble madly.

The hour is up and he gathers his belongings. My hand aches with writing, and I have pages of notes to mull over. I don't quite know what to say but I know that I don't want Him to go yet.

The café door swings open. I look up and gasp. It's Geoff and Evie. What do I say? They are going to see us sitting together and ask lots of questions. I blink hard to check it really is them and automatically do what is necessary. I take a deep breath and beat a hasty retreat. I am without ammunition and need to protect myself from imminent disaster. "Oh, it's my daughter!" I say breezily. "Better get off." I leap out of my chair, grab my stuff and sprint across the café to greet my family. As I kiss Evie hello, I steal a peek at Him. His blue eyes signal confusion and hurt. I see him hover undecidedly by the table for a moment, and then I watch him go.

That's that, then, I think as I head for home. *I screwed up good and proper. He must have thought I was so rude, not saying thanks or goodbye and rushing off like that.* My chagrin increases as the minutes pass. *I've been such a muppet. He'll never want to give me his time again. Perhaps that's my sign. Yes. I'd better forget all about him, from now on. I have some notes to help with the fifty-first challenge, so I'll try to go it alone.*

I pull in at a quiet layby and rest my head on the steering wheel. *I know why I acted as disgracefully as did. It's because... I* stare into space. "I cannot and must not communicate with you again. Farewell," I whisper dramatically under my breath. "I'll never forget, but perhaps it's best if I try." I turn the ignition key and head for home.

Saturday, 7.00 a.m.

I am supposed to be bag-packing in support of the Brownies at our local supermarket from half past nine, so I have dragged myself out of bed and showered. I am now sitting in the kitchen, attempting to feel more alive than I actually feel. When Geoff appears, bang on his usual weekend get-up time, I make him a cup of tea and hand it to him with a kiss – trying to be a good wife.

"I'm still pissed off that you went behind my back and bailed at Blackpool, you know?" he huffs. "And I'm disappointed that the blender's become an expensive *objet d'art*. He shrugs his shoulders, wanders over to the Bowl of Chance and Opportunity and peers into it. He delves his hand into the bowl and draws out today's challenge:

GIVE YOURSELF A SPRING CLEAN. HAVE A COLONIC IRRIGATION.

He raises his eyebrows. "That'll get you back for Blackpool, and it's miles better than that 'helping the low-lives' one," he mutters, before leaving the room to wash the cars.

At Work. Monday.
Amazingly, I have discovered that Hairy Nina has this treatment on a regular basis. I call her Hairy Nina because she openly embraces her natural beauty and refuses point blank to wax, shave, pluck or bleach a single strand of her facial hair. I think she is completely mad, yet brave in the extreme. We discuss her colon-cleansing experience over lunch. "So, what happens, exactly?" I ask, forking spaghetti bolognaise into my mouth and trying to avert my eyes from her moustache and mono-brow.

"In a nutshell, a trained person sticks a speculum up you and flushes you out with warm filtered water. It's fascinating seeing what's been sucked up. I'm sure I noticed something shiny in the viewing chamber the first time." She takes a spoonful of pasta bake. "Oh, and you might have your stomach massaged gently to dislodge any gunk stuck to the sides of your colon. It doesn't hurt, though."

"It sounds rather unsavoury to me," I reply, somewhat perturbed. I stop eating, my appetite having mysteriously disappeared. "How do you feel afterwards?" I ask, guarded.

"Tired, but in a nice way – as if I've had a good workout. Some people feel like they're reborn."

With that, we return to work. I secretly Google 'Colonic irrigation'. I have so many questions running around my head. I want to know if it really hurts; what it looks like and if it's as bad as having an enema. If it is, there's *no way* I'm having one. I suffered one of them in labour and nearly fainted. I note down the name of a couple of interesting looking YouTube videos to watch later.

9.00 p.m.

I've just logged into YouTube when Pippa comes into the kitchen, her appendage firmly attached to her hand, and looks over my shoulder to see what I am up to. "You're not, are you?" she shouts over her music.

"Not yet," I reply cagily, pulling her earphones from her ears. "I'm researching and am about to watch a clip to virtually experience what it's really like. Care to join me?"

"*Gross.* Why would I want to see *that*? I'm off."

I watch the clip in silence and knock back three shots of Drambuie. Wine is not enough.

Thursday.

Nina holds my hand in the clinic's waiting room because I am trembling. I don't think I can… I keep thinking about the clip and the possible side effects. I remember the enema when I was in labour. "Nina, I know I'm a wuss, but I simply can't do this. I don't think I'm going to learn anything of value. Don't try to persuade me otherwise. Please take me home."

I fail the challenge, and I don't care.

Week Three. Friday, 5.00 p.m.

SWING WITH THE MON-KEYS.

I can't bring myself to think about this challenge yet. The last one was so awful and, given Geoff's reaction to my recent ones, I've fibbed about failing it. I turn to a favourite failsafe coping mechanism – baking – for relief from my mental disarray.

As I roll out the dough for an apple pie, my thoughts inadvertently return to Him and our meeting in the café last Friday afternoon. It's been eating away at the back of my mind. I'm ashamed at my appalling behaviour and lack of manners.

Regardless of the fact that I have decided to never, ever see or talk to or text you ever again, I think I should make amends and apologise, I decide, while frantically cutting out the rounds.

The phone rings. "Hi, Grandma."

I put the phone onto loud-speaker and continue with my work as Grandma rolls out her usual spiel.

"What are you doing with yourself, *bubelah*?"

I take a deep breath. I need cheering up and decide to tell the truth and see what happens. "I'm going *swinging*," I shout into the receiver.

"Ooh! Swimming! I won medals for that. The boys used to say I was the best swimmer in town." I stifle a giggle. I'd just die if I held the title 'best swinger in town'.

Much later that evening, I am finally strong enough to acknowledge my challenge. This one is easy to arrange, thank goodness, but I'm going to have to be brave to go through with it. My thoughts turn to the Mon-Keys, as they are the people I need to make contact with.

I first met Mrs Mon-Key through my hairdresser, Becca, one December. We were both having our Christmas trims, and we all got rather tipsy on supermarket own-brand fizz. Back then she was known as Miss Mong. Over the next few years, we would bump into each other at Becca's, and it was there that she met Mr Key. She was having her hair bleached, and he was having highlights to disguise his silver fox streaks of grey. Romance blossomed over the hair dye, and they married soon after.

Mrs Mon-Key likes to present herself to the world as a flamboyant and *extremely* glamorous lady. She adorns herself in statement necklaces, her hair is always elegantly coiffed into a white-blonde beehive, and her make-up is simply stunning. She trowels on foundation that is slightly too dark for her skin tone and ends around her jawline, her cosmetically enhanced lips are permanently stained bright pink, and she never leaves home without her trademark long, thick black false eyelashes and the dreaded HD brows.

Her husband, a placid and generous man of around the same age, has a sense of style that is as interesting as his gorgeous wife's. He favours *bright* Hawaiian shirts (worn open to the waist to reveal a steel-grey hairy chest), a man-tan, and skin-tight trousers that leave *nothing* to the imagination. He reminds me of a seventies porn star.

It is obvious that the Mon-Keys are deeply in love. Whenever I see them together, I can't help smiling at their obvious continuing fascination with each other. Some people might find it embarrassing to see this constant show of affection, but I like it. In fact, I sometimes feel quite jealous of what they share. I smile to myself. I have a hair appointment for Evie arranged with Becca tomorrow. I'll sort it all out then.

Saturday morning.

Evie is in the chair and Becca is snipping away. I casually ask when Mrs Mon-Key will be in next. "You're in luck. She's due in an hour," replies Becca. She lowers her voice. "They're hosting a *party* tonight." She winks.

Evie stares at Becca through the mirror. "Why are you whispering about a party?"

"Nosy," I laugh. "It's a special party and they want to keep it a secret," I lie. Becca and I exchange knowing glances. It's *special* alright.

10.50 a.m.

Mr and Mrs Mon-Key make their grand entrance. He holds open the door to Becca's salon, and his dear wife floats in, parading a voluminous multi-coloured Grecian kaftan à la singing legend Nana Mouskouri, coupled with four-inch white diamanté wedge shoes, a floppy straw hat and a pair of huge round plastic-framed sunglasses. Her husband follows her, carrying her bags and struggling to keep a sausage dog under control.

"Hellooo," she cries. "Come *faire la bise*, darling." She theatrically air-kisses Becca three times. "Mwoah, mwoah, mwoah."

She spies me and Evie. "*Ciao*, darling – and this must be your mini-me?" She raises her sunglasses and examines Evie's face. "Oh, you are just gorgeous, honey bun," she smiles. She motions to Mr Mon-Key. "You can take care of Bratwurst, if you like. Pass her the lead, darling."

While Evie is busying herself with their pet, I pluck up the courage to ask Mrs Mon-Key if she can help me. "Why yes, darling, *tonight*. Experience the joys of super-swinging at our one-hundredth party masked ball. Pass her an invitation, Mr M."

"Er, tonight?" I take the invitation from Mr Mon-Key and put it in my pocket.

"No buts. You and Becca will have *such fun*. You can wear these." She rummages in her handbag and hands us two shiny, bejewelled masks with elastic tied around the back. "It makes it all the more interesting if you can't see who you're shagging," she says bluntly. "Wear whatever you like – anything goes, but you'll probably be better off in PJs and dressing gowns this time. Oh, and don't bother to eat beforehand, as there's a buffet. Be at ours for eight. How wonderful that we met today. We must celebrate. Pass the fizz, Mr M."

Evie's asleep when Becca dumps a second empty bottle of Prosecco into the recycling bin. My mobile vibrates. It's a text from Geoff demanding to know where I am, as it's gone lunchtime and he hasn't eaten yet. It sounds a bit angry. A few of the words are in capitals. I stare drunkenly at the message and press Delete.

7.00 p.m.
I have made my peace with Geoff in one of the best ways I know how – serving up his favourite meal (prawn red Thai curry, followed by apple pie) and plying him with beer. I am dreadfully anxious about tonight.

"Why are you ready for bed so early, and what's with the mask?" he asks. "Am I on a promise tonight?"

"Nooo, I'm… er… at the Mon-Keys' later, in aid of my latest challenge. But I'd rather not go," I say half-heartedly.

"YOU have an invite to their hundredth shag-fest?" he asks incredulously.

"How do you know about that?" I say, surprised.

"What planet are you on?" He stares at me in disbelief. "YOU are going to the most fucking amazing event ever and you don't want to go? You're not even a member."

"It sounds scary and, well, creepy, and not something I'd ever do." I shrug. "And how do you know about it, anyway?" I repeat.

"Their parties are legendary. It's every guy's dream. Bloody wish I could come," he says wistfully. "Get some action – a threesome or a gang-bang. Jess tells me…"

"STOP!" I yell, covering my ears with my hands.

"You're such a prude," he smiles, shaking his head in amusement. "Bring back some top tips. Go and learn how to use a whip," he sniggers.

Blimey, I think to myself as I wash up. *What on Earth am I going to see? What have I got myself into this time?*

8.30 p.m.
Becca and I are at the party, dressed in our not-so-sexy pyjamas and dressing gowns. Mine are purple with a white reindeer design and are topped with a fleecy pink dressing gown. Becca

is in red cotton stripy pyjamas with matching dressing gown. Our masks are secured, and we feel comfortable and – most importantly – anonymous and safe. The Mon-Keys greet us masked, but we know who they are because they are wearing name badges, like at a convention.

"Welcome, darlings!" cries Mrs Mon-Key, air-kissing us three times. "Shoes off!" She drops them into a rack behind her and hands us a glossy leaflet each. "Here's a map of the house. Drinks are straight ahead, and the buffet is through there." She indicates to a room off the hallway. A laminated sign headed *Information and Rules* catches Becca's eye.

"Should we read through the rules?" she asks.

"Yes, at your leisure," instructs Mr Mon-Key, ushering us away from the reception desk and into the hallway. "We're not charging you tonight, as it's your first time. However, when you leave, we'd be extremely grateful if you'd complete a feedback form. We're always striving to continuously improve our service, you know."

The doorbell rings again. The Mon-Keys drift away to greet more guests, and we are left alone.

We go to read the *Information and Rules*:

1. *Condoms – varied types in the red labelled boxes in each room.*
2. *Respect sexual preferences.*
3. *No petting in the buffet room.*
4. *Wash your hands before touching any food in the buffet room.*
5. *If a themed room is full, kindly wait your turn or go elsewhere.*
6. *The Hush Room is for relaxation, low-level chatting and sleeping. Anyone abusing this will be asked to leave.*
7. *The toilets on the Ground Floor are not for sex UNDER ANY CIRCUMSTANCES.*

8. Respect confidentiality and anonymity.

Concerns or questions? Dial 0800 113322.

"It's a slick operation," I remark. I don't quite know what else to say.

"Come on," hisses Becca, accepting flutes of champagne from a passing scantily clad masked male waiter. "Let's explore."

We enter the buffet room and stare in disbelief at the sight of two *enormous* trestle tables, groaning with food. Large printed signs in bold hang above each. We go left and read:

FINGER BUFFET.
DON'T FORGET TO WASH YOUR HANDS.

Our eyes alight on a range of hot and cold dishes to suit all tastes including several tempting puddings. We look to the right and I snort with mirth.

FINGERING BUFFET.
PAPER PLATES ONLY. NO CUTLERY ALLOWED.

An impressive display of foods, tins and jars, including cans of squirty cream, chocolate spread, jam and peanut butter greet us. Bowls of cold baked beans and custard sit invitingly. Tubs of posh ice cream are stacked in a mini freezer alongside bags of ice cubes and tubes of yoghurt. You cannot miss the huge fruit bowl piled high with bananas, grapes and strawberries. It's difficult to take it all in. Dumb-struck, we knock back two glasses of champagne each.

12.15 a.m.
We sway our way up to the second floor and the 'dungeon', a

dimly lit room kitted out with exact replicas of the equipment described in the novel *Fifty Shades of Grey*. It's mega-impressive.

Becca and I play about with the toys. I clock that she looks *extremely* interested in a set of handcuffs and the whips. She also looks *extremely* interested in a guy standing in the room close by, and he looks *extremely* interested in her. Leaving them to it, I decide to investigate the 'playground'. I gently rock to and fro on a swing, enjoying the laid-back vibe.

And then I hear a familiar voice. It can't be, can it? It's my sister Jess, and she's gently whipping a man called Mr Steele. My hand goes to my mouth, and I sneak closer to better listen in to their conversation, glad that my mask is concealing my identity.

"Mr Steele," she moans, "tell me about physics. I just *love* to hear you describe Newton's laws of motion. Let's put his theories to the test." *Oh my God, Claire. Your secret lust, your daughter's physics teacher, is getting it on with* my sister.

I hide behind the penis-shaped conifer, howling with laughter. That has made my night.

At four in the morning, we collect our shoes from Mrs Mon-Key and thank her for an excellent party. "I had the best time ever," says Becca, blushing profusely.

"Excellent, darlings. Here's our membership details and payment plan." Mrs Mon-Key smiles and moves away.

Saturday, midday.

Geoff's relentless probing into the goings-on at the party is draining. I tell him as much as I want to, leaving out key details about Becca and my sister.

"Are you sure you didn't get it on with anyone?" he asks for the third time. "I'm crushed."

"No, I didn't," I reply, disgruntled. "Why? Are you disappointed that I didn't commit adultery?"

"You've wasted a fantastic challenge. It wouldn't have been

adultery, darling. You had my blessing, for one thing, and it wouldn't have meant anything; shagging a stranger. It would have been a mind-blowing experience. Most women I know, with a few exceptions like puritanical Claire, would have got right in there and brushed up on their skills – like Jess and Stanley do."

"What?" I say incredulously.

He makes an obscene hand gesture and laughs. "I'm definitely calling you Prudish Parker from now on." He winks as his mobile rings and strolls outside to take the call.

I sit at the kitchen table feeling distinctly uncomfortable at what he has just said. I ring Becca.

"And how the devil are you, this afternoon?" I ask wickedly.

"Fine, I'm fine." Becca sounds hungover, yet chilled.

"Can I ask you something?"

"Okay."

"Do you honestly believe that people have regular one-night stands without it damaging their long-term relationship? Can they compartmentalise it in some way?"

"Well, that's what I did last night," she replies without hesitation. "Do I feel I cheated on my Stu? No, actually. I believe that this experience will enhance our relationship. I love Stu, not that other guy. He and I were just horny and in the moment. It was certainly a night to remember.

"Listen, Amy," she sighs, "It was a one-off. I believe that life is for living, and you only get one shot at it. I don't want to have *any* regrets and I want a shedload of fantastic memories at the end. As long as I'm not obviously hurting anyone, what's the harm in it? It doesn't mean anything significant to me and I know it never will. If others criticise me for thinking like this, that's their problem. I know you say you'd divorce Geoff if he ever cheated, but would you really? I see things differently. Just look at Mr and Mrs Mon-Key and their fantastic marriage. If they were monogamous, I bet that they wouldn't be as happy. They'd probably be divorced or stuck in a rut, as so many long-term relationships become, spending their nights fantasising about celebs or somebody else and knowing that that's it *forever*. No more moments of pure passion and fortyish bloody years relying on sex toys, booze, web porn and sex novels to get their kicks."

I write up my diary entry on my laptop and reflect on the events of the last few days. As I recap and think of Him, my stomach somersaults and my legs turn to jelly. Becca's views on monogamy echo in my head. She had been describing *me* – a sad married, fantasising about a stranger. Why? I could have got it on with anyone at that party. I had the ideal opportunity, but I didn't… What if he had been there, though? I push the thought from my mind and concentrate on composing the text to say sorry for being so rude when we met at the café.

> Hi, how are you?
> I am sooooo sorry.
> It was rude dashing off after
> our meeting on Friday.
> Hope you can forgive me coz
> that's not normally like me.

I add a smiley face…

> Thanks again and sorry it's taken
> so long to text you.

conclude the text…

> You were lovely.
> Hope we can keep in touch
> and you can give more awesome
> top tips for my 51st challenge.

and press Send.

Week Five. Adriano's Restaurant. Friday, 9.00 p.m.

"What's this getting at then, Girls? Watching the entire box set of *24* in forty-eight hours was great fun last week, but this?

ENRICH THE LIVES OF THOSE YOU LOVE.

It's obvious who the most special people in my life are. It's just that I can't think of ways to *enrich* someone's life." I take a sip of wine.

"You could enrich your husband's life by learning how to use a whip like Jess supposedly can," Bea jeers.

"God knows what Stan and Geoff talk about when we visit," I shudder. "At least I'm never in the room when they *bang* on about their social life." I smile at my joke. "No, I want to do good, in the community, perhaps? I'll focus on people who would really benefit from my knowledge and experience," I conclude. "If you think of anything, let me know."

Claire is sitting to my right. She puts her mouth up close to my ear. "So, how'd the meeting with Him go?" Her question takes me by surprise and my finger goes to my mouth. Flashing her a look of annoyance, I discreetly check to see if anyone has overheard.

"Meet Monday?" I mutter, desperate to change the subject.

"Ok, half-ten at Tea and Tranquility," confirms Claire. "We'll talk then."

My gaze falls on my mobile. *Why haven't you messaged me? Should I delete you from my contacts? Perhaps it didn't send.* I scroll down to the message I sent to Him and catch my breath. *It did bloody send. So why haven't you replied? That's so rude. I thought you liked me?* For some reason, I feel quite upset.

Saturday morning.
Pippa and I are baking sultana wholemeal scones as a treat for Geoff. I've noticed that he's become a bit snappy, and it's been making me feel anxious and guilty.

"You're full of surprises these days, Mum," Pippa says. "Look at what you've achieved and what you're achieving. You're surprising me, and you must be surprising yourself every week. I think you're discovering a new you – in a good way. At first, I was scared that the challenges would change you, and you wouldn't be 'Mum' any more – but that hasn't happened. Last time I spoke to Grandma, she said that you're a butterfly emerging from its chrysalis, and she's right. You are happier than I have ever seen you, and I hope that at the end of the year you don't go back to being how you were. You're not unhappy and bored."

I stop in my tracks. What she's just said has made me feel unexpectedly emotional – so much so that I am about to boil over. I make an excuse to leave the kitchen, leg it to my safe, secure place where I can lock the door (the downstairs loo) and begin to cry. My body shakes involuntarily. Adrenaline pumps through my veins, and my head throbs with the tension of silent sobbing. My pain feels so raw; it's as if I am mourning a loved one. I dare not let anyone see or hear me like this, so I lie face down on the carpet, trying to muffle my suffering, rhythmically bashing the carpet with the palms of my hands. *What is wrong with me? My emotions are all over the place. Perhaps I'm just tired.*

I wait for the storm to abate, splash my face with cold water and return to the kitchen to take the scones out of the oven. The timer is bleeping.

Home baking does the trick, and over lunch Geoff's mood improves dramatically. However, when I try to engage him in conversation about my challenge, he becomes very obviously uninterested. "Hmmm… interesting," I remark to him as I Google the meaning of 'Enrich'. "Who'd benefit from my help? I need to find people who will gain something from my knowledge and experience."

"Why not give it a rest this week, Amy, eh? It was nice to see you back in the kitchen earlier. It's time to test a scone or two,"

Geoff salivates. "I trust they are packed with fruit?" He pats me on the behind and goes to find some jam.

"Thanks, darling," I mutter, mildly irritated.

Monday, 10.30 a.m.

Claire and I sit down to chat. She can hardly contain her excitement. "Well?" she says, "What happened when you met? Is he out of your system?"

I sip my coffee and reflect on that meeting in the café; how I felt, how time flew, how lovely he was and how I treated him at the end. I remember word for word the text I sent apologising for my rudeness and the coded message willing him to stay in touch.

I tell Claire everything. I don't hold back this time. I need to talk, and I trust her. "I feel as if something has been unlocked deep inside of me, Claire," I say sadly. "I want to forget Him, believe me, I desperately want to move on – but I can't yet. Meeting him made things worse, if anything," I admit.

She nods and waits for me to continue.

"Nothing has changed, nothing at all. I am *in lust* with a young scruff-bag whom I don't know. It's mental. But I don't want to be in lust. Can you understand that? It's affecting my safe, predictable world, and it's mentally exhausting. My mad challenges are giving me quite enough to think about without added complications – in a good way," I smile broadly.

On the outside, I portray a vision of calm. Yet on the inside, I'm a wreck. My heart is racing and my stomach is clenched. I sit on my hands to stop myself from chewing on my finger. "I am in pain and ecstasy at the same time, Claire. I think about him too much, and every time I do, I feel full of purpose, energetic and *alive*. I love it. There's a part of me that wants to hug him and thank him 'cos in spite of everything, all this damn pain and angst, I feel wonderful."

Claire's eyes are very bright. She looks close to tears.

"There is something about him," I say almost inaudibly.

"There is something about this man that I have connected with – but I have to disconnect from him." I look at her evenly. "So, I have decided that to put an end to this pointless lusting, if I can discover something I really dislike about him, hopefully something that I really hate, this something will make me see sense and realise that I've been premenopausal and pathetic and that my life is good as it is."

Claire reaches for my hand and squeezes it. Her voice wavers with emotion. I really feel as if she understands, but how could she? "Give it time, Amy. One way or another, something will happen. Everything happens for a reason, – it's part of God's plan. We may not understand today or tomorrow, but eventually, The Lord reveals why we go through everything we do. I will pray for a sign."

"I bloody pray your God gives a sign soon," I laugh.

Noon

"Have you a minute, madam?"

I've been accosted by a woman in the street representing Elderly Cumbria. She hands me a leaflet advertising training on social media and informs me of the social, emotional and cognitive benefits for the elderly. I listen intently.

6.00 p.m.

The plan is to be away visiting Grandma in her Manchester care home until Thursday afternoon.

"Why on Earth, Amy?" declares Geoff indignantly. "You see her once a year, don't you? Your place is here. This house has been in chaos recently."

"There is something important I need to do," I reply. "It's my *challenge*, and it'll be good for you to cook for the children for a change."

"I am not being drawn into that conversation, Amy. I was kind enough to agree to spawn children. They'll eat when they're hungry. When I was a child, I was expected to feed myself, and I turned out alright. I have better things to do than spend all my time running around and mollycoddling them like you do." I let him rant and rave and use his Pointy Finger.

"Well, I need to do this, Geoff. You'll be fine. Claire said she'd help out, and it's only for a few days."

I cross my fingers behind my back and smile sweetly. Inside, I am seething at his lack of understanding and compassion. And what was that he said about our children?

I run upstairs to pack.

Tuesday, 9.00 a.m.
The fridge is full of microwaveable ready meals, and guilt has persuaded me to bake a crumble for Geoff. I leave the children fifty pounds for 'feeding emergencies' and go to the train station.

That afternoon, over tea and cake, I ask Grandma and her friends what they get up to during their day.

"Well, *bubelah*, we watch television, we eat, we sleep and on Mondays the hairdresser comes," replies Grandma.

"A nice young couple sing every Wednesday afternoon, and there's bingo on Tuesdays," interjects Grandma's friend.

"Do you see your friends and family often?" I ask.

The group falls silent.

"Amy, don't drive me *meshuganah*," says Grandma. "You know full well that we don't see anyone as often as we'd like. We can't walk, let alone drive or catch the bus – and as for shopping, I can only dream about getting to Bromley's these days. We rely on others for most things now," she smiles. "At least we've got satellite TV, though. All those marvellous channels."

The senior staff confirm that there is adequate internet access and broadband. My idea won't work if they haven't. I carefully explain my plan to them.

Wednesday.

Five third-age-appropriate PCs have been located, and we're good to go. I'm delighted that the staff in charge have agreed to designate a corner of the dining room as the care home's very own 'internet café'. All residents are informed of the improvements to their environment and the associated benefits. Everyone has been invited to participate in taster sessions for getting started on the internet. I can't wait for them to join Facebook and dabble in some internet shopping.

I spend the afternoon teaching Grandma and her friends how to make the most of Skype. It takes *hours* and is one of the most frustrating and rewarding challenges that I've undertaken. However, the look of pure joy on their faces when they finally get the hang of it and see their loved ones live on the screen brings a lump to my throat. Grandma stares and stares at the image of Pippa waving to her. She puts her face really close to the screen – so close that her nose is touching it – and taps the image. "Is this *real*?" she says, stunned.

I feel very emotional.

Thursday.

Twenty-five care home residents are merrily surfing the net, Skyping and chatting on Facebook. There is such demand that the staff have had to enforce a strict rota. I've been assured that they will continue to coach new residents and will keep me informed if they are ever in need of further assistance. They thank me for my kindness. I thank them for being so open-minded. "It's no problem at all," I say. I'm so glad that I was given this challenge and that I finally understand what it means. I am proud and thankful that I have been able to enrich their lives.

I go to say goodbye to Grandma. It's time for me to leave this challenge behind and revert to normal life. I find her dozing in the Day Room. I'm sure she's lost weight since the last time I saw her. Terrible sadness engulfs me. I have a strong premonition that time is running out for her. I stand by her side, watching the steady rise and fall of her chest as she sleeps, wanting to capture this moment for ever. The clock chimes. "Bye, Grandma," I whisper lovingly and kiss her on her forehead. She doesn't stir, but I think I see a faint smile play across her lips as I turn away.

I reach the door, hear a cough and turn to see her shoulders shaking as she laughs silently, her brown Paddington Bear eyes twinkling. "Give me one of those Sky calls when you get home."

8.00 p.m.

Geoff is so relieved to see me that he hands me a bottle of Pinot Grigio on his way out to the pub. I accept it dispassionately. It doesn't feel like a gift of love or appreciation, and I feel extremely sad. Pippa and Evie squawk with delight that I'm home. "So, how was it without me? Did you cope? Dad hasn't really said. I've only seen him briefly."

"We lived off whatever you left in the fridge, and Dad forgot to collect me from school one night," Pippa laughs. "And he tried to force us to eat some soggy mixed veg stuff that he attempted to make in the wok. It was full of courgettes, mushrooms and peppers – gross. He's lived with me all my life and he still doesn't know what I like and don't like."

"Perhaps he'll appreciate me more now, then," I respond flippantly.

Evie eyes me critically. "He moaned a lot, so maybe. It was so cool what you did for Grandma and her friends," Pippa smiles. "I'm happy you're home though. We need you here."

I feel so choked up with love for her, I'm speechless. I hug her hard and go to write up my learning on my laptop.

May

Week One. Friday lunchtime.

HAVE A SECRET SNOG WITH SOMEONE YOU LIKE.

Bea and I meet in town to discuss my latest challenge dilemma. "Another 'bad things' challenge that Geoff will relish and that you think is just plain wrong?" Her acerbic tone cuts me to the quick.

"Well," I reply tentatively. "Isn't having a teenage-style snog with someone I find attractive defined as cheating and the first step on the slippery slope to marital misery?" I chew on my finger in silence.

Bea snorts derisively.

"*But*," I continue at speed, "I keep telling myself that it's only a snog and it doesn't say anything about using tongues or anything, so perhaps I can get away with a quick peck on the lips – or cheek, even?"

"You're over-analysing it, pet. Sometimes, you're exasperating," Bea replies good-naturedly. "All you have to do is find a nice guy or girl and give them a kiss. It's no big deal. The worst that can happen is that you catch herpes or turn bi – ha. Anyway, your husband gave you permission to play away at the Mon-Keys' house. This is nothing in comparison."

We discuss my options: go to a dodgy nightclub, get drunk and flirt unashamedly with strangers in a pub, pick somebody up from a dating website, throw a party or go to a party where I don't know many of the guests. We take a vote and make a decision.

8.00 p.m.
Bea has taken control of the situation and persuaded one of her friends from out of town to invite us to her 'celebration of divorce' party that weekend.

8.30 p.m.
I receive a text from Him:

> How are the challenges going?
> I'm going to a Divorce Party
> tomorrow night.
> That'll be a challenge ;)

Are we going to the *same* party?

> Really?
> I'm going to one of them too.

The reply comes instantly:

> Are you going with anyone?

Woah, I think. *He's coming on to me.*
    I force myself to put my phone away without replying. It's absolutely possible that we're going to the *same* party. How about a snog with Him?

Saturday, 7.00 p.m.
I'm sitting on my bed, surrounded by my entire wardrobe. Clothes, shoes and bags litter the room. After spending two frustrating hours on trying to create the 'right look' for tonight, I'm exhausted, and I don't know if I can be bothered to go. Geoff's lifting weights in the bathroom. "Another pointless challenge you're rushing off to do? I hope you're going to clear

that lot up before you go, dear, or it's going to charity," he shouts across to me.

"We really do need to address your ataxophobia, *darling*." I yell after him. "And they are not pointless. I'm learning loads, thank you."

He doesn't even know what this challenge is, I hiss under my breath. *Bet you'll give me a medal when I do it though. I bloody am going to do it – and damn well enjoy it.*

In desperation, I call Becca. She's a fashionista and will know what I should wear. We agree that, given the parameters of the challenge, I should aim to select items that will ensure I am only 'available' from the neck up.

7.30 p.m.
Dressed in leggings, a long-sleeved top and a leather jacket, I feel comfortable yet dowdy. However, once I add my prized eighty-five-pounds-in-the-sale silver sparkly wedges, I feel so much better. And teemed with matching tote (slightly more than eighty-five pounds and not in the sale) as possible use in self-defence should I need it, I am ready for anything.

The party is in full flow when I arrive. I'm greeted by the hostess, whom I don't know, and push flowers and a bottle of Cava into her hands to atone for crashing her party. Thankfully, I am spotted by Bea and swept away for a much-appreciated glass of fizz. I spend the next hour drinking, dancing and chatting about girly stuff. I don't mention anything about getting my teenage snog. That would be lethal.

10.00 p.m.
Still no sign of Him. I wander upstairs, wondering what I can possibly do to engineer my challenge secret snog. I've decided it just has to be with Him if he is here. He fits the challenge criteria, and this is the golden opportunity I've been waiting for

103

to get him out of my system. One snog, and then I will be free of lust and free of another challenge.

I'm blindly picking my way past the hordes of party-goers littering the dim hallway when I do a double-take. That's Him, going into one of the rooms on my right. My pace quickens. I can do it now – in privacy. Then, afterwards, I can explain and he'll understand and we'll both laugh and feel okay about it all. Brilliant.

In my haste to catch up with Him, I stumble over someone's leg, lose my balance and fall into the room. A hand from inside steadies my fall. *His* hand. *Oh my God. I couldn't have planned this better. This is it. I'm going to have my secret snog right now.* Weak with anticipation and befuddled with alcohol, I close my eyes and prepare to lose myself in the moment. All these weeks spent daydreaming are about to become my reality. I can't wait to breathe in the yummy smell of Him.

Something is not quite right. As he pulls me closer, I get a faint whiff of what can only be described as mustiness. You know, as if somebody has washed their clothes, not dried them properly and put them away in a drawer. I sniff again and feel slightly nauseous. My face brushes against his jumper. This is definitely unpleasant. Perhaps if I can get to smell his face, it will be better. Oh yes, I am sure it will be better, He is *so* gorgeous.

I try to focus and get back in the zone. He is holding my hands… I can feel his breath on my face… closer… closer… and then it happens; my passionate teenage snog. Only it isn't passionate at all.

He suckers his lips onto mine like a squid and stays there, motionless. I don't quite know what to do. He does not move, I do not move. I try to move my face slightly to the left. His face moves with me, his mouth still firmly attached in the sucker position. Then, without warning, the vacuum is released and he begins to whisper a completely incomprehensible string of gibberish into my right ear.

This is bizarre. I strain to understand what he is saying. Is it in a foreign language? Before I have a chance to put my translation hat on, I feel a strange wet feeling. Shit. He is licking my ear. His entire tongue is… this is gross… it is moving all around… and inside… and round the back… lick, lick, lick. God, if he mews like a cat in a minute, I am going to scream. I can't bear it. I sense that there is dribble on my neck.

That's it, game over. I *so* need to get out of here. Feigning a coughing fit, I convincingly splutter that I need a drink, feel my way to the door and *run*.

I bump into Claire at the top of the stairs, grab the drink from her hand and down it in one. She looks at me in awe – I *never* do that – oh, and I ask her if she can sniff me to check if I smell alright.

"Hon?" she enquires sympathetically.

"Sniff me here." I point to my neck. "What can you smell?"

"What do you mean?" she laughs.

"Do I smell, well, musty?"

"What?"

"Never mind," I smile wateringly, turning to go downstairs. Actually, I am *not* ok, but I can't tell her that.

Perhaps that is it, then. At least I can tick that *bad thing* off the list now. I should be pleased, but I am not pleased at all.

I reach the bottom of the stairs and turn to go back into the lounge. Then I stop and stare. He is in there, chatting to a group of people. He is not upstairs. Has he been upstairs, then? Did I miss him coming downstairs? Did I?

The wine has completely gone to my head and I feel confused and fuzzy. I sidle up to the group, who are deep in conversation, and gently pull one of the girls (whom I vaguely recognise from the school gate crowd) to one side. I whisper urgently in her ear. "Have you all been here for long?"

"Ages."

"Nobody's moved away or gone upstairs?"

"No."

"None of you?"

"*What?*"

"Can you smell a musty smell around here?"

"You're odd."

Who have I snogged? Musty Man is not *Him*. Where is this ear-licking man I've wasted my teenage snog on? I have to know.

I spy Cate across the room and sprint over to where she is standing. "Come with me," I say. "We need a Girls' pow-wow, right now."

We congregate in the hall, and I briefly explain what has happened.

"Are you sure it was a man?" asks Bea, giving me 'the eye'.

"It was *definitely* a man," I reply firmly.

The hunt for Musty Man is on. We split up into pairs and discreetly sniff as many male guests as we can. Reconvening in the kitchen ten minutes later, we are none the wiser. I am determined to find out who he is. Maybe not tonight – but I will.

10.30 p.m.

It's karaoke time, and the hostess is subjecting us to a delightfully awful rendition of Gloria Gaynor's *I Will Survive*. Claire has taken Bea home early, as she has a headache.

I sit on the stairs, slugging down glass after glass of rum punch and obsessing about how I can achieve the right teenage snog with Him before I leave this party.

Bolstered by alcohol, I make a decision to go for it and coolly saunter across to say hello. As he catches sight of me heading towards him, he breaks into a broad grin and waves. He smiles into my eyes and says he appreciated my text.

Ooh, I think. *He really is pleased to see me. He is being so friendly.*

This is my first opportunity to really examine Him up close. He is as scruffy as ever, dressed in a faded plain brown hoodie and grubby jeans. I note the tattoo. He really is not my type at all, and he stinks of whisky.

Why do I want to even do this? I wonder. *What is my fascination with Him?*

And then I begin to talk. I tell him at length and in great detail about the challenges that I have faced. I cannot stop talking. I think that I am talking complete crap, but he is listening attentively and asking lots of questions, and he is laughing – which is good. Perhaps he is just being kind. He is very kind.

Midnight

I am still talking *at* Him.

I notice the time. I need to go home. Even though my inhibitions are very much lowered, I can't bring myself to ask him for a snog. It's not going to happen. I prepare to say goodbye.

"Amy?" he interrupts me. "Before you go, tell me something. How do you feel about this teenage secret snog challenge?"

The words tumble out of my mouth.

"You know," I say in earnest. "I am married with lovely children. I'd never do anything to hurt my family, but I have *always* been so damn sensible and this year, I don't want to be. I'm realising that the husband I married is a bit of an arse, and I'm frustrated with what my life has become. This year is about having harmless fun and exploring myself."

I catch my breath and carry on.

"Last year, the mere thought of snogging a stranger – let alone somebody I fancy – is something that I would never, ever have dreamed of doing in a million years – being married and all that. Yet, for some reason, this snog challenge was specifically chosen for me, and it's my duty to carry it out as best I can. And do you know something? When I first read it, well, I was so scared and at the same time desperately excited to legitimately be able to um… have a go? And, well, I am so pissed off with my husband. He never calls me gorgeous… So how about a snog, then?" I shut up.

He gawks at me and is about to say something when Cate bundles me outside to our waiting taxi.

Monday, 9.00 a.m.
Thinking about what happened on Saturday night brings me out in cold sweats. On the way to work, I take appropriate action. In the car, I select *Crush* from my MP3 player on repeat and whack up the volume. Driving off at speed, I sing all the pain, guilt and longing out of my system. Of course, I alter the lyrics – an old habit of mine. It makes the track so much more meaningful and personal to me.

> *It's just a phase, a snog, a kiss,*
> *It's crazy, God I can't resist,*
> *D'you see me? Let's go get it on,*
> *Heyyy.*

> *I'm diseased. What's up with me?*
> *Need this snog, Him. Can't you see?*
> *Just a quick moment, Him, heyyyy.*

> *Just one time, behind the door.*
> *Come on now, please, that's the score.*
> *No strings, commitments oh, hey.*

> *No ties, no lies,*
> *A challenge filled with butterflies.*
> *Let's go. Just one old snog – for me… (oh, please!)*

By the time I get to work, my voice is hoarse and my cheeks are streaked with tears. But I do feel better.

Week Two. Friday, 7.45 a.m.
Geoff reads out my challenge between mouthfuls of muesli:

GO APE! ALLOW YOUR BODILY HAIR TO GROW AND EMBRACE YOUR NATURAL BEAUTY. THIS CHALLENGE MUST BE UPHELD FOR ONE MONTH.

"One month?" I complain, bemused.

"Well, we have to see your 'tash in all its glory. Can't wait to parade you around town. Hand your shaving stuff over, wifey."

The full horror of the challenge sinks in. Bloody hell – it includes facial hair. This is too much. I can cope with hairy legs and armpits; you can hide *them*. However, a hairy face is not a good look unless you are male or a furry animal. Hairy faces are visible and ridiculed. Even Cate carefully monitors the length of a single hair growing from a mole on her chin and plucks it out the minute she feels it. It's just not done. But what can I do? I dutifully hand all razors, bleach, tweezers and lady-shave to Pippa for 'safekeeping'.

Monday, 7.00 a.m.
I examine my legs, arms and armpits for evidence of hair. Yes, it's sprouting nicely. After a shower, I carefully sniff my armpits for the slightest whiff of body-odour. All okay so far.

Tuesday.
Over a work lunch date with Hairy Nina, I bring up the subject of facial hair in the hope that she can give me some top tips. Nina is a revelation. She informs me that she hasn't removed any bodily hair for two years and that it has definitely changed her life for the better. "In some cultures, body hair is considered a beauty essential," she says in a matter-of-fact tone. "It displays confidence and self-assuredness in oneself. My partner loves me, ergo he loves my hair – wherever it may grow. He says that going *au naturel* is sexy and makes me unique."

"Don't you get teased?" I ask. "And what about when you're at the swimming pool?"

"If you are secure in your womanhood, you won't care what narrow-minded people think. I refuse to remove my hair because some small-minded bigots decided that it is the right thing for women to do. What gives anybody the right to tell anybody else how they should look? People like me for who I am. It's their problem if they can't see through the hair and respect and admire the person beneath."

"Not sure *my* husband will find my newly grown mono-brow and moustache sexy, Nina. I don't have your self-confidence. I like to fit in. Perhaps this challenge is directly related to my insecurities about conforming?"

"Possibly. However, from what you say, it might be trying to tell you something about your husband and his, um, influence over you... perhaps."

Wednesday.
I've been feeling unconfident all day, made all the worse because I totally forgot that I was due a facial hair wax tomorrow and I'm sure that the dreaded hairs are enjoying a growth spurt. I lie out in the garden under an overcast sky and hope the sun bleaches them – even a tiny bit would be helpful.

6.00 p.m.
The house is empty so I treat myself to a quick cup of coffee before I start on the evening meal and properly consider the Mystery of Musty Man. I am seething. "That bloody man *stole* my secret teenage snog. I am going to find out who he is and give him a piece of my mind. He will feel remorse," I say tersely, scrunching scrap paper into a ball. "That kiss was supposed to be special, *unique,* and now it has *gone*. It has been ticked off the list. It is done."

I pace the kitchen in frustration. *That snog was meant to be with Him. I was going to use it to put my lust interest to bed. I* smile at the double entendre. It was supposed to be the event where I would find out that he was smelly or the snogger from hell.

I kick the fridge in annoyance. I was so drunk that I can't remember what I talked to Him about, what he was wearing, what he was drinking, if he was smoking and if he smelt alright or not. I might have found something that I hated then but I can't remember anything except that I talked *at* Him. I shudder. *Oh God, I talked at Him and I… I…*

There is one thing that I distinctly remember. I admitted that I wanted a secret snog with him. I'm definitely going to have to find something to dislike about him so that I can get over him – and fast.

Week Three. Sunday.

Nina kindly emails me a link to an article portraying a gorgeous eighteen-year-old, arms raised above her head, proudly displaying her dark, ape-like armpits in all their glory. Her message reads: Hope you find this picture inspirational.

Nope.

I sneak out of the house. It's time to:

DO SOMETHING ILLEGAL.

I drive to the large roundabout at the edge of town, check there's no traffic about, say a silent prayer and slowly drive round it the wrong way. Then, I put my foot to the floor and fly down the dual carriageway as fast as I dare.

Unscathed and relieved the challenge is over, I quietly let myself back into the house, trip over Pippa's 'strategically' placed boots and jar my back. Doubled over with pain, I hobble into bed, cursing her.

Monday.

The reward of excruciating lower back pain after last night's escapade has given me the best excuse ever to sign off sick from work, become a recluse and by chance, turn into an avid watcher of the shopping channel *Simple Pleasures*. In fact, in just two hours I am named live on air as their number one online shopper! So much for saving money – I am spending it in fistfuls and enjoying every minute of it. "Well," I tell Evie, as I commit to purchasing another hundred quid's worth of designer cosmetics. "It can always go back." (As if…)

I daren't look at myself for longer than absolutely necessary in case I freak out. Geoff finds the whole situation highly amusing, remarking that he quite likes the fact that I'm beginning to look 'unacceptable' and 'unappealing' and constantly reminding me that I have to go to work next Monday. Every time I recall a remark he made to Bob last night about me having a great 'cock-tickler', I wince. What can I do to disguise it?

The news is on. There is a heated discussion in progress between politicians about air pollution in East Asia. It spurs me into action. I know what to do. I will pretend that I have a *horrendously* bad cold and cover my nose and mouth with a mask. I search through the children's dressing-up box for their doctors-and-nurses set and I pull out a green surgeon's face mask. It's a bit crumpled, but it will do.

I go to bed feeling slightly better.

Week Four. Monday, 8.00 a.m.

Pippa is manically searching for school books, shoes, and her PE kit while Geoff meticulously polishes his shoes. My eyes dart to the clock. She has seven minutes before she misses the bus again. *You're never going to make it*, I think, resignedly, unlocking the car.

"Can you drive me?" she calls, flinging muddy trainers into a plastic carrier bag.

"Will you take her for once, Geoff? I need to get to work early."

"*Mum*?" implores Pippa, flouncing into the kitchen and forcing text books into her school bag.

Evie is by my side, looking smug. "It's Monday, Mum. Read your challenge. She jumps up and down with glee. "It's so cool."

"I will, after…" I notice that Geoff has disappeared.

"After *I've* run madam to the bus stop," I bark, stuffing the paper slip into my pocket. "and take that yellow hoodie off, Evie – where's your proper school jumper? WILL YOU GET IN? IT'S OPEN!" I bellow to Pippa. "We've had this behaviour too many times this year, and I am at the end of my tether. If I have to drive you all the way to school again, I will ban all screen action for the week. Do you hear me?"

She saunters past and blithely asks if my face is feeling warmer thanks to the extra layer of hair. I bite my lip and start the engine, trying hard not to lose it.

Fortunately, we arrive at the bus stop on time. We sit in silence. I am stewing over her behaviour and Geoff's lack of empathy. I break the silence first. "Well?" I begin.

"Well what?"

"Haven't you anything to say to me?"

"Not really," she retorts.

I am about to go into meltdown when I happen to take the challenge from my jeans pocket. I read it and my temper miraculously subsides. "Listen to this," I smirk. "My challenge is for us to:

HAVE A FREAKY FRIDAY."

Pippa looks nonplussed. "What's that, then?"

"You'll find out tonight," is my parting shot as I metaphorically kick her out of the car.

9.15 a.m.

I sneak into my office and fire off an all-staff email:

> Due to the unfortunate fact that I'm full of cold, I have cancelled all my meetings for the next few days. I really don't want to contaminate any of you, so I will work quietly in my office. If you wish to communicate with me, please ring or email. I will let you know when I am better.

I stick a copy onto my office door – just in case. Then I tie my face mask and wait.

11.30 a.m.

Oh, this is going *so* well. I have managed to successfully avoid all my colleagues and Nina has kept me informed of any gossip. I celebrate with a cheese scone.

11.34 a.m.

A 'high importance' email pings into my inbox. I read it with horror. I have completely forgotten that the CEO is coming to our office *this afternoon* to present me with an award for the two-and-a-half grand I raised for the organisation's nominated charity last year. I feel faint and grip the table. How am I going to deal with this one?

I read the attachment detailing the itinerary kindly sent from our PR department three times.

> 14:00 Josh Cummings CEO to meet Amy Richards in the Boardroom. All staff to be present.
>
> 14:15 Presentation of cheque to Charity Fundraising Director by Amy Richards and official photos.
> Photo selection for Intranet Newsletter and External PR.

There is absolutely no way I can get out of this situation without getting myself into a lot of trouble.

To try and calm myself, I stare doggedly at images of cats on my mobile. Do I wear the mask? Should I do a runner? Can I survive this with my hand clamped across my mouth? Do I – *dare* I – show my face?

2.00 p.m.

I am summoned to the boardroom. Everyone is there waiting for the presentation to begin. I am brave and face the music, welcoming everyone with a bright hello. The room falls silent. Everybody stares.

Steve the trainee breaks the silence. "Cold gone?"

"Much better, thanks. Stay away, though. I'm still infectious," I mutter.

Fortunately, the photographer rushes in to prepare me for the photos. She takes me to one side and hands me a tissue. "Wipe your top lip, dear. Have you been drinking hot chocolate?"

Oh, my Lord. How can I admit that it will not ever wipe off? I decide that the only way to go is to tell a white lie. "Regrettably," I reply sadly, "my hirsutism is a temporary side-effect of my medication." I laugh nervously and stroke my top lip gently.

"Still, your husband and children will be proud when they see you in Friday's *Advertiser*. It's a special colour edition, too."

Proud? Colour edition? It's been bad enough coping with Geoff's constant teasing, but it's everyone else's reaction that bothers me. What if my newly acquired caterpillar is seen by Him?

I turn to the photographer. "I can't be in the paper," I say calmly, "because."

She touches my arm sympathetically. "Hey, there's no need to be embarrassed. We can photo-shop the pictures, then nobody need know. Remind me afterwards to tell you about laser treatment. It worked wonders for my mother's self-confidence when she went through the menopause and sprouted hair in odd places. She used to say that her hairiness was due to medication too."

2.45 p.m.
I have persuaded my boss that due to my unfortunate physical condition (the side effects of my medication), I am psychologically fragile. He has agreed that I may work from home for the rest of the week. Result.

Head Teacher's Office. 3.30 p.m.
For Freaky Friday to succeed, school has to be on board. I'm not prepared to admit failure a second time. I already feel bad enough about bottling out of the colonic irrigation challenge. It's on my list of 'things to resolve before December'.

"So, Mr Cope, the plan is for my daughter and me to swap places for twenty-four hours. I will be her and she will become me, and we will experience each other's worlds," I enthuse. "She's old enough to be exposed to the stresses, challenges and joys of adulthood and parenthood. I think it'll be good for her, don't you agree?"

Mr Cope nods. Sales pitch over, I wait.

4.00 p.m.
He has been persuaded! Freaky Friday will become 'Wacky Wednesday'.

I track down a copy of the film (1976) and download it. I've seen the one from 2003. However, in my humble opinion, it's not a patch on the original.

Bea is a key player in this challenge. I brief her on her role and invite her round to watch the movie with us. "Now remember," I say, over a coffee, "You will live under my roof for twenty-four hours and shadow Pippa twenty-four seven. Unless she's doing something downright dangerous or illegal, you must not butt in – oh, except for when she's having a wee – you know, stuff like that."

Bea's eyes light up. "God, Amy – I just love it!" she says excitedly. "How do I deal with a credit card situation?"

"I have transferred two hundred pounds onto her debit card. She can't go overdrawn with that, and if she *does* use it all up and tries to spend more, well, that's a valuable life lesson, isn't it?" I laugh. "She has to learn that money doesn't grow on trees." My eyes crinkle with mirth as the full implication of this challenge hits me. "I don't know how Geoff will take it, though?"

"I take it that the novelty of your year is wearing off? Never mind, pet. You leave Geoff to me, and stay strong."

Late that afternoon, while Geoff is at Bob's, Pippa and Evie are made to watch the movie with Bea and me. Bea's sworn them to secrecy until all the arrangements are in place because she's sure that the instant Geoff knows what's in store, he'll do everything in his power to scupper the challenge.

Pippa's chuffed to bits that she's going to take centre stage. As I pass the study on my way downstairs, I overhear her nattering away on Skype. "I'm going to be Mum for a whole day… eat what I like… go shopping… watch crap TV… get my hair and nails done… yeah… forgot about a facial… might have her credit cards…"

Monday evening.

Geoff, Evie, Bea and I finalise the challenge, which officially begins tomorrow night. Geoff is particularly belligerent. "I would never have agreed to this if you'd bothered to ask me first. You've been uncompliant within the terms of our marriage agreement again, Amy."

Bea tsk-tsks. "Amy didn't say anything earlier, Geoff, because I knew how you'd react, so I told her not to. Anyway, you can't get out of it now. I've announced it on Twitter. Pull out, and I'll tell everyone what a killjoy you are." She continues with a sadistic chuckle. "You do realise that Pippa will be sleeping next to you in your bed, don't you?"

"What?" he scowls.

"Well, yes, pet. We have to make this as realistic as possible.

When I wake her at midnight, I'll take her into your bedroom, and Amy will disappear into hers. Hope you've some appropriate pyjamas. You can't exactly lie next to her naked."

"Where will Bea sleep?" asks Evie.

"On the camp bed in the hall," I reply.

"Better get some PJs then, Dad," says Evie. "Or Bea will see your willy, ha ha ha! Can I talk to you when you are here, Bea?"

"No Evie," says Bea firmly. "I'm going to be 'invisible'. I'll wear all black, like a mime artist. You can talk to your dad, but you must act as if I am not there. The only person who can talk to me is Pippa, and the only time I will talk to your dad or mum is if there is a problem."

"You are all going to have to try your hardest to treat Pippa as if she is me and me as if I am her," I say solemnly. "Now, is everybody clear?"

"Geoff?" Bea raises her eyebrows.

"I don't have a choice, do I, Bea?"

"No, pet, you don't."

Wednesday, 0.01 a.m.

The challenge has begun. I am in Pippa's bed and she is in mine. I wrinkle my nose in disgust. Wish I'd washed her duvet and pillow. They reek of teenager.

7.00 a.m.

My bedroom door is flung open. Pippa, hands on hips and wearing my favourite work suit and quite a lot of my make-up and jewellery, eyes me scathingly. I bite my lip. I must say nothing. I lie there as she would.

"You know the time," she announces. "You will be late if you don't get up now. Why didn't you set your alarm?"

She sounds *exactly* like me. I want to laugh, but I don't. I have to take this seriously, so I grunt and say what she always says every single morning. "I'm *doing it*, Mother. Okay?"

118

8.00 a.m.

"Where's Dad?" I whisper to Evie.

"Gone to work, Mum. He can't bear it. Pippa is very grumpy."

"Where's my packed lunch?" I ask Pippa. She looks up, alarmed. I can tell she's forgotten about it. "You'll have to do without it today, as I have run out of bread," she lies. "Here's some dinner money." Pippa delves into her purse, which I know contains around ten pounds in coins, and hands me four pounds. I grunt, sit down on the floor and slowly put on my socks and shoes, exactly as she does, every day. I know that she is going to have to drive me to school now. I have missed my time slot to meet the bus.

"Bugger!" she exclaims. I hide a smile. "I'm going to have to drive you all to school, and today my shift starts at nine." She flies around the house, checking the doors and windows are locked, spends slightly too long admiring her reflection in the hall mirror, grabs my favourite handbag and pushes us out of the house and into the car, where Bea is in the driver's seat, waiting. As I get in, she scrutinises my face. "Wipe it off right now, madam, or I will do it for you."

Blimey, I think. *I'm not as harsh as that when I'm being the make-up police. Well-spotted, though.*

Pippa hands me the wipes that I conveniently keep in the glove compartment and watches as I scrape the foundation I'd used to try and conceal my moustache and the blusher off my face. Oh God, now my face is clear of make-up, I feel very self-conscious. *Stay in role, Amy. One day of pain, but think of the gain...* I keep my mind firmly on my mantra and climb into the back seat of the car.

9.00 a.m. MUM'S DAY

It's registration. Pippa's peers don't seem to be at all concerned with my bushy 'tash and brows, which is refreshing, and I soon forget all about it. They're more amused that I'm in school with them for the day. I sit next to Pippa's best friend, Cara, and try to engage her in conversation. I want to experience as normal a day in her life as I can.

The kids chit-chat about the latest cool vlogs and sport. They taunt each other while their form tutor shouts a lot; trying to keep control of the class, take the register and make some key announcements all at the same time. *Nothing's changed since I was at school then*, I think, and I smile.

10.00 a.m.
God, what a boring English lesson! The teacher's voice is sooo monotonous and I'm not surprised that most of the class is fidgeting and mucking about. I tune into the lads' banter going on behind me and strain my ears to pick up on what they are saying. It's much more interesting, extremely rude and very funny.

1.00 p.m.
Being surrounded by so many children in the playground feels intimidating, and the noise level is deafening. I attempt to buy a cup of coffee alongside my meal and am politely informed that it's not allowed. I am offered water and take two headache tablets.

2.00 p.m.
I have a wonderful time reliving my youth, playing netball as wing-attack. I give it all I've got. After fifteen minutes I am completely exhausted.

2.45 p.m.
The school nurse treats me for grazes to my knees and elbows. I think I've also strained my shoulder. She offers me an ice pack and a chocolate digestive. I accept gratefully.

3.30 p.m.

It feels like I have been in school forever. I have caffeine withdrawal symptoms, and my knees and right shoulder feel sore. I don't want to go to Pippa's usual after-school activity tonight, which is choir, but I have to because I don't want to break the rules of the challenge. I turn up in the music room and am met by the music teacher. "Mrs Richards. Let me offer you a lovely mug of filter coffee. You must have had a very interesting day…"

4.45 p.m.

I now remember how much I adored choir at school. We belt out selected numbers from the musical *Les Misérables* and, very quickly, I realise what a wonderful time I'm having. I lose myself in the music and feel my tension ebb away. *I must start singing again*, I think. *Why did I ever give it up? I think Geoff persuaded me shortly after we got married…*

5.15 p.m.

School is deathly quiet. Everyone has gone home except for me. Pippa has forgotten me. I send her a text, sit on the bench outside the school gates and fully enjoy the moment. I'm in no hurry.

6.00 p.m.

I keep out of the way, which is what Pippa would normally do, by sneaking a flask of tea upstairs into the study and catching up on my emails and social media notifications. I can't smell any cooking, though. I clearly hear Geoff addressing Pippa. "Is tea on? Hope you've made a fruity pud for your dad, Pippa? Give me a shout when it's ready, I'll be vacuuming my car." I want to slap him. Is this what my children see and hear? Is this the role model they should have? I feel sick.

7.00 p.m.

"Is tea nearly ready?" I ask Pippa. "I'm hungry."

"It's on its way alright. Leave me alone. I'm busy," she snaps.

"May I have a packet of crisps, then?" I whine, just as she would. She gives me a look of fury and I scarper. *Great. Now, perhaps you understand just a little bit more*, I think as I shoot upstairs.

8.00 p.m.

Critically surveying my bowl of lukewarm soup, bread and butter, rice-crispy cakes and watery jelly with satsumas swimming in it, I vow to teach Pippa some cookery basics. Geoff is unimpressed. "Is this *it*?" he growls. He glares at her and leaves the table.

8.30 p.m.

I know that Pippa has gone out. At least Bea is with her, so she can't get into too much trouble. I take a shower, grab a banana and retire to my bed to watch iPlayer.

PIPPA'S DAY

I've made breakfast, got myself dressed and both 'kids' off to school, fed the fish, cleared away the breakfast things, and now Bea's driving me to Mum's workplace. I'm already exhausted and want a sit-down.

Dad didn't help one bit. In fact, he just did his own thing and then went to work without saying goodbye even. Why? Why didn't he offer to help – or just do anything, in fact? Why didn't he kiss any of us goodbye or wish us a nice day? Isn't that what married people and families do? Mum always kisses us goodbye and tries to make conversation, even though I tend to ignore her.

I don't have time to think about this any more, as I have arrived at Mum's office. I feel quite scared. I don't know what to expect. I'm greeted by Mum's boss and shown around. He treats me like an adult, which is nice. I'm to act as receptionist – answer the phone, transfer messages and calls and complete any IT work that is handed to me. Somebody shows me to my desk, and I'm left to start. I feel very important. I sort out my penholder and look at all the files on my computer.

11.00 a.m.

Having drunk three cups of coffee since I started, I feel a bit hyper. I'm missing the playground chat. I'm hungry, too, but I've forgotten to bring a snack, and some snotty woman told me that I'll have to wait until lunchtime before I can go out and buy anything. I'm super-bored and start playing games on my phone. The snotty woman notices and reports me. I'm told off. It's against company rules. I feel rather lonely. Nobody talks to each other about anything interesting. Everybody looks stressed and sad. I vow to work harder at school and get a job that is nothing like this one.

I realise that I miss people and having a laugh with my friends. I sneakily ring Mum's beautician and book a manicure with polish and full facial for four o'clock. That makes me feel a bit better.

Midday.

Bea arrives to drive me out for my half-hour lunch break. I'm not allowed to talk to her, which is super-depressing, as I really want some banter. I ask her to take me to the bakers.

This is more like it. I buy two sausage rolls, a packet of crisps and a jam doughnut and wash it all down with a can of full-sugar coke. *Ha, Mum,* I think. *Can't stop me now.* I have hated this morning, but this makes up for it.

1.00 p.m.

Back at my desk – my 'prison' – feeling tired and sick. I shouldn't have eaten so much, and I could do with a nap. I have been given a pile of papers to input into a database. It's repetitive work, and I can't bear sitting in one place for so long. I dream of being back at school.

2.00 p.m.
Freedom. Bea picks me up in her car and takes me to town. It's time to shop until I drop.

I have spent a hundred pounds on clothes and make-up when my mobile rings. It's Daisy Hill Academy sounding rather angry. I've forgotten to pick up Evie. It's going to cost me ten pounds if I collect her now. However, if I pay twenty, I can leave her until six. I try to ring Dad. He just says he can't help as he is working and to get on with it. I beg him to pick her up at six. He says he can't, but he won't say why and hangs up on me.

I know that he can leave work right then if he wants. I think he's just being pig-headed or lazy. In fact, he never picks us up or takes us anywhere unless Mum gets in a right strop or it fits in with his plans. I feel angry and frustrated and decide that he can pay the twenty pounds charge. He's really pissed me off. I understand why Mum gets frustrated with his lack of co-parenting.

4.45 p.m.
Harmony presents me with a bill for ninety pounds. I can't afford to pay it if I'm going to go out tonight, and I really want to do that. I try to ring Dad, but it goes to voicemail. I beg Harmony to wait until next week, when I'll get Mum to settle up. She gives me a talking to about personal responsibility and money management and says I should go and get a Saturday job.

5.15 p.m.
I have forgotten to pick up Mum from school. I daren't ring Dad again. Anyway, what's the point? I ask Bea to make a u-turn, and

we go to get her. As we drive along, I'm sure I see Dad hugging a woman. She looks familiar. I think she's one of Mum's friends, but I don't have enough time to see who it was.

5.45 p.m.
"What's for tea?" Sis is at my side. Shit, I don't know how to cook. I open the fridge and spy a tray of raw chicken thighs. They'll do. Now, what about pudding?

6.30 p.m.
I check on the chicken and realise that I've turned on the mini top oven and grill instead of the main one, which is where the chicken is. The poultry is still raw, and there's a burning smell coming from some bacon fat left in the grill pan. I start to worry a bit. The smoke alarm goes off…

7.00 p.m.
Mum's nagging me to hurry up with tea. I'm trying my best, but it's hard work keeping everyone happy. Dad is being a pig and putting me down. Why won't he help? I'm tired and fed-up of his demands. I'd planned to have a bath and lie soaking in Mum's fancy bath oil and then get dressed up to go out, but I have too many other things to do. I sit down to read the online newspaper. I want to cry. Mum is acting out me, whingeing and stomping around. This is how mean I am to her. It's terrible, and I feel deeply ashamed.

8.00 p.m.
Dinner is served.
"That's a well-balanced meal. Eat it up, everyone. You've got some of your *five-a-day* there," I say more loudly, "and, I made a fruit pudding."
Dad's reply is brutal. Is this what Mum has to put up with every day? This wouldn't be tolerated in school. It's bullying. I sit down and think about our family and our daily routines.

Mum looks at the food on offer and leaves the table. Evie eats without looking at me. I feel sad that my efforts have been ignored. I feel bad that I gave them such an awful meal. I need to learn some basic cooking skills.

8.30 p.m.
I tell Dad that I am going out with a friend and do a runner. I can't be bothered to ask about homework or how everyone's day has been, like Mum always does. I just want to get away and be free. I feel tired and run ragged. Bea drives me to Adriano's. Wish I could have a Pinot Grigio.

* * *

11.30 p.m.
I peek over the bannister to try and see what's going on. I don't want to draw attention to myself and I don't think I want to get involved. Bea is talking to a large hessian potato sack that she and Geoff are carrying from the car into the house. As they set the bag down on the floor, it moves slightly and a hand reaches out of it towards Bea. I realise that it's an *extremely drunk* Pippa who is unable to stand. As she tries to raise herself, she retches and passes out.

Saddened and horrified, I get into my and Geoff's bed and try to sleep. I drift off, praying that she has learned as much as I have from this challenge.

The next morning, Pippa doesn't go to school. She is in bed nursing a hangover and I am caring for her. It gives us an opportunity to evaluate Wacky Wednesday. "So, tell me about your day," I ask her over a cup of peppermint tea.

"Mum, I have learned such a lot. This challenge has been the best and the worst," she continues, blushing. She pauses. "Have you spoken to Harmony yet?"

"No, why?"

"Oh, well I… we… I owe her some money," she says in a small voice. "And," she continues, "I think I owe Aidan and Mario an apology too. Don't ask me any more, I'm very embarrassed. Bea sorted it out." She looks flustered. "Mum?" Her lip quivers.

"Yes, darling?" I don't know what else to say. She has obviously suffered enough, and harsh words from me won't help.

"Mum, I need a hug," she sobs, holding her arms out to me. "I'm sorry for thinking you had it so easy. It was hard being an adult, having to remember so much, doing jobs you must hate and dealing with us… No wonder you go out with your friends when you can or have your nails done… no wonder I got… drunk." She puts her head in her hands and tears splash through her fingers. "I love you, Mum. You go out and treat yourself because it's a release from the pressures you're under, don't you? You do it to get away from us and all the stuff that sits there waiting for you all the time… and Dad doesn't do much to help." She wipes her eyes on her sleeve. "Why are you married to Dad?"

Lunchtime.

My whole face and whole body are the same shade of pastel pink paint as Evie's bedroom walls. However, that is a small price to pay, for Harmony has waxed me clean and I am fur-free. I had to cough up another fifteen pounds for an extra pot of wax so that Harmony could finish the job, but I don't care because I feel *so* much better. Secretly though, I feel pathetic and hypocritical. The Go Ape challenge showed me how easily my self-confidence, self-esteem and behaviour were affected when others made me aware of my differentness. Yet, interestingly, when I was in school, being 'different' wasn't an issue, and I was accepted for who I was – hair and all. I leave Harmony's salon deep in thought about the effects and consequences of prejudice.

Later that afternoon, I quiz Bea about her time with Pippa. "Well, pet, apart from her appalling time management skills, complete inability to manage a budget, and extreme drunkenness 'cos they sneaked booze into Adriano's and downed it in the ladies' toilet, it went very well," she laughs. "I'm sure she's learned a few valuable lessons. How did your day go?"

"I learned tons," I say. "I put up with a lot of crap. You were right when you said I'm stuck in the mould of a nineteen-fifties housewife. I've become a bit of a punch bag, and for some reason I selflessly work my life around my family while Geoff fits his family in around his life. Why did I let him persuade me to give up my singing group? Why must I go to bed when *he* says at ten-thirty? Why can he only have sex on Friday and Saturday nights? What if I felt like a midweek quickie?"

"I think you should get him tested for Asperger's and while you're at it, read up about Narcissistic Personality Disorder," she replies.

"What?" I reply hotly. "It's not that bad."

"If you say so, pet."

"Yes, I do," I reply. "I know you and he don't get on, and he has his faults, I have an ever-growing list of issues that need resolving," I laugh, "but it's all doable."

"We'll watch this space, then, pet."

"Oh, yes," I reply menacingly. "It's going to be explosive."

June

We are well into our quota of Pinot Grigio and delicious pasta main when I hear a familiar voice close by. I look up quickly to see who it is and choke on my drink. *He* is here; standing by our table and talking to *Bea*. I had completely forgotten about the six degrees of separation theory. How on Earth does Bea know *Him?*

I have a real urge to cough. I try to control it and spectacularly fail. The back of my throat is tickling. I am going to have a major coughing fit in front of Him. No, no, *no* – I must choke quietly. I think I'll disappear for a minute.

Pretending to drop my fork onto the floor under the tablecloth, I slowly slither in a snake-like fashion downwards to join it. Ah, now I can cough and hide in peace. I strain to catch the conversation and hope I'm not discovered…

"Hello," I say sheepishly as Claire's head appears under the table.

"What are you doing down there? Get up!"

I slither back up, trying to appear calm. He is looking straight at me and smiling. "Nice to see you again." He takes a swig of his beer, and his cornflower-blue eyes crinkle at the corners with what I interpret as genuine happiness to see me. I smile back, holding his gaze, and adrenaline courses through my body. I think the wine is causing me to experience a teenage moment.

"We must catch up properly. You were awesomely drunk at that divorce party." He laughs and turns back to Bea.

Ohh! He's smiled right into my eyes. We've definitely just shared a moment. I can feel my face reddening and check to see if any of my friends have registered what he just said. Phew. Claire's texting, Cate's at the bar and Bea hasn't noticed. Anyway, I can't speak. If I do, I will cough again.

He chats animatedly to Bea for a few minutes. His buzzing mobile interrupts their conversation, and he wanders off to take the call.

"Now, *he* is such a lovely man," says Bea. "I'm desperately trying to find him a girlfriend, but it's proving tricky."

"What's wrong with him?" I ask as nonchalantly as I can, fanning my face in an attempt to cool down.

"Look at him. He's on the pop too much… and he's never exactly dressed to impress the ladies, is he? He could improve on his personal hygiene routine too, although today he's okay," she sighs.

Well, that's a bonus. I accidentally snog a man who wears musty clothes while lusting after a man with a possible aversion to water and washing machines. Somehow, I am going to have to get up close, check his hair and sniff him. Perhaps he smells alright? If he smells, if I can tell he's been wearing the same clothes for days on end, if I can tell he has chip-pan greasy hair or worse, then there is no way on this Earth that I will ever entertain a snog with him. I can't snog a manky man, and that will be the best reason *ever* for deleting him from my life.

During dessert, my mind wanders to what he said to me earlier. What did he mean when he said *catch up with you sometime, you were awesomely drunk at the party?*

I bet he's intrigued by my obvious alcohol-induced hints that I'd like to snog him. I smile to myself. And then I remember something. Bea left the divorce party early. If only she'd been there, how different things might have been. Just my luck.

Saturday, 5.00 p.m.

The trill of my phone interrupts my train of thought while I'm typing up my challenge diary. It's Claire's landline number. Geoff's voice startles me. "Why are you at Claire's? You should be here. We're running out of time."

"Yes, I know." There is a pause. "Anyway, I rang to say I'm sorry I'm late, and I'm on my way. You'll never guess what's happened. I've received an exciting email this afternoon. We're being reorganised. I think I'm in for a promotion. If this comes off, I'll be made."

I register his enthusiasm and eagerness, yet I only feel apprehension and a distinct sense of foreboding. We've been in this position before. The word 'reorganisation' always means 'trouble'.

As he rabbits on about possible future organisation structures, pay scales and colleagues who might be affected, I rummage in the Bowl of Chance and Opportunity for my challenge and make an attempt to draw the conversation to a close. I've had enough of it all for now, and I don't want to even think about *it* until it happens. I learned that lesson the last time. "Just please try not to get too excited," I caution. "It might not go as you imagine. Just get home. We're going out, remember." I hang up and close my eyes for a moment before looking down at the challenge slip sitting in my lap. It reads:

DECLUTTER YOUR LIFE.

Today is Bea's fortieth birthday, and Geoff and I have been invited to her house to celebrate along with around eighty others. The party theme is 'Around the World with Eighty Guests'. We have been requested to bring a dish from any country of our choice and to dress accordingly.

Geoff's take on Mexican – complete with Sombrero and bushy, drooping moustache – is completely ridiculous but does he love his look. He struts into the kitchen, makes us all aware of his presence with a loud "*Hola!*" and persuades Evie to post several photos of him on Facebook.

I am a Japanese Geisha Girl, complete with 'authentic' wig that looks awesome but is becoming a bit of a problem. I've only had it on for ten minutes, and my head and the back of my neck are already itching. I can't stop adjusting the damn thing and continually scratching my scalp.

"Hurry up!" I say irritably as I scratch. "We're late. I promised Bea we'd be there by eight for pre-party drinks. What were you doing at Claire's?"

"Stop itching your head, Amy. It looks as if you've got nits," he says, pretending not to have heard and to be preoccupied with straightening his crooked moustache.

8.13 p.m.
I am livid and no longer talking to Geoff, who is reclining on the sofa, supping a can of lager and engrossed in the footie. He stubbornly refuses to move until the match is over. "Fifteen minutes, Amy," he pleads, his eyes glued to the match. "It won't make any difference. It's a party, we won't be missed. SHOT."

Be assertive, whispers my inner voice.

"Darling, it is not okay, and we will be missed," I try to say calmly. "It's Bea's fortieth, a special occasion, and I am one of her best friends. I should be there to support her. Now, I appreciate…"

My good intentions rapidly disintegrate as he blatantly continues to ignore me. I begin to pace the room as fast as I am able, given my restrictive Geisha Girl costume.

Not again, I fume inwardly as I pace awkwardly. *I don't feel that you respect me or my friends and, to top it all, you are drinking when you're supposed to be the one driving.*

My laptop is lying open on the side. I make a quick note about what's going on before shuffling back into the kitchen and asking Pippa to let Geoff know that I have gone – but *only* once the match is over.

As I make to leave, I happen to notice his car keys lying on the table and gently *push* them down the back of the radiator. "That'll teach you," I smirk with glee, pulling my dress up over my knees, scooping up my own car keys and making a quick exit before I am spotted.

Claire opens the front door to me. "You're late, Ames. Awesome outfit." She studies me more closely. "You okay? You look flushed."

"It's the wig, Claire. It's like I'm wearing a hot water bottle on my head. But I'm not going to take it off. It took ages to find online. You look gorgeous too. Flick your castanets at me, you sexy Spanish Señora."

She stamps her foot, shakes her Flamenco dress, clicks a castanet on her right hand and shouts "*Olé!*" A crowd of guests applaud in appreciation.

"Where's Geoff?" Claire enquires.

"Tied to the damn footy. Who knows if we'll see him later. I'm so bloody annoyed with him, and I don't want to spoil Bea's night." I smile at her and scratch my head. "Come on. Perhaps a glass of Pinot Grigio will help cool my temper – and my head."

A Grecian Goddess hugs us from behind. It's Bea. She leads us into the kitchen, which is packed with her family and friends, exclaiming animatedly about the effort that everyone has made with their costumes. I can tell that Bea is already wired. She's always entertaining (and often quite unpredictable) after a few drinks, causing me to wonder what might happen tonight.

"Hi, you." She hugs me hard. "I take it that your lovely husband is glued to the football, like mine? He'd rather be watching the match upstairs on his own than celebrating his wife's fortieth." She chuckles and winks slyly. "I'm not concerned though, Ames, because I have a plan. I'm going to clear the dead wood from my life and start again. Why don't you join me, pet? Cleanse your life of the shit you've accumulated – *all* of it."

She drifts away, and I take a sip of my wine and rub my head. Has she just implied that I should get rid of Geoff? No, I can't have heard right. She's probably had far too much Prosecco and is feeling a mix of euphoria at being the centre of attention on her special day and royally pissed off with her husband.

As Claire and I head towards the living room, our attention is drawn to two A3 pieces of paper taped to the wall, headed:

Bea's Life Cleanse.
Ideas for a new way of living without
clutter and crap.

"That's a coincidence," I say, scratching hard at a very irritating wig-itch. "This week, I'm to declutter my life and Bea's just said that she is going to do the same now that she's in her forties. Remind me to come back and read this list later, Claire. It might give me some ideas."

10.00 p.m.
Bea appears, supported by Cate. She is so drunk that she can't walk straight. "Amy Risshards. Come and look after this Arab Sheik for me, pleshe? He doesn't know many people and I said that you are verrrry good at looking after people because you did so well when you looked after those poor people in the shooop kitchen, didn't you, pet." She pinches my left cheek affectionately. "And, he will cheer you up because your husband is such an arse and you deserve better, mush better."

"Do I know this Arab, Bea?" I inquire, slightly put out at her insistence that I need to leave Claire, yet equally intrigued by the mystery party-goer.

"I don't reeeemember."

Just as Bea is about to take me to meet the mystery guest, she is whisked away to blow out the candles on her cake.

"Where is Bea's husband?" I whisper to Claire and Cate. *And where the hell is mine?*

Geoff eventually turns up at ten-thirty. He finds me dancing in the lounge, puts his arm around me and kisses me on the cheek. I can smell more than one can of lager on his breath. I stop dancing and turn to him, my eyes cold and my expression fixed.

"You are rather late."

"Sorry about that, darling. The babysitter didn't arrive, and I came by taxi," he explains, not quite meeting my eye.

"I think you came by taxi because you are over the limit," I say evenly. "And who is looking after our children?"

"Stop nagging," he barks. The kids will be fine for a few hours on their own, and I'm here now, aren't I? Don't go off on one. People will notice."

I bite my finger, determined not to make a scene. It's Bea's party and I don't want to cause any trouble. Before I can reply, Claire and Cate grab my arms, looking distressed. "Sorry about this, Geoff – we have a *friend emergency*," smiles Claire, dragging me off.

"What's going on?" I half-shout over the music as I try to shuffle as quickly as I can, given the restrictions of my Geisha outfit, towards the rear of the house.

"Shush," warns Cate. We creep to Bea's spare bedroom. It's quieter at this end of the house and quite dark. As we inch closer, we can hear a female mumbling and a deeper male voice chuckling.

"Perhaps Bea and her husband are having words about why he's been watching the footie upstairs," I whisper.

"No, he's crashed out on the bed," whispers Claire into my ear.

The three of us crowd around the door and earwig into the conversation. "I think she's taking off her bra," says Cate, horrified.

Bea's voice is clearer now, obviously being intimate with a stranger. "Do it now, before it's too late and I am too old... I wanna feel passion... Put the va-va-voom back into my mundane life."

Cate sneezes.

We scarper to the nearest place of safety, the downstairs loo, where we huddle together, watching in abject horror as Bea's husband, escorted by some woman we don't know, marches purposefully past us towards the spare bedroom, looking thunderous. We look on with bated breath as the door is thrown open and they go inside, slamming the door shut behind them.

"Fuck," I breathe. "What has she done?"

An hour later, we find Bea's husband alone in the spare bedroom, staring out of the window, his eyes puffy and red from crying. I hold out a glass of champagne to him, but he waves it away and turns his back to us.

"So, ladies. Were you aware that my wife had a one-night stand tonight?" he says quietly. He does not wait for our answer. "I know that we've not been happy for a long time and that I was upstairs earlier. I realise I take her for granted but a sordid bang *in here*?" He shrugs. "I can't stay married to her now. This has changed *everything*. I won't sit back and forgive her like some blokes might, even though I've been a complete bastard to her. You are her closest friends. Do you understand why I can't be with her any more?"

I try to reason with him. "This must have happened because she's unhappy for some reason. You've admitted that you take her for granted. Perhaps if you tried to make amends, you could get back to how you were?"

"That's impossible," he replies in a cold, clipped tone. "We married before God. Beatrice has broken the commandment *Thou shalt not commit adultery*, and now, whatever I feel about myself and us and what we have become, whatever I did wrong – and, believe me, I have made many mistakes – my faith will not allow me to let this one go. Claire, you will understand where I'm coming from."

He moves towards the door. "Perhaps it's for the best, anyway. Perhaps it was inevitable. Excuse me."

11.30 p.m.

Bea is ready to make an impassioned speech. She stands on a kitchen chair, her eyes glittering dangerously, her husband by her side. It is obvious to everyone that all is not well. A hush falls over the crowd as she raises a bottle of champagne to her lips and takes a glug.

"It's my fortieth year and high time I sorted out what I want from life, because I'm halfway through. So, I decided that my birthday present to myself would be to declutter my life." She smiles and takes another drink. "I don't do gossip, and I don't like rumour, and so *we*," she motions to her husband, "have decided that I will tell *you*," she motions to us, "my dearest family and friends, how I am going to clear the crap, the excess and the un-nec-ess-ary from my life."

The room is in deathly silence.

"Firstly, I want to raise a toast to my husband. I want to thank you for giving me twelve years of marriage, one fantastic child and years of *total shit*."

We laugh uncomfortably. Nobody quite knows where to look. Bea raises her arms, oozing confidence and speaks with conviction. "I am decluttering my life of my husband. Tonight, I had a fling. Tonight, I *purposely* broke my marriage vows, and I'm no longer going to be a wife. My husband has set me free. As of tonight, I am going to be a free Bea." She laughs at her joke for a minute. Then her mood darkens.

"My fling tonight was the best birthday present ever. I have hurt my husband, for which I am truly sorry, but there is a lot of stuff that he has done to me." She turns to him, and her tone becomes brittle. "Your *faith* didn't stop you from doing stuff that perhaps led me to…" She stops abruptly and takes another gulp from the bottle. "Anyway, as of tonight, I am Bea… free… me… cheers." She raises her glass.

Nobody moves.

"Come on. It's my birthday and I'm *forty*. Turn the music up and dance."

What more can we do? It's her party. We dance.

Before Geoff and I leave, I remember to read the suggestions Bea's guests have made to help her declutter her life. Out of the corner of my eye, I notice an Arab Sheik kissing Bea goodbye in the hallway. Bea waves me over to say hello.

"Ameeeee, pet," she slurs. "This is the Arab I wanted to introduce you to earlier." She turns to the Sheik. "Have you met my dearest friend?"

I turn to find myself looking into cornflower-blue eyes. I blink hard. I know those eyes. Where have I seen them? And then it hits me. It is *Him*. They are *his* eyes, the eyes of *Him*.

I bet I could have grabbed a secret snog if I'd only met him earlier tonight, I shout inwardly. *I could have decluttered my life of him had I known he was here, right under my nose. Why didn't I interpret 'declutter your life' to mean 'rid yourself of toxic people in your life', like it says on the flipchart list over there?* I scream at myself. *I could have devoted this week to changing his status from lust interest to critical friend and book guru. I could have worked on finding lots of habits and personality traits I dislike about him. I could have moved on. Why have I been so blind? That's yet another wasted opportunity to wash that man out of my hair,* I screech.

He, of course, has absolutely no idea what I am thinking. In my head, I'm shouting and screaming and tearing my hair out, but outwardly, I am the epitome of 'cool' – and furiously tearing at my scalp.

"*Konnichiwa*, Amy. *Kanpai*." He raises his glass of whisky in a toast and takes a gulp.

"Sorry?"

"That's 'hello' and 'cheers' in Japanese. Nice wig. Bit hot, under there is it?" He laughs as I scratch.

"Um, yes," I reply, still rattled at meeting him like this. "But it makes the outfit, so I'm braving it."

"Started writing?"

Hey, he remembers. That's impressive. Most men I know wouldn't remember stuff like that from one day to the next.

I smile. I am on safe ground, talking about my year and my writing. My nerves evaporate. "Everything's going really well, thanks. Should I really start thinking about the fifty-first challenge so early? I thought I might wait a bit."

"It's never too early to start thinking about it," he replies. "Is there a plot? Do you have a story arc? Who is your protagonist? That's if your chosen genre's fiction, of course."

My mouth gapes. I'm completely flummoxed. I don't have a clue what he's going on about. I itch my scalp again. I think it's bleeding. All I can muster is an "I don't know," as I catch a glimpse of his muscular arms and my lustometer rises from lukewarm to steaming.

"Well, you told me all about it at the divorce party, so I reckon you're sitting on a lot of choice material already. Shame you're leaving now. Text me when you're ready. Don't leave it too long though, eh?" He winks.

"Actually, I have loads of questions for you," I stutter.

He's standing so close to me that I can smell the whisky on his breath. This could be my chance to steal my snog and have done with it. Geoff is nowhere to be seen. My brain is whirring. I feel a tugging on my sleeve.

"Taxi's here."

I come to with a start. "Oh. Bob? Thanks a lot for delaying Geoff at yours this afternoon."

Bob looks confused. "I was here, helping Bea this afternoon. Claire did mention that Geoff dropped by. He's left his jacket at ours, by the way. Bye."

Geoff appears, looking fed-up. "Come on, I'm tired. I thought you wanted to get back, as the kids are on their own?" he grumps, ignoring Him. "And I think that after her performance tonight, you should declutter Bea from our lives." He takes my arm and pulls me away to find our taxi.

Sunday.

Bea and I are sitting at her kitchen table, dunking chocolate biscuits into mugs of steaming hot tea and candidly discussing her future. She is philosophical about the whole event. "We are where we are, pet. Last night I plucked up the courage to publicly announce that my marriage was a bad habit and that it was time to break the habit and deal with the shitty stuff. At long last, we are putting the wrongs right. No more stress and no more pretending." She hands me the two sheets of A3 paper from her party. "Cate told me about this week's challenge. Here, you take them. I don't need them. I am decluttering my own life by renouncing wifedom and embracing singledom. I'm going to enjoy being me again."

My eyes fill with tears. "You were together a long time. Don't you regret that it's over?"

"Don't feel sad for me, pet. Life's a learning experience. I live with many regrets, but they are part of my game of life. Every little thing we do – every choice and decision – can cause unpredictable effects elsewhere. It's called the Butterfly Effect. When you chose to examine your life, you became that butterfly. You flapped your wings, and I'm absolutely sure you're learning a great deal more than you could ever have imagined you would.

"It's what we *do* with what we learn that makes us who we are, Amy. Too many people make choices and decisions that in time don't work any more, but although they whinge and complain or suffer in silence, they don't do anything to improve their lot. Why? Are they too frightened? Perhaps it's the fear of the unknown, or they're too concerned with what others will think... eh, pet?" She sips her tea.

I'm unnerved. I think she's trying to tell me something, yet I'm too scared to broach the subject. I don't want to hear what she might say.

"I have changed," Bea says, studying her graduation photo closely. "I met my husband just before this was taken. We'd taken our Finals. We got jobs, earned enough money to rent a flat together, and the pressures of life that are with me now weren't there. I'm sure you remember what you were like when you first met Geoff? We were carefree. I knew that Christianity was important to him, but religion never came between us then.

"Around two years into our marriage, our gorgeous daughter came along and we became a proper family. When she turned two, his career went through a difficult patch and he was forced to live away a lot – freelancing in the Midlands – so he joined the local church for companionship. He ended up being away from us for most of the week, every week, and I had to become more resilient.

"For ten long, hard years, I cared for our daughter without much support, while he focused exclusively on building his career. My beautiful girl and I bonded and became very tight-knit. My husband wasn't ever too bothered about our lives, really. He was preoccupied with his own. As long as when he was home, the house was tidy and welcoming and he could relax, see his mates, be looked after and have sex with me, he was happy. She and I didn't mind, though. We knew he had to go away again, and so the time we spent together became quality time. We did a lot of fun things.

"Then, when she died..." Bea's eyes take on a faraway look, and her voice breaks. "When she... everything changed. He turned to his faith, and it began to affect our relationship. Whenever I tried to explain how shit I felt, he turned to prayer and quoted from the Bible – like Claire does. He told me to get a grip. He said that we still had each other, that we had God in our lives and that I should move on."

Bea pauses. "And I did try, Amy. I tried to rationalise things. You know me. I'm not very romantic. I did my damnedest to keep things in perspective and be a good wife. But too much had changed."

"We moved here. I found a job and met you lot. I had counselling and even tried to embrace his religious beliefs. I did everything to try and live my, no, *our* life again. However, over time, I grew to realise that this gnawing feeling of discontent deep in the pit of my stomach was not going away. I couldn't be the wife he wanted me to be. We had grown apart, and although we were friends, that magic something had gone. Last night, I felt alive. I felt release. I don't want to lose those feelings."

She looks at me, teary-eyed. "I am forty. I have considered my future, and I am not prepared to sacrifice my happiness. I don't want go to my grave as a martyr. I don't think it's fair on anyone if I spend the rest of my life living a lie – married to a man whom I care for dearly but whom I don't love in the way I once did. Am I expected to? Why should I? For whom? For him? For the sake of convention? Because it's written in the Bible? Because I will be financially worse off and forced to depend on the state and my own resources to make ends meet?"

She begins to clear the table. "You are a good person, Amy. I know that I will lose friends over what has happened. People can be cruel and judgemental when they haven't the right to be, and too many will judge me harshly. I think that you get it, though, and I hope that we will remain close."

A tear trickles down my cheek. She has touched a raw nerve, yet I cannot talk about it. Not yet. I need to make my own choices and decisions. "Bea, I will always be your friend," I say, a lump in my throat. "I understand. I really, really do."

Monday evening.

My *Declutter Your Life* list is taped to the kitchen window. I call my family into the kitchen. "Behold," I announce proudly. "Let me read it out to you."

GROUND RULES

- *Everything I own must be useful or there because I really love it.*
- *I will cull my cuddly toy collection and cookery book stash and create scrapbooks of prized recipes.*
- *I will dump or donate the kitchen gadgets I never use.*
- *If I haven't worn a piece of clothing etc. for a year, it will go.*
- *I will tidy and categorise my PC files and documents.*

"Great," applauds Geoff. "Here's to a tidy house. I thought you'd go further with it, though. I'd be happy to suggest lots more decluttering that you could do. So, when do you plan to do all this then? I reckon it'll take a year or two."

His hands go to his hips. His eyes are mocking. His sarcastic tone is all too much and I feel the resentment rising. I clench my fists and bite my tongue in frustration and disappointment. For a split second, I consider doing a Bea and adding him to my declutter list.

Thankfully, Pippa comes to my rescue. "Well done, Mum," she compliments, kissing my cheek. "I think it's cool. I'll help you to declutter, if you like?"

"Thanks," I smile, an atom of resentment dissipating. "I suggest we draw up a plan of attack and start tomorrow. Let's do it over popcorn. *That's* the way to be supportive," I remark to Geoff. "Can't you just be pleased that I'm making the effort?"

I turn to Pippa. "Just give me five."

I run to the kitchen and make a quick note of Geoff's reaction and my feelings on my laptop – before I forget.

Thursday.

The garage is piled high with neatly stacked boxes and bin liners full of things to sell, donate or dump. My kitchen cupboards are no longer stuffed full of gadgets I never use, and my favourite cookery books are neatly displayed. I have even let my favourite dress and matching heels go. The dress is too small and the heels were badly scuffed – but they held lots of great memories.

"Only the PC to sort, and that can wait," I say proudly. "Thanks for all your help, Pipps. I could never have done it without you. Let's show Dad what we've achieved."

I hug her and go to find Geoff who follows me out to the garage and casts his 'professional' eye over the scene before him. "Isn't it a great improvement? My team-mate and I have worked really hard, and I only have the PC to deal with now. Then I shall be well and truly decluttered."

"Yes..." He pauses. "I have to admit that our house does look better, Amy," he says, his eyes firmly fixed on the boxes and bags. "Please ensure you do something with all... *this*... or else all the clutter will simply have been transferred from one place to another, won't it? Don't forget."

"I'm not going to leave it all sitting here," I exclaim, "and I plan to declutter regularly in future."

"Really? Are you sure this 'challenge' isn't another one-week wonder?"

It's taken one sentence to successfully suck the enthusiasm out of me again. I feel deflated, tired and irritated. "Why, oh why aren't you just happy or pleased for me, Geoff? Why is there always a 'but' or a dig at me or a caveat or... or... an 'I thought'?"

"Calm down, dear," Geoff replies under his breath.

"Oh, *go away.*" I barge past him and storm upstairs to take my frustrations out on my laptop.

Pippa has overheard our heated conversation. "Leave it all there in the garage for a couple of days, Mum," she says quietly.

"Yes," I say with passion. "I bloody well will, just to annoy him."

11.25 p.m.

I want to talk to Geoff; to clear the air. I hate conflict, and I've been told that you should never go to sleep angry or mad at your partner. But he is asleep, and I know better than to wake him.

I felt G disrespected me today. And why does he think my challenges are one-week wonders? I type. *I don't. Some of them seem ridiculous, but they are making me think. They are challenging my opinions and beliefs. I'm gaining a new perspective on life. I'm trying out new things and meeting new people. I am only sorry that Geoff can't see it, and it saddens me. Perhaps he will in time.*

Week Three. Saturday afternoon.

Mrs Harmer is *the* renowned tarot reader and psychic round here. Everyone rates her, and the best news is that she has agreed to come over to my house tonight at five. "Yes!" I thump the table with delight. Last week's Experience Disability challenge (when I had to do everything without using my thumbs) was enlightening, but this one:

CONSULT A CLAIRVOYANT AND 'SEE' THE FUTURE

… is *relevant*. I sincerely hope she will tell me how to curb the lusting and provide comfort that all will be well at home. I text The Girls:

> 5pm Tarot, tonight.
> £20 a reading.
> Bring and Share tea.
> Text back what you are bringing.
> I'll provide the wine.

5.00 p.m.

Mrs Harmer is settled in my bedroom, ready for her first client.

I have decided to go last. As each of The Girls has their reading, the rest of us tuck into the food and wine.

7.00 p.m.

Claire's eyes are swollen from crying. Cate is comforting her. "She's wrong – she has to be. He must care, because he said I was wonderful and he gave me… Oh, Amy."

"Can I help?" I say.

"I'll be fine in a minute. It's nothing…" she hiccups.

"It's something about an old flame who has used her or is using her," Cate says. "*Whatever,*" she mouths to me.

"Amy, your turn, pet."

"How did your reading go, Bea? I hope it was better than Claire's. She's in a right state," Cate asks.

"I'm supposed to fall head over heels in love and have a baby. I'll believe it when I see it – especially the baby. Anyway, pet, you're on. I'll stay with Claire."

I take a deep breath and go to find Mrs Harmer.

"Shuffle and select seven cards," she says. "Hmmm. The Fool, swords and cups. You are working on a creative project. Do not stop." She pauses briefly. "Visualise two tomato plants. You are enthusiastically feeding the first with nutrients required for growth and good health. In return, it is rewarding you with vigorous growth. This is pleasing you, but it will never reward you with fruit. I see Blossom drop." She leans forward, her eyes impassive, her tone measured. "The other plant is wilting. Lord Rhizoctonia solani, Lady Cancer and the Japanese Knotweed twins are at work. Be mindful."

I yawn, bored by the gobbledygook she's spouting.

Mrs Harmer catches her breath, tuts disapprovingly and rubs her eyes, distinctly ruffled. "Someone you know abuses alcohol, my dear. Perhaps they drink for Dutch courage? I see many bottles." Startling green eyes lock onto mine. "Pick two more. Your eyes are open, yet you are fast asleep. Enabling many to achieve dreams is commendable. However, I fear that their happiness may be at your expense. Wake up and tend to your plants."

She folds her arms over her chest. "When your son's Venus Fly Trap becomes infected with grey mould, he will call you for help."

"But I don't have a son," I say indignantly.

"Take heed of my messages and the future is yours. Do you have cash on you?"

I leave the room, my head spinning. I don't believe a word.

Week Four. Adriano's Restaurant. Friday, 8.00 p.m.

LET THE DICE DECIDE.

Now, this is a cool challenge. Years ago, Bea suggested I read Luke Rhinehart's *The Diceman*, and it really appealed to my dark side. To actually get the chance to try it out is thrilling. At Adriano's, Bea describes the meaning behind the challenge.

"A bored psychiatrist decides to spice up the daily grind of his life and lets the throw of a dice decide his actions and the course of his day. Once you hand over your life to the throw of a dice, anything can happen. So, Ames, how are you going to play this one then, pet? Tame or *extremely* dangerous?" She nudges me suggestively.

"Well," I reply excitedly. "Firstly, we need to decide on different things I have to do for each number on the dice. For example, if I throw the dice and it lands on number one, it might mean that I have to… well…" I hesitate. Well? *What?* "Help me decide my dice-play."

After much debate, this is what we come up with:

1 = Live without technology.
2 = Ravage my husband's wardrobe and burn his favourite

t-shirts and vests that he loves so much and that I
cannot stand.
3 = *Go make-up free.*
4 = *Chat up a man or woman in a pub and get their*
number.
5 = *Wear no underwear.*
6 = *Steal something.*

Tomorrow, I will let the dice decide.

Saturday morning.

Geoff has no idea what this challenge is, thank God, and I have no plans to ever tell him about it. He's at a university alumni reunion in Leeds all weekend, and when he gets back, it'll all be over. I wait for him to leave, find a dice and sit in silence, rolling it around in my clammy hands and willing fate to be kind to me.

"Please dice," I whisper lovingly. "Be generous." I shut my eyes tight and I roll… It's a four. I have to go to a pub, chat up a man or woman and get their number.

The phone doesn't stop ringing all morning. Everyone's ultra-keen to advise me on chatting up a stranger. Bea is surprised at how nervous I am. "But Amy," she says. "You are such a sociable person. You, of all people, shouldn't have any trouble chatting somebody up, especially in a pub. Once you've had your three glasses of wine, you're up for anything, pet. This should be a doddle."

"You see," I explain, chewing on my finger, "I have never, ever actually chatted up a stranger before. I have never needed to. I've had so few boyfriends and they always came onto me. I don't know how to do it?" I continue in a small voice. "And," I continue in an even smaller voice, "I am scared."

"I know exactly how to help you," she says. "Meet me at two in T and T."

Bea turns up with a tall, dark stranger in tow. "This is Rom. He's Italian, from Naples and staying with my friend. I thought he'd be able to help you practise your chat-up lines."

"Hello," I say nervously.

"*Ciao, bella!*" replies Rom in a drop-dead gorgeous Italian accent, kissing my hand. "I amm 'ere to 'elp you become a sexy seductress of man, no?"

"I only want to chat someone up, not shag them," I laugh.

"Shag?" Rom looks confused. Bea explains what a shag is and his face clears.

"*No, tesoro,*" he says, wagging his finger at me. "You do not want to make the love wiz 'im. You must try to make 'im feel that you want the, as you say, shag wiz 'im. Zat is 'ow you must chat to 'im. Zen he will give you 'iz *numero di telefono. Andrà tutto bene.* It will be fine."

I am sold. "Come on then, Rom. Teach me!" I cry. And everyone in the café looks round at me in surprise.

An hour later, I'm finally putting my own stamp on the seductress persona. It doesn't come easily to me, but I'm better able to use body language, touch and eye contact to convey 'I am seriously interested in you' and have learned some rocking lines of introduction. Although Bea is insistent I try, I've decided that chatting up a woman will be too difficult. I'm going to target a man.

Claire readily agrees to accompany me to a local well-known 'pulling' pub for support and moral guidance. The venue is already packed when we arrive, and there's a good vibe. We sit in a corner sussing out the talent. She insists on taking a photo of me in the pub 'for my scrapbook', which is nice.

It's great being away from my normal Saturday night routine of tea and telly, but my challenge is sitting like a monkey on my shoulder and I can't relax. The only saving grace is that a disco of sorts is playing damn good music, and after two large glasses of wine and a pep talk from Claire, I've loosened up enough to give it some on the tiny dance floor.

10.00 p.m.
I'm parched and acutely aware that time is running out. I simply *have* to get on with it and find a suitable guy to chat up. I leave Claire dancing and stagger to the bar for Dutch courage and to prepare myself for action.

It's super-busy at the bar. There's a lot of pushing and shoving to get served, and as I push my way forward, someone splashes lager over my right arm. Now I can add 'l'eau de lager' as one of the weapons in my arsenal of chat-up tools and techniques.

I fidget impatiently as I wait my turn, my senses heightened to the high levels of testosterone around me. I'm acutely aware that a man in a mid-blue woollen jumper keeps glancing in my direction.

Right, I say to myself. *He'll do. He looks nice enough, and he's playing straight into my hands.*

I begin to tentatively play out what Rom taught me earlier. I tease my hair, bat my eyelids at him, smile shyly and... I am rudely interrupted by the bartender shouting at me above the din. "Sorry? Oh, a large Pinot Grigio, please."

I'm fumbling in my purse to pay when I hear a deep voice to my left. "I'll get that for the beautiful lady."

Who has just called me a beautiful lady?

I turn in the direction of the voice and almost faint as I see the bartender handing Blue Jumper Man my drink. "I didn't mean to startle you," he says apologetically, passing me the glass. "It *is* okay if I buy you this, isn't it?"

"Yes, of course," I splutter. "That's very kind, thanks."

Our hands touch briefly and I jump. I am so damn nervy. It's the thought of what I must do. We make obligatory small talk. "I don't often come here," I say, and then I remember the challenge and add: "but I'm glad I did". I smile into his eyes. *Rom would be proud of me.*

"Me neither," he replies, giving me the once-over. "I'm glad I did, too. What's your name?"

This is going too well, I think to myself as I pretend to be interested in his conversation and apply some honed eye contact techniques, ensure my body is turned towards him and smile encouragingly. *He's a bit pervy, but never mind.*

"What are you doing afterwards, Amy? Fancy a night cap in town?"

That's a bit forward, I think. However, tonight I don't care. It couldn't be going any better. This is *the* question that Rom and I have prepared a killer answer for. "Aww, I'm really sorry. I have to go soon, but we can swap numbers and keep in touch?" (*Rom is applauding.*) I give him my number. He sends his directly to my phone. Job done. It's time to leave.

"Goodbye, beautiful lady," he says cheekily, leaning over to plant a kiss on my cheek. I don't object. Well, he has said I am beautiful and helped me to achieve my challenge. However, just as he makes to kiss me on the other cheek, we are rudely interrupted by a friend jumping on his back. "Watch the lady, you fucking pisshead," says Blue Jumper Man, pushing him off. "Sorry about that, Amy. Please ignore my ignorant brother. He's a complete prat when he's pissed."

I look up to see who Blue Jumper Man is referring to. I don't believe it. It is *Him*, here in this pub and he is talking to the very man I am chatting up. This is just too much. It's uncanny.

"Brother... You're *brothers*?"

I stare at Him, lost for words. "Do you know Amy, then?" he asks Blue Jumper Man playfully. He has a certain look in his eye which I can't quite decipher.

"I do now," grins Blue Jumper Man, leaning in to plant another kiss on my cheek.

I am so stunned at the news that these two are related that I lose my balance and my hands land on Blue Jumper's waist. Yuck. His jumper is damp. I tear my hands away and wipe them on my jeans. He must have been caught by the flying beer too.

"Laters, babe!" shouts Blue Jumper Man as I speed-walk back to Claire, who has recorded the whole incident on her phone.

"Yes, see you soon, Amy," his brother echoes.

"Who was *that*?" giggles Claire.

"That was…" I stutter and, without waiting for Claire, I turn and run outside to find a taxi, completely dumbfounded.

July

LEARN THE ART OF ASSERTIVENESS.

I usually feel nervous at the start of training courses. It's the fear of the unknown that gets to me. Today, however, I am glad to be away from home, focused on something much more important than fretting over whether Blue Jumper Man will text or phone and how to play it if he does. The thought of picking up top tips on how to manage Geoff better is my priority, and I am euphoric to be here.

Our trainer, Eloise, is a boldly dressed woman in her forties. Seven bangles – the colours of the rainbow – adorn her right wrist, and whenever she writes on the flipchart, they jangle and catch the light, which is ever so slightly distracting. She stands at the front of the room in a smart red fitted suit accented with a brightly multi-coloured scarf and black tights. Her hair is bobbed. Not a strand is out of place.

"She looks assertive, all right," delegate Tony on my left whispers to me. "Wouldn't like to get on the wrong side of her."

I giggle and Eloise frowns. Her hands move to her hips; her gaze (which seconds before was kind and friendly) is icy. *Perhaps I'm not going to enjoy this as much as I thought,* I ponder. Eloise scrutinises me for what seems like hours before breaking into a smile. Her eyes soften and she speaks to me kindly. "How do you feel?"

"Must I?" I reply, trying hard to remain professional.

"Please don't be shy." Eloise sits down and waits. The other delegates laugh nervously.

"Upset and uptight," I say quietly.

"And why is that, Amy?" probes Eloise.

"Because you were standing there right in front of me in a bright red smart suit and you gave me a *look*. You made me feel like I was a child, like my eleven-year-old daughter when she has done something naughty. I don't know you and I feel intimidated. The way you looked at me made me feel very small, and I wanted to go home. In fact, if this continues, Mrs... Miss..."

"*Eloise*," whispers one of my colleagues.

"Yes, Eloise... I think that I might have to leave right now because I know that I will not learn *anything* with a trainer who treats me like you just have... oh!"

I remember where I am and crumple into my chair, eyes lowered, waiting to be given my comeuppance. I'd been so excited about today, and now, thanks to my big mouth, I'm about to be ceremoniously expelled from the course before it's even begun and probably advised to take an anger management programme instead.

There is silence and then a round of applause. I wait, stunned. "Good. That was very expressive and articulate," nods Eloise. "If I were put in the same situation, without knowing how to deal with it, I might have done exactly as you just did. Thank you for starting off our day with a *great* example."

And that is how the course begins; with Eloise describing 'the three Vs' – that our body language (visual), tone of voice (vocal) and the words we use (verbal) give off signals about us.

5.00 p.m.
Armed with a bunch of really cool techniques to test out, I leave for home on cloud nine; the lyrics to D:Ream's *Things Can Only Get Better* in my head on loop. It feels like I've been

in counselling. It's blindingly obvious what's wrong with my marriage. For the first time ever, I've identified how easily Geoff pushes my buttons and why that impacts on our relationship – in a bad way.

I've confessed to Eloise that the same thing happens with my mother and with my sister Jess, as well as with other significant people. I'm in a pattern of behaviour that I find almost impossible to break – but if I am to have a healthy, happy marriage, I have to. I can and I will.

"I get it," I say to my reflection in the bathroom mirror. "I'm never going to be like Bea, but if I change my behaviour, then Geoff's will change too, and things will improve. We will communicate in a loving way and treat each other with respect – and he will be more receptive to me. He will be willing to listen without criticism or derision." Perfect.

Just you wait, world, I think to myself. *The worm has turned.*

Just three hours later, my euphoric bubble has burst. Reading back my course notes and my diary entries, I am at a low ebb. I don't think doing this will be enough. Just a few short hours ago, I was certain that assertiveness would be my panacea, but there's a bunch of other really challenging stuff to tackle, and right now, it all feels too much. God, I'm so stupid. Is there really any point? What if I try this out on Geoff and fail?

Hey, soothes my inner voice. *Slow down. This is just the start of things to come. Take small steps and keep the end in mind, and you will succeed. Assertiveness is just one tool in your toolbox.*

And if it doesn't work, what am I supposed to do?

The familiar sound of a text dropping into my inbox interrupts my train of thought. I reach for my phone. It's from Him. I gasp, and as I open the message, that familiar feeling of trepidation and excitement punches me in the pit of my stomach, lifting me out of my dark mood instantly. It reads:

Recovered from my bro's snog?
I'm gutted. ;)
How's you?

Wow! I didn't expect that. He sounds dead chatty and keen, I giggle to myself. I fire back a witty reply:

Just been on an assertiveness course.
Can't believe I'm over halfway through.
I'm gonna sort out my husband.
Ha Ha.

You don't come across like a
shrinking violet to my bro and me.

Ooh, the cheek, I cringe, laughing to myself. I feel quite giddy, and I'm definitely glowing on the inside. What should I say next? Something about Blue Jumpers? No, I'd better not go there unless I have to. I feel bad for having led Mr Blue Jumper Man on, and I don't want to encourage him further. I'm still praying he doesn't get in touch.

A second text pings in.

So, tell me more?
I'm interested.

Now, if anybody else had responded in that way, I'd be straight on the phone talking nineteen to the dozen about what I've been up to and what's been happening lately. We'd have a really cosy chat. However, this is Him. I *so* want to call Him, yet something is stopping me.

My inner critic cuts in. *If you keep texting and talking to him, you are a step closer to finding out something about him that you dislike, and then the spell will be broken. You will be able to declutter Him from your life. Take the chance. You have nothing to lose and everything to gain. Just do it.*

A second inner critic cuts across the first. *If you keep texting and talking to him, you are a step closer to building an emotional relationship with him. You are more likely to seek out and find things that you have in common. You will find it more difficult to declutter him from your life and sort out your relationship with Geoff. There is every chance that you will want to connect with him again and again. You have everything to lose. Don't do it.*

My finger goes to my mouth. My conscience has been pricked with a very sharp pin. This is *the* ideal moment to stop our friendship in its tracks…

I'm not building any kind of emotional attachment to him – I've absolutely no intention of romance. It's a friendship and a business relationship and nothing more. Anything else simply isn't going to happen. I laugh. *I suppose an emotional relationship is like having an affair – just without the sex. And we definitely aren't doing that. Dreaming about stealing a quick secret snog and harbouring lustful thoughts is one thing, but that's not an emotional relationship, is it? It's total rubbish. I'll try to be assertive.* My heart is fluttering as I text:

> Too much to say in a text.
> Can I ring you?
> Then I can delight you with
> tales of my antics, ha ha.

No response.

Twenty minutes later. Still nothing.

"Okay," I yell angrily at my mobile. "Be like that. What the hell is up with you? I thought we were in conversation? Am I your entertainment when you're at a loose end or without a better offer? Is that when you contact me? You are seriously doing my head in."

I am mad. I feel let down and I know that I should just call it a day and tell him to jog on. The urge to delete his number from my phone is overwhelming. I can't bring myself to do it. I stare at his number. I stare at the Delete Contact button. My finger hovers over it yet I can't quite press it and permanently end our relationship. I fling it onto the floor in disgust. In a flash, my sense of joy has been flipped on its head and I feel intense emotional pain – the same pain I felt when my first true love dumped me because he said he couldn't fit in with my life plan.

10.30 p.m.

As I hear Geoff's footsteps coming up the stairs to bed, I turn onto my left side, facing away from him, and pretend to be asleep. I can't deal with his questions and digs and 'I thoughts' right now. I need time to process my feelings.

Okay. I'm still in lust with Him. He doesn't know that, though, and that's not a good enough reason to act in haste and frustration and permanently delete him from my life, is it? I think I will regret it if I let him go. I don't get why, but I feel I need to stay connected to him and so, right now, I'm going to listen to my intuition. And anyway, I can delete him whenever I want to. I definitely will do after he's helped me get going with my fifty-first challenge. I have control.

Week Three. Saturday, 8.00 a.m.

This is *the* weekend that I cherish in summer. I whisk my children away from the daily grind, and we step away from reality, put our insignificant stuff into perspective and unwind. Nothing and no one from our everyday lives is allowed to invade our space, and ensuring this includes having a total ban on electronic devices. Escaping into the open arms of a swanky hotel with spa in the city is a great tonic, and we always ensure that we have the best time ever.

There is method in my madness, however. This is a treat with a purpose, for it's how I try to keep us connected and close – to strengthen the sense of family and unity that was acutely lacking in my own childhood. And it kinda works. We always return feeling rejuvenated and much closer. Best of all, I get to learn a lot about my children and their lives; things that I would never usually find out.

My Skype alert goes off. "Hi, Grandma."

"Amy, *bubelah*." Her frail face appears on the PC monitor.

I stare intently into her heavily lined eyes. "You don't look so good, Grandma."

There's a long pause. "Oh, don't you worry about me," she smiles. "Tell me about your challenges."

We return to familiar territory.

"Well, last Thursday I buried a time capsule in the garden, which was fun. And this week, I'm going busking, which does not sound like fun."

"You're doing what this week?"

"Busking," I shout down the computer. "Becoming a street entertainer. If people like me, they'll give donations."

"Donations? Mrs Perkins gives donations of blood, and she gets a cup of tea and a biscuit afterwards. Most civilised." Pippa stifles a giggle and gesticulates wildly. "I have to go, or I'll be in trouble with your great-grandchildren. I'll be in touch early next week."

Her face disappears.

"Have fun," says Geoff as we make to leave. "What time will you be back?"

"Whenever we finish," I laugh. "Why?"

"Oh, no reason," he replies airily. "I might be out. Don't worry about cooking for me."

"Okay," I reply. "Gotta go. See you."

Sunday.

We have gossiped, laughed, pigged out and shopped until

I literally did drop from exhaustion and had to revive myself with litres of coffee. We are spent up and blissfully happy – Zen-like, even. Such is the feeling when we have been away. It's just heavenly.

We meander through the crowds, taking in the atmosphere and marvelling at the talent of the street performers entertaining the masses. "Next challenge?" remarks Evie.

Ah, I'd completely forgotten.

"I'm not confident enough to sing or dance, and I don't play a musical instrument. What on Earth could I do?" I snap.

"Why don't you ask that guy from the soup kitchen?" suggests Pippa, noticing my change of mood. "Didn't you say he was a busker?"

Of course. I sigh with relief. I'll ask Pete.

9.00 p.m.
There's no sign of Geoff as I pull up onto the driveway. I message him to let him know we're home and chivvy the children into the house.

11.45 p.m.
Geoff shakes me awake, takes me into his arms and holds me close. Grandma has died.

Monday afternoon.
Geoff says he can't get time off from work at such short notice, so I go to the funeral alone. I'm secretly relieved. He wasn't close to Grandma and I don't want to have to spend my time (a) looking after him and (b) stopping him from being rude to Jess and pissing me off. He's never got on with my family, and I don't trust him to hold back, not even at Grandma's funeral.

Upon my arrival, I awkwardly embrace my mother and Jess. We congregate in an oppressive, stark, whitewashed room, ready to mourn Grandma's passing. As the service begins, my fingernails gradually dig deep into the palms of my hands; the discomfort of it stops me from breaking down. *I have known you for all my life*, I think. *You are one of the few who knew me inside and out and loved me unconditionally – and now you are gone.*

My mum and Jess are stoic. However, before long, I cannot help but weep openly as I recall the special things that made Grandma who she was. I silently thank her for always being there for me. *Unlike some*, I think, shooting a dirty look at my mother, who visibly stiffens and sneers at me before averting her eyes.

Thankfully, the service is short, and Grandma's casket is prepared for burial. As tradition dictates, I follow the coffin to the graveside, stand in respect as prayers are said and watch as she is lowered into her final resting place alongside her husband.

Seminal moments from my childhood flood back. I hear her voice comforting me after Dad walked out on us. "Don't cry, *bubelah* – have a bagel." My tears fall once more.

Jess comes over to comfort me. "Amy," she says, putting her hand on my shoulder. "One of the last things Grandma said to me before she passed away was about your challenges and adventures." She takes a scrap of paper from her pocket and reads from it. "She asked me to tell you not to give up on them, to keep an eye on some frenemy of yours – whatever that means – and said that you must donate blood this week, even though you would be sad. She was insistent that you demand a cup of tea and a biscuit afterwards. Who is this 'so-called friend' that Grandma referred to, Ames?"

"I think she means Claire, but she must be muddling her up with somebody else. Claire's the perfect friend."

"Oh yeah," cackles Jess. "She's definitely one to watch."

"Stop taking the piss out of Grandma. Get in the car, Jess. Mum's waiting. I won't have you wind me up today about her or Claire or Geoff," I snap.

"Sorry, Amy," she retaliates. "You've always been such a good judge of character."

"NO MORE." I cover my ears with my hands and running to the waiting car.

Tuesday, 5.00 p.m.
Pete spots me hovering in the doorway at the soup kitchen. "Hey, you!" he cries delightedly, giving me a bear hug. "Fancy a brew?" He makes the tea and pushes a biscuit into my hand.

"What's up?" he asks, concerned. "You look bushed."

"It's been a tough week," I reply. I fill him in about Grandma.

"Ah, I know what it's like to lose somebody you love," he empathises. "When I lost my wife, my world fell apart." He looks at me, his eyes dulled. "Amy, do you ever wonder why I'm here and why I busk?"

"It has crossed my mind. You don't really look as if you, well, belong here," I reply, blushing.

"My wife had an affair and left me. Before that, I had a good career, we shared a wide circle of friends, we lived comfortably – you get the picture – and we were great together. But when our lifestyle changed, it tested us. Through no fault of my own, I lost my job and took temporary positions to keep us solvent. I was no quitter, but we were forced to downsize and eventually defaulted on our mortgage. We lost our house because we couldn't sell. It was in negative equity. Cara became depressed. She decided she couldn't cope with the changes, so she cheated on me."

His light, matter-of-fact tone turns brusque, and he picks angrily at a scab on the back of his hand. "I didn't see the warning signs. I trusted her. There I was, working my butt off, and all the while she was lying and scheming. Eventually she cut her losses and ran off with some dick 'cos he could give her all the fucking inconsequential stuff – the status and bling and security – that I could no longer provide, Amy."

He bangs the table with his fist in frustration. "We live in a country where it's acceptable to throw out and replace our stuff without a second thought. When did it become okay to dispose of people so casually too? It's not alright to bail out when things get tough or don't go the way we want them to. Doing something purely for personal gain is not justifiable in my book. Cara wasn't happy so she disposed of me, legitimised it and moved on. It wasn't like that in my parents' day. They worked through the ups and downs of life. Isn't that where the phrase 'make do and mend' came from?"

What a bitch, hurting Pete like that. I'd never cheat, I affirm silently. *It's not worth it. All that secrecy and guilt and the constant fear of being discovered, not to mention the risk of picking up a nasty disease – and the gossip.* I shudder. *No man's worth that.* I tune back into Pete, who is still ranting.

"Anyway, I dealt with the crap by blocking out the past with drink and doing some terrible things. I simply existed, and I didn't care, Amy. Now I understand that I needed time to grieve before I could move on, but back then I pushed the self-destruct button." He looks me squarely in the eye. "I busk to make ends meet. It makes me happy to play my guitar, sing and give others pleasure. I live in a caravan on a mate's farm. I don't see my kids because they won't see me, and I work here to make amends; to help others going through bad times and to stop them taking the same road I took."

"You seem content, Pete?"

"It's all an act, Amy baby," he replies, shrugging his shoulders. "I'm happy, safe and valued when I'm here – but away from all this?" Pete motions around himself. "I feel worthless, without purpose, direction and love. Thanks to her, I can't get close to anyone anymore. Not surprisingly, I have mega trust issues, you know? Without trust, you have nothing. However," Pete smiles, "on a more positive note, I've taken the first step and acknowledged my problems. I'm in counselling and I've cut down on my drinking. I'm no longer that ostrich ignoring my issues. So, that's all good. Excuse me, my scab is bleeding." He goes to find the first aid box. I follow him into the kitchen. "Pete, I came here to ask you for assistance with my next challenge. I can't do this on my own, and I think it'll be good for you too."

I explain.

"So, will you busk with us? It'd be nice if we could learn some of Grandma's favourite songs and sing in her memory? The only thing is that we need to do it by Friday or I'll fail, and I can't afford to do that – for Grandma."

Wednesday, 4.30 p.m.

Pippa, Evie, Pete and I are at the soup kitchen amicably planning my challenge with Bianca and her mum. A number of tracks are now downloaded onto my MP3 player. The girls have borrowed tambourines from school and successfully blagged Eastern-European-style character skirts, gypsy-style blouses and character shoes from their local dance school.

We practise singing and dance routines until the soup kitchen opens. We aren't perfect, but that isn't what matters. As Pete says, if we make an effort, the crowds will love us.

Thursday afternoon.

We meet in town at Pete's regular busking spot. "I never knew you busked here, Pete," I say in amazement. "I walk past all the time, and I've never noticed you."

Pete laughs. "Lots of people don't notice us, Amy baby. They look anywhere but at us. It doesn't matter."

We set up our equipment. Luckily, it is a dry afternoon. Pete picks up his guitar. "Ready, Amy?" asks Pete kindly, strumming his guitar.

"I think so," I grimace.

"Okay – let's rock for Grandma!" he cries, and off we go.

A small crowd gathers to listen to our catchy tunes. We encourage everybody to join in with our dance moves. By the end, we're all breathless, as is the audience. As they applaud and shower us with coins, I look to the heavens and smile. "Hope you enjoyed the show, Grandma."

Afterwards, we decamp to a local café and order the obligatory tea and biscuits. Pete counts up our takings. We've made just over a hundred pounds. "It's all for you, Pete," I say, pushing the pile of cash towards him. "Accept it with love and use it unwisely – but not on alcohol," I giggle.

"What will you buy with it all, Mr Pete?" asks Evie.

Pete thinks for a minute. "I am going to put it all away and use it to buy a suit, shirt and tie," he says carefully. "For when I start looking to get back into more regular employment." We whoop with joy, applaud and toast his bravery with cups of tea.

"Do the toast now, Mum!" shouts Evie.

"Okay, guys – raise your tea cups," I smile. "Here's to Grandma. Sleep tight, *bubelah*."

When I get home, I find a text from Pete:

Amy baby, don't be an ostrich.
Face your fears, don't run from them.
You have friends to support you.
Your challenges are there to guide you.
Listen to the messages they send.
Do what is right, not what is easy.

Week Four. Friday, 9.30 a.m.

Family Richards leaves for Cyprus tomorrow, and today is about packing, cleaning and managing meltdowns. I am feverishly writing to-do lists in preparation for today's annual guaranteed day of woe when Cate pops round. "How'd you get Geoff to agree to Cyprus?" she asks in amazement. "I thought his heart was set on Austria?"

I grin sheepishly and fess up. "I booked it without telling him the day after we got back from my challenge at Blackpool, where I had to ride The Big One. I was so mad with him and his conniving ways and pig-headedness. I knew that he would have talked me round and I would have regretted it. However, seven sun-filled days away from the pressures of everyday life will do us good. It'll help us to bond as a family, and Geoff and I will have time to talk and become more appreciative of each other."

"Will you go – to Austria, I mean?"

"One day. It's the focus on walking I'm not sure about. I like walking – just not Geoff's walks. However, now that I have newly acquired knowledge and skills in assertiveness, when the conversation comes round again, I'll be better able to stand my ground and turn it into a win-win," I chuckle, feeling smug.

"How?" laughs Cate.

"We were told to begin with the end in mind, and I have a very clear image in my head of what the end is."

I reel off my list of conditions:

"No remarks about drinking responsibly. That guilt-trips me. No commenting on what we eat – *all holiday*. His healthy eating obsession has to go on hold. And finally, one complete day off for me. I always ask for time to myself on holiday and never seem to get more than half an hour. I will have one full day where I get up *when I want*, I do what I want and I meet my family at an agreed time in the evening. The thought of being able to sit and read a book from cover to cover in peace without constant pestering or feeling guilty for doing so is the one thing that I miss most about holidays before children."

I notice the time. "Sorry, I have to go. I just know that if we leave home without diarrhoea tablets, one of us is sure to come down with the runs." I smile. "And I can't rely on Geoff to remember."

4.45 p.m.
Evie and Pippa have been tasked with putting their holiday clothes into neat piles, ready for packing. The tears and tantrums begin.

7.30 p.m.
I am using wine therapy to keep calm. The girls are each building a tower of totally unnecessary stuff to take away. I haven't even started packing.

7.45 p.m.
A difficult conversation results in a rapid prioritisation of their mountains of stuff. The pile shrinks by a third. I have almost finished the bottle of wine and have still not started packing.

"Suitcases?" requests Pippa.

"As usual, poppet, I am waiting for your father to discuss this. He's told me that we have a weight limit and so packing in the right way is very important. This year, we can only take two cases. He's bringing them down in a minute."

I eye the amount of stuff waiting to be packed. At this rate, I'll be taking next to nothing, as there'll be no room in the case. I just know what's coming next.

Geoff ceremoniously wheels a perfectly packed suitcase into the spare bedroom, complete with neatly rolled shirts. As I predicted, there isn't room for anything else in his. I observe the case that he has selected for us. My stressometer spikes, and the fact that I have been drinking empowers me to speak up.

"Don't tell me that we have to try and cram all our stuff into *this,* while *you* gloat that *you're* ready to go and that *your* shirts will arrive in pristine condition?"

Pippa and Evie start to complain. Geoff bites back and orders them to halve the amount of stuff they want to take. His Pointy Finger comes out to play. I sit there and watch. The scene is typical. I drink more wine.

Five minutes later.

The situation is escalating out of control. Geoff is throwing our clothes around and making inappropriate comments. I am about to get mad when I stop and remember my assertiveness training.

"Darling," I rest my hand on Geoff's arm. He stops talking and pointing. "You've packed your clothes so well and in good time," I gush. "However, we have three other people's clothes to somehow pack, plus a lot of other family essentials. I don't think that the case you have given us is big enough – and perhaps your case is designed for one person only? You said yourself that we can only take two cases and we have a weight limit, and I am sure that we could do this differently?"

I pause. Geoff looks okay so far. "I feel upset that you have sorted yourself out and left everything else to me. We have spent a long time organising what we should take." I mentally tick off the stages of the four-stage 'How to be Assertive in Conversation' framework from the training course. "This frustrates me and makes me feel like you don't understand or appreciate us," I continue. "So, do you think that we should, no, we *could* sit down together, discuss our holiday organisation and share the load?" I show him the lists of jobs that still have to be done before I can go to bed.

"Now, Amy," he says as if addressing a child, "when you speak to me like that, it is so loving that I am quite willing to consider your point of view and be helpful. All you have to do is ask without getting so uppity."

"Why should I have to ask?" I reply. "It's pretty obvious, isn't it?"

"Not to me," he says. "Women are better at this sort of thing. You know what needs to be done. Now, let's discuss this rationally, shall we?"

I want to smack him for being an arrogant, sexist pig and somehow turning the conversation to his advantage. However, at least he has agreed to help out, so I give in. By half past nine, the cases are packed.

Saturday, 5.00 a.m.

On the way to the airport, I read out my challenge to my family:

GO SCUBA DIVING.

Geoff bangs the steering with the palms of his hands and the car swerves violently. "Brilliant choice. We finally have another challenge of substance. Always wanted you to try that, and I'm sure we'll find somewhere for you to have a go."

"Brilliant? You know that I hate putting my face underwater, I'm not a strong swimmer and I can't see well without glasses or contact lenses," I reply glumly.

"You need to try, Mum," comes a voice from the rear of the car. "You always say that we shouldn't knock it until we've tried it."

"I do," I sigh. "Won't be saying those words of wisdom again in a hurry."

Tuesday.

I want to disown Geoff. Everywhere we go, he busies himself searching out scuba diving opportunities for me. We haven't found anywhere yet, and I hope that I can delay the challenge until we return home. I've secretly messaged Cate and discovered that I can have a taster lesson in our local swimming pool. That would do fine.

Wednesday, 2.00 p.m.

Taking a stroll around the harbour, Geoff casually mentions that our holiday rep has found a company offering scuba diving adventures at sea. "I don't think so," I say firmly.

"Dad!" interjects Pippa, "Let Mum do what she wants. She needs a break. Stop telling her what to do."

"Well, I think you should, Amy," he replies, ignoring her. "I thought that you wanted to face your fears? Don't tell me you're going to bottle out? Tell you what, why don't we just go and find out about it? No pressure." He smiles seductively and I agree. Why not?

The owners of Cypridive speak basic English and are incredibly enthusiastic about taking me out. They ply us with the local Aphrodite white wine while enthusing over their passion. Their hospitality seduces Geoff and, without my knowledge, he books us both onto a dive tomorrow at eleven o'clock. He pays up front. There is no going back.

"Just remember, Amy," he says, when he finally gets around to informing me. "Life shrinks or expands in proportion to one's courage."

"Blimey – that's deep, coming from you," I say. "Who said that?"

"Anais Nin," he replies proudly. "Jess told me about her. She was one of the first prominent women in the Western world to write erotica. There's a lot you don't know about me, Amy," he smiles. "Now, come and help me to choose a handbag for my PA. She hinted that she'd love a red leather tote, whatever that is."

Thursday, 11.00 a.m.

Geoff and I, four other tourists and two Cypridive reps are on our way out to sea – to who knows where. One guy steers the tiny motor boat while the other kits us out ready for our dive. The range of clothing available is limited, and everything I try on is too big. I attempt to use this fact to get out of the dive.

"No, no, lady." Stephan waggles his index finger at me. "A leetle big but fine." He pulls at my wetsuit and winks. "Very sexy, Mrs Aimeeee."

"How do I look?" I shout to Geoff above the drone of the motor. He gives me the thumbs up. We are handed fins. Again, I think that mine are too big, but as I've never worn fins before, I carry on. As I waggle my feet around, I notice Geoff and Stephan deep in conversation and pointing to my feet. It makes me slightly anxious.

The boat stops and the engine is switched off. We have arrived. "We are in the middle of the ocean," I whisper to Geoff, panic-stricken. "I don't want to do this… I don't want to…"

"Leetle lady." Stephan pulls me across to the side of the boat. "You take this belt of weights and I give you the mask. Put on please."

I do as he says. He stands back, admires me and, turning to his colleague, says something in rapid Greek. They laugh. I turn to Geoff, who won't quite meet my eye. Before I can say anything more, we are asked to sit on the side of the vessel looking into the boat, and Stephan gives a short talk about what we are about to do. I can't understand him very well and am preoccupied with my mask. I don't think it fits properly.

"Now you, leetle lady. I poosh you into the water and you wait."

"What? I've never…"

"Opa!"

He shoves me violently, and I topple backwards into the sea. *Oh, my Lord. I'm going to drown.* I surface, spluttering, and grab hold of Geoff, who is shaking with laughter.

"And now we go," announces Stephan, diving gracefully into the water. I cannot *go*. I try to move my feet, but they don't activate my fins. My fins move independently of my feet. I cannot control where I am going.

"You come with me." Stephan takes my hand in his and drags me behind him for the entire dive. It's all I can do to concentrate on keeping a tight grip of his hand. I don't see a thing – I can't see a thing. I focus on floating behind him, avoiding *stuff* in the sea. I can feel myself hyper-ventilating and make an attempt to slow my breathing. It's reverberating in my head.

Suddenly, I find I can't move any further. My right fin is entangled in something that looks like fishing line. I try to kick it away from my fin and alert Stephan, yet he is oblivious to my plight and tries to drag me onwards. I become hysterical. *Shit, I'm going to let go of Stephan any minute. My arm isn't a piece of elastic. It's going to give.* Somebody grabs my fin and cuts the fishing line, and I 'ping' back to Stephan.

I clamber back into the boat, crying with relief that it is over. Unfazed by the incident, Stephan hands round glasses of cheap fizz and takes photos in celebration of our achievement. I am so traumatised by the event that I down both Geoff's and my drinks. All I want to do is to get off this vessel.

7.00 p.m.

Over dinner, Geoff theatrically presents me with a bottle of fizz to celebrate the successful completion of my challenge. "I knew you could do it," he crows. "All it takes is for me to give you a push (get it, girls? a push) now and again, Amy, and you achieve greatness. Now, that was an *appropriate* challenge with great learning potential. It's confirmed to me that it's high time you became more adventurous. As I've said before, I think that you are ready to embrace a job that stretches you and expands your network and your horizons."

"Let's have a look at the photo," I say, blanking him.

"Really?" Geoff looks nervous.

"Yes." I want to see what I looked like in my wetsuit and mask. I hope I resembled Jacques Cousteau.

Pippa searches for the photo on Geoff's mobile. I see her expression change from amusement to shock when she finds it. "How could you let Mum go out looking like this? Everything's massive on her. It could have been so dangerous. Oh, Mum, you do look funny though. Look, Evie." They double over with laughter.

"Hand it over, please," I demand, staring daggers at Pippa. She relents reluctantly.

"You must admit, it is rather amusing," quips Geoff. "It did the job though, eh wifey? It gave everyone a good laugh."

I stare at the photo for a long time. Oh, it is *awful*. You can't see my face because the mask is so big and what is that black balaclava thing on my head? I don't remember that at all. My wetsuit is bagging everywhere, I look scary. My feet. Those fins…

Simmering with rage, I assertively pour the nearly full glass of beer, which Geoff had just started to enjoy, over his head. "Don't you *ever* do something like that to me again, you pig," I say quietly. "You knew how dreadful I looked, and Pippa's right – it was bloody dangerous. I have learned something of value from it but it's nothing to do with learning to scuba dive or whatever else *you* think I should have learned from it. You took delight in arranging this challenge so that you could have a laugh at my expense, and that's inexcusable. You went too far this time, and I won't tolerate it again. Come on, girls."

I turn on my heel and stride off, leaving a soggy Geoff to his empty glass.

Week Five. Saturday, 7.00 p.m.

"You faced your fear, and here's the evidence. Now you'll never forget it." Geoff hands me a framed photo of my scuba diving challenge and a glass of the Aphrodite wine we so enjoyed in Cyprus. "Cheers to that."

No, I won't – and I've learned some valuable lessons that I'll never forget either, I add silently. *Cheers to that.*

"I've picked my next challenge," I say, quickly changing the subject. It's to:

INDULGE IN A SECRET PASSION.

"Do you have a secret passion, Amy?"

"That's a toughie. I don't think I'm passionate about much, really. Passion. It's an emotive word."

"Oh, you *can* be *passionate*," Geoff smirks. "You were passionately angry about scuba diving and passionate with lust when you were drunk not so long ago, ha ha."

"Oh, go away," I bristle.

"*And*," he carries on, undeterred. "You have a real passion for shopping, scones, crisps and general untidiness. Those socks have been living on the floor over there for weeks. And, let's not forget one's passion for Pinot Grigio." He eyes my empty glass accusingly. "That's two you've had tonight. One too many glasses, perhaps, wifey?"

"Don't go there," I warn. "I might be your wife, but you're not my keeper, and your views on many things were duly noted in Cyprus. Not now, please. *And* this house is homely, not untidy."

Geoff looks as if he is about to say something, but he holds back. "Have you started job hunting? A new career with more status and cash in your pocket will fire you up. Pippa worries how you'll be when the challenges come to an abrupt end in December, you know."

My finger goes to my mouth. I *agree*, I think. *I know and kinda worry about that too, but taking on a new job is not the answer.*

My secret passion challenge came to me at three in the morning. If I'm honest, the question of whether I made the right life-partner decision has been preying on me more and more. Perhaps, if I revisit my past, it'll help me to reconcile my marriage. But dare I do what I want to do, and how will Geoff react?

The next morning, I consult Bea. "I'm thinking about tracking down William, my ex-boyfriend. He played an important part in my life pre-Geoff – well, I dumped him for Geoff, didn't I – and I'd like to find out where life has taken him," I explain, over a mid-morning coffee and apple scone. "Wouldn't it be cool to reminisce? Do you understand what I mean, Bea?"

"That's an interesting secret passion, Ames. I presume this includes checking him out against that list of perfect partner criteria you had, to see if you made the wrong choice eh, pet?"

"Between you and me, um… it has sort of crossed my mind if my 'What I will do to ensure I am successful and nab the essential lifelong partner' criteria list was flawed. Did I dump William for the right reasons? This is my opportunity to play detective."

Bea looks pensive. "I reckon you'll learn a lot from this challenge – just as long as you *don't* start imagining you're eighteen again and shag him as a 'social experiment'", she laughs. "Don't be too disheartened if he refuses your request – it *is* crazy – and promise me that if you meet up, it's in public and you remain stone-cold sober." She makes to leave. "My house move is arranged for the second week in August. Book out the whole day; I need all the help I can get."

"Don't worry," I reply, kissing her goodbye. "I won't forget."

Geoff finds me lying outstretched on my bed, crying with laughter as I read about a particular cringe-worthy event from my teenage diaries. He tries to look over my shoulder. "No, you may not," I reply, disgruntled. "These are my secret diaries from another time dimension, and it is my intention that they remain private forever," I announce dramatically.

"That's ludicrous. You're my wife. We should share everything. I wouldn't mind if you read my diary. Have you got something to hide, then?" he accuses.

"Of course not," I say. "It's not crucial for you to know every single detail of my life. If you read any of it without permission, I'd consider it an invasion of my privacy. Anyway, these are from many moons ago."

"Well, I don't agree, and I don't like your attitude. Married couples shouldn't have secrets, and you shouldn't be thinking any different." He slams the bedroom door behind him.

An hour later, Pippa pokes her head around the door to check that I'm still alive. "Any advice on relationships from back in the dark ages?" she laughs.

"Now you come to think of it, yes I do," I say. "Come over here and let me describe how *not* to end a relationship..."

Geoff barges into our private conversation with a commanding "Ten-thirty. Bedtime," and disappears into the en-suite. We hear the tap running. I catch the sound of a sharp intake of breath and watch as Pippa loses her temper.

"That's super-rude, Dad. Don't you have any respect?" she hollers through the door. "We were talking. Going to bed a few minutes late won't kill you, will it?"

Geoff opens the door to the en-suite, toothbrush in hand. "This is my bedroom, and I always go to bed at this time. I think that you've been up here long enough, and you're done with your inconsequential girly chit-chat."

"What? Are you sexist, just rude or a total control freak?" she yells.

My heart is in my mouth as I battle to temper the desire to join forces with Pippa and have it out with Geoff, but I swallow the bile threatening to spew from the depths of my stomach. I know my time will come, but it must be the right time – and that is not now. "Go downstairs and give us a minute," I say quietly to her, going into the en-suite and closing the door behind me.

"Listen, Geoff. I know you don't understand or agree, but this mother–daughter conversation is important, and we haven't finished, so why don't you go to bed and relax as you like to do, and we'll go downstairs. I'll be up shortly. Promise I'll be quiet."

Geoff stomps back into the bedroom in a sulk. "Those socks still haven't been put away. I'll bin them if they're still there tomorrow," he threatens.

12.30 a.m.

Time stands still as Pippa and I study photos of William over a packet of Haribo. I well up as I tell her my stories. Intense love for my child envelops me. The wish to educate, protect and empower her is overwhelming. "Nothing really changes from generation to generation," I explain lovingly. "People fall in lust or love every minute of every day, and when it happens, it's just the best. Will it lead to a happy ever after? Well, we all kiss a few frogs before we hopefully meet our forever prince or princess. Then, it's a case of crossing your fingers and hoping that the love spell cast is potent enough to withstand the test of time."

"Should marriage be for life?" she asks.

"Well, to be absolutely honest," I say, "marriage is a lottery. Saying 'I do' doesn't guarantee a lifelong partnership of love and romance, whatever anybody says. Look at Bea and what's happened to her. She didn't marry thinking she'd be getting divorced now, but she is where she is," I sigh.

"How did marriage change you and your life, Mum?"

I choose my words carefully. I want nothing more than to vent my frustrations but if I do, I might corrupt her young, impressionable mind – something that would be inexcusable. "People get married for all sorts of reasons – usually because they are in love. Life's a mystery. Things happen – things you never dream of when you start out, but life goes on regardless. It's when you come up against difficulties or change and you have to make choices and decisions that life becomes more complicated."

I don't want her to know any more.

"Promise me you'll never be afraid to make difficult choices and decisions. Life's too short, and I don't want you to live with regret, married or not. I'm sure you will make good choices," I say, planting a kiss on the end of her nose. "Choice is the greatest power we have. Now, go to *bed.*"

Monday.

I've been battling all night with the thought of contacting

William. I clearly remember the last time our paths crossed (at a friend's sixtieth, many years ago) and the emotions he stirred up. However, time has moved on, and things are different now. It still takes a sesh on my mindfulness app before I dare pluck up the courage to call him. It goes straight to voicemail. "Er, hello. Remember me? It's Amy... Rich... Parker... um... I was reading my old diaries and thought I'd give you a call... perhaps catch up after all these years... You have my number... um... so hopefully you will ring... And this isn't a pervy call, so if you are in a relationship, please don't feel I'm trying to... um... rekindle romance... so bye." I hang up, exhausted and shaking.

Adriano's Restaurant.
The Girls meet up at Adriano's on a Monday because it's the summer holidays. I tell everyone about my potential rendezvous. "Ooh, I'm super-impressed. I'd love to do what you're doing," Cate says wistfully. "But I'd be too shy."

"I've done it," confesses Claire boldly, her eyes shining.

Bea sits up. "Really? When?"

"At a school reunion, just before I got married. Well, I'd just found out that the man I thought loved me had gone and proposed to somebody else. Don't go there. It's a story I'd rather forget... and I just happened to meet Ben. You know, Ben the Bonk with the bulging bollocks? He was my humongous love interest back in the day."

She stares into the distance and hesitates momentarily. "I *knew* who he was as soon as I clapped eyes on him – even though he was almost bald – but I saw through all that. In my opinion, nothing had changed, and it was just like I was fifteen again. We got pissed and had a 'moment.'" She blushes.

"I take it that's before you found religion, pet? Well, this week it's Amy's turn to be a hot *milf*."

"Bea, that's gross."

"You can take it, Claire. And being called a milf is a

178

compliment. Go kick ass, Amy," retorts Bea. "You're on a year of self-discovery and adventure. Just keep off the wine, and you'll be fine."

Tuesday
I'm to meet William tomorrow. I take a day's holiday from work and spend it on making myself look absobloodylutely fabulous. It costs a bomb, but it's worth it.

Wednesday, 8.00 p.m.
William is instantly recognisable. His once straw-blond mane of hair has thinned and now falls like gossamer around his shoulders, and years of smoking has ravaged his complexion, but the instant I see his smiling face I am teleported to another galaxy. I smile at him fondly, and as he gives me his trademark lopsided grin, any hint of guilt or nerves disappears.

"Rat Face!" he cries, hugging me hard. "Looking good, babe." He runs his hand through his hair and a fine shower of dandruff drifts onto the collar of his black polo shirt. "Your usual?" he smiles, and before I can reply, I find myself staring at a glass of wine and a packet of salt and vinegar. *One glass won't matter*, I reason. *It'd be rude not to, and I really don't fancy him at all.*

9.30 p.m.
Having drunk more than my safe quota of wine, my tongue has loosened considerably. I'd forgotten how well we got on, and it's fun remembering the fantastic times we shared. We make small talk until I decide to pull the trigger. I take aim. "*So, enough of the past...*" And fire. "How do you think I've turned out?" I grin, Cheshire Cat-like.

William takes a drag on his roll-up. "You, Amy Parker," he pauses and laughs easily. "You were independent, fiery and brimming with ambition and ideas – the girl who would heartlessly dump anyone who didn't match up to her criteria.

I'm surprised you live the life you do now. I never imagined you as a wifey and selling your soul to follow some executive husband's dreams with the obligatory two-point-four kids in tow. If the Amy I knew is buried deep inside, you must be bloody dissatisfied a lot of the time – dry-cleaning his suits and silk ties. I know you wanted security and status and to escape your mundane childhood, but I don't get why you sold out. It must have come at quite a cost. You don't sound too happy." He sees my crestfallen face. "Sorry," he shrugs. "But you did ask. You've gone from Rat Face to Mat Face."

"Is that really what you think?" I reply, aghast. "That I'm a doormat now?"

"Oh, babe," he replies, kindly. "You are exactly the same as you were back in the day, but the life you describe is far removed from what I imagined. Another wine?" He goes to the bar and I'm so upset that I leave before he returns.

Thursday evening.
Claire calls me, bursting to know what happened.

"William said I'd sold my soul to follow my executive husband's dreams."

"And?"

The enormity of this moment is huge. My voice breaks as I try to explain. "Opening my 'ex-box' opened my eyes. I've learned that, for some reason, I took up the mantle of 'wife' to feel safe, loved and a 'somebody'," I laugh. "I had a list of criteria to ensure I went with my head and not my heart; to ensure that I chose with care – or so I thought. On *Don't Tell the Bride*, they say that getting married is the best day of their lives. I think they should do a follow-up a few years down the line, called *What They Didn't Tell the Bride*, ha ha."

"I don't understand what you mean, Ames? You *are* a somebody – a friend, a mum and Geoff's wife – with a family that others would die for. You just need something to give you back your lust for life... and talking about lust – what's the latest with Him then?"

At the mention of Him, I cheer up considerably. "He's doing my head in," I smile. "We text each other intermittently, and we were in a conversation a bit ago, but as soon as I asked if I could ring him, he didn't reply. I felt really let down."

"So?"

"I need his help. Is there something wrong, Claire?"

"*So whoever knows the right thing to do and fails to do it, for him it is sin. James 4:17,*" she quotes. "I think this has gone on for too long, Amy. If this continues, you are going to get hurt, and you're gonna hurt Geoff. Are you sure there's no hidden agenda that you're not admitting to? Are you certain you're not getting off on this texting game? What is he giving you that Geoff doesn't? You know what to do, Amy. Put the fifty-first challenge and Him on the back burner and focus your attention on what's important – the here and now."

10.30 p.m.

I know that Claire is right. My four statements of intent are written in bold on my laptop. I say them aloud, ticking them off on my fingers.

I will sever all contact with Him for four weeks.

Should he get in touch during this time, I shall ignore him completely.

I will uncover something about him that extinguishes any potential further lusting.

I will forget all about having a secret snog with him. That challenge is over.

Then I will return to normal.

I go to bed full of determination.

August

"Happy birthday," sings Evie, handing me my birthday cards. Geoff's reads *To my beautiful wife, my world* and informs me that he's on an early morning hike. As Evie busies herself preparing a special birthday breakfast for me, I remember to select this week's challenge. It reads:

GO INCOGNITO AND HAVE AN ADVENTURE ALONE.

GO WHEREVER YOU CHOOSE. COVER YOUR TRACKS.

USE CASH.

MOBILE: FOR EMERGENCY USE ONLY. TURN OFF LOCATION.

PASSPORT: IF GOING ABROAD.

LEAVE 09:00 MONDAY AND RETURN BY FRIDAY MIDNIGHT.

I glance furtively around the kitchen to see if anyone is taking any notice of what I am doing. The coast is clear. I read on.

YOU MAY TELL ONE CLOSE FRIEND THAT

YOU HAVE GONE.

DO NOT DISCLOSE WHERE YOU ARE. THE FRIEND WILL BE YOUR EMERGENCY CONTACT SHOULD YOU NEED THEM OR SHOULD ANYONE NEED YOU.

ON TUESDAY MORNING, THEY WILL INFORM YOUR FAMILY WHERE YOU ARE.

Midday.
Geoff sees me manically cleaning. He's delighted.

1.00 p.m.
I've done an online supermarket shop that will arrive later. I can't leave my family to starve while I'm gone.

3.00 p.m.
I write to-do lists for each family member.

3.30 p.m.
I remember that no one is supposed to know that I have gone. I burn the lists.

8:00 p.m.
Over dinner at our local Chinese restaurant, Geoff passes on some 'birthday advice' along with my present. "I've invested in a three-year gym couples' subscription to encourage you to keep in shape and get rid of your hibernation overhang. I've given Adam Anthony one too. Jess thought it a great idea."

I put down my chopsticks, outraged.

"Don't start, Amy. I should be able to say what I want to you, and you should accept feedback with good grace. Any other wife would be grateful for the advice and appreciate this gift. It cost a bloody fortune, almost as much as this meal, in fact."

"You both thought what? No, you thought wrong, and what are you doing spoiling that boy? You think more of him than your own kids, always treating him," I say, utterly dismayed. "I can't believe you've bought me that and commenting on my…"

The last thing I want is a stand-up row on my birthday – about my weight – in a restaurant with my children looking on, so I count to five, thank him with a kiss and store the incident away in the 'for later' file.

Geoff shivers. "It's bloody chilly in here. I've mislaid my jacket."

"It's at Claire's," I reply, busy scooping egg fried rice into my mouth.

He tilts his head to the side and clears his throat. "You might be right. Can you pick it up for me when you next see her? Now, how about a glass of fizz before we go? Waiter? A glass of champagne for the birthday girl, please. Only the best for team Parker, eh, Amy? Drink it up quickly, darling. It's late, and I'm knackered."

Calm down, Amy, ignore his comments, I say to myself as I force myself to knock back my drink as quickly as I can. I'm bloody glad I'm going away tomorrow, because the way I feel right now, I could do something to him that I deeply regret.

Tuesday, 10.30 a.m.

On the ferry to Amsterdam, I've met a lively Stag party who've kept me entertained with tales of their laddish lives. I love this kind of banter. You can learn things you'd never imagine likely or possible, and lads, when prowling in packs (and especially after a few beers) just love to boast about themselves and their exploits. As we disembark, they ask me about my plans. I make them believe that I am raising money for charity and returning home shortly. They are well-impressed, and I feel bad.

It's a beautiful day, and I amble towards the Centrum feeling content. In fact, I have almost forgotten that nobody at home has the slightest idea where I am, and I only remember that I am a fugitive when I see a child across the street who closely resembles Evie. My itinerary is mapped out – which is good, as what I am about to do is completely out of my comfort zone. I am determined, however, to Experiment, Experience and Grow.

First stop: the Sex Museum. It's packed with people of all ages and all nationalities, studying and sniggering over the various artifacts on display. It doesn't take me long to get in the zone, pushing my way through the hoards of museum-goers to take a better look at the focal display entitled *New and Exciting: Sex Toys Through The Ages*. I stare at a multitude of what can only be described as sexual instruments of torture, trying to imagine what they could possibly be used for. "I simply can't believe that people ever used this stuff for pleasure," I remark pleasantly to an elderly couple standing next to me. They look at me strangely. "No?" says one of them as they pass through an unmarked door on my right.

My curiosity gets the better of me, and I follow them – only to be greeted by a writhing mass of groaning bodies in a poorly lit room that smells of sweet incense and human sweat. I can't quite make out what is going on. "Hi," I say to a middle-aged woman wearing an official-looking badge. "Is this an interactive show?"

"This is an interactive *area*. They are taking pleasure with replicas of the toys you will have seen outside in the new display. Please join in. It is for everyone. You leave your clothes over there." She motions me to move forward.

"Ah! I don't really think this is for me quite yet – but thank you all the same. Where's the exit?" I stutter.

"Over there." She motions towards the other side of the room. "Take care to avoid the people."

Shielding my eyes with my hand to ensure I don't see too much, I deftly step over objects and writhing bodies, desperate to get out. Somebody pulls me into a passionate embrace. I feel an object vibrating against the small of my back and panic. I do the only thing I can think of under the circumstances; I stamp on their toes. Hard. They release me and I run.

2.00 p.m.

I'm desperately hungry but know that scones don't exist over here. Anyway, I'm determined to try the local speciality – cake infused with cannabis. It's on my list of key things to experience. However, I have absolutely no idea how to tell normal cake and cannabis cake apart. After a fruitless half an hour examining cakes in café shop windows, I decide to ask for advice at the Tourist Information Office.

I hear a shout. It's the Stags from the ferry. They cross the road and embrace me warmly. "We thought you were going straight home once you'd reached the city, Amy?" slurs Josh, the Chief Stag.

"Um, I decided that since I, er, came all the way here, I might as well explore for a couple of days."

"Join us, Amy," he smiles, picking me up in his arms and carrying me down the road to the nearest bar. "You can be our Stagette." And that is how I join the Stag party.

"Got anything to eat, Josh? I'm famished." He delves into his backpack and hands me a brown paper bag. "There you go," he grins. "Space cake will do the trick."

"That's an unusual name," I reply. But I don't question it. I don't normally like chocolate cake, but this is exceptionally good and I wolf it down.

I only realise what I've eaten as a feeling of total calm and relaxation gently washes over me and I drop to my knees with an irresistible urge to lie down and stare up at the hazy blue sky. "I can see Pippa's face in the clouds!" I giggle, squinting upwards. "She's smiling down on me. Helloooo! At least you know where I am. Cate will have told you by now, and this must be a sign that all is well."

The Stags join me. We lie in in a row, staring up at the sky.

The following night, as is customary, we investigate the Red Light District. The Stags find the whole event highly amusing, but I don't. I'm intrigued yet just a little uncomfortable at such blatant advertising of sex. I stand apart, watching a female carefully ironing a shirt. I have an urge to enter her world and experience what it's like to stand in her shoes, behind the glass. She stares me straight in the eye and smiles. I smile back and using sign language, I ask if I may speak with her. She invites me inside.

Sammy from Leatherhead and I sit on her shocking pink sofa, and I listen intently as she talks candidly about her life as a sex worker. "I enjoy it, Amy, simple as that. Over here, I think that my work's respected, and because prostitution is legal and regulated, I feel safe. I also do it for other reasons. I mean, I work the hours I want from home, there's no office politics to piss me off, every day's different, my services are valued and I get great satisfaction from giving pleasure to people who might otherwise not experience it."

"That's exactly what Becca, my hairdresser, said when we were discussing the benefits of being a Sex Chat Line Operator," I smile. "I completely get where you are coming from."

Out of the corner of my eye, I'm conscious of a man staring intently at me, the intensity of his gaze burning through the glass. Curiosity gets the better of me and I steal a glance in his direction. I do a double-take. A triple take. It's *Pete*. I run into the street and hug him hello.

"Amy," says Pete, quietly. "We need to talk."

He shows me a Facebook post on his phone. I stare at the phone. I stare at Pete. I stare at the post. I stare at the Stags. Everyone stares at the post and they all stare at me. Pete gathers me into his arms. "Why don't you tell us all about it so that we can sort it out?"

"It's me. It says I am *missing*? I'm not missing, I'm supposed to be having a secret adventure; going incognito. I told Cate... she was telling Geoff... Oh, my Lord."

Pete puts his head against mine and takes my hands in his. I stare into his kind, sad eyes. "Amy baby, please don't worry."

12.45 a.m.
Everyone knows why I am really in Amsterdam. Pete phoned Geoff and the police in the UK to let them know that I am safe and well. I speak to Cate briefly. "Ames, I feel dreadful. I totally forgot. There was a cyber-security breach at work – I had to drop everything and fly out to our HQ in Stornoway. Your husband has been horrible. He's threatened to section you for leaving him and your children like that. I've tried to explain, but I don't know if he understands."

"Don't beat yourself up about it, Cate. We'll talk when I get back. Just make sure that I've been taken off the official Missing Persons Register." I end the call and can't help but burst out laughing at the absurdity of it all.

We toast the fact that I am officially found and that the trip has been 'a blast' (as Josh called it). We take loads of photos for posterity. I turn to Pete. "What exactly are you doing here?" I ask. "You can't have been sent to track me down?"

"I'm busking to earn some dosh and taking a break at the same time," he explains. He pauses. "You look really happy tonight, Amy baby, as happy as when you were with us all in the soup kitchen. Have your challenges become your way of running away from your troubles? Use your insights to be strong and face up to what is stopping you from having a good life. Don't be like I was."

He turns away. I am desperate to cry in his arms and tell him about the thoughts and secrets that are eating me up. I want to admit that what Pippa said on the Freaky Friday challenge is branded in my heart and haunts me every night. Why did I marry Geoff? Why am I still lusting after Him? But I can't. I stare into Pete's sad eyes and hug him tight.

Week Two. Friday, midnight.

I have been home for half an hour. No one is in. I feel strange, out of place, unsettled. I sit at the kitchen table in tears; a glass of Pinot Grigio by my side, typing up the events from the past week. So much has happened. I can't quite take it all in. I'm missing it already. And then I hear the front door slam and the clatter of feet, and my children run to me. They throw their arms around my waist and welcome me home as only families know how. I feel the love, the relief, the sense of belonging. I realise how much they mean to me; that I have missed them more than words can say. Geoff is not with them. He is at Claire and Bob's. I start to cry.

Saturday afternoon.

Cate came round earlier, bearing gifts to assuage her guilt. My other friends have visited out of concern and love, and I have cried myself out in their arms. Geoff has not been kind. He returned home drunk at two o'clock this morning and spent a good half an hour guilt-tripping me about my actions. He woke early and went downstairs without a word. Pippa discovered a note by the front door informing me that he's playing in a golf charity tournament in Scotland and will see me tomorrow.

As I open a box of chocolates left by Cate and pop my favourite into my mouth, I remember that my mobile has been off since last Monday. I fish it out from the depths of my bag and switch it on. Amazingly, it still has charge, and I gasp at the number of unread texts waiting for me. I scroll through the messages, starting with those sent on the day I left for Amsterdam. Many of them make for painful reading. None are from Geoff. However, amongst them all is a text from Him.

Where are you, Amy?
Are you safe?

He has reached out to me and shown that he cares, which is more than Geoff did. I feel that familiar rush of adrenaline and am taken aback by the intensity of my emotions. They are as strong as ever. I want to talk to him and thank him and tell him how I feel. *I will not text him,* I resolve. *It's not allowed.*

Two minutes later.
I reread his text and feel that warm glow deep inside of me. "I will *not* text him," I say aloud, putting down my mobile.

Two minutes later.
I pick up my mobile… I put it down.

Two minutes later.
Oh, sod it. I have to text. I can't concentrate. My stomach is taut. *Perhaps it'll go away if I text? And this is an extraordinary situation, after all.*

> Hi.
> Thanks so much for thinking of me.
> I am at home now.
> All fine.
> Challenge over.
> Got excellent material for my book.
> I can send what I have so far if you like?
> Amy :)

I wait for a reply, but there is nothing. The Bowl of Chance and Opportunity catches my eye, and I select my next challenge in an attempt to push my disappointment aside.

A FRIEND IN NEED IS A FRIEND INDEED.

Relief. Tomorrow is all about helping Bea to move house. She is a friend in need and fits the challenge criteria perfectly.

Sunday, 8.00 a.m.

When I arrive at her house, Bea is sitting on the parquet floor in her cold, dim hallway, surrounded by cardboard boxes and weeping quietly. Outside, it's teeming with rain, and a bitter wind whips through the trees. It's been like this since last night – a depressing sight in mid-August. Her house feels cold and hostile. The electricity has been disconnected, and candles flicker wildly in the breeze. Peeling off my sodden raincoat, I sit at Bea's side and wind my arms around her. "Here. I knew that today would be difficult, so I brought you something to cheer you up." I hand her a box of her favourite liqueur chocolates. "Go on, open them."

"Why not, pet." Bea smiles through her tears. She unwraps the box and we scoff the lot.

By ten o'clock, Bea's friends are arriving in a constant stream to help her pack up, and she is busy allocating jobs. "Would you mind detoxing my personal stuff, Amy? Just do what you did to yours, pet. You know, when you had to um… declutter," she says. Her eyes flash. The word 'declutter' has evoked memories of the night of her fortieth birthday, the night she decided to declutter her life of her husband. Today marks the culmination of that process. She is leaving her family home behind.

She recovers her composure. "Go to the spare bedroom and bag up whatever's brought up to you," she says, handing me a box of binbags and labels. "I've sent someone up to help you."

The spare bedroom door is shut, and so I knock gently before opening it. "Hello? Hell…" I see my assistant. My assistant fastens his eyes upon me and a wide grin spreads across his face. "Beautiful lady. This is an unexpected pleasure."

This can't be real. I don't want to see you, of all people, right now. I'm supposed to be in a Him-free zone, and you are related to

Him. Not only that, but I might have to explain about my Let the Dice Decide challenge and how I used you...

I realise that I am cowering by the door and gripping the handle tightly. I can't quite believe that I have to work with Blue Jumper Man – who, incidentally, is wearing another blue jumper. I don't know whether to laugh or cry.

Blue Jumper Man is sorting books. His hair and clothes are dripping wet. "You should really take that wet jumper off. If you don't, it'll start to smell as rank as this room, and you'll catch cold," I say without thinking, my nose wrinkling in disgust.

His eyes dance suggestively. "Yeah, it's a bit stale in here. But as it's so cold, I didn't want to open the window to air the room. But if you'd like me to undress for you..."

"Only take your jumper off if you have clothes on underneath," I squeak. "I might take fright, and you'll freeze."

I avert my eyes as he pulls his jumper over his head and throws it onto the bed in the corner. If he's naked, I will have to leave. What would Geoff say if it got back to him that I'd been alone with a semi-clad bloke? The six degrees of separation theory would make sure of that, and then I'd be in big trouble. Fortunately, he is wearing a polo shirt underneath.

"Okay for you?" he smirks. "Reputation intact?"

"Oh, piss off," I breathe shakily.

He laughs. "You're right, Amy, I feel *so* much better," he winks. "Come on, there's stacks to do."

5.00 p.m.

"Bea, I've been thinking about all the stuff I've bagged up for you today and how I can help you make some money to spend on your new place, perhaps. I still have all my stuff stored in our garage, you know, from the challenge when I decluttered my home?" I hesitate. We're back to that decluttering challenge. "Anyway," I continue at speed, "I keep meaning to do a car boot sale, so how about we do one together and I'll gladly donate all the money I make to you. What do you think? You know, a friend in need and all that."

Bea hugs me. "Aww, thanks, pet. You've taken a weight off my mind. I was worried how I was going to replace what my lovely ex-husband has snaffled." She rattles off a list of household items that her husband has taken with him since their split. It includes half of her CD collection. She is especially annoyed about losing Madonna.

"Never mind, Bea. It's only stuff, and stuff is easily replaced. If we can sell half of what we have now, you'll be okay." I smile. "Can I smell pizza? I bet you haven't eaten much all day. Come on, you've gotta keep your strength up." I take her hand and lead her into the kitchen.

9.00 p.m.

The (after) party is rocking, and I have drunk far too much wine. Somebody opens the front door, and the bitter draught reminds me that I've left my coat upstairs in the spare bedroom. I decide to go and get it. It takes three attempts and a lot of uncontrollable giggling to stand up in my heels, so I take them off. "God, I am dangerously drunk," I titter, staggering over to the staircase. "Up we go now, up, up, up into the sky," I sing. "I am climbing in Austria, Geoff," I chuckle to myself as I navigate the last few stairs on my hands and knees.

I crawl the length of the hallway to the spare bedroom and reach up to grab and turn the door handle. On my third attempt, I successfully sway inside. "There's my coat. Oh, Blue Jumper Man's forgotten his jumper," I slur. "I wonder if it smells of Him?" I pick it up gingerly, close my eyes, bury my nose in the sleeve and breathe in deeply. My eyes fly open. I recognise that smell. Oh, my Lord! I sniff the jumper again to be sure.

The Mystery of Musty Man is solved.

Week Four. Adriano's Restaurant. Friday, 9.00 p.m.
For some reason, I'm feeling off-colour. I toy with the stem of my wine glass, half-listening to Bea's excited chatter. I'm definitely not in the mood for challenge chat but this week I've to:

BREAK A RECORD.

And I need help to do it.

"Heard the latest about Josie Jamieson? She's really doing my head in with her string of posts online, boasting about a new business she's set up with an *amazing* woman she met at some parking enforcement event in Wigan. Does anyone know about it?"

"Whoever she's working with must be strong-minded, Bea," I yawn. "Jess would give her a run for her money. I could never imagine those two hitting it off, though."

"Who gives a damn what she's up to, anyway?" smiles Bea. "I'm glad she's left the governing body and her stranglehold on the school. Only wish I'd taken a photo of the moment when her dress was caught up in her thong, showing that school coat of arms tattoo on her bum, and sent it to *Teacher Weekly*," she giggles. "Hi, Claire."

"Sorry I'm late, guys. I've been carrying out a nightmare review on the church summer school. Pour me a glass of Pinot Grigio, Ames." Claire dumps her red leather tote on the table. There's something familiar about it, but I can't think what.

"That's a cool bag," remarks Cate.

"It's gorgeous, isn't it? It was a present." Claire strokes it lovingly. "I bumped into Geoff yesterday, Ames. He told me you hated last week's car maintenance course challenge."

Bea chuckles. "I can't believe that, pet. I'm gonna enrol on it. Getting down and dirty with greasy mechanics sounds like lots of fun, and I'm up for that now."

Claire sighs disapprovingly. "You're not even divorced yet, Bea."

"Claire, stop being so disapproving. Just because…"

I step in quickly. "Girls, I've important news. Last Saturday at Bea's, I solved the Mystery of Musty Man." There is stunned silence.

"Are you referring to that man who stole your secret snog at the divorce party we went to in May?" says Claire, agog. "How?"

"Yes, I am. You remember back in June, when I Let the Dice Decide?"

"Course we do. You pulled a man in a blue jumper in the pub."

"Well, Blue Jumper Man and the secret snogger are one and the same – the mysterious Musty Man – and his real name is Jason. Exhibit One." I pick up a carrier bag that's been sitting by my feet and pass it to Cate. "Feel free to sniff."

"Oh God," blurts out Cate. "That's *really* awful." She throws the bag to Bea, who sniffs gingerly, grimaces and passes it to Claire.

"Oh, rank," she mutters. "You stood by him in a pub and let him kiss you smelling like that? Didn't you realise?" She sniffs again and retches. "It smells like he's washed it and put it away before it was properly dry. You'd remember that smell anywhere."

"Precisely. That's exactly what I thought when he… we… he snogged me in the dark. I thought that it was a garment that had been put away while still damp."

"But Ames," says Cate. "How come you didn't realise who he was that night in the pub? It's so pungent."

"I didn't get close enough to sniff his jumper then, unlike on the night of the secret snog at the party in May, when my nose briefly buried in his jumper and I got a good whiff of it. In the pub, he leaned forward and kissed me on my cheeks, so my face was nowhere near."

I take a bite of my bread and think on. "When my hands touched his jumper in the pub, it did feel damp."

"It'd been raining hard that night," adds Cate. "Maybe you thought it was damp because of the weather."

"Spot on. I didn't put two and two together," I laugh.

"When exactly did you realise that Musty and Blue Jumper are one and the same?" smiles Cate.

"He left his jumper at Bea's, and I brought it home for safekeeping. So that's that. Would you mind returning it to him some time, Bea, and perhaps dropping a gentle hint about hygiene? Now," I say, "onto more important matters. What's my party piece? My challenge is to be a record-breaker."

Bea laughs heartily. "How about the ping pong ball one you rejected from the Learn a Skill to Impress challenge? It's dead impressive to watch."

"That's just vulgar, Bea. It'd ruin Geoff's reputation," tuts Claire. "Isn't he trying for a promotion?"

"Yes, supposedly," I reply guardedly.

"Oh, Claire," Bea cuts in. "Don't tell me you are subtly taking the piss out of Amy's husband for once?"

"Sorry?" Claire replies. "I don't know what you mean?"

"Knowing Geoff, he'd like nothing better than for his wife to get down and dirty, pet." She pauses. "Shame, I thought I was on for a first, then. You know, you making fun of him?" she teases.

"Oh, shut up, Bea," mutters Claire crossly, "You know he's an old friend. Amy, I was thinking more along the lines of an eating challenge. Something to do with crisps or scones, perhaps? I'll Google 'eating challenges' on my phone."

I go into finger-gnawing mode as the table is cleared and the sweet trolley is wheeled into view. I am racking my brain for ideas. "Here's one," Claire says, squinting at her mobile. "In two thousand and one, someone set a record for eating individual cold tinned peas in three minutes. You needn't eat peas, and three minutes seems a bit excessive, but we could find something else... like..." She scans the sweet trolley. "These." She points to a cake overloaded with blueberries. "How about seeing how many blueberries you can fit into your mouth in one minute?" she says excitedly.

"It's an interesting idea – but a bit dangerous, don't you think?" I muse. It sounds like a choking disaster waiting to happen. I don't much like the idea of having somebody on standby to perform the Heimlich manoeuvre. Let me think about it."

"Amy," sighs Bea. "I can just see the headlines now. Mad mother embarking on adventure and self-discovery for her fiftieth – buried by blueberry misadventure. You are always *so* cautious and sensible, pet. Do something impulsive for once."

"You are over-exaggerating," agrees Claire. "We *could* hold a competition to see how many blueberries we can eat in a given time limit, the winner being the one who ate the most. It says here, on this website, that the official record for the most eaten in one minute is one hundred and sixty-five."

At long last, I feel a familiar spark of excitement. This has the making of an excellent challenge and will take my mind off the complex emotional rollercoaster ride I'm on. I beam at my friends. "That's the one, then. I'm not sure if I'll try to break the world record, but we can set a record for eating blueberries that will stand in our village. Will you all take part?"

"Absolutely," they reply in unison.

"Let's crack on then and do it... on Wednesday."

On Saturday morning, Evie and I eagerly digest the rules and regulations – should I wish to formally challenge the world record. There's a part of me that would so love to be a bona fide world-record-breaker. Grandma would be so proud. Geoff takes a peek at what we are up to and snorts derisively. "*Another* brainless challenge, Amy? You could do so much better." Arms folded, he continues to read over my shoulder, sniggering. "At least there's added health benefits. Little chance of piling on the pounds scoffing blueberries, eh?" he taunts, pointing to my stomach. "And although there's no way you'll do it, if you manage to eat that many, I reckon you'll increase your IQ by at least ten points."

Without warning, an internal volcano that has been simmering deep inside of me erupts, and fiery, frothy frustration spills from between my lips. "How can you stand there, pointing that finger, ridiculing me and talking about failure and how stupid it is when I haven't even had a go – and in front of Evie, too? Other people believe in me. They don't put me down. But *you...*"

I feel my body tensing, fists clenching, heart splintering. *Breathe, calm, don't say anything silly...* I can't control myself this time. "Listen here," I hiss. "I was set this challenge for a reason. It's about pushing boundaries and striving to achieve. It's about being the best one can." I wait for him to come back at me, but he is silent. "This is a good challenge for me. I haven't tried to achieve my full potential for many years now. I'm not even sure what my potential is any more – I think I buried it years ago. But this year, I'm exhuming a gobsmacking amount of information about myself."

Remembering Eloise's assertiveness training, I stand up before I lose it. The dreaded tears are threatening, and I want to remain strong. "In fact," I state, my hands flat on the table, leaning towards him. "This challenge has given me an idea. I'd like to organise an annual family community event where people can compete against each other to set and break records. You know, a bit like the Olympics, but with a more eclectic range of challenges – like standing on one leg for as long as possible while balancing a beanbag on their head, perhaps. This event will be about giving children and adults an opportunity to learn and grow. What I mean is, they'll be able to experience stuff in a fun and safe environment, learn from their experiences and, as a result, grow as individuals. Their confidence will improve, and their horizons will broaden." I flee upstairs, launch myself onto my bed and lie on my back staring up at the ceiling, feeling totally frustrated.

11.30 a.m.

At the supermarket, Evie bombards me with intelligent questions and observations about the challenge. "I think that you should have a go, and then we'll know if you can do it," she says gravely. "You need to eat one hundred and sixty-six blueberries in one minute to win. That's a lot," she adds in a serious voice. "What if you turn blue?"

3.00 p.m.

Evie and I are on a secret adventure. I am about to try a test run, to see if I can down one hundred and seventy blueberries in one minute flat. "Ready, Mum? Stop chewing on your finger," she scolds. She gives me a cuddle. "Don't be nervous. If you can't do it, at least you've tried. You always tell us to have a go and that it doesn't matter if we don't succeed."

"Yes, I do, don't I?" I say absentmindedly, staring down at the bowl in front of me. It doesn't look very appetising. In fact, the thought of putting them into my mouth makes me feel distinctly queasy. "Okay, let's do it," I say, focusing on the task in hand. I take a deep breath. One... Two... Three... Go!"

One minute later, Evie counts forty uneaten berries. "Never mind, Mum – it was a good try."

"It's okay," I croak, sipping a glass of water and dabbing at my streaming eyes. "I gave it my best shot."

Thirty minutes later.

Evie is holding my hand in sympathy as I retch into the toilet bowl. "Eating fruit shouldn't make you sick, Mum. Did you wash it properly?"

"Water," I gasp.

"Dad," she shouts. "Mum's puking a lot. Can you get her a glass of water, please?"

Geoff's head appears around the door, and he takes in the scene. "What's going on in here?" I can hear the irritation in his voice.

"Mum tried to break the blueberry-eating world record," says Evie, forlorn.

Another wave of intense stomach-cramping makes me vomit again...

Sunday, 7.00 a.m.
The puking has continued all night long. My mouth is dry. My throat's so sore. I want to brush my teeth, but I can't move. I nudge Geoff. No response. I elbow him harder.

"You'll have to do everything today," I breathe weakly.

He grunts.

"Aren't you up yet?" Pippa is at my bedside.

"Dying," I reply feebly. "Dad will have to get up for a change." I attempt to pull the duvet off him.

"Dad," shouts Pippa. "You can see that Mum's ill. Get up."

"Get ready," I whisper. "Drama club starts at half-nine." I close my eyes to stop the room spinning.

Pippa kisses me lightly on the forehead. "I'll make you a cup of tea."

Through half-closed eyes, I watch her tiptoe round to Geoff's side of the bed, where he is lying motionless. A look of steely determination is set upon her face. I bite my lip, trying not to laugh as she picks up the glass of water sitting on his bedside table and deliberately pours the contents over his head. "There!" she shrieks, dashing down the hallway as he swears furiously. "You're up now."

Brilliant, darling, I think, pretending to be asleep. *Glad you're assertive.*

Wednesday, 7.00 p.m.
The contestants are crammed around my dining room table, sitting before plates onto which two hundred blueberries have been counted. There's a buzz in the air, and the excitement is palpable.

At the eleventh hour, Evie persuaded Geoff to join in as 'Challenge Compère' (because if he doesn't, everyone will wonder where he is). He struts about the kitchen sporting an 'Official Compère Crown' made by her, and solemnly reads out the challenge rules and regulations (to ensure everyone is clear on what constitutes 'good form').

"Hurry up and open the champers, somebody? We have to toast the challenge," pipes up Mrs Mon-Key.

"Epic," grins Bea, glaring at Geoff. "Why didn't I think of that? This is supposed to be fun, and it's a bit too serious for my liking. Here – allow me, Mrs M."

"Madam," stutters Geoff, horrified. "*I* think we should toast the winner *after* the contest."

"*You think what, darling?*" Mrs Mon-Key's eyes widen. "Oh no! We don't do bossy. Come over here, sweetie."

Geoff hesitates.

"Come here," she repeats more firmly, patting the chair next to her and gesturing for him to sit down. "You have to learn not to be so officious, you delightful man," she gurgles, taking his hand in hers and stroking it provocatively. "You are too strained. Relax," she purrs. "A tinsey-winsey glass or two of champers will help us all to enjoy the evening, eh Amy?" She winks at me.

"Blimey, do they know each other?" whispers Claire, her eyes fixed on them. "She's a bit forward, isn't she? He'll hate that."

"They've never met, but it's good fun watching him being tamed by the man-whisperer," I giggle as he quietens down.

Mrs Mon-Key looks thoughtful. "Cate and Claire, darlings? Would you search out some nibbles? I quite enjoy a little something to chew on with my aperitif."

She watches them go into the kitchen, and her expression changes to one of unadulterated excitement. She gives her husband a covert nod, and he quickly refills Geoff's glass.

"Drink, my darling," she instructs Geoff, her eyes hypnotically transfixed on his. Geoff takes a gulp of his champagne and grins.

"*All* of it now," commands Mrs Mon-Key, her eyes sparking. "Good boy." A devilish smile plays across her face. "I've heard, darling, and I understand what you need. You'll soon be full of good spirit again." She leans forward and whispers something into his ear. Geoff's eyes glint appreciatively.

10.30 p.m.
"Everybody, lishen up!" bellows Geoff. Muffled 'oohs' resound around the room, followed by raucous laughter. Geoff has miraculously morphed into a loveable Christmas pantomime actor, rousing his audience into a frenzy. His crown has slipped around his neck and now resembles a spiky necklace. "You have one minute to eat ash many blueberriesh as you can – but there ish a twisht!" He reveals a packet of cocktail sticks from up his sleeve. "No hands may touch the blueberriesh, only the coshtail stick. Three… Two… One… "

One minute later.
Thank God it's over.

11.30 p.m.
I must have dropped off to sleep, as I am brought to by Mrs Mon-Key announcing the winner. "By a very small margin, our champion is our darling Amy."

Rising unsteadily to my feet I make an attempt to give the victory speech that I prepared yesterday, in case I did win. But it won't come out right. "I would like to sank you for… I can't remember what I should sank you for," I giggle. "Wheresh Geoff?"

I scan the room for him. He should be by my side, puffed up with pride and sharing my joy, but Claire tells me that Mrs Mon-Key and Bea put him to bed before the results were announced. If I think about it too much, I know that I will cry again – this time with despair. Making my excuses, I go into the garden, where I pace agitatedly back and forth, flicking through my phone contacts, searching for somebody who will want to hear my news and be excited for me. My finger hovers over Him. I smile. He believes in me. He's told me so. He won't laugh at me or make me feel inadequate. He will make me happy and applaud my efforts. I bang out a text and press Send.

September

"A drunk man wants to speak to you." Evie passes me the phone.

"Hello?"

I listen, hang up, look to the sky and take a deep breath.

"Mum?" Two worried faces stare into mine.

"Dad's been made redundant. That means he's lost his job. I need to pick him up from the pub."

10.30 p.m.

Geoff is slouched over the kitchen table. I attempt to be a good wife and comfort, reassure and provide hope. But he is furious. Noxious utterances fly from his mouth like shards of glass. Whatever I say smacks against a high force field he has created and ricochets into the ether. Nothing can help right now. He needs to talk, shout and blame, and I am his punch bag. A few minutes later, I hear him on the phone and the front door slamming behind him. I let him go. What I'd really like to do right now is to reach for the Pinot Grigio, but I know that alcohol isn't the answer, and I mustn't use it to get rid of this big fat reef knot that somebody has kindly tied in the pit of my stomach. I start to clear the mountain of washing-up sitting in the sink. Right now, I feel helpless, and I can't help wondering if Claire's God is punishing me…

Monday.

For some inexplicable reason, in times of crisis, I have a need to reconnect with my family, and even though Jess is totally off the wall, I know that she went through similar with her husband a year or so ago, so she will understand. "Shit happens – it's life," Jess says flippantly. "What are you afraid of, sis?"

"What if he can't get another job? It's a huge part of his life. Radio 2's recent feature about the over-fifties being unable to find work in the current market scares me to death."

"Stop catastrophising," warns Jess. "Not all men his age are like the ones described on Radio 2. There are loads of jobs out there. Okay, his ego will take a bashing. He'll have to take a cut in salary and work alongside people beneath his station," she laughs loudly, "but perhaps that's a good thing. He always used to do my head in with his boasting about posh hospitality events and his going on about your fancy company cars. Take it from me – this redundancy is a blessing in disguise. He was well on the way to a heart attack or an affair."

"What on Earth gives you that idea?" I say, aghast.

Jess sniggers. "You know. When the cat's away and all that. Just remember why Dad left us. Geoff's told me that you're *extremely* busy these days. Don't you ever wonder what he's up to and with whom?"

"Jess, I am not going there. Geoff is *nothing* like Dad. He's not having, had or about to have an affair, nor is he on the way to a heart attack – and you've got the wrong end of the stick, as usual. He's been made redundant. His work and my challenges have not caused problems with his health or our relationship."

"You know best, sis. Anyway, redundancy can be an opportunity. It was for us. I take it you don't know I've gone self-employed?"

"No! You've never held down a real job. What do you do?"

"I am gainfully employed in the social care sector, spreading joy and happiness all around."

I hear her hooting with laughter for some reason, and I suddenly remember why I rarely speak to her. Her sense of humour grates on me. Unless I terminate our conversation *right now*, we are going to have *words*.

"I really don't need you to take the piss out of me now, Jess. Thanks for your advice. I must get back to work." I close my eyes and make an 'mmm' sound to relieve the tension I feel. As I reopen them, I see my colleague, Hairy Nina, observing me as she washes her hands.

"Nice vocal toning. I didn't mean to overhear, but is your husband looking for work?" she asks.

"Why?"

"He's an accountant, isn't he? Finance restructured recently, and I know they're looking to inject new blood into the team. Take a look at the intranet. There might be something there for him."

I immediately text Geoff.

Finance Dept are recruiting.
Ring and have a chat.
Amy x

The minute I get home from work, I take Geoff a cup of tea, ready to hear all about the call. He is on his e-reader.

"Well?" I ask brightly.

"What do you think I should say?"

What? Does he really need me to hold his hand just to pick up the phone?

I spend the next ten minutes motivating him to make the call.

5.30 p.m.
Geoff bounds up to me, waving an email in my face. "I'm in!" he whoops.

We read the email together.

"Well, you're not in quite yet. It says here that you will have a competency-based interview *if* you pass two psychometric tests." I read on. "They will be emailed to you at nine tomorrow morning, and you must complete them by midday. You will be informed by five whether or not you will be called back on Thursday for a formal interview."

"So, what happens if I don't get the required pass mark?" asks Geoff.

"It'll be a case of 'thanks, but no thanks', regardless of how good a track record you have or how nice a guy you are," I say simply. "That's how they shortlist these days. I don't necessarily agree with this strategy for recruiting somebody at your level, mind. I think that really good candidates often slip through the net."

He looks crestfallen.

"Hey," I say, giving him a hug. "You're smart. You can do it."

"But I haven't ever done tests like these. I'm disadvantaged before I've even begun. I bet there are loads of younger guys going for the same job who will have taken shedloads of them."

I think for a moment and become energised. The new and improving Amy Richards is going to use talents that have lain latent for too long to ensure Geoff has the best chance ever to land that job. "Okay," I say firmly. "Pass me the iPad and the phone. We're gonna prepare you good and proper. There's no way that some poxy ability tests are going to stop you getting into that interview room. I know that you are good! I'll use my Miss Marple investigative skills to suss out the type of tests you'll have to complete. Come on. Let's see what's out there on the web."

"Thanks, Amy," he replies, giving me a bear hug and smiling into my eyes. It feels good. It reminds me of times past. I smile back warmly.

When I return home from collecting Pippa from a dance class, I discover Geoff analysing sample test questions on the PC over a beer. "Good, you're back," he snaps. "The amount of information available is pretty lame, the sample questions are shit and there's no opportunity to time myself trying out an online test. Do you have any ideas?"

"Give me a mo, I've only just got *in*," I cry, kicking off my shoes.

"But *this* is *important*. Come on, you're good at this," he wheedles. "That's one of the reasons I married you. As soon as Claire introduced me to you, I knew we'd make a great strategic partnership and you'd help me get on in life. Help me to nail this job, and we won't have to cut back on the kids' activities."

"Sorry?"

"Well, I've worked out that if we stop the dancing and swimming lessons, we'll be okay for a bit."

"But they *love* all that so much, and if I cancel the direct debits, then…"

"Amy," he reprimands sternly. "Kids don't need all this entertainment. I thought that this would be the easiest way to trim off the fat, and it'll do them good to stay at home and play. That's what *I* did when *I* was a child. Now then, is it plum crumble with nutty topping tonight?"

My eyes moisten as I stomp into the kitchen. Earlier, I had a glimpse of what we used to be, but now it has gone again. I take off my coat, make myself a cup of coffee – the first I've had since coming home – and start on the mash for shepherd's pie. *I won't let them suffer*, I whisper under my breath. Once we've sorted out your job, we're going to sort out our life. *Why don't you cut back on your sodding golf or boozing down the pub for a while? That'd save us a fortune. I don't want to compromise my integrity. I have strong moral principles, but…* I steel myself and make the necessary call to Ability Testing HQ.

6.10 p.m.

Evie has been ceremoniously kicked out of the study, and Geoff is seated in front of the PC. "Watch," I announce proudly as I log into my Outlook account and open an email from Ability Testing HQ.

"What am I doing, exactly?" he asks.

"I have here," I indicate towards the PC, "the *actual* two tests that you will sit tomorrow morning."

"You have *what?*"

"I spoke to Ability Testing HQ and informed them that I'm considering setting up my own business and becoming an accredited tester, but that in order to assess the suitability of their tests, I really would like to have a go at doing them myself." I point to the email on the screen. "And here they are. The tests for you to have a go at – *right now.*" I open up the link to the first test, and we read the instructions.

"How long have I got to complete this?" asks Geoff, his eyes widening as he scans the instructions. "And how will I know how well I've done?"

"Ah! I have thought of *everything*," I say proudly. "I asked if I could be given the maximum amount of time available to have a go, and the person I spoke with agreed. When you do the test proper tomorrow, you will have twenty minutes, but... tonight we have *fifty* minutes for each test, which will give you quite enough time to have a really good crack at each question."

"No way!" exclaims Geoff under his breath. "Wow, Amy, how did you blag *this*?"

"I simply asked, and they said yes. And what's more, if you do the tests and submit your answers before seven tonight, we'll get immediate feedback on the results. So, I suggest you get on with them right now. The log-on details are there, look. And remember that you are me. Have fun."

Wednesday.

Geoff's passed the tests. I heave a sigh of relief. Only an interview to go, and then this nightmare will hopefully be over. His track record at interviews is good. However, he might be a little rusty, and the letter did say it would be competency-based. I text Cate:

> Any chance that you can come round
> and help prepare Geoff for an
> interview?
> We need to whip him into shape.

> My pleasure. 8pm?
> Make sure he has the Job Description
> and Person Spec. to hand.

Thursday.

"I'm not going to wish you luck today, as you don't need it," I smile to Geoff as I leave for work. "Just be yourself and remember the super-sexy answers to the questions Cate practised with you last night. Don't forget to ring me as *soon* as you know the outcome." I make to leave. "Oh, and go *easy* on the aftershave. Feedback saying that you were rejected because you suffocated the interviewers simply *will not do*." I laugh, and go before he has time to reply.

Once in the safety of my car, I allow waves of uncertainty to wash over me – but only for a moment. Music therapy will save me from myself once again. "This morning, I shall mostly be singing to the awesome *No Worries*," I say aloud. "You are my affirmation of the day."

As Simon Webbe's soothing voice fills the air, the feelings of helplessness and pain lift from my shoulders and my positivity returns. *This redundancy might signal the start of something better for us all. Even if Geoff doesn't get this one, doors might open for him. I feel we've really connected this week. He's been so much nicer.* I turn up the volume on my stereo, wind down my car window and sing with Simon about not having worries.

5.00 p.m.

Has he got the job? The continued silence from Geoff is agonising. We agreed that he would ring me when he had any news, and I am determined to wait for him to do so. I delay going home, opting for a glass of wine in a local pub to quash the inevitable catastrophising. *Every day is different,* I reason with myself. *Nothing lasts forever. Things happen for a reason, and I know I'll be alright.* I reach in my bag for my purse, and my latest challenge slip catches my eye.

SPLASH THE CASH! BUY SOMETHING REALLY EXTRAVAGANT.

I simply *daren't* go out and blow a significant amount of cash right now. It wouldn't feel right. For the first time since my year of self-discovery and adventure began, a challenge feels like a burden. It saddens me. I play with my phone, willing Geoff to call or text. I down a second glass of wine… and then a third.

A warm fuzziness envelops me. I fancy a light-hearted chat with somebody and scroll down my list of contacts. My finger stops on Him. *How are you? Have I been in your thoughts at all since I drunk-texted you after the blueberry challenge. I loved your witty reply. It made me laugh out loud… I miss your texts. I want you to call me awesome and gorgeous again… I know I've totally failed to stick to the four statements of intent I made back in July, but…*

Without a second thought, I ring his number. It rings once, twice, three times before I realise what I am doing, chicken out and end the call. *What the fuck was I thinking?*

I sit, shaken, staring at my phone, warm fuzziness replaced by crushing chest pain. *Do not ring back. Please do not ring back.* I turn it onto vibrate, hail a passing taxi, and make for home.

"Hello?"

The house is in total darkness. Bad thoughts whizz through my head. *What if Geoff's committed suicide and is hanging in the hall? What if he's taken an overdose and I find him slumped in the kitchen or he's stabbed himself to death and is lying in a pool of blood?* I take a deep breath and open the kitchen door slowly.

"*Boo!*"

"*Aaaaagh!*" Light floods the room.

"Surprise!" Evie shouts. "Look, looky *look.*"

The kitchen table is laid ready for a special occasion. Candles, cutlery, table confetti and napkins are in place. I notice a small, perfectly formed vase of flowers, an uncorked bottle of red wine and glasses. A large cake dominates centre stage. "Read what's written on the cake." Evie drags me over.

"It says: Thank You Wife and Mum," I say, "and there are three hugs and kisses."

"Sis and I made it," laughs Pippa. "*And* we got Dad to get a takeaway too, so *you* wouldn't have to *cook.*"

Geoff looks rather pleased with himself.

"Well, Geoff?

"I got it."

"You got it?"

"The job, idiot. Subject to references and all that shit. The formal offer arrived late this afternoon, and I have accepted it." He picks up Evie and swings her from side to side singing "I got the *job*, I passed the *tests*, I walked the interview. I was the dog's bollocks."

"You mean *we* did it," I say.

Geoff puts Evie down and fishes in his back pocket. "Here." He hands me an envelope.

I rip it open. "Why have you given me a blank cheque?"

"Why do you think, Mum?" Pippa's laughing. "What's your challenge?"

"To buy something extravagant," I reply.

"Well, here's your blank cheque," says Geoff. "The girls didn't want you to fail this challenge and persuaded me to let you splash some cash tomorrow."

Pippa butts in. "No, Dad, that's not very loving. This is a *gift* to say we love you, Mum. We love that you've done *so much* to help Dad to make sure that we don't have to leave our house, our friends and our schools. She even missed her fave TV show for you, Dad, and Mum *never* does that," she giggles. "*We* really *appreciate* everything you've done, don't we Dad?" She gives Geoff a look. "*Say* it, Dad. Tell Mum how much you appreciate her," she snarls.

"I thought that was *obvious*," he replies huffily, pointing to the cheque.

Pippa stares at him in disbelief and turns to me.

"Now Dad's got a job, you can go and spend spend spend without feeling guilty." She sits by my chair and hugs my legs. "Wish *I* was you," she chuckles. I stare at the cheque.

"Why didn't you text or call, Geoff?"

"Eh?"

"You promised. I was going *crazy* worrying. After all I've done, you couldn't be bothered to let me know what was going on?"

He sits tall in his chair, arms clasped across his chest. "I forgot, Amy. I'm a bit thoughtless at times, and I was busy. Here, don't start tantrumming. I've given you a blank cheque, haven't I? And the girls baked a cake and persuaded me to buy pizza against my better judgement. You know how much I loathe fast food and eating that stuff won't help reduce your hibernation pouch. If things don't go your way…"

"*Dad!*" shouts Pippa.

The atmosphere is charged. Evie starts to cry. "Dad let us

have pepperoni," she sobs. "That was a *nice* thing to do. We *never* have that."

I catch my breath. What was he busy doing? I'm itching to delve deeper, but this is not the time to make a scene. But I want to – very, very badly. I want to rip his bloody blank cheque up and yell and scream. Does he really believe that he can buy my love and appreciation with *money*? And as for him allowing us to have a pizza takeaway (including a pepperoni topping) – how bloody generous. But… everything is back in place: he has a job, so I can stop worrying, and things will improve once he's settled in. Of *course* they will, thank God.

"It's fine – thank you *so* much, guys. It's a wonderful surprise," I say, picking up the cake knife. "Here, cut it with me everyone. Close your eyes tight shut and make a wish."

The four of us take hold of the knife, our hands placed one on top of the other. We carefully cut the cake as one, and make our private wishes. Mine are brutal.

Week Two. Friday, 7.00 p.m.

With bated breath, I reveal my extravagant purchase to my family and wait for their comments. For some reason, I have an overwhelming desire to justify what I've bought, but I say nothing.

"Of all things, you chose *a handbag*?" Geoff says. Pippa throws him a look of distaste. "That's so insensitive, Dad. You wouldn't understand. Mum, I think it's lovely. Can I borrow it sometimes?" she asks wistfully.

"Well, at least I didn't buy a car or a yacht – or a holiday for *one*," I jest. "I could have, you know, and I was sorely tempted to do a Shirley Valentine and run away to the sun for seven days of rest and relaxation. Anyway, it was *my* choice. I wanted something that I could keep forever and pass down to you children. I've always had a secret lust for a designer bag, and this was my chance. So, jog on," I reply.

Geoff gives an exaggerated yawn. "Pubbing it at nine to celebrate my fantabulous job. I'll need a lift after tea, Amy. I'll stay over at Bob and Claire's."

The mention of Claire's name jogs my memory. "Speaking of Claire and bags, she has a red tote that looks remarkably like the one you bought for your PA when we were in Cyprus," I say.

"Ah. I wondered when you'd spot that," he smiles, scratching his nose. "I gave it to Bob to give to her. He'd forgotten their wedding anniversary, and so I helped him out. You won't let on to her, will you?" He busies himself with his mobile.

"Well, *that's* alright then. For a moment I *did* wonder."

Geoff looks up. "Where's tea? It's getting late."

9.00 p.m.

On my return from dropping Geoff down the pub, Pippa's waiting for me, looking grave. "Mum, I need to talk to you. Don't you think Dad's going out a lot... every weekend... without you?"

"Perhaps it's a bit excessive at the moment, Pippa. But remember, Dad's been through a lot recently. He's been working away most weeks and dealing with the stress of losing his job. It's not been easy for him, and the weekend's the only time he gets to see his mates."

"Why *did* you marry Dad?"

Her pointed question catches me off-guard, too tired to construct a diplomatic response. "I'm trying to work that out, darling. Do you have any ideas?"

"I don't think he treats you well. I never really thought about it until that Freaky Friday challenge, but since then I've noticed lots of times when he's taken you for granted and been... well... *mean.* That chat we had ages ago, when you were looking at your diaries and we talked about your exes – well, I remember you saying that being a wife changes people and their lives, but you never said *how* it changed *your* life. Is *this* what it means to be a wife, Mum? That you live your life around *Dad?* He brings in

215

most of the money, but *you* work too. You do almost everything else, in fact. Dad does and says what *he* wants to all the time. I think he has the best of *all* worlds at the expense of everyone else. *You* are his minion. Well?"

I pull her close. "I know that Dad and I have… issues, Pippa. All marriages go through rocky patches, and this is one of ours. Now that he has a new, less stressful job, I'm sure that things will change for the better. Please try not to let it worry you." I take her hands in mine and stare into her eyes. "I'm really glad you came to me and we can talk more openly now. I promise you that we are fine and we will be fine." I have to get out. I feel stifled. "Can we park this conversation for now, darling? We need to prepare for Bea's car boot tomorrow."

Taking a bottle of wine and my laptop into the bathroom, I lock the door and sit against the radiator to drink and think. Then I type and type and type.

Note to self:
Never forget that every day is different and that positive things come out of the most desperate of situations. Hold onto dedication and positivity.

Is Geoff going out a lot?

Is he neglecting the children?

Belittled? Taken for granted?

He wants the best of all worlds at the expense of everyone else?

We have a strategic partnership.

His minion?

Is this my future?

Saturday, midday.

Bea's car boot sale has not been a success, and I have a raging hangover. To boot, Geoff has sent me a voicemail informing me of his whereabouts for today, tomorrow and into next week. I listen to it impassively and sigh aloud as the message ends.

"Well?" asks Bea, counting her meagre takings.

"Geoff sounds like he's dictating a memo to his PA. He's even specifying his packed lunch contents to take away with him. He's on some course all next week."

Bea looks impassive. "Let him make his own packed lunch, pet. You're not his mother."

"But it's my job," I reply indignantly.

"Is it?" For a split second, she looks as if she is going to say something more, but for some reason she changes her mind and the subject. "Sod husbands and sod this car boot. I'll treat you to lunch, Ames. We're worth it."

1.30 p.m.

Tucking into garlic bread at Pizza Pizza, I seize the moment and quiz Bea about Blue Jumper Man and Him. "I still don't know why your friend Jason stole my secret snog, Bea." I fiddle with my napkin. It's difficult to look her in the eye. Bea chews slowly on her garlic bread and studies me, intrigued.

"I find it interesting that Jason snogged you, pet. He's a very private person and usually reserved. It was completely out of character for him to do something like that." She laughs heartily. "I know that since his last toxic relationship ended, he has partied a bit more, though. Perhaps the snog with you was some kind of release? Tell me about it again, pet. The thought of being grabbed without any warning and passionately ravished by a stranger in complete darkness sounds awesome. What a story to tell when we're old wrinklies."

And then we hear a cough… followed by a familiar voice. Our eyes lock in abject horror. Blue Jumper Man Jason is sitting at the next table to us. I want to die right now. If I could don Bilbo Baggins' invisibility ring and disappear...

"D'you think he's heard?" I whisper urgently to Bea. I feel sick. Bea is unperturbed.

"Dunno, pet. Let's see, shall we? Act normally and say hi. Jase?"

"Bea! How are you?" He sees me. "And my Beautiful Lady."

"On your own, Jase?"

"I'm grabbing a quick bite before driving to Glasgow to pick up the remains of my pissed brother from the airport. God knows if he's alright. Only he could go away and leave his mobile at home."

"Come and join us, pet."

Before I can protest, Jason is seated at our table, sharing our food, our wine and our conversation. I heave a sigh of relief. If Jason's brother has been away without his mobile, he won't have seen that I've rung him. Perhaps he'll ignore it.

Geoff texts me. "Oh guys, I have to go. I'd completely forgotten that I said I'd pick Evie up from the cinema." I ask for the bill and put on my jacket. *Now I'll never know about my snog,* I lament silently. *This was the ideal moment, and now it has gone.*

"One minute, pet." Bea looks shifty. "Jase, help us solve a mystery."

"Anything for you, gorgeous," he replies gaily.

"Bea, it's fine. Leave it," I say heavily.

"No," insists Jason. "I'm intrigued."

I opt to accost him before Bea can do any damage. "Why *did* you snog me at that divorce party?"

Jason leans back in his chair and claps his hands behind his head, clearly enjoying the moment. "You want to know if I had any *intentions* that night?"

"Well, yes and no," I reply crossly. I am not enjoying this conversation, but I have to deal with it once and for all. Then at least I will have closure. "My challenge was to bag a secret snog. You stole it, and I have to know why, because you ruined my plan. I wanted it to be with someone else," I complain. "Did you know? About my challenge, I mean. Did you do what you did on purpose?" I give him a penetrating stare.

"Do you want the answer you want to hear or the real answer?" he replies easily.

"*What?* Of *course* I want the real answer, Blue... Jason," I almost shout. "Why would I want any other version?"

"Okay. I didn't know about your challenge. However, I had no intention of snogging you until I saw you. It was a moment of madness. Will that do?" he says.

"No, that will *not* do," I assert. "Why did you do it? I *need* to know."

"It was my opportunity to make somebody else jealous," he replies simply. "Amy, I don't fancy you. I'm really sorry. You're cute and awesome – but I used you, I'm afraid. Please *don't* hate me," he pleads, taking my hands in his.

I laugh, and the tension is broken. "How could I hate you for not fancying me?" I reply. "But, why choose me?"

"Because the person I really want to snog is someone you know, but she wasn't at that party," he replies sheepishly.

"So, you thought that if you snogged Amy, then she would tell her various friends and somehow you and this mystery lady you fancy would get it on?" interjects Bea.

"Kinda," Jason replies. "I didn't quite know what to expect, but I knew that Amy would tell her friends – what girl wouldn't? I hoped that somehow I could use the snog tactic to get Amy to introduce me to her at some point."

"But it went a bit wrong, *didn't it*?" giggles Bea.

"It did, rather," smiles Jason. "I don't know if Amy's even told her, as she wasn't at the party, and I'm not even sure how close you are to her, Amy. I watched you getting angry and ratted and soon after I decided to call it a day and left."

"God knows what I would have done if I'd found you, Jason," I say. "It was a good thing that you went when you did." I think on. "What about when I chatted you up in the pub that night? We exchanged numbers. Was that another attempt at getting in with this girl?"

"I couldn't believe my luck when that happened, Amy. I decided that if I could get to know you better then, eventually, you might invite me to an event where I could get her number. I'm still hoping. Interestingly enough, I've since found out that you were using me too – weren't you, Amy?"

There's an awkward silence.

"Yeah, I'm really sorry," I sigh. "I take it you know about my Let the Dice Decide challenge, then?"

"It's fine, Amy. Let's call it quits, eh?"

"Moving on," says Bea merrily, "You're still burning a candle for one of Amy's mates then, Jase?"

"I sure am, but I don't know how to snare her in my net."

"And you won't tell us who it is, pet?"

"No. I find this kind of thing difficult," replies Jason. "I want to get to know her better. I think she's gorgeous, but I need to do it in my own time and in my own way."

My mobile vibrates with a shouty text from Geoff. It's definitely time to go. "Leave it with us, then," I smile. *One mystery solved and another begins*, I chortle to myself. *What a plan he had. Pure class.*

Sunday morning.

"Not so many left now," I reflect sadly, tossing the remaining slips of paper around the Bowl of Chance and Opportunity. I close my eyes and select one of them:

BE A SECRET MILLIONNAIRE.

"This is impossible. I'm not a millionaire," I say harshly to the goldfish.

"Who decided on this for me and why? What am I supposed to do? Rob a bank or fleece Geoff? The show is all about mega-wealthy people splashing their cash to help the disadvantaged. That's laudable, and if I had a squillion pounds I would gladly do likewise, but I don't, so I can't."

I tear open a packet of crisps and feed them mechanically into my mouth, feeling desperate. Pippa wanders into the kitchen, singing along to music on her mobile. "Crisps. Yum." She opens the family treat cupboard and scavenges inside.

"*Excuse me.*" I pull her earphones from her ears and give her a stern look. "I don't think so. You've just had breakfast."

"Oh, sorry," she replies airily. "But can I take this for later?" She holds up a chocolate bar. "You'll be a mum in a million and I'll love you forever." She skips out of the kitchen.

"Pippa?"

"Mum?"

"Repeat what you just said."

"When?"

"Just now, you muppet. You said something like 'let me have this and I'll be a mum in a million.'"

"Don't you like being complimented?" she replies indignantly.

"Sit here a mo." I show her my latest challenge slip. "It says here that I'm to be a Secret Millionaire, you know like on the TV show. Just now you said I was a mum in a million. What did you mean by that?"

Pippa hugs me. "You *are* a mum in a million. You're special because you are loving and generous and selfless and kind. You do so many wonderful things for us all. What about doing good turns and putting smiles on lots of faces? You don't need to do big things. Remember when I lost my bus fare home and a stranger gave me the money? That's the sort of thing I mean. It was really kind."

We've nailed it. It all makes perfect sense. My brain shoots off on a hundred tangents as I dissect my challenge, and my heart fills with elation as I mentally list some of the people I want to 'treat'. This challenge is going to be awesome.

1.30 p.m.
The Secret Millionaire is ready to go.

Now I really think about it, there's not enough neighbourly love in this world, I reflect while brainstorming a list of good deeds to perform. *Everyone is too damn suspicious of everyone else. When somebody does something nice for us, we wonder why. We can't simply accept it's because we're being thanked or appreciated. We immediately jump to the conclusion that there's an ulterior motive.*

I chew on my finger, deep in thought.

And these days we're all too busy to take time out of our chaotic lives to be nice to each other, except when we are made to do so, like at Christmas and for birthdays and other key events. I am going to change all that. In fact, if it goes well, this might become something I do more often.

"Amy, can I run some ideas by you for this presentation?"

"Ah – glad you're back, Geoff. I'm just writing up this challenge and then I'll start on dinner and vacuum the lounge. How was the Stag do last night? Hope the groom was well-behaved."

"Eh? Oh, it was great," he replies casually. "Now, you can do that in a minute. I have to get this finished." He pushes his laptop across to me.

"How about I look at it properly in half an hour's time?" I suggest. "Do you think we could have a chat about…"

He doesn't let me finish. "Amy, this is my *work*. It's important. Just look at it and tell me what you think."

"Waiting half an hour won't make any real difference, and it'd really help me," I reply assertively. "And it's better if you leave something for a short time and come back to it. You see it through new eyes. We can talk things over while I prep the veg."

"*Amy!*" he cries, banging his fist on the table, "You used to enjoy doing this for me. You've got the rest of the day for all that other trivia. Stop being so *contrary.*"

I shut up. I give in. I feel undermined again. The words 'minion' and 'petulant child' shout out to me, but I keep quiet and do as he asks because he has shocked me and although I want to do something about this, I still don't quite know what that something is.

3.00 p.m.

An extra-large notice informing others to *Keep out or be prepared to die a horrible death* (with smiley face beneath) is stuck to the study door. I am completely focused on preparing for my challenge. I beaver away, singing along to Abba at full volume. I am happy.

Geoff bangs on the door. I lower the volume. "Amy, come *out.* Are you still preoccupied with this bloody challenge?"

"Yes – and it's a good one, Geoff."

"Fucking *hell,*" he explodes for the second time today. "Aren't you taking this just a bit too far? Your exploits are getting in the way of us and our lives. Come for a walk. I haven't been out yet today and I could do with some exercise. If we go now, we'll get the best of the weather, and we'll be back for five, which'll still give you plenty of time to do whatever you have to do in preparation for Monday. Your challenge can wait, can't it?"

My eyes narrow. I have picked up on the tell-tale personal pronoun 'I'. This is not about us. It's all about him again – his frustrations, wants and needs. *Nice thought to get me back for five,* I think angrily. *That's match kick-off time, and oh yes, that gives me plenty of time to get you organised for Monday…*

I open the door a crack, determined not to lose my rag. "Thank you, but no. I appreciate that you have decided to spend time with me right now, but as you know, if I don't crack on, *I* won't be ready for tomorrow. I haven't even started on the fruit

223

cake you said you'd like to take away with you – and I won't be able to carry out my challenge either, because I won't have finished what I'm doing. Once I get this all done, I'll be able to relax. Why not ring Bob or one of your friends or go on your own or, even better, why not help me?" I remember Bea's words. "*You* could make your cake for once?" I suggest.

And, shutting the door purposefully, I sit with my back firmly pushed up against it so that he can't possibly force his way in.

"I'm not spending my valuable weekend baking. It'd take me hours, and it's *your* job, Amy. Why can't you all do what I want to do for a change? I've this bloody important course starting *tomorrow* and a few hours spare before I have to drive down south – which I'd like to spend with *you*, talking stuff through like we used to. You're so wrapped up in yourself and these challenges. You never *used* to be like this. It's you and the kids, you and your friends, you and a challenge. You have bucketfuls of spare time to indulge in all this other pointless crap. What's happened to *my wife?*" The petulant child stomps off, muttering some rather unpleasant words under his breath.

Two minutes later.
My resolve to be strong weakens.

He's worried about his new job and wants to share with me, I think. *Perhaps he's right and my challenges have got in the way. There should have been a Buyer Beware clause for us to sign up to before this all began. Beware of the possible consequences before you delve into your Bowl of Chance and Opportunity. It's more than a game; it's life-changing in more ways than you might think. If I were to go with him it would make him happy. It would build bridges between us and I could use the time to tease out where he's been and why he's neglecting the children. It's true that I don't have half the time for him I used to have. That's so selfish of me. I should be supportive and there for Geoff, especially now, while he's finding his feet. I have failed Geoff. I'm even complaining about making his cake, and I never used to do that.*

I go to look for him, but he has already left. I have no way of contacting him either. He's left his mobile behind.

Monday, 4.30 a.m.
I wake with a start, my phone alarm vibrating under my pillow, and dress quickly. Pippa sees me skulking around the kitchen.

"Mum?"

I spin around. "Oh, it's you," I whisper, shocked.

"It's challenge stuff, isn't it? I want to come."

I can tell she means business. "Alright then," I say in a low voice. "Grab your slippers and dressing gown, madam, or you'll miss it."

I put my fingers to my lips and, like Santa and his Elf on Christmas Eve, we slink from doorstep to doorstep, depositing bottles of wine and envelopes.

"What are these for?" whispers Pippa as we wind our way around the close.

"Gifts to thank people for being good neighbours," I reply proudly. "I have written personalised messages, thanking them for being... well... it depends on who they are really. I wanted them to know that I'm not pranking them. My gesture is heartfelt." I consult my list. "We need to hurry or it'll be wake-up time, and I mustn't be discovered."

7.10 a.m.
I keep making silly excuses so that I can pop outside and check on who's found their surprise and almost jump out of my skin when Mr Draper, my eccentric eighty-five-year-old next-door neighbour (and Neighbourhood Watcher extraordinaire) throws open his front door.

"A *very* good morning, Mrs Richards. Why are you about at this fine hour? Catching the worm?" He notices his gift. "What's this, then? A ration parcel?"

I pretend to tie my shoelace.

"Mrs Richards, come hither and see what some lovely person has left for me. I have been given a bottle of wine and a short message thanking me for being such a dedicated Neighbourhood Watch citizen." He puffs out his chest and smiles broadly.

"Now, this is quite something, Mrs Richards. Never in my whole time living here amongst you good people – and I have lived here for over twenty years, let me tell you – never have I been thanked for performing a job that I consider to be of vital importance in this cold and heartless world in which we live. Reminds me of the war."

He extracts a grubby handkerchief from his trouser pocket, wipes his eyes and blows his nose loudly. "Whoever has recognised my service to our community has cheered me up no end. It's as if I have received the *Légion d'Honneur*. In fact, I shall write to our local newspaper and voice my grateful thanks to this *inconnu*."

He changes the subject. "While you are here, Mrs Richards, a thought has crossed my mind. Would you be so kind as to do me a small favour later this afternoon? My usual transportation befriender who assists with my weekly supermarket shop is unavailable today. Would you mind taking their place, please, and help me peruse the shelves? I will gladly treat you to an iced bun and beverage by way of recompense. They serve a superlative pensioners' afternoon tea on a Monday. Say four-ish?"

Now, normally at four on a Monday, I am just preparing to sit back and enjoy a quick 'nana nap'. But this week, the Secret Millionaire is in town. "No problem at all," I reply. "I'd be delighted."

"*Affirmative*, Mrs Richards. Oh, Santa Claus and Rudolph – I spy more packages. Were they parachuted in the night, per chance? This is so mysterious and such a *delight*."

I leave him ruminating on the subject and run back home. What a result. One small act by woman, one giant leap for mankind, I laugh, misquoting Neil Armstrong and feeling like I am floating along on a cloud of happiness.

At four-thirty, I pick up Mr Draper and take him to the supermarket. As an avid people-watcher, I can't wait to observe his shopping habits. Mr Draper is smartly dressed in a double-breasted slate grey woollen suit complete with waistcoat and black satin bow tie. His hair is slicked back, and a distinct smell of aftershave wafts in the air. "We're only going shopping, Mr Draper. I never dress up, let alone spray on perfume to delight the sales assistants," I laugh as I unlock a shopping trolley from the bay.

His eyes twinkle. "Thank you for complimenting me on my attire and scent, Mrs Richards," he replies, studying a silver pocket watch. He stuffs his handwritten shopping list into his trouser pocket. "We'll shop later. Come on, come on," he says, suddenly agitated, "it's time for tea." He hurries off in the direction of the café and I follow.

By the time I have parked the trolley, Mr Draper is nowhere to be seen. I scan the queue at the café and gasp. The place is crammed with smartly dressed pensioners.

I hear Mr Draper calling me over. "This way. Listen out for the whistle. My hearing aid is a bit dicky."

"Whistle? Why is a whistle going to sound?" I ask in astonishment. Right on cue, there is a loud blast and a tannoy announcement.

"*Odd numbers move 'round one place as usual, please. You have five minutes, ladies and gentlemen. Don't forget to ask your carers to help you fill out your feedback card. Happy dating.*"

"I'm an even, so I may stay put," he says. "This is your place, Mrs Richards. Have a bun. Shall I pour?" Mr Draper motions for me to sit down and hands me a mug of tea. I take it without speaking, completely overawed. He pushes a card and pen into my hands. "Please put a tick against number twelve and comment, 'yes please, nice eyes."

"Are you alright, deary?" An elderly lady to my right, sporting a baby pink fascinator topped with silk flowers and embellishment, touches my arm. She looks as if she is off to a wedding reception.

"Oh… yes… I wasn't expecting…" I stop.

"He hadn't told you, had he?" She nudges Mr Draper. "Oh Dickie, you are a one. You hadn't told this young lady about our special afternoons, had you?"

Mr Draper grins. "Never too old to meet the ladies. Keeps us young and active, eh, Mrs Barker – and this is the modern way, isn't it?"

Mrs Barker's fascinator wobbles as she giggles. "You are a card, Richard Draper," she gushes.

"You come here to engage in speed-dating, Mrs Barker?" I ask.

"Yes, although we call it 'not-so-speedy-dating'," she smiles.

The whistle blows again. *"You have ten minutes to get to know your new partner. Best of British."*

I watch enthralled as Mr Draper and his new partner, number thirteen, begin chatting. *It's charming, really,* I think to myself. *Everyone is having fun, and it's miles better than sitting at home alone with the TV and radio for company.*

Afterwards, everyone mills around aimlessly. It's obvious that nobody wants to go home. "Where will you go with your dates, Mrs Barker?" I ask.

"That is a problem, my dear. We can't do anything exciting. Most of us rely on others to take us around, and the bus service is poor."

"What would you like to do?" I sense the Secret Millionaire coming out of hiding.

"Oh, go to a tea dance like I used to during the war," she replies dreamily. "And I haven't visited the pictures in years. That would be a lovely treat too."

"I used to take my ladies to the pictures and buy them ices.

That film about Alan Turing would really cut the mustard," interjects Mr Draper.

The two of them giggle together like teenagers. My brain begins whirring. *Amy Richards, you are about to make dreams come true...* I bang my glass with my fork.

"Quiet everybody, please."

The room falls silent. Thirty pairs of elderly eyes are on me. "I have had a wonderful time here this afternoon. I never knew that speed-dating was so popular with more mature folk, and it's awesome that you are obviously having fun meeting new people. Mr Draper and Mrs Barker have expressed an interest in going to the cinema to see *The Imitation Game*, you know, the film about World War II and Alan Turing. I have been informed that you don't have many places to go and socialise, and so tomorrow night, I will lay on a bus and take you to the local cinema in town. Please see me now if you are interested, and I'll arrange pick-up and drop-off points along the way so that everyone can come along."

"What about the cost?" whispers Mr Draper.

"I will pay for the bus and negotiate a special rate with the cinema. It depends on how many of you want to come, of course, but I don't think it'll be too much of an issue."

Thursday evening.

Geoff won't be back until tomorrow, and my girls are on sleepovers, so I'm free to indulge in an early night snuggled up in bed with the radio for company and writing up my diary. I read a thank you note from Mr Draper. The cinema trip was such a success that he has taken it upon himself to organise monthly film nights in the future.

I smile to myself as I remember the palpable excitement on the bus, the raucous sing-song on the way home and how happy everyone was. Grandma would have loved it! *What a great experience,* I reflect. *Highly rewarding.*

I go to bed feeling blessed.

A cathartic heart-to-heart with Claire (about everything that's been going on in my family life of late), has resulted in her kindly organising lunch at a local child-friendly gastro pub that offers an incredible range of mocktails and ice creams aimed unashamedly at the tween and teen markets.

"The family that plays together, stays together," I murmur, picking at my fingernails as Geoff pointedly criticises the lack of vegetables, comments on the amount of carbs we've consumed and complains about the cost of the starters.

"Aww, you love him really," grins Claire, noting my mounting embarrassment. "As does Mrs Mon-Key. Since the blueberry-eating challenge, she hasn't stopped singing his praises. Have you started helping her with her accounts yet, Geoffrey?"

"Are you? You never said?" I say, perplexed.

"She asked, and I agreed. It's no big deal and doesn't take up too much of my time. Her terms are excellent, Claire," he smirks.

"I'm sure they are," Claire smiles.

"Why didn't you tell me?" I plough on. "How come my friends know about this but your wife doesn't?"

Claire smooths the waters before he irritates me further. "Does it matter, Amy? Geoff's doing her a favour, that's all. I agree that he should have mentioned it, though. You really should communicate better with Amy, Geoff. At least let her know where you are when you're away. Now, let's change the subject. Show us your challenge."

The slip of paper reads:

SPEND A NIGHT IN A HAUNTED HOUSE.

"Fancy joining me?" I ask, looking round the table expectantly.

Geoff chokes on his beer. "Count me out. Load of bollocks."

"Well, I'm up for it," says Claire. "And I bet the rest of The

Girls will be, too. We could hold a séance or try the Ouija board like we did at school, remember?"

"Over my dead body," I frown. "Spending a night in a haunted house is one thing. But no boards, please. They scare the living daylights out of me." I remember the blind panic I felt as I heard a glass scraping over the table one time. "However, we must have the right location. No venue, no challenge," I chant.

"The answer is right *under our noses*," Claire giggles. "I work in a building that was once used as a mental hospital," she explains. "It's thought that a lady dressed in a long nightshirt floats around the building and *talks*. Everybody believes it."

"*Nooooo*," I breathe. "Well, that's decided then – as long as you can get the go-ahead? Just remember that we need to do it by Friday."

"I'll try. Even if it means we do it as a fundraiser for our charity of choice or something. It'll be worth it."

"Cracking plan, ladies," laughs Bob. "Don't forget to watch '*High S-ghoul Musical*' while you're there and buy food from the 'ghost-ery store."

"Bob," I groan. "Okay, I've one big favour to ask you guys? While we are away, send us *lots* of motivational and comforting texts. I know I'm going to need them. They'll *really* help me."

"We can do that, can't we mate?" says Bob.

"Most definitely," affirms Geoff. "No worries."

Tuesday, 8.00 p.m.
Exploring the nooks and crannies of this sprawling building is frightening yet *exhilarating*. We snake our way along a maze of stark and draughty corridors and through a myriad of abandoned spaces, looking to commit to where we will set up camp for the night. We don't feel the cold. We are united in our cause – to survive the night in a haunted hospital. A heady cocktail of adrenaline and strong black coffee has got us this far, and there is no way we are giving up now. We decide on a dank,

whitewashed room, which could have been used as a ward back in the day, and change into our onesies.

"It's damn draughty," shivers Cate, unrolling her sleeping bag. "Hope the candles don't blow out."

Bea is busy unzipping a coolbag. "Get that down you, pet," she says kindly, passing Cate a glass. "You'll soon warm up after a dram or two of something special and these treats, pet. Ta-da!" She unveils several bottles of alcohol and packets of nibbles. "Got to recapture the days of our misguided youth," she grins.

The goodies are a welcome distraction. None of us have eaten properly all day. Nobody has had much appetite. Cate's busying herself with the contents of a carrier bag. I wander over to investigate. She holds a ten-inch-tall brown plush dog aloft. "This is no ordinary dog – this is a *special* hound," she laughs. "Say hi to the Cosmotron Three Thousand, tonight's interactive investigator. Nice to spook with you, to spook with you, *nice*," she laughs, imitating Bruce Forsyth. "My friend Weird Dan is into this sort of stuff. When I told him what we were up to, he agreed to loan me this cute thing."

We gather round to admire the dog. "Dan's informed me that using something familiar and attractive to a… a whatever, may entice it to make contact," Cate explains. She takes out her iPhone and scrolls through her messages. "Ah, here it is. Dan says that the dog will detect something called EMF… blah blah… his nose lights up when he senses spikes… and when he senses changes in movement, vibration and temperature, he speaks and his ears *flash*." She looks up, wide-eyed. "I wonder what the Cosmotron might say? He might scare *us* away. I'll switch him on." She inserts two AA batteries into the dog's stomach and sets him down on the floor. "Wake up. Time to do your stuff."

"A *light's* come on!" screeches Claire, grabbing hold of my arm. "He's spotted something *already*."

"*No*, silly," Cate replies, laughing. "That light on his tummy shows he's working."

We all giggle with relief. "Time for more alcohol, methinks," I say, taking a look at my watch. "Yep, Girls, it's deffo wine o'clock. Now, where's that crate we brought with us?"

It's incredibly stressful trying to ignore the Cosmotron Three Thousand while waiting for something to happen and so, to keep our spirits up and prevent us going insane, we resort to a lively game of charades. The dog's cuteness has waned somewhat. There's been absolutely no sign of any paranormal activity, yet every so often, it speaks without warning, making us jump in fright.

Cate's mobile vibrates. "Dan's checking up on us. Oh, he's such a charmer," she giggles drunkenly. "He says he's totes jealous and has reminded me to tell you all to switch off your mobiles, as they interfere with stuff. So, phones off, Girls." We do as she instructs.

"Why do you call him 'weird'? Must be a bloody weird bloke to be texting you at one in the morning," I slur. "How do you know him? You've never talked about him, and we've known you for *ages*. What's he like? He might be a good catch for Bea, if he's available," I chuckle.

"Yessh," replies Bea, topping up everyone's glasses. "I am ready for a bit of lusting. Not loving, though. Love is too much trouble, but I would *lurve* lust right now. Is this Dan hot? You, Cate, are a sheep in wolf's clothing, mishes, pet. Have you had a moment with him that you've kept quiet about? *In vino veritas*. From wine comes truth. We're having the wine, now give ush the truth."

"Bea, it's a wolf in *sheep's* clothing," Cate smiles. "Well, Dan is um… *unique*. We're just friends. I'm up for inviting him over, though, if you're agreeable. It'd be good to use his expertise and help locate some ghosts. It's all been a bit quiet so far. He might say no, and for all I know, he won't even reply. He's dead unreliable like that. But then again, how many single blokes would turn down the opportunity of spending the night with us? Now that *would* be weird."

Thirty seconds later.

"Blimey, he's on his way," she gasps, "and he's bringing along some mate of his called Dave."

"Nice one," laughs Bea. "Just make sure he brings more booze too."

It's two in the morning, and our makeshift disco is going strong when Weird Dan and Dave turn up bearing gifts of beer, vodka and tonic. The ward has been fully transformed into a eighties disco heaven. Rotating disco balls reflect against the walls and ceiling, and classics from the decade are blasting out.

Cate alerts us to their presence, and I sway cross the room to welcome the lads – with Bea in hot pursuit. Cate hugs Dan and smiles at Dave. "Welcome to Amy's latest challenge," she shouts over the music, pointing me out.

Bea wastes no time in settling in the newcomers. She assertively links arms with them both and practically drags them towards the designated bar area. "Have a drink and join the party. I don't know why we've never been introduced?" she says, giving Dave one of her brazen seductive looks. "Girls, I'm gonna make some new friends, and perhaps a friend *to the end*," she adds offhandedly.

"Don't go getting too friendly with them, Bea. Cate," I wince. "She's used our *code*."

"Bea, did I just hear you right? Did you just say you were going to be friends to the end?" I ask, curious. "Yes to friends, but perhaps not to the *end*?" I mouth deliberately, raising my eyebrows.

Bea smiles and tosses her hair. "Ah, Ames, you are always so sensible and right. No worries, pet. We'll be just fine." She turns her attention back to the boys. Cate and I exchange glances.

"That's a load of bull," she whispers to me. "She's already decided what she's gonna do. I only hope that those lads can handle her. Dan's rather naïve. She'll eat him *alive*."

Dan turns to Cate. "Where's the Tron? Has there been any paranormal activity or spikes?" he asks.

"He's over here, but absolutely nothing's happened, nothing at all."

It's that time of night for drunken, *meaningful* discussions about whether the paranormal really is 'a load of bollocks', as Geoff so eloquently put it earlier in the week. Dan has visibly relaxed. He sits opposite me, chain-smoking and excitedly talking us through a pile of magazine articles he's brought along that describe different types of so-called paranormal visitations in detail. I half-listen to him through my drunken fog, watching him and his quirky mannerisms. He doesn't seem that weird to me. He reminds me of an overexcited eight-year-old waiting for Santa to arrive on Christmas Eve. I like that – it's endearing. *In fact,* I muse as I listen to his stories, *I wonder why he's single? In some ways, he reminds me of Him. It's that easy-going manner and tone of voice...*

I sit up with a start, and my heart skips a beat. I smile inwardly. *Oh, Him. Where are you, and what are you up to? What did you think when I tried to call you? Were you happy that I did?* I brood. Once again, I feel an overwhelming urge to reach out and connect with him. I know I can't, as our mobiles are out of bounds, but I *so* want to. And if I could...

"Claire. Come over here. I need to ask you something important."

"What is it?"

"It's about Him and me. *Hypothetically* speaking, if you were me and whatever you tried, you just couldn't get him out of your head, what would you do? What if you felt you'd connected in some way and didn't want to break that connection, even though you knew you should?" Alcohol loosens my tongue further. "What if I'd really snogged him and liked it too much? What if I still want to snog him? What if he's become that fucking addiction we sort of talked about?"

"Do you think he has? Become an addiction, I mean? Please don't tell me you've lied to me all this time and been snogging him – or worse," she whispers. She sounds totally shocked and close to tears. I realise that I've gone too far and that she doesn't get it. Her expression and tone of voice is condemning. For the first time since I confided in her, I feel quite uncomfortable, and I bend the truth to get out of trouble and protect myself.

"Course not," I reply emphatically. "That's all behind me now," I backtrack. "I think about him now and again – well, he is my fifty-first challenge buddy, after all – and we've texted each other a bit, but *nothing else* has happened. However, the fact that I secretly harboured feelings of lust for so long has made me question myself and my fidelity."

I see obvious relief written on her face. "Oh, Ames, my prayers have been answered. The Lord has given you the strength to find your way to safety. You must stop torturing yourself, hon," she says, rubbing my arm gently. *"No temptation has overtaken you that is not common to man. God is faithful, and He will not let you be tempted beyond your ability to resist but with the temptation He will also provide the way of escape, that you may be able to endure it.* The snog never happened and, although you worried me there, I never believed for one minute that you – of all people – would risk everything you've worked so hard for, just for a tryst. If you feel that bad inside, sit down with Geoff and talk it out. I know he needs you. He'll understand."

She digs me playfully in the ribs. "In all honesty, I think you are acting weird because you're in the middle of your menopausal mid-life crisis, fuelled by this madcap year of yours. It's forcing you to dig deep within yourself and challenge everything in your life – even stuff that doesn't *need* analysis. But this is an *extraordinary* year, hon; you must keep things in perspective. I'm glad there's not long to go until you can get back to some kind of normality. Next January, you'll take stock and realise how ridiculous you've been – mooning over some stupid bloke. I think you'd deeply regret it if Geoff were no longer beside you and vice versa. I envy what you have." She turns away for a brief moment and coughs.

"You okay, Claire?"

"Yes, Ames. Swallowed the wrong way. Now, where were we?"

"Do you really think everything I'm feeling and doing is down to my hormones?" I reply, hopefully.

"Yes, I do," she replies confidently. It's all about the hormones at our age. Even Bob frogmarched me to see my GP, who kindly diagnosed that I was *on my way* and casually added that it might take up to eleven years before I am officially through it."

"You're on your way to where?" I ask.

"Prebloodycisely. According to my research, I am on my way to a potential loss of sex drive, vaginal problems, migraines, weight gain, mood swings, a furry face and forgetfulness. I feel incompetent and unwell, but who can I tell? Who'll understand?

"I desperately hide all the crap I'm feeling and muddle through. But one day I will return to how I was, and I will be happy again and, Amy Richards, so will *you*."

I hug Claire tightly, but she pulls away, takes my hands in hers and looks me straight in the eye. "I know you want this *Him* to help with your final challenge, but you are strong and intelligent enough to do it on your own, Amy. I want you to cut ties – permanently – with Him, and I know, deep inside, that you do too. Do it for your lovely husband. Make a pledge to end it right now. Here, put your hand on your heart and swear to me," she says with gravitas.

I hesitate. It all sounds a bit melodramatic, and Claire's behaviour is unnerving me. I've never seen her like this before – so insistent – almost manipulative. It must be the drink talking. I do as she wants to keep the peace.

Claire appears satisfied. She turns to Dan. "May we switch on our phones just once?" she asks. "Ames and I need to check for motivational messages."

"Go on, then – but be quick," Dan laughs.

We fire up our mobiles and wait for the messages of support to ping in. Everyone has messages from friends and loved ones – everyone except me. Dan notices my crestfallen face. "Husband forgotten about you?" he enquires.

Sadly, that's probably true, I sigh to myself. I quietly retire to the ladies' to compose myself. I feel deeply let down. *Why didn't Geoff text me this time? We need to sort this out*, I reflect grimly. *He's taken me for granted for too long. Pippa's right, I am his bloody minion.*

I walk slowly back to the main room, pour myself a consolatory glass of wine and throw my mobile into my bag in disgust. A freak cold draught hits me across my back. "Sorry, did I leave the door ajar?" I ask absentmindedly.

"No," says Cate, giving the door handle a wiggle. It doesn't move. Her brow furrows as she tries it again. "Hey, Dan, come and open this for me," she asks, slightly panicked. "It won't budge."

The Cosmotron Three Thousand springs to life. "Hush, everyone," Dan commands, his eyes gleaming. "There's nothing to worry about."

Nothing to worry about? I wail internally. I am frozen to the spot. My breathing quickens. My finger moves instinctively to my mouth, and I begin to chew methodically, my eyes darting around the room, watching and waiting... Everyone except Bea and Dave looks as petrified as me. They are oblivious to it all.

Cate makes a noise like a strangled cat. "Dan?" she screeches, desperately tugging at the door handle. Dan wrenches it open. "Sorry, Ames. This is too much for me. Claire, stop that texting and *come on*." She grabs Claire's arm and flees to the safety of her car.

Bea sidles up to Dave, who is strumming on his guitar, removes a cigarette from the corner of his mouth and takes a long, deep drag on it. "Last woo and men standing," she slurs, swaying to the music. "Smoking is another experience that I renounced years ago and rekindled," she breathes seductively. Dave flashes her a look fuelled with unmistakable pure unadulterated lust. "Come on, Bea-youtiful," he drawls. "Let's go explore this place and declutter it of a few ghouls." There's absolutely no mistaking his intentions. He struts purposefully out of the room signalling for her to follow, and Bea runs after him.

That leaves me, Dan and the dog. I cannot remember the last time I felt this vulnerable. *Was it in Amsterdam?* I ponder. *At least I knew the Stags a bit,* I smile, remembering the fun we had. *I hardly know Dan at all, and why does Cate call him weird? What if he did something weird, right now?*

I pour myself a glass of wine, trying to mentally list what Dan doing something weird might look like: taking off all his clothes because he needed to get closer to nature, or donning some strange ghost-hunting outfit to help him to get into role. That would be well, weird. What if he talks in a foreign tongue to 'visitations'? *That one would really set me off,* I shudder. Perhaps I should ask him what it is about him, right now.

Dan is messing about with the door. "The door's fine, Amy," he says, taking a pen and pad from the back pocket of his jeans and making some notes. "You're Geoff Richards' wife, aren't you? I met him at the Society Dinner this year. He's an inspirational and funny guy. He told us all about your year of 'non-conformity and insubordination' in a great speech about Privacy, Regulation and Compliance. Amy? Have you heard what I've just said?"

"Yes…" I reply shakily, "… I have… Dan? Do you see that dim glow over there by the radiator?"

"No, I don't – but the Tron has spiked, so something's going on." He examines the dog carefully.

I shut my eyes, count to three and open them again. The glow appears to be slowly moving across the far side of the room. I rub my eyes and look hard. "I really can see somebody floating there – over there – Dan? Now, don't you dare start chanting or talking in tongues, or I will leave *right now.* She is young… white gown… there… and I can hear her… she is talking to me."

Dan pulls me close. I sense his presence and come to. Inside, I'm bricking it, but Dan's calming influence is making me strong. I stare into his eyes, squeeze his hand and feel his joy permeate through my body as he realises a lifetime ambition.

Thursday afternoon.

I'm back home on the sofa, feigning sleep. I don't want to talk to anyone right now. Yet again, a challenge has taken me on an emotional journey. It's difficult to return to normal life – whatever that means – and I cannot forget how deeply hurt I feel due to Geoff's complete lack of consideration towards me. I somehow have to get him to put himself in my shoes and appreciate my point of view, but I need to choose my moment carefully… Geoff appears at my side, holding the house phone. "It's Bea."

I open one eye and take it from his outstretched hand wordlessly. I can't help myself. "You didn't text me."

"Unfortunately not…"

I open both eyes. "What does that mean?" I sit up, ready to have it out.

"It's no big deal. I didn't. I forgot, okay? Stop hectoring me," he sighs, clearly exasperated. The conversation comes to an abrupt halt as Evie throws open the door and runs across to hug me. "Poo, you stink, Mum," she laughs. "Is it the smell of fear? Dad said you'd probably have it."

Beware, Geoff. It's you who should have the smell of fear, I think grimly as I shoo them both from the room. *I can't believe that you just said what you did, even after Claire made a pointed comment about being a better communicator. Thank God you're away from tomorrow.*

I turn my attention to Bea. "Hi."

There's a pause. "I think I'm in love, pet."

"No, you're not." I retort. Take it from me. In lust, yes – but love, no. It's called limerence. I read about it in…"

Bea cuts in. "This was different, special. We connected. I feel alive. I can't stop thinking about him. That clairvoyant, Mrs Harmer, said I was going to fall in love, and I have."

My eyes roll. "She said a load of garbage and earned a bomb that night. Get some sleep. See you Thursday."

"Okay," she replies grumpily. "But I am *in love*."

What is going on with us all? Is she menopausal too? I wonder as I press play on my MP3 player and Mrs Harmer's *Go Comatose in 5* starts up. I burrow under my throw and tune into her hypnotic voice. *Time to relax and sleep*, I say to myself, mantra-like. *Relax and sleep… relax… slee…*

Week Four. Friday, 10.30 a.m.

Waiting in line to order my coffee, I feel a sharp tap on my shoulder. I almost collapse on the spot. It's Him, standing behind me in the queue, and his mesmerising cornflower-blue eyes are staring into mine. Compose, calm, breathe… I manage a wan smile and hum that dreadful catchy tune from the Disney film *Frozen* under my breath. Anything to lower my heart rate. "Hello. Nice to see you… again." *God, that's so stilted, Amy,* I cringe, furtively taking off my fleece jacket.

He shakes his head from side to side. There is a pause. "You phoned, Amy?"

"Um… sorry… misdialled," I lie, scuffing the floor with the toe of my shoe.

"Ah, easily done. So, how about a dinner date? I'm freed up and firing on all cylinders." He shakes his head violently again. My stomach contracts at the word *date*. I take a deep breath. My heart is pounding and my palms are drenched with sweat. I stare fixedly at his nose. I cannot bring myself to look into those hypnotic eyes again. He doesn't appear to notice my state of disquiet.

My brain and mouth disconnect. "Yes... we will... soon... I'm not quite ready yet... lots to sort out... but I will be ready... um... in two weeks' time," I gabble. "However for our... um... *relationship* to work, it's vital that you think really hard and tell me something – or hopefully several things – about yourself that I might not like, or even better, something I'd *really* dislike about you."

I stop.

What have I just said? I can't believe I've gone and done that – I need to go, scarper, vamoose – right now.

"Sorry, say that again?" He bangs his right ear with his palm. "This ear infection has buggered up my hearing. What should I tell you?" he asks, his eyes narrowing in concentration. Just then, his mobile starts ringing.

"Hmmm, nothing, no nothing, forget that," I stutter. *Thank you, thank you, God. He hasn't heard me. He is hard of hearing. I have been reprieved.*

"Madam?"

It's my turn to order my coffee. When I look back to reply he has gone.

Adriano's Restaurant, 8.00 p.m.
I've purposely arrived early at Adriano's to snatch some 'me' time. September is always a stressful month, what with the start of a new school year – let alone all the other activity that I'm caught up in. My emotions are all over the place. I briefly touch base with Geoff and Jess by text before looking at this week's challenge slip:

THROW CAUTION TO THE WIND – BE SPONTANEOUS AND RECKLESS.

I bet Bea's behind this one. She's always joking that there's something wrong with me because I don't 'do' impulsiveness and I'm never reckless. I've experienced and witnessed the after-effects that come from people acting in the heat of the moment, and I vowed long ago that to be successful in life and avoid costly mistakes, I'd focus exclusively on achieving my dreams by using my head and not my heart. Geoff's always admired me for not making rash decisions or taking uncalculated risks as it means he knows where he stands with me. In hindsight, however, I think that Bea may have a point.

I thought I knew exactly what I wanted from life and how to get it, I think sadly, *but now I'm not so sure. Was my 'What I will do to ensure I am successful and nab the essential lifelong partner' list a crutch – because I was scared of being trapped into a life like my mother's?...*

Later that evening, The Girls bombard me with suggestions to unleash the reckless and spontaneous inner me. I've hardly eaten and am on my fourth large glass of Pinot Grigio, listening to their advice through a happy drunken haze.

"Steal something."

"Flash your boobs."

"Start singing, and we'll join in."

"Snog a stranger." That one gets my attention.

Snog a stranger, I smirk. *Another snogging challenge alert. I could snog Him – third time lucky? It would be spontaneous and reckless and legit. Dare I try... tonight?*

At least then, he'll be out of your system for good, justifies my inner voice, *and nobody need know. Your reputation will be intact, and you'll have satisfied your thirst, so you can get on with your life, guilt-free.*

Yes. I'll explain to Him why I want a snog, so there'll be no misunderstandings on the lusting front. We'll have a laugh about it, and that will be that. And, hopefully, he'll be a rubbish snogger or smell or something, which would be even better. I need to be more drunk... another... one more... right, Amy, do it, do it, do it!

I pick up my phone. I put it back down. I pick it up again. Luckily, nobody is taking any notice of me. They are too busy discussing a trip to Manchester that we plan to make in the new year. I take a *deep* breath… *Spontaneous and reckless,* I shout internally. I send a text.

> Hi. Ears better?
> I have a tough challenge
> and I think you can help.
> Please text back.
> Amy.

A reply flashes up on the screen.

> What is it?

> I've to be spontaneous and reckless.

> Where are you?

> At Adriano's.

He does not reply.

10.30 p.m.
Still no reply.

I can hardly bear it and check my phone every few seconds. I've lost count of the glasses of wine I've consumed. He can't do this to me. I have to leave soon. I won't be able to do this tomorrow. It's tonight or never. Do you hear me, Him, tonight or never, ever, *ever.*

10.45 p.m.

> Rendez-vous at the Kings Arms

in 20 minutes.
Look for a red Mini.

Oh my God. That's a ten-minute walk from here. I should leave *now*.

I am so uptight, I could vomit. I must compose myself. Making the weak excuse that Geoff is giving me a lift home and I can't be late for him, I guestimate my proportion of the bill, throw cash onto the table, grab my belongings and speed-walk to our agreed meeting place. It's the only way to rid myself of the adrenaline surging through my body. I feel jittery and excited and *reckless*.

I arrive at the pub to see a Mini waiting for me. He flashes his headlights as I approach and winds down his window.

"Jump in. Don't look so nervous. I'm really looking forward to helping you with this challenge and I know exactly what we're gonna do. Is this spontaneous enough for you so far?" he says, glancing at me coyly.

I remove an empty bottle of vodka from the passenger seat, get in and sit on my hands to stop myself from finger-chewing. "Where are we going?" I splutter as we pass Adriano's and I see Claire and Bea waiting for their lifts. I could swear they're staring straight at me.

"Not far. Trust me. Tell me about your evening."

He pulls over in a quiet layby on the outskirts of town and switches off the engine. I stop talking. I can hardly breathe. We are alone.

"Amy," he says quietly, staring straight ahead. "Do you remember anything about what you said to me at the divorce party a while back?"

I blush. *That* party. The one where I told him that for some reason, I really wanted to snog him. I daren't look at him. If I look into his eyes, he will see what he mustn't ever see.

He chuckles quietly. "I remember what you said. Every word. Enjoy your challenge, babe."

245

And then, it happens. It really does happen. He takes my hands, pulls me towards him roughly and snogs me.

And it is perfect.

Sunday, 2.30 a.m.

It is no longer perfect.

Geoff snores contentedly, while I toss and turn. *Why oh why did I do it?* My insides are coiled so tight that my core is aching. I've battled with my emotions all weekend, trying to rationalise the situation and concealing my conflicting feelings from the world. What I did weighs heavily on me.

I lie curled up under the duvet, sniffing lavender oil and listening to a podcast entitled *Unwind, Uncoil and Be Free.* But nothing can help right now. Turning onto my left side, I poke my feet out of the duvet in an attempt to push the thoughts of last Friday night's snog of snogs into the dim recesses of my mind. But they keep sneaking back, driving me demented.

It was a damn good challenge, I think. *And the outcome! I'd never have foreseen I'd get my secret snog like that. It was spontaneous and reckless. It was exciting and dangerous. I felt alive. That night, at that moment, I was Amy, not Mrs Richards, not Mum, not wife. I was me.*

Geoff mutters in his sleep, and my stomach knots with guilt. *What would Geoff say? Will he quiz me about why I was out so late? What if he rang anyone to check up on me? And if Claire saw me?*

My inner critic kicks in: *Stop right there. You did what you needed to do. It was a challenge, nothing more. Now you can move on.*

I turn onto my other side. *Stop thinking about it,* I reprimand myself firmly. I can't. I don't want to leave it behind quite yet. It feels too soon, and I know I'll never experience anything like it again.

I stare at length at my husband, a steady flow of tears

trickling silently down my cheeks. I force myself into his shoes. How would I be feeling if he had done similar and I knew about it? I know the answer. I'd be feeling totally wretched, and I would despise him for his infidelity.

What shall I do? I think. *Forget? How could I forget all this; it's an integral part of my year of self-discovery.* I sigh deeply and make a decision. *It's alright to indulge myself tonight, but tomorrow morning, I will not think about it again. Distance will be my healer, and my challenges will be my distraction.*

Then it comes to me. I will take control of this situation and work it through with my head and not my heart by formulating a SMART objective: *specific, measurable, achievable, realistic* and with a *timescale.* My boss would be proud of me.

By the end of November, I will be able to talk to you on the phone and text you without feeling lust. I will be able to treat you as my writing critical friend – which is how it was meant to be all along. My new mantra will be: It's all about the book and not the boy.

I slip into my dressing gown, creep downstairs and get it all down on my laptop. As the words appear in print, I feel a sense of purpose. Then, exhaling slowly, I close my eyes, press play on my mental video clip and relive every single detail from last Friday night.

Monday evening.
In celebration of the fact that I have my Evidence-Based Master Plan – 'From Lust to Dust', as I am now calling it – I throw myself into making a Christmas cake to the sound of a CD I recently unearthed. It is called *Uplifting Music for Release From Those Moments.* Thankfully, it's doing what's on the tin. I'm definitely having a 'releasing' moment belting out the lyrics to *Bitch* by Meredith Brooks.

Catching a glimpse of my reflection in the sparkling oven door, I smile. "Hey, Meredith, you're singing about *me*," I say aloud. "I am a parent, a spouse, a confidante. I'm a pic'n'mix of good and bad, and I should be *unrepentant* for being all of those things. I am who I am, and *everyone* should accept, embrace and love me for it – especially Geoff." I put the cake into the oven and set the timer. "If Geoff really cares, he won't make me feel bad for wanting change. He won't drag me down. He'll love, support and encourage me. I only want for us all to be happy. He has to acknowledge that I'm... what's the word...? *Repressed*."

I check the definition on Google:

oppressed, subjugated, subdued, tyrannised, ground down, downtrodden, inhibited, frustrated, restrained, introverted, suppressed, held back, held in, kept in check, muffled, stifled, smothered, pent up, bottled up, unfulfilled.

At last. I have described myself in my own words. It feels right.

October

Pippa finds me rummaging in the kitchen cupboards on my hands and knees. "Why are you cleaning so early in the morning, Mum? That's not normal."

I sit back on my haunches and announce that I am on a 'B' day. My challenge is to:

LIVE THE DAY BY THE LETTER B.

I draw an imaginary 'B' in the air.

"What?" she replies incredulously. "Have you been on the Bucks Fizz again, like last Christmas Day? Dad!" she shouts, "Mum's been drinking alcohol in the morning again. She's acting all *weird*."

I lie on the floor, clutching my sides. *Hee Hee. I can legitimately get bamboozled on booze, and I have a bottle here.* I chuckle at the number of 'B' words I've found before pouring myself a small glass of the fizz and downing it quickly.

"How about eating this?" Evie's holding a box of All Bran.

I recover my composure. "Bran would work," I reply, "but I don't really like it. However, today," I say, noting packets of breadsticks and bourbon biscuits lurking at the back of the cupboard, "as my challenge is to live by the letter 'B', I will breakfast on breadsticks, bourbon biscuits and Bucks Fizz."

"May I share your challenge and eat biscuits with you?" pleads Evie.

"No," I reply sternly, "Bad for your health and your teeth. Only those on challenges are allowed to do this, and for one day *only*. You could make me a hot drink beginning with 'B' though."

Geoff puts his two cents in, a plastic smile glued to his face. "I suggest *black* coffee and a *bang* on the *bonce* to make your mother see sense. I thought that you might have selected *blueberries* or a *banana*, Amy. That would have constituted two of your five-a-day."

"Yes, s'pose," I mutter. "However, I *thought* that it wouldn't be so much fun, and fruit didn't come to mind. Oh, get into the spirit of it, Geoff. You can be such a…" (I mouth the word *bastard* at him).

Geoff slams his e-reader shut. "Right. I've had quite enough of this. I'm off to the Mon-Keys' and possibly golf with Jay. I hope you haven't forgotten that my boss and his wife are coming over tonight for dinner?"

"Who's Jay?"

"Don't change the subject, Amy. God only knows what you are going to serve up! Does being on a 'B' day mean we'll have to endure whatever you stumble upon that begins with that letter?"

I nod.

"Well, please remember that I'm trying to impress tonight," he concludes grimly and turns to go. I can tell something isn't quite right. Some expression in his eyes, a certain hint in the tone of his voice. "By the way, you know that god-awful track you're playing incessantly?"

"Bitch?" I giggle. "That's a 'B' word too."

"I think that track's about menopausal women. Those lyrics sum you up perfectly, Amy. Get yourself some HRT. I'm missing my former wife. See you."

I chew angrily on my finger. *He's missing his former wife? Why? Doesn't he like any part of the new me? Well, it's not even the new me, it's just me – the me I was before stuff got in the way. I must have been like this when I met him, mustn't I? How can I tell him I feel repressed when he says things like that?*

"Oh!" I gasp. I have just remembered something important. Snatching up my car keys, I dash to the front door. Luckily, he is leaning against his car, chatting animatedly on his mobile. "Leave me your BMW for the shopping, Geoff. I can't use my Mini – it's an 'M.'"

Geoff rolls his eyes, snatches my car keys from my outstretched hand, stomps across to my car without a backwards glance and drives off.

Pfft. I'll show him, I think angrily.

10.30 a.m.
It's time to hit the supermarket.

I start up the BMW, load Blondie into the stereo and make my way to Bigger Bargains, where I scour the shelves for 'B' products.

Brussels sprouts, baked beans, bulgur wheat, butter, beans, bagels, blueberry jam, blueberries and back bacon make their way into my basket.

Wow, this is easier that I thought, I smile, cheerfully throwing a bag of blackberries in for good measure. *We won't starve, and Geoff has his healthy options too. A few Brussels and beans will sort him out. He'll be blowing off all evening, which will be awesome entertainment for his boss.* I spy the alcohol aisle. *Ooh! Good choice, Amy. Bollinger and Bellinis!*

Back home, I unload my shopping while downing a black coffee. My phone alerts me to my waxing treatment at midday. Waxing doesn't begin with a 'B', so I ring Harmony to explain.

"Harmony, I have a *big* dilemma. My wax is today, but my challenge is to live the day by the letter 'B'. As the word wax begins with a 'W', and you, Harmony, your name begins with an 'H', you can't wax me today; it'd be illegal."

Harmony thinks for a moment. "How about a Brazilian? Our new waxing technician's available at quarter past twelve. He's highly competent and, what's more, his name is Ben – and he's bald!" She chuckles. "How does that sound?"

"That sounds *the best*," I laugh.

12.15 p.m.
Bald Ben welcomes me, his bald head covered with a beanie. "Bonjour," he smiles. "Harm's told me all about you."

"Ben? Ben the bonk with the bulging bollocks?" I blush.

Shit, it *is* him. *The* Ben who Claire bonked in the toilets at her school reunion is about to see my most private parts and *Brazilian* me. His face breaks into a broad grin. "Amy Parker. Nobody's called me that for *years*," he sighs. "Those were the days." His tone changes. "This way please, madam."

Ben leads me into a treatment room and asks me to undress. I lie on the bed, eyes tightly shut, a towel covering my lower body. Oh, the embarrassment. It's inconceivable that Ben is about to see me in all my naked glory. The Girls are going to have a field day when they hear about this one, especially Claire. Goodness – I wish I had some booze right now.

3.00 p.m.
In Bromley's, I order a banana milkshake to recover from my trauma and text Claire about her ex-beau, Ben:

Had a close encounter with
your ex-schooldays lust.
Today I am mostly buying B things.
Brief you tonight.

Who? Ben?
Spill the goss.

I am about to
Buy Birthday

bears for your girls.

Glad you've messaged me.

We need to talk.

Bears would be brill.

3.30 p.m.

I make a beeline for a sales assistant in Bear Heaven. "I'm after bears whose names begin with a 'B'?"

She points to a bear on a nearby shelf. "How about Barnaby Bear with a very big head?"

"Sorry? Barnaby with what?" I gulp hard.

She picks up a Barnaby Bear and waggles his huge stuffed head from side to side.

"Ah, got it!" I laugh. "I'll take two… no, make that three. I'll give one to my husband for Christmas. Can you insert blueberry scented beating hearts into two of them, please, and may I record a private message for the third?"

I follow the sales assistant to a quiet corner, where I record my message for Geoff's Bear. It takes ages before I'm calm enough to put on a sexy, husky voice. I press record. *"Beat my bottom, boy. I've been a bad bear… a bad, bad bear. Look at my big, big head."*

8.30 p.m.

Geoff's boss and his wife, together with Claire, Bob and Geoff, are enjoying my evening devoted to the letter 'B'. It's all going extremely well. Geoff stares agog as I proudly serve Bollinger accompanied by a starter of broad bean and Brussels sprout dips. It is followed by beef and butternut squash stew with basmati rice and rounded up with Bellinis and a medley of blackberries and blueberries.

We play Boggle, Buckaroo and Battleships and end the evening bladdered, belting out tracks from Blondie, Blur, the Bee Gees and Bronski Beat. At the end of the evening, I regale everyone with a colourful account of my day and present Claire with two Barnaby Bears. "Did that really happen?" Bob asks, laughing heartily at my tale of the sales assistant's double entendre.

"Yep. I don't think she quite realised what she was saying," I giggle. "She was foreign." On the spur of the moment, I present Geoff with his bear too and accidentally press the bear's heart. I grab Claire's hand and hold my breath as Bad Barnaby speaks…

"Beat my bottom, boy. I've been a bad bear… a bad, bad bear. Look at my big, big head."

I cover my eyes and peek at Geoff through my fingers. He is shaking with laughter.

When Claire is looking for her coat, I casually ask what it was she wanted to talk to me about. My heart is in my mouth as I wait for her reply. "Eh? Oh, no, it was nothing important." She smiles and rubs her nose. "We've said 'bye to Geoff. Hey, great evening. Give me a hug."

I heave a sigh of relief.

11.45 p.m.

"Are you on HRT? You were amazing tonight – the Amy I used to know. Is my strategic partner back? I must have impressed my boss with that display. Come to bed."

I pause. The warm satisfied glow I used to get when Geoff praised me for my hosting skills isn't there. I feel like his glorified housekeeper. *And, now the housekeeper receives a reward, doesn't she?* I grimace as I climb in beside him and he puts his arms around me.

"Mrs Richards," he yawns. "Tonight I'm bushed, so your 'B' day bedtime bonk is aborted. You're off the hook." He kisses me lightly on the cheek and turns away from me.

"That's not like you? What's brought this on?" I say, astounded. "Are you alright?" Geoff grunts quietly in reply. Seconds later, I hear the sound of gentle snoring.

I lie in bed feeling troubled. Geoff never turns down the opportunity for sex on a Saturday night. He's let me 'off the hook'? That's unheard of. My heart rate rises and my insecurities crowd in. There must be a reason why. I don't know if I dare broach the subject. Geoff must know something. What if he confronts me about Him? Oh God. What's going on?

Week Two. Saturday, 2.30 p.m.

FORGO YOUR CREATURE COMFORTS AND SPEND A NIGHT UNDER THE STARS.

Being the proud holder of a Girl Guiding *official* Camp Permit badge supposedly qualifies Pippa to lead wild-camping adventures. Today, she is in charge, excited at the challenge of cultivating a love of 'getting back to basics' in me. "Don't bank on it," I say cagily, swatting at an imaginary insect.

I've not been a fan of camping since a disastrous school trip to Dieppe. It put me off for life. Ah, the memories. It rained continuously for the five days that we were there. The campsite turned into a veritable mud bath, we morphed into mud-coated savages and, worst of all, the palaver of getting up in the night and peeing in the cold and then having to try to remember which was your tent... I shudder involuntarily.

Tonight, I've been press-ganged into spending a night under the stars, in the wilds (our local woods). If I was on my own out here with crawly beasties for company, I'd have to be sectioned by morning. "What if an animal creeps up on us in the middle of the night while we're sleeping? When I was in the Yosemite National Park, bears would rip open tents with their claws to get at food – including toothpaste, of all things. It's true," I assert as she chuckles. I swat again.

"Oh, *Mother!*" she giggles. "There's nothing there. It's all in your *head*." She expertly unpacks groundsheets and sleeping bags. "You won't find any bears or poisonous spiders – nor any of those creepy crawlies from *I'm a Celeb*. And, there's no fear of midges either at this time of year. Come on," she shouts over her shoulder, "It'll be dark soon, and you'll be well pissed off if we don't get organised. It's supposed to be fun – and at least it's not raining."

My mouth drops open. She is *never* like this at home – and not a mobile or a screen in sight. "I bet this challenge is to get me back for loving *I'm a Celebrity, Get Me Out of Here*," I mutter as Pippa hands me a smelly green tarpaulin. "It wouldn't surprise me if Geoff has had a hand in this one and dropped a few critters in for fun. At least being here will prevent me from breaking my 'From Lust to Dust' plan."

Pippa takes me on a 'site familiarisation tour'. I am very grateful for this, as I have a fear of getting lost – anywhere. My sense of direction has never been the best. "Take this whistle. If you are unsure of where you are, blow three times and I'll know to come and rescue you," she says handing it to me. "Wear it at all times and use it if you need to."

"That's impressive – and so kind of you. I'm liking this awesome alien," I giggle, hanging it around my neck and giving her a hug. "I'd love to see a bit more of this *at home*."

"Aww, thanks, Mum. Do you think you could try to um… stop complaining now? It's a bit immature."

I make a decision. "Okay, you're right. I am being childish, and I'll try to get involved. If I do, I might just begin to enjoy it." A sudden thought crosses my mind. "Did you bring a portaloo?"

"*No*. Here." She passes me a spade. "Get digging over there." She points to an area a fair distance from our camp. "And after you're done, replace the turf. You do realise there's no toilet roll either?"

"Yes," I lie. "I don't want to *go* – well not yet, anyway. I was just asking," I retort. I resolve not to go until I get back home.

4.30 p.m.

Now, this is more like it. Head torches on, we forage for our tea. We have found a few apples nearby and now, at Pippa's request, I am busy picking puffball mushrooms. "The challenge says that you should be a hunter-gatherer, and we will use them to make a *delicious* tea," she explains.

"I never knew you could *eat* these," I remark. "They're not poisonous, are they? I remember your father getting excited about mushrooming one time, and if it hadn't been for Bob, he'd have ended up in A and E," I laugh.

"These defo aren't going to kill us," she replies. "It's Mr Draper's recipe. He said they swore by it during the war, so I decided that we should give it a go."

"Ooh. If it works out, well, that's another cheap and nutritious meal to try," I laugh. "Now, what about water?" I continue.

"Over there, from the stream," indicates Pippa, "but boil it first so that it's safe to drink. Use this canister."

I don't half feel useless. It's as if we are back in the Freaky Friday challenge where we reversed roles. Today, Pippa is taking the lead. She is the parent and I am the pathetic child.

Sunday, 1.00 a.m.

The chain around my neck is strangling me. I take it off.

3.30 a.m.

I need a wee.

3.45 a.m.

Oh, I *need* a wee.

4.00 a.m.

I go to take a wee. *Wow, it's dark*, I reflect, stumbling outside to find a suitable spot.

4.04 a.m.

How do I get back?

4.06 a.m.

Where is my sodding whistle? I panic.

4.09 a.m.

"Mum?"

"Thank God!" I cry.

Back under the safety of the canopy, I feel quite silly. I was convinced that I was lost in the woods for an hour or more, but according to Pippa, it was more like a five-minute thing. She chastises me for ignoring her instructions and puts me firmly in my place.

6.30 a.m.

Waking up cold, damp and aching from lying on the hard ground, I remember what I hate about camping. The magic of last night has passed, and I'm ready for a hot shower. As we wait for Geoff to pick us up, I sense a tiny knot in the pit of my stomach. I haven't seen him for much of the past week. We've both been busy doing 'stuff' and have not had time to talk. I'm still worried about why he aborted our usual weekend bonk, but I've decided to keep quiet about it. If he wants to raise the issue, he can.

"Have you had a good time?" asks Pippa.

"Yes, I honestly have, darling. It's awesome seeing you so independent and doing something you enjoy. Spending quality time with you, without your mobile and um… other distractions, has been wonderful." I pause. "I felt free and… unrepressed."

"Other distractions? Like Dad, you mean? Yeah, it's been good for you to get away from him. You've chilled. Bea said he's a millstone around your neck and your marriage is a car crash waiting to happen. I didn't understand what she meant at the time, but I think I do now," she replies flippantly.

My curiosity is piqued. "Really?"

"Do you really love Dad – or just the life he provides, Mum? Dad's always been like he is. Evie and I laugh it off and get on with stuff in spite of him, but you're the one who married him, and you must have known…" She stops mid-sentence. "Dad's here."

"Did Bea say anything else?" I probe.

"Yeah. She said something really weird – that something small's created complicated things, but that I shouldn't worry because chaos is good and leads to order and opportunity."

"When was this?"

"Dunno. Not that long ago. I think she called it the Butterfly Effect. She was super-drunk at the time – flapping her arms about like wings and laughing a lot. Come on, Dad's waiting."

Bewildered, I follow her to the car and Geoff drives us home.

11.00 a.m.

"Have you been cleaning the outside of the house while I was away?" I shout across to Geoff, who is jet-washing his car. I point to an array of items strewn across the garage floor.

"Eh?" He follows my gaze.

"Well done, you!" I applaud. "Using baby wipes is an interesting idea."

"I cleaned *all* the windows and ledges. Even though I've been feeling a bit off – since last weekend, actually," replies Geoff smugly.

Ah, that explains why he was so tired that Saturday night and avoided sex.

"Shall I put this lot away in the garage? Where's the bucket, Geoff?"

"No, it's okay. You carry on," he replies. "I'd better feel alright tomorrow for the big piss-up conference. Hope the drugs Jay gave me do the trick."

"Golfing Jay? You let a friend give you…? What pills? Do you think that's wise?" I caution.

"They won't kill me. Hopefully, they'll sort me out. Save your lectures on drug-taking for the children, please," he replies. "I don't need it, Amy. I've got to leave at lunchtime, and it's a bloody long drive to Norwich. Do you think I could use that bag you took away with you? Could you get it for me, now?"

I take my bag upstairs, unpack and tidy our bedroom. As I make the bed, I notice a packet of amoxicillin antibiotics on Geoff's side. Three have been taken. I shake my head in disbelief at his behaviour as I put them back where I found them.

Week Four. Adriano's Restaurant. Friday, 9.30 p.m.

"So, pet, when we were last here, we helped you decide how to be reckless and spontaneous. What did you do?"

I panic. What should I say? I plump to tell a half-truth. "I can happily report that I was totally reckless and spontaneous as was requested and can provide evidence if necessary," I lie.

Bea raises her eyebrows. "Was it worthwhile?" she probes.

"I think I enjoyed it as much as you enjoyed the Haunted House challenge," I smile sarcastically.

"*I know*," she mouths across to me.

"*You know what?*" I mouth back.

"What you *did*." Bea winks.

"And what *was that*, exactly?" I flash a silky smile.

"What are you two up to?" interrupts Cate.

"Nothing," I giggle. "Just having a bit of fun across the table."

Is Bea having me on? She knows Him. He might have told her. Would he? Perhaps he told Jason too? For the rest of the evening, we trade knowing glances and I feel ever so slightly anxious.

11.00 p.m.

Bea grabs my arm and slurs into my ear. "Back to mine, pet."

There's no escape.

Midnight.

I don't care any more. I trust Bea. She knows Him. She definitely thinks that Geoff is a bit of an arse. She will advise me. She hands me a mug of hot chocolate.

"Amy?"

"Yes?" I wait expectantly. My stomach tightens.

"I'm late, pet."

"What?"

"I'm as regular as clockwork."

"Okay?"

"I have a test here."

"Take the test, Bea."

"You won't go, will you, Ames?"

"How late are you?"

"Late enough."

"Take the test, Bea."

"Now?"

I take her hand. "You need to know."

"It's Dave's, from the Haunted House challenge."

"Really?"

"Absobloodylutely."

She shrugs her shoulders and goes to the bathroom.

She returns smiling.

"So?"

"This is a sign, pet. I haven't been able to get pregnant since she died, and then this happens in my fortieth year. I decluttered my life, removed the stress and… voilà! Who'd have thought that an idea you had a year ago would lead to such unlikely consequences. Ah yes – it's that Butterfly Effect." She waves two pregnancy indicator sticks in the air. "I'm keeping this baby. I have finally been blessed with the opportunity to be a mum again, and I'm accepting the challenge."

"What about Dave?" I ask.

"I'll talk to him," sighs Bea. "I'm not giving this baby up, though – Dave or no Dave." She grins and pats her stomach.

"Bea, we'll all be there for you – you know that, don't you? It's a big decision, mind, and you have to be absolutely sure," I say, embracing her.

"I know, pet. And now I'm off to bed. Sleep tight."

Saturday, 7.00 a.m.

"Amy? I know what happened that night, you know. You snogged Jason's brother."

There, it is out. I concentrate on picking a speck of dirt off my jeans.

"Jase told me, Ames."

The doorbell rings. It's my taxi. "Bea? I need to ask you something."

"It was a challenge. Nothing more, pet."

"It's not about the challenge. It's about Geoff and me and something you said last night."

The doorbell rings again. "Go on, pet. The taxi's waiting." She pushes me out of the door. "Take a leap of faith and trust your instincts, Amy. You don't go out to find love, it finds *you*. Think about it."

She goes inside quickly and slams the front door shut behind her.

I arrive home to have Pippa and Evie dragging me excitedly into the kitchen.

"Mum, you have a new challenge!" giggles Evie, thrusting a challenge slip into my hand and dancing around the kitchen. I have to:

WEAR THE WRONG TROUSERS FOR FOUR OR FIVE HOURS.

"Is it about *Wallace and Gromit's The Wrong Trousers?*" she asks.

"Perhaps. We should watch it and see if that helps," I suggest. "Now, get yourselves upstairs and throw me down your dirty school clothes, please. You both know the rule that if a wash isn't on by three, there'll be no clean uniform – and right now, the washing machine is empty."

Piles of clothes fly over the bannister.

"There's mine!" calls out Evie.

"Thank you," I laugh, picking the items up one by one. I notice something that isn't hers. "Evie? This sweatshirt belongs to Zac in your class. You must have been wearing his clothes all week. I can't believe we didn't notice. I'd better text his mum."

"Were you wearing boy clothes, then?" jeers Pippa. "If you did, then you were a *boy*."

"No, it's a sweatshirt that belongs to a boy. I didn't turn into a boy just because I was wearing his clothes," retaliates Evie, her face reddening.

"*Girls!*" I yell.

They fall silent. "I know what my challenge is!" I cry with delight. "It's nothing to do with *Wallace and Gromit*, but it is to do with wearing trousers. I am to wear men's trousers and convince everyone that I am a man."

"You're going to need to wear man clothes," giggles Evie.

"And get a man smell," adds Pippa.

"I think I'm going to need more than just clothes and BO to turn me into a bona fide bloke," I sniff. "What are you doing?"

Pippa's tapping furiously on the family iPad. "This blog has tips on how to disguise yourself as a man."

We sit on the floor and she reads it out to us. I notice the time. "Come on, we've got an hour or so. Let's go to the charity shop and see what we can dig up."

6.00 p.m.

I am officially kitted out with a great set of 'man clothes', including hat, polo-necked jumper to hide my lack of Adam's apple, baggy jeans and trainers. Pippa helps me to bind my boobs with bandages from the first aid box. She critically assesses me. "There's one thing missing," she says candidly. "A *you-know-what.*"

"What's one of them?" I ask, preoccupied with appraising myself in the bedroom mirror.

"A willy."

Our eyes meet.

I take four pairs of socks from Geoff's drawer, fashion them into the right sort of shape and stuff the socks into where I think the appropriate place is for them to be. They move about a bit when I walk, so I wrap them in a couple of pairs of my knickers. "There," I say, jiggling about. "That feels okay. Might as well be well-endowed. Where's Dad? He's gotta see this."

"He's playing golf with his friend Jay. He'll be back tomorrow. He said you knew about it," remarks Pippa.

"I don't remember him telling me that at all – but never mind. Now, where's that bucket with all the stuff in he used for cleaning recently? They'd make convincing plumber's props."

I go to dig them out from the garage, but I can't find them. I make a mental note to ask Geoff tomorrow where he stored them.

8.00 p.m.

My male persona is taking shape nicely. Evie has suggested I call myself Shaun (as in *Wallace and Gromit*'s *Shaun the Sheep*), and I've decided to be a plumber. I don't know anything about plumbing, but I reckon I can blag it.

I know that to really pull this off, I need to act blokeishly. I spend a happy half an hour practising some key man-isms: crotch-scratching and making inappropriate crass noises such as slurping and spitting and snorting. I can't get the belching quite right, though.

I ring Claire and ask her to rate my prowess in man-isms by spitting, slurping, snorting and swearing at her down the line. "It'll be a doddle," I say convincingly. "All blokes talk about is sport, gaming, sex and drinking. They don't go for deep conversation. I'll just grunt a lot and sup my pint," I giggle.

"Just as long as you don't forget you're in role and request a glass of wine, Amy, or you're be rumbled good and proper. Goodness – you sound dead realistic. In fact, you're making me feel ill. You'll fit in brilliantly at a footie match," she chortles. "There's one on tomorrow. I'll ask Bob to take you."

Excellent.

Sunday morning.
Ten minutes into the match and I'm totally out of my comfort zone.

"Alright, mate? Bloody cold today." Some guy on my right has acknowledged me as a man. That makes me feel so much better. If anyone guesses...

"Freezing my bollocks off," I grunt in reply.

Bob nudges me gently. "Nice one, Shaun," he whispers. "One nil to you."

At half time, I'm desperate for a wee. "Bob," I whisper, "I need a... um... piss. I'm going to have to use the men's, aren't I? Please come with me. I don't know what to, erm, expect." I stifle a giggle.

Bob guffaws loudly. "Okay, Shaun, let's go." He pulls open the door to the men's toilets. I take a deep breath to calm myself and retch at the stench.

"Bloody hell!" I choke. "It's worse than when I went camping with school to France years ago, and I thought *that* was bad enough."

"Keep in role, Shaun," laughs Bob.

My heart is pounding in my ears. What if I'm discovered? I could get arrested for this. What if I see someone I know? What if I see someone I know's *willy*?

Breathing through my mouth, I attempt to swagger into the toilets. I give my surroundings a quick once-over. Three men are at the urinals, and all have their backs to me – good! I slip into a cubicle and hover as I wee, trying to ignore the strange grunting coming from next door. *What about hand-washing?* I wonder. *Is it the done thing?* Nobody is by the sinks, and there's no soap. *Gonna have to be blokeishly unhygienic then, unless...*

"Bob, wash your hands – so I can, please?" I mutter. "I can't bear to leave without doing so, even if there's no soap."

"Oh, Shaun," he sighs. "Come on, then."

We make to leave. I am so busy trying to catch sight of just one willy for posterity that I smack straight into somebody.

"Watch where you're going, pal."

I turn to see who it was. It looked just like *Him*.

"Bob, get me out of here – quick!" I squeak.

"You look pale," grins Bob when we are back in the stands. "You're doing great. Another pint?"

"Not bloody likely – another pint will mean another *piss*," I shudder, pointing towards the gents (and possibly another meeting with Him). "I'll wait, thanks."

A problem with post-match bloke etiquette is that I am supposed to drink beer – and pints of the stuff – at speed. Bob takes great delight in seeing me struggle to keep up with him and his mates. Before long, the bar is propping me up as I concentrate intently on the lad-banter and behaving in a blokey way.

"Stop sipping your pint," whispers Bob.

Ah yes... no sipping. Forgot.

6.30p.m.

Cue the bawdy sing-song. I'm feeling warm from the beer,

relaxed and happy, and I can feel my blokeish persona slipping. By pint number four, it's all a bit of a blur. I swear I can see Geoff chatting to somebody who looks remarkably like Josie Jamieson.

7.00p.m.

I am very blokeishly sick in a flower bed outside the pub.

Monday.

I awake to a bloke-sized hangover, my vibrating mobile reverberating in my ear. I squint at my texts and gasp. I've been sent an image... WHAT? It's of *Him* giving me a fireman's lift. You can't see my face, but there's no mistaking it's me. My arms are dangling behind him, and *he* is grinning from ear to ear. And, oh my Lord! Geoff is there, glowering in the background... and I'm sure that's Josie Jamieson standing next to Geoff. I didn't know they knew each other?

I flop back against the pillows, feeling totally wretched. The accompanying message makes me feel suicidal:

> Amaaazing challenge.
> You are some (wo)man.
> Bob took this as a momento.
> You crazy drunk.

What the hell must He and everyone else think of me now? Me! A bawdy drunk dressed as a bloke with a massive dick. And in front of Josie Jamieson, too. It's going to be all round school today... all round everywhere by tonight, and I'm going to be the laughing stock of the neighbourhood.

At least you can plead that it was a challenge, says my inner voice. That's true. I can't remember anything, and Bob was looking after me, so I wouldn't have done anything untoward. Would I? I pray that I didn't come out with something inappropriate or vomit over Him. I'd better say sorry and explain.

I remember my SMART objective. I can't make contact with Him until the end of November. For the first time ever, I don't actually want to reach out to him. I feel so ashamed. In fact, I don't know if I can ever speak to him again. I stare at the pathetic image of me in his arms. Why isn't Geoff carrying me? I examine the image of Geoff. He looks so angry. What was he doing there, anyway? I see Josie. I think back to what Pippa said – that our marriage is a car crash waiting to happen.

A note left on the pillow informs me that Geoff will see me on Friday. A tightness grips my insides. I've been so stupid. Where did it all go wrong? It wasn't meant to be like this. I sense that the safe, secure world that I've worked so hard to construct is collapsing around me, and I sob into my pillow, feeling a total idiot and wishing that things were different.

9.30 p.m.

The only person I've felt able to speak to about the whole sorry event is Cate.

"Amy, today's tittle-tattle is tomorrow's chip paper. Let Mrs Jamieson gossip. It was a challenge that went slightly wrong, that's all. Bob was totally irresponsible allowing you to get drunk like that. He knows your 'three glasses of wine and you're out' quota," she sympathises. I burst into tears.

"Hey, you're working yourself up into a state for no good reason. So, some kind stranger is carrying you," she soothes. I daren't tell her that he's a bit more than a stranger. "You're not snogging him, are you?" she continues as I find myself retching, still sick from this morning. "And why shouldn't Josie know Geoff? Perhaps Bob introduced them. He used to be a school governor at Daisy Hill. You're in public, aren't you? In fact, Amy, I'd be more upset that it's not your husband who's looking after you. I'd challenge him on that."

"So, what should I do?" I hiccup.

"Geoff's away, isn't he? I'd leave it a few days and then, once the dust has settled and you're feeling calm, talk to him, Amy. Indulge him. Take time out to reconnect, and I'm sure he'll come round."

I end the call, vowing to do as she suggests.

Thursday.

A package arrives, addressed to me. I rip it open, and Geoff's socks and my knickers tumble out. A Post-it note attached to one of the socks reads:

You left these awesome undies. Can't wait to help you de-code this one, ha ha.
Give me a bell x

I am so shocked that I get straight on the phone to Claire. *"He's* seen my knickers," I blurt out.

"What?"

"Does Bob know *Him?* They were in the same pub when I was being Shaun, and he has not only given me a fireman's lift, but he has seen and *touched* my granny greys."

"You've lost me there. Hang on." I hear her and Bob conversing.

"Bob says that the guy found you puking outside the pub and came to your rescue," she reports back to me. "They didn't speak, but he was very caring towards you, and Bob thought he knew you well. Does that help? Gotta go. God bless."

As I stare into the opened package at the remains of my 'package', a warm glow spreads through me. *He looked after me. He cared about me.*

It should have been your husband caring for you, though, goads my inner critic. *This is all wrong, Amy, and you should put it right.*

"I know," I say aloud. "I need to talk to Geoff – and I will – but what about Him? I need to explain to Him too – but I can't." I stare doggedly at my SMART objective and repeat it three times under my breath to ensure I stick to it.

5.00 p.m.
I want to text Him. I go for a run.

6.00 p.m.
I want to text Him. I lock my mobile in my car.
  Damn.

Week Five. Saturday morning.
Evie and I have been searching for an elusive Halloween bat costume (age 11) for two hours solid, and I'm gagging for a caffeine fix and a sit-down. My new 'pleather' boots are pinching. We make it to Bromley's top-floor café, dump our bags at a free table and take five, waiting for Pippa to join us. Evie unfolds my challenge slip. It reads:

GO AGAINST THE FLOW.

"What does that mean? It's *your* challenge," she asks.
  "I think it's about doing the opposite of what you'd usually do. Not conforming," I explain. I have a flashback to my words many months ago: *No, to conformity!* I crane my neck to try to catch a glimpse of Pippa on the escalator. "Your sister's late," I say. And then I have THE idea.
  "You see that escalator. People are coming up the up one and going down the down one, aren't they?"
  "Yes."
  "So, if I went up the *down* escalator or down the up, I would be going against the flow," I say triumphantly.
  Evie's eyes widen. "Do it, Mum. See how quickly you can."
  Fire burns in my belly. "Why not?" I giggle. "If I do it now, my challenge will be done."
  Amyyyy. This is a Bad Thing. What if you get caught? chastises my sensible inner voice.
  Oh, go on – no one will notice, impels my inner devil.

"I'm going to run down the up," I announce. "I'll start at the top of the store and fly down the four floors to the basement in one go. Come on."

I leave Evie in the basement ready to record the event on my mobile. "When you see me, press that button," I giggle. "Okay?"

I hare down the up to the fourth floor... to the third... then the second. Shoppers are staring and pointing. I avoid their gaze, absolutely determined not to fail or fall – and it's bloody hard work.

"Mum?"

I glance sideways to see Pippa staring in astonishment and terror as I stumble past. Once in the basement, I cannot speak. "Need... water..." I pant. "Such... fun... though." A wave of dizziness overcomes me, and I close my eyes briefly.

"Mum?" hisses Evie urgently.

"What?"

"Excuse me, madam?"

I open one eye. Oh God, it's a security guard and she doesn't look impressed. In fact, she looks distinctly angry. Quick. Think. Options? I choose to faint.

Later that afternoon, when I overhear Pippa recounting the events of the afternoon in graphic detail to Geoff, including how I completely ruined her street cred, I take refuge in our bedroom. Two hours later, he finds me still there, lying outstretched our bed, trying out my latest stress-busting technique as suggested by Becca, my hairdresser.

He marches stormily into the room. "Amy, what are you up to?" he barks. "The kitchen floor could do with a mop, and we need to talk."

"P... ing... pa... n... P... ingu... Pint. Got you!" I snarl to my mobile.

"Amy." He comes over and hovers purposefully by my bedside. I tense.

"I'll mop it in a minute, Geoff. How was your week?"

"Why'd you do it?"

"Do what?"

"Run the wrong way up the escalator."

"Down, you mean. I ran down the up," I correct him.

"Oh, whatever," he replies crossly. "It was dangerous and bloody stupid."

"I didn't think I'd get caught," I reply cautiously.

The words I so vehemently uttered way back last October before my year slam back into my head.

… I must experiment and experience… I will challenge myself and get to know myself better. It's time to break out of my comfort zone and try out new things – stuff I secretly dream of doing but never believe I can or should. No to convention and conformity.

"My challenge was to go against the flow, so that's what I did. It was something I've always secretly wanted to do, and it was harmless fun. The store saw the funny side of it and let me off with a caution," I giggle nervously.

"Sod that. You could have done something more worthwhile," berates Geoff. He stares at me, steely-eyed. "You've changed. You're not the Amy I thought I knew. The woman I married would never have done anything so fucking stupid. She'd have been sensible and measured. She would have thought through the impact of her actions on me, I mean us – and that includes the children. Very few of your so-called challenges have been a justifiable use of your time, and Christ knows what you've learned of value. However, I've been learning a lot about you, and I don't like it." He pauses to read a text message.

"Are you referring to what happened in the pub?"

"Enough, Amy. I don't want to hear your excuses. I will wait for this godforsaken year to be over, and then we'll see how it goes," replies Geoff coolly, striding from the room. I hear feverish tapping on a mobile and the front door slam.

Where's he gone now? What has he learned about me? Has anything been said about Him and me and stuff? What did he mean, I should have thought up something a little more sensible? We'll see how it goes…? I need to talk to him, to explain…

I try him on his mobile, but it cuts to voicemail. I don't leave a message. He'll know I've called, and I'm sure he'll ring back once he's calmed down.

I go to try and locate the mop and bucket. The bucket is tucked away in one corner of the garage, neatly filled with a coil of rope, some garden twine, a packet of baby wipes, two tea towels and a half-filled bottle of baby oil. *Ah well, at least Geoff's been doing something to help out, and I should be grateful,* I think, emptying the contents out onto a shelf. *But God knows what he's been doing with this lot.*

9.00 p.m.
Geoff hasn't called me back, and he's still out somewhere. I casually surf the net, randomly clicking on 'marriage rescue' sites for guidance. One, in particular, catches my eye.

RELATIONSHIP TROUBLE?
Significant others going somewhere you don't want to?
Battling against them?
Stop! Change direction. Go against the flow.
Your partner will notice your efforts and respond more agreeably to your heart's desire. What have you to lose?

Very true, I think. *When I do something for Geoff that he values, like baking scones or going on one of his walks, he is automatically more appreciative and nicer to be around. So, let's find something special, something significant, that he'd love. Cate said to indulge him too, so that's what I shall do.*

I feel better already.

And then we'll go out for dinner and discuss everything over a bottle of wine like we used to, I smile. *Marriage Recovery Plan Phase One: Initiated.*

Sunday morning.

Geoff is engrossed on the family iPad.

"You came in very late last night – or was it this morning?" I say lightly, handing him a cup of coffee. "I wanted to talk to you. I've thought long and hard about what you said yesterday."

He does not acknowledge me. I plough on.

"There's nothing in the rules to say I can't do two different activities to achieve a challenge, so I have gone against the flow for the second time this week and booked us a short walking break in Croatia. We can talk and spend quality time together. We leave on Tuesday. I've cleared it with your boss and arranged childcare."

Geoff looks up. His eyes shine with pleasure.

Two hours later.

The history page randomly pops up on the family iPad while I'm reading up about Croatia. My eye is drawn to a list of *pornographic* websites. *Whoa!* We have our very own Porngate scandal. Who has been watching porn, and lots of it? There can only be two suspects: Geoff or Pippa. But which is it and why? I interrogate Pippa.

"It's not me. Have you spoken to Dad?"

"Not yet," I admit. "I'm worried what I might discover."

"It's no big deal, you know," she says unabashedly. "The boys at school watch porn all the time. I bet the stuff Dad's been looking at isn't half as bad as what they see."

"Great. That makes me feel better," I laugh. But inside, I remain ill at ease.

I accost Geoff.

He denies it.

I try to explain.

"Show me the history," he replies offhandedly. "I don't know what you mean".

The iPad is out of charge.

"It's ok – it'll wait," I remark casually.

Lunchtime.

I fire up the iPad. The history has been deleted. I charge to Pippa's bedroom and thrust it under her nose. "No history of porn. Did you delete it? My proof has gone."

"Mum, it definitely wasn't me," she whispers back savagely. "Hang on. Where's Dad's iPad? It's synched to the family one, so if you check the history on that and the Croatia website is there, you'll know it's him."

Brilliant!

I do as she says. Yes. The Croatia website is there, and the rest of the history mirrors the family iPad. Porngate is solved. I go to find Geoff, who is engrossed in the FT.

"Porn? Deleted history? You?" I say acerbically.

"It's not been unknown," he replies, his eyes fixed downwards.

"So was it you?" I am confused.

He stands up and massages his temples. "It has been known. God, I've got a headache," he mutters.

"Probably due to watching too much porn, darling," I reply pithily as I watch him pop two headache tablets.

I am about to give him a piece of my mind when I remember Croatia and my Marriage Recovery Plan Phase One. I take a deep breath and do what I would not normally do. I do not question him any further, nor do I rant and rave. I show no emotion. I go against the flow.

His mobile pings, and a notification catches my eye:

Mon-Key on hook.
Hang noose.

November

Week One. Friday, 7.00 p.m.

REDISCOVER THE LOVE OF YOUR LIFE.

This challenge is nothing to do with hobbies or interests. I think it's a coded message about guarding against the curse of Empty Nest Syndrome. I'm being asked to dissect my marriage and strengthen my relationship with Geoff, in preparation for a future of fun and frolics together (minus children) until death us do part.

Niggling thoughts that have been tinkling away in the background for months boom in my head, and my inner critic throws out question after question.

Where is our marriage heading? Have we neglected our relationship? Have our children enhanced it or are they the only bonding factor? Can we salvage our marriage?

Sighing heavily, I put my head in my hands and think. Whoever assigned me that last challenge could see something I couldn't. It was a subtle way of showing me how controlling Geoff really is. And Marriage Recovery Plan Phase One certainly didn't go as well as I hoped. In Croatia, he never once asked me what I wanted to do, and he refused point blank to talk about anything of significance at all.

It wasn't always like this, was it?

In the beginning, we were bonded together with superglue. I smile to myself. We did everything together. We went out all the time, and I loved being with him. I distinctly remember agreeing that if children came along, they would enhance our relationship but never define it, and we'd never become child-focused.

I think back to dinner parties where couples talked incessantly about their kids and Geoff sat in silence, a look of total boredom emblazoned across his face. I recall the jokey conversations between us afterwards, when he intimated that should I become one of those women, he'd divorce me. How we *laughed.*

I search out photos from the early days – holidays, outings, events. We are a team, smiling for the camera.

Really? Were you smiling with joy, Amy?

When babies came along, I remember feeling stupidly tired, frustrated and needing 'me' time – but however often I asked, there was plenty of 'we' time, but never 'me' time.

What was 'we' time? Did you go along with his plans and projects?

I shut my eyes tight. If I'm honest, I did.

Why?

Because that was the only way I felt I could have 'me' time. When I was with Geoff, I could shut off for a few minutes because the children were with *us.* And when he was at work or away, I developed coping mechanisms. He rarely ever did what *we* wanted to, and when he did, I felt guilty for making him participate when it was obvious he didn't enjoy it...

So?

We ended up doing more without him. Whenever he was around, I opted for the quiet life. I went along with whatever he wanted. I spent my life giving *him* purpose, motivation, direction, sex and outstanding puddings using wholemeal flour. In return, he rewarded me by being loving, undemanding and generous.

What does he give you in return now?

My brow furrows and I chew on my finger. We are four distinct individuals whose lives are intertwined. We live in the same house, but his life is far less connected to ours and essentially, he still does exactly what he wants when he wants, regardless of anyone else's needs and desires. I have allowed him to mould me into his minion, and now I feel repressed, unloved and unappreciated. I don't feel how I think a wife should feel.

My heart swells as I think about my children. I love my life and role as a mum, taxi service, coach, confidante, cook and mediator. I adore my friends and my life. My job is okay too. It's a rollercoaster ride – exhausting – and at times I despair. But when all is said and done, I wouldn't want it any other way except that... The words stick in my throat...

I do love Geoff, but I don't love our marriage. I have monogamy and permanence and status and freedom, and I don't have an 'efficient' relationship with my children, like I was forced to endure with my mother. I have what I have craved since I was a child. I thought everything was fine, but I now have evidence and clarity of thought that proves it is not fine any more.

Amy, crows my inner voice. *You've neglected your marriage intentionally and used your children as an excuse to withdraw from Geoff.*

I am honest with myself. I think that we have both neglected our marriage *unintentionally* over time. He's gradually lost touch with us and our lives. I have been all things to our children because he has rarely agreed or wanted to step up to the mark, and I have never challenged him. Nowadays, for the most part, we live parallel lives.

Is this how you want your marriage to be, Amy?

"No," I say firmly. "It is not."

And what about Him? Why are you drawn to Him? He is representative of a part of you that is missing in your marriage, isn't he? If you rediscovered the love of your life, would the fascination with Him disappear in a puff of smoke?

I stare out of my kitchen window, massaging my sore finger. *Right. I'm going to try again,* I think. *Marriage Recovery Plan Phase Two will be to successfully rediscover the love of my life. Then I will be rid of Him, and our marriage will be back on track. I will do it. It's just – how?*

Saturday, 10.00 p.m.
I meet The Girls at the pub. "Ideas on how to rediscover the love of my life, please. I'm working on improving my relationship with Geoff."

"Didn't you rediscover the *magic* in Croatia?" says Bea with a touch of irony.

I am economical with the truth. "We had a pleasant few days away, but I didn't come back feeling any different really, except for glad that we're back on an… um… even footing. I certainly didn't think we recaptured what we had back in the day, though, and that's my focus now."

"Revisit those significant places and do those things you did together in your first heady days of *lurve*," giggles Claire. "Five years ago, Bob took me back to the church where we married. It brought us so much closer. The memories might spark something."

"Good idea, Claire. Relive your first date, your first snog and your first shag, and see if that fixes your marriage, pet." Bea is stony-faced. "Pot calling the kettle black," she mutters under her breath.

Sunday afternoon.
It's all planned.

Geoff's Outlook calendar has been interrogated, and tomorrow afternoon and evening has been reserved for our date night. *I bet he'll have something to say about that, though,* I think. *He'll hate going out late on a week night, of course. Well, tough. I have to do this before Friday, so tomorrow it is. And anyway, if he cancels without good reason or complains me into the ground, then I'll know where I stand.*

I have looked up the walk we went on and the place where we had our first kiss. I have booked the cinema and our 'first date' restaurant. It's impossible to see the first film we ever watched together on the big screen, but never mind.

1.00 p.m.

I am summoned to the study. "What's this in my Outlook for tomorrow? Please don't do it again without asking. Tsk, Amy! You know it's a week night?"

"Well, yes. However, I thought that we might be spontaneous and spend some quality time together. We used to go to the pub quiz on Tuesday evenings, and Monday is as good a day as any."

"For a date night?" He eyes me quizzically.

"You can read then," I laugh.

"Don't be facetious, Amy. But why?" he continues. "I'd prefer a weekend. I'm supposed to be somewhere tomorrow evening."

Ah yes, I think, remembering the notification I saw on his mobile. "Can't somebody else get the key, Geoff?"

"Sorry?"

"I accidentally saw a message on your phone reminding you to collect a key on Monday. It said to hang loose. That's good advice. You should take it easy, considering you were on antibiotics recently."

A wry smile works its way across his face. "That's an idea," he says wickedly.

I pretend to be oblivious to his demeanour. "Great. It's good for one's wellbeing to be spontaneous. I learned that from a challenge," I smile. "And I promise you that by the end of it, you'll be totally chilled. So ask somebody else to fetch the key, and be here for three."

Monday, 2.30 p.m.

Date dress, make-up and hair ready.

3.00 p.m.
No Geoff. No text message. No voice mail. *Nothing.*

3.15 p.m.
I leave Geoff a voicemail.

3.30 p.m.
Geoff rushes in, dishevelled. I am underwhelmed.

3.45 p.m.
Feeling uneasy, I drive Geoff to the country park. He has not commented on my dress, hair or make-up, and he has made no effort with his appearance. He is wearing the same pair of chinos and shirt he has been in all day. The only difference is that he stinks of aftershave.

Trudging around the country park in the gloom of a November afternoon, I attempt to make conversation, but I can tell that he's not in the mood. What can I chat about? Talking about the family is off-limits today. "How was your day?" I ask, taking his hand.

His mobile rings. "Gotta take that, sorry." I listen into the conversation as we walk along. "I'm with Amy. No, mate – it's nothing special."

I feel my frustration mounting.

5.30 p.m.
Geoff takes my hand for all of five minutes in the cinema. I don't feel able to snog him. The feeling just isn't there.

7.30 p.m.
At dinner, we reminisce about our first date. We smile into each other's eyes as the waiter comments that we have ordered the same dish, and we share private jokes as we recall our first meal together, the one when we did exactly the same. This is

better. This is the man I fell in love with. At last, we're really getting on.

Ten minutes later.

Geoff takes my hand. "Put your knife and fork down a moment."

Ah, here we go. Romance alert! What is he going to say or do? The anticipation is exhilarating.

"I've been meaning to give you this for a while now, but it's never been the right time, Amy."

"Yes?" I say breathlessly. *Come on, come on,* I yell to myself, my heart almost jumping out of my body.

He pulls a piece of paper from inside his jacket pocket.

"Tickets?"

"Not quite," he replies, his voice trembling. "It's so exciting, Amy. Here." He passes a letter to me. I finish reading and drain my glass.

"Are you serious? Australia?" I say incredulously.

"Isn't it great? Top-up?" He reaches for the bottle, smiling broadly.

"But *why*?" I demand, my anger rising.

"Because it's a once-in-a-lifetime opportunity, and it'll be good for us all. I have done this for us, for our family. I think it's for the best."

I stare at him in complete disbelief. "You went and did this behind my back, without a word?"

"I thought it would be a brilliant surprise. It's what I really want to do, and I thought you'd be delighted for us. We've relocated before, haven't we? When the children were small."

"But that was *then* and this is *now*," I reply heatedly. "Things have changed, and back then…"

"Back then *what*?" he interjects. "You've never complained about moving away before. Once you get your head round the idea, you'll be raring to go. This time we'll be able to afford a house with a pool. We'll have sunshine instead of this bloody endless drizzle, and you won't have to work for a while, either. Just imagine it, Amy. I've got until the end of December to decide, but it's a no-brainer."

"But I won't have my life – *this* life," I whisper.

"You'll have *me*," he smiles.

No, I won't. You will be busy cultivating your career and social life, and I will end up doing everything else. I will be back where I started at the beginning of this year, I think. I will have to start again, make new friends, deal with all the issues surrounding our children. I will lose my friends, my support network and my job. I will remain repressed; back as the dutiful wife and mother. I will be put firmly back in my box, which I think is where you want me to be.

"Being with you – just you and the children – is not enough right now," I say calmly.

I take a long look around the restaurant, the place where *we* began and the place where *we* just possibly might end. I take a deep breath and look at him with determination. "I don't want to go, and I don't want to talk about it – not even to the children. Come on, we're leaving." I march purposefully out of the restaurant, leaving him sitting at the table.

11.00 p.m.
We are not on speaking terms.

Week Two. Friday, 4.00 p.m.

"I was supposed to rediscover the love of my life – my husband. However, what I actually discovered is that everything I hold dear – the loves of my life – are about to be whipped away by the so-called love of my life without consultation or discussion, Cate. I have learned *so* much, I don't know where to begin. It was such a significant area for us to explore. We could have ironed out the kinks in our relationship. I went all out to try and bring us closer," I sigh.

"Your date didn't quite go as expected, then?"

I shake my head, lost for words, as I recall what happened. It's thrown me into inner turmoil, and I swing between the desire to engineer his near-death experience and a plan to beg HR to tell him they made a mistake and the whole thing's off. I spend all my free time daydreaming about how to make *it* go away.

"So?"

"He could change his mind, the job might be pulled or something might happen to make sure we stay, perhaps?" I reply flippantly. "I just don't understand why he did such a selfish, self-centred thing? There must be a reason behind it? I thought he was happy in his work? I thought he loved his life?"

"Oh, Amy," replies Cate sadly. "What will you do?"

"Nothing for now," I state resolutely. "I'm trying to erase the whole conversation from my mind until the end of December, when my year of challenges will be over. I'm under the impression that he has until the start of January to decide. I can't go near him right now without him somehow trying to bring up the damn conversation, though. He's desperate for me to give him the decision he wants."

Manipulator, control freak, selfish bastard.

"What's he asking?"

"Oh, stuff like: 'why don't you like Australia?' or: 'tell me the things you dislike about your life here', or even: 'don't you want to let us all have a good life that we will enjoy?' He's even taken to leaving specific websites up for me to read – you know, to appeal to my better nature – ones that describe the country and the benefits of living there, blah blah blah."

"Why do you think he's doing that?" she probes.

"He's busy working on trying to change my mind, and it's doing my head in. He's trying to manipulate me and make me feel guilty for saying that I don't want to go. He thinks I spoke in haste because I was shocked, and I'm sure he's of the opinion that I will come round in a day or so, 'cos that's what usually happens," I shrug. "But this time, what he's doing is only serving to strengthen my resolve. I simply don't understand where this sudden desire to emigrate came from."

I drain my coffee cup.

"And he's chained to his mobile. Forever receiving and sending texts."

"Really? What do they say?"

"I don't know. Anyway, I'm not going to be emotionally blackmailed, and I won't give my final decision about our move abroad until the end of the year."

"What about *his* decision? He's accepted the job, hasn't he?"

"As far as I know, he has. That was *his* decision – not *our* decision," I spit. "God knows what else he hasn't told me. I wouldn't be surprised if the one-way flight tickets are sitting in his wallet right now, and if he's informed the schools and arranged our house sale. To think that he's been merrily planning and scheming and making decisions that affect not only our lives but our children's lives. He has completely ignored our needs, and he's disrespected me *big time*," I rant, tearing my napkin into shreds. "Has marriage removed my voice and right of choice? I will decide whether I go or not, and I will base my decision on the right reasons. *God*, I need another coffee."

"My shout," replies Cate, getting up and going to the counter.

"Let's change the subject, I say on her return. "We have better things to worry about. What do you make of *this* challenge?

DO SOMETHING WORTHWHILE FOR A CHARITABLE CAUSE:

RAISE AT LEAST £500, FEED FIFTY-ONE OR MORE GUESTS AND PROVIDE LIVE ENTERTAINMENT. (Over 3 weeks).

"Three challenges? That's demanding."

"Nah. After yesterday's revelations, nothing is too tough. The end of the year is nigh, so let's go out on a high. This challenge is the perfect excuse to channel my energies into something positive. I'm going to throw a big bash, Cate. In three weeks' time we're gonna party like its 1999 and I'll bag another three challenges," I chuckle.

Cate hugs me.

"Oh, Ames, thank God for your sense of humour. You know we'll all help you as much as we can – not just with this event, but with everything. You know what I mean."

"Thanks. I'm going to need all the help I can get," I reply, my eyes shining with tears.

Yep, I'm gonna need all the help in the world to get through the next few months, I think sadly as I drive home in total silence.

* * *

"I think we should tell her. We can't wait much longer. She deserves to know."

"Why, Cate? Do we really need to hurt her?"

"Are you out of your mind, Claire? We can't sit by, knowing about this. We could help diffuse the shock, help her make decisions, support her, you know – deal with the fallout. Geoff's been a right nob."

"We know that, Bea. You said that what goes on at Mrs Mon-Key's stays at Mrs Mon-Key's. If we said anything, we'd be breaking the rules."

"Who gives a shit about rules, Claire? Amy's our friend. What he's gone and done is unforgivable. One way or the other, it's gonna destroy her – and what about the children? What he's gone and done is beyond belief. Fucking dick."

"He's being so blasé about it all. It's only a matter of time before it gets out. Does he think he can cover it up? I mean, it's quite a plan he's put together, but if we don't act…"

"Cate! What are you saying! She's married, with obligations!

She was doing so well, refocusing on her relationship. The Lord told me they could come through this…"

"Pffft, Claire. I respect your religious beliefs about death do us part and all that other nonsense, and if Amy decides to stick with that bell-end, that's her business. However, it's our duty to tell her… Anyway, what about *his* obligations?"

"Sorry, Claire. I agree with Bea there. Amy has to know the truth before it's too late. The question is how and when."

Sunday, 10.30 p.m.

"Bedtime?" enquires Geoff, hovering by the lounge door. "I don't think we concluded date night with the first-night bonk. Let's recreate it tonight."

"Soon," I reply, my eyes glued to the TV screen. "This is interesting." I cannot look at him without feeling raw pain.

"I always find that sex is a good stress-buster. We've not had a shag for ages now," he flirts. "I'm sure I can make you like me again."

The thought of him coming anywhere near me is sickening.

"We've not had date night since the evening you so kindly informed me that I was moving abroad," I say. "And you never want sex on a Sunday, so why tonight? Sorry," I smile sweetly. "I'm just not in the mood."

"I'm away on a training course until Friday now," he huffs.

"I know," I reply, in as cool a voice as I can muster. I don't want a conversation right now.

His eyes bore into me. "Right. I am going to bed. Come on." He switches the TV off.

"Sorry?" I reply sharply. "I know that it's your bedtime, but *I'm* not ready to go up yet. Please don't make me feel guilty for not going to bed when you want to." I switch the TV back on. The atmosphere is choking me. I want to light the touch-paper, but now is not the right time. As far as I am concerned, this conversation has run its course for now. "See you Friday. Sleep well," I say, turning away.

I listen hard and only relax when I can clearly hear his footsteps climbing the stairs. I flop on the settee, my stomach somersaulting with a mixture of alarm, guilt and anger.

I'd run away if I could.

Monday evening.

Over Pinot Grigio and nibbles at home, I unveil my plan for this challenge to The Girls and my children. "This year has involved so many fantastic people," I enthuse. "I'm ashamed to say that I haven't kept in touch with a lot of them, and so I've decided to invite my significant *others* to a megatastic party."

"Cool," says Claire. "Can you remember everybody you've encountered and their contact details?"

My wonderful year of non-conformity flashes before my eyes. I can't help it – tears spontaneously course down my cheeks. The thought of actually being able to see everybody again is overwhelming, and my heart is pulled apart with joy.

One hour later, we're agreed on the charitable causes (the Alzheimer's Society and Grandma's care home) and that the theme will be the seventies and eighties.

"Auctions of promises raise quite a bit," suggests Bea. "I won a naked male cleaner once. I paid twenty pounds for him, but he never *followed through*. It was most disappointing."

"You mean he never *turned up*," I say, rolling my eyes. "*My kids are in the room*," I whisper fiercely.

Bea laughs loudly. "Oh, pet. There was definitely no turning *up*, ha ha."

"Moving swiftly on," I sigh, "anyone up for a *retro sweet sale*?"

"May I sell the sweets, Mum?" requests Pippa.

"Of course. You and your sister must be there," I smile.

By nine o'clock, we are done.

Week Three. Friday evening.

The only way to describe my life right now is frenetic. My mobile never stops ringing. To-do lists occupy my every waking hour, and rainbow-coloured sticky labels plaster the study walls. It's probably a good thing, as this way I don't have time to think about Geoff and all the crap. On the outside, it looks like we're the perfect family. Geoff and I are such good actors. Scratch beneath the surface, however…

I call a planning meeting. "Okay," I start. "We've filled ten tables and need at least one more."

"Invited your sister?" asks Claire.

"Not yet. I better *had* invite Jess, though. Actually, I bet she'll get on really well with the Mon-Keys. Geoff can do penance. I'll sit him between Jess and Josie Jamieson on Mrs Mon-Key's table," I reply scathingly.

"What about Weird Dan, Dave, Jason and his brother?" adds Bea. "Shouldn't they be invited? They've played a significant part in your year of self-discovery and adventure."

"You can't leave them out," smirks Claire.

"I haven't seen Dave for a while. He's in a bit of a state over the baby, but we are talking, and if I were to see him in a social setting, it might smooth the waters," says Bea.

It might smooth the waters… Yes. It might smooth the waters enough so that I can talk to Him sociably and sensibly. It is getting close to the end of the year, and seeing him at an event would be a good icebreaker, I think.

"Okay. Go ahead and invite them."

Thursday afternoon.

Fourteen tables are dressed for a retro charity gala event. Glitter balls and decorations shimmer. The retro memorabilia table is set, and lava lamps add glamour and atmosphere. Pippa is busy pinning signs to the wall advertising the retro sweets stall, while Evie pours flying saucers, blackjacks, fruit salads and chocolate mice into large plastic containers. The raffle prizes are labelled. I feel immensely proud as I cast my eye over the wonderful hampers that Pippa has conjured up. First prize is a food and drink hamper, second is a pamper hamper, and third is a large teddy bear.

Week Four. Friday, 8.00 p.m.

The raffle and retro sweet stall are doing a roaring trade, and there's lots of laughter as people survey the memorabilia table. The Girls are doing a great job as my co-hosts, topping up empty glasses and putting everyone at their ease. I can tell that it's going to be a good night.

"Glad to see your husband's well-occupied, Margot Leadbetter," observes Claire wryly.

"Glad you know who I am," I enunciate in an upper-class voice.

"So what *is* the craic with Geoff?"

"I decided that as I don't want him to have any opportunity to discuss you-know-what, the best policy is to keep him busy all night. And it's working." We look over to where Geoff, dressed as Mr T from *The A-Team*, is doing a sterling job as Chief Photographer. I smile as he takes snaps of Grandma's care home staff and various friends emulating Abba. *Oh, Grandma. I wish you were here,* I smile to myself. *You would have been in your element.*

"Time for dinner, Amy," whispers Aidan in my ear. "Where's Geoff sitting? He's not on your table?"

"No – Table 4, sandwiched between Josie Jamieson and Jess. I hope they keep him out of my hair." *And that's an understatement,* I think grimly.

8.15 p.m.

Everyone is seated and commenting on the menu: 'Porn' (Melon) Cocktail, Coq au Vin or vegetable stew, and 'Fallen' Angel Delight – all in memory of the Sex Chat Operator challenge.

I drink in the atmosphere. The level of chatter is deafening and reassuring. I quietly congratulate myself on how I handled meeting Him again. I replay the moment of introduction in my mind. *Yep, I gave good eye contact. I was friendly. I didn't kiss him, and he didn't try and kiss me.*

The 'how-should-we-say-hello' issue had been secretly troubling me. Shaking hands was so much more formal and detached, and I didn't feel anything, well, lustful. Perhaps I have finally fallen out of lust and can sign off my SMART objective.

I hear Aidan introducing me on the mike. It's time to make my speech. *Can I do this without becoming emotional?* I wonder. It won't be a good look if I blub now. *There will be absolutely no crying until after eleven*, I tell myself firmly. I take a deep breath and begin, my voice cracking with emotion.

"We connected through this crazy Year of Adventure and Self-Discovery, and every one of you here tonight is special to me. I want to thank you for helping me to learn and grow." There is a smattering of applause. "I am thankful that this challenge has reunited us in celebration and friendship and united us in a common cause – to achieve November's challenge. Now, before we eat and party, I'll announce the winner of the Best Outfit competition. The prize is a highly desirable bottle of Blue Nun."

9.30 p.m.

It's live entertainment time. Oh, my Lord. I am going to do something completely out of my comfort zone; something mad. And in front of Him.

"Ready, Ames?"

"You've forgotten your rapperesque dollar chain, Ewan." I place a handmade silver foil super-sized dollar sign necklace around his neck. "Now we are ready," I chuckle. "Do you think it'll work?" I chew on my finger, jiggling around on the spot in nervous anticipation.

"It's gonna be the best, Amy. Come on, it's *showtime!*" Ewan and his mates run onto the stage to huge applause. Ewan takes the mike. "Hey, everyone. We helped Amy with her moshing challenge back in January, and we've agreed to help her again tonight. Amy's put this together, and she's dead nervous – so please give her a big clap."

The opening bars of *Dirty Cash, The Adventures of Stevie V* start up on loop and the lights dim. The air is heavy with anticipation, the bass is pumping and people are clapping.

"Here," Ewan hands me a bucket. "Sing, and collect that cash."

> *"Give up your cash, that's all that we ask for,*
> *As much as you can, you know the score.*
> *Help Amy with her challenge, please,*
> *We're begging you on bended knees.*
> *Empty your pockets,*
> *Your purses and wallets,*
> *Dosh, Wonga, Loot, Green,*
> *Give it up for Amy's dream."*

We sing in unison as I sashay around the room, cajoling my guests into throwing their loose change into my bucket.

10.30 p.m.
The disco is rocking, and I'm on a high as I introduce Pippa and Evie to my friends.

"*Amazing* routine, Amy," slurs Weird Dan, giving me an impromptu hug. "My article's finished. Fancy meeting up some time to check it over before I try to publish?"

"I'd love that," I reply warmly.

"Eh up, Jase!" shouts Dan over the music as he wanders past. "Won yourself that bird yet, mate?"

"You know each other?" I ask.

"We were at school together," replies Dan.

Memories of that meeting in Pizza Pizza, when Jason

admitted using me to try and hook up with one of my friends, remain graphic. "Who is it then, Jason?" I ask.

"You'll find out soon enough." His Tommy Cooper Fez falls to the floor.

"I want to know now!" I laugh, retrieving it for him. "Cool hat."

"Fezes are awesome. My ambition is to play the word Fez as many times as I can on Wordie. D'you play Wordie, Amy?"

His voice startles me. *Act normally*, I admonish myself. *He's in your ex-box.* I stare once more into his cornflower-blue eyes and feel myself weakening. Nothing has changed since the day I first met Him. Even dressed as the Six Million Dollar Man, he is having an effect on me. "Never," I lie, "and you? Nice outfit by the way. Most appropriate," I titter.

"It's most fun when you're hammered," he snickers, swigging his beer. "What's your username, then? I'll give you a run for your money."

"Amyr21," butts in Claire.

"Hey," I hiss.

"Oh, why not? Especially after what your bastard husband said about moving abroad," she mutters fiercely, her hand tugging at a chain around her neck.

"Glad you agree with me for once – about my husband, I mean," I laugh. "Where is he?"

Oh no, I think, as I catch sight of Geoff cavorting to the Human League's *Love Action* in a threesome with Jess and Mrs Mon-Key. It's all a bit too full on for my liking.

"Claire? Do me a favour and go and tell those three to stop that ridiculous display of lust action to *Love Action*? It looks like they're filming a porn movie. Still, at least they kept him occupied. I must thank them later."

December

Lord, do not be far from me, I mutter under my breath. *You are my strength. Come quickly to help me. I am breaking the rules, but...*

The pub door swings violently open, making me jump, and I find myself nervously finger-combing my fringe in preparation for what is to come.

"Clarabell. To what do I owe this pleasure? I trust this won't take too long. Places to go and people to see."

I squirm under his gaze but keep my voice neutral. "Why don't you sit down, Geoffrey?" He pulls up a chair opposite me and smiles.

"Well?"

"I know about your Saturday nights," I say quietly.

"What do you know about my Saturday nights, exactly Claire?"

I sip my coffee. "This is really hard for me. I've gone behind everybody's back to meet you and talk about this, because I care. I've prayed daily for you and Amy and your marriage, and I really thought that things were improving until I heard about all this. Did you really think you would be able to keep your latest game secret? I didn't want to believe Bea when she first told me, and Amy had convinced me that you were working on your family problems, but..." My voice trails off.

"Busybody *Bea's* been spreading gossip, has she?"

"It's not *gossip*, though, is it?" I gulp.

"Explain yourself, Clarabell." The smile is replaced with a condescending sneer, and I flinch at the steely note in his voice.

"I don't understand why you *keep* doing it?" I state calmly. "And this time, well, it's deplorable. 'Marriage should be honoured by all and the marriage bed kept pure, for God will judge the adulterer and all the sexually immoral.' Please do the right thing before it's too late."

"And what do you suggest I do?"

"Well, you could go to counselling or the church for support and guidance, perhaps?"

"How thoughtful of you," he replies coolly. "I'd rather you didn't tell me what you *think* I might like to do. I know exactly what needs to be done, and I'm not the one who needs *help*."

"Sorry?"

"It's my *wife* who needs help, and I am sorting her out. Did she put you up to this?"

"What?" I'm taken aback. "I'm here of my own free will. I'm your greatest ally, and I've always been there for you, haven't I? I came to terms with why you married Amy instead of me a long time ago, but that doesn't mean that I don't still love you. Who else would have helped you to cover up your past *indiscretions*? Without me, your life would be in tatters."

"I've always been grateful to you for that, and I appreciate your discretion in helping me keep Amy blissfully unaware of our relationship and specific aspects of my private life. Don't I reward you for your efforts?" He points to my red leather tote and the fine gold chain around my neck. I finger the chain lovingly.

"You do, I'm sorry. I've spent all year listening to her bleating on about it all, and I've acted like the perfect friend. I think I've persuaded her that what she's going through is perfectly normal for someone of her age and that she'll pull through. The last thing I want is for you two to split up, because I know how much you need her – and you are so special to me. I'm determined she doesn't do anything silly. What about you and me?" My voice cracks. "What more can I do?"

He chuckles and leans forward, unflinching. "Don't go giving me those puppy dog eyes. We will leave very soon. It's taken longer than I anticipated, but she's coming round to the idea now. A fresh start is what she needs – without *unnecessary* distractions."

"You think that by moving her abroad you're going to solve everything?" I croak. "You're deluded if that's your game. Running away won't help this time. The reason why you're emigrating is nothing to do with Amy and her wellbeing. It's all about *you*." My eyes harden. "Listen to me. Where are you going to go the next time and the time after that? I don't know what I can do to mitigate the scandal that's going to hit the streets very soon, but Australia is not the answer. It sounds like a great plan, but it won't work. Please don't go. I need you in my life – and what about Adam Anthony? See sense, and let me help you and Amy while there's still time. We'll work something out, like we've always done."

In desperation, I try to take his hand, but he shrugs it off. "What *about* my nephew?" he says scornfully, getting up from the table. "I'll still be able to keep in touch with him through Jess, and Amy will remain none the wiser."

"But what if…" Geoff grabs my hands and tugs them sharply, his voice hardly audible.

"Pull yourself together, woman. I appreciate your concern, but there is no need for this. If you really want to help Amy and my children, I suggest you focus your energies on supporting us through our relocation. I am doing this with the best of intentions, you know, and in part, it is to do with Amy and her, erm, *wellbeing* – as you so tactfully describe it." He smiles and puts on his jacket. "However, our future plans are of no concern to you or your cronies, and if you'll excuse me, I have to leave."

"For some $Jx2=OH!$?" I reply sadly. His eyes flash menacingly, making me suddenly afraid.

"Tut tut, Clarabell. That behaviour won't do you any favours with me; you know that. I'll be in touch."

Saturday, 6.30 p.m.

"Are we eating tonight?" harrumphs Geoff from behind his e-reader.

"Why don't you make tea tonight for a change?" I reply offhandedly, tapping away on my mobile. My last challenge was to become a Microsoft Office Wizard, and I'm pretending to practise my skills when really I'm playing Wordie.

"You do the shopping. You know what there is," he replies.

"Go and have a look and see? That's what I do," I say, tapping away. "It'd be nice to switch it up a bit at the weekend. I'd love a night off from meal planning and cooking." Inside I feel quite sick and take a large gulp of my Pinot Grigio as I wait for his response.

Geoff goes on the attack. "Do you realise how long you've been on that app? One hour," he replies curtly. "Totally unproductive time that could have been spent making our evening meal, using that gym subscription I gave you for your birthday to rid yourself of that flab you're still lugging around, or discussing our relocation that you appear to be avoiding. What's the next strategy you're going to employ to avoid everyday life, darling?" He tries to snatch my mobile out of my hand. It falls to the floor. He picks it up and slips it into his back pocket.

"I'd like my phone back, please?" I ask politely.

"When you've agreed to stop using that app as your current *avoidance strategy*, Amy. I think that you've been living in *suspended reality* for too long, resulting in a psychological disorder. Others convinced me that your *bad behaviour* is down to the menopause, but I think differently now. The good news is that your *problem* is treatable and you will be sane again. You just need to see your GP to get the ball rolling. In six months' time, when you're having treatment and we're living our new life, you'll thank me for sticking by you." His mobile vibrates.

"I'd like *my* phone back, please?" I repeat slowly, my anger mounting.

"Not yet. I want you to realise that I'm no longer prepared to carry on making allowances for your behaviour and attitude towards me. Do you agree that you've been avoiding things?"

"Yes," I reply truthfully. Inside, I am livid.

"Well done."

Geoff pats me on the head and offers a sympathetic smile. "That's step one in curing you. Girls," he smiles broadly. "Your mother has acknowledged that she is ill. She's on the mend."

He stands over my chair. It's overbearing. "Now, Amy, will you agree to discuss our relocation later this week?"

"Yes," I lie.

"Great. Then you may have your mobile back." He places it on the side.

I down my glass of wine, willing him to go.

"Drinking too much is an avoidance strategy."

I close my eyes.

"That's another."

"What is?"

"Closing your eyes to block me out. See what I mean? I'm going out in an hour or so and need to eat." A flicker of amusement passes across his face. "Actually, I'll get my fill elsewhere."

"What's wrong with staying in, Dad?" asks Pippa. "You're out every Saturday night. Where do you go?"

"Somewhere I feel happy and with people who appreciate me and my worth," he replies, stomping out of the lounge.

I stare after him, glowering in defiance but saying nothing… yet.

9.00 p.m.

"You okay, Ames?"

"It's Saturday night, I'm fine and on the wine now that *Geoff's* out." I let out a brittle laugh. "Claire?"

"Sorry. Got distracted. Hey, it's the first week of December. A couple more challenges and then what? I won't be sad when it's over, you know. Your exploits have become a huge part of our lives, but I'm not sure if it's been a… *constructive* process? In some respects, it's been developmental, yet going about it the way you have has come at a cost." Claire sounds odd, distant, uptight. There's another silence.

"Let's just say it's not turning out as I imagined," I say. "I don't know how I'll feel when I reach the end, Claire. It's a bit surreal. Nothing will ever be the same again. Are you there? Claire?"

"So, what's in store for you this time, Amy?"

I read from the slip of paper. It says:

RETREAT RETREAT.

"You're *not* emigrating?" she gasps.

"*No.* I'm not changing my mind and going along with Geoff without good reason," I reply sharply. "Something that happened earlier this evening has confirmed my interpretation of this challenge. I am going to withdraw, unplug and take a digital detox."

My gut tells me that this challenge isn't about doing anything wacky. It's a golden opportunity for self-reflection. I never get the chance to sit and think for any decent length of time, and given my current situation and the fact that the end of the year is coming, I am ready for it.

"I can see why you want to do that, and I think it's worthwhile – but what about Pippa and Evie?"

"Geoff can cook and clean and deal with everything," I reply coldly. *Let's see how long it takes for him to resort to avoidance strategies,* I think. "Will you keep an eye on things while I'm gone?"

"Um, I don't think I can, Amy."

"Why?"

"Ames… listen. I have to go. Have a great time and make some good decisions – some rational decisions. I'll pray for you. Bye."

What was that all about? I wonder as I hang up. *She was acting very strangely.*

Sunday, 4.00 p.m.
I'm almost ready to go. Living like a hermit, I'll only require the basic necessities. Renouncing technology and fripperies sounds great, and I'm sure I'll return relaxed and reinvigorated. With this in mind, I packed the following:

- *Onesie.*
- *Toiletries.*
- *Underwear and a change of clothes.*
- *Food and drink.*
- *Money.*

An hour later I repack, adding:

- *Mascara.* (I feel it's wrong to leave it behind.)
- *Perfume.* (For use as an air freshener if the house smells musty.)
- *A toilet roll.* (I'm not taking any chances.)
- *Bathroom cleaner and cloths.* (I abhor a dirty bathroom.)

10.30 p.m.
I've found my very own desert island in the Lake District. Someone who rents a house on an island in one of the many local

lakes has agreed to loan it to me. I just have to work out how to get to the house from the mainland. There's no transportation, you see.

My daughters and I sit together in the study, drinking steaming mugs of hot chocolate, discussing my dilemma.

"Go in this – a *swan* pedalo. You'd look like a bird on the lake. No one would see you. You'd be invisible." Evie shows me images of graceful swan pedalos at the Olympic Park in London. "They are big and stable and you pedal them like a bike..." she reads.

"Well done, Evie. Dilemma solved," I giggle.

There is an aggressive bang on the door from Geoff. "Shouldn't we be in bed? You all know the rule."

"Boring predictable fun-sucking millstone," mutters Pippa as we file past him.

"That is all the more reason for us to move away," he comments loudly so that she can hear. "She needs new friends to teach her some *respect*."

I inform Geoff that I am abandoning the family and returning on Thursday evening.

"Why are you doing this?" he asks.

"It'll be good for me," I rationalise. "It will help me to... erm... think things through."

His face lights up.

"What a *fantastic* idea. I'm delighted that you're finally seeing sense. You go away to think. Make some notes and we'll discuss everything when you get back. I'll work from home this week. I'm sure I can swing it," he gushes, rubbing his hands with glee. "Once you've had time alone, without *that lot*, I know you'll see the benefits and appreciate that it's a move I must make. Here, take this bundle of websites and articles that I've printed off for you to read." He pulls a bulging plastic wallet from under the bed. "I've had this ready for you for ages. HR said that it will help you to feel more comfortable with the idea of going and answer all those irksome questions you probably have," he smiles.

"What do you mean, once I've had time *to think without that lot*?" I ask.

"Well, you know. Without *influence* from those *friends* of yours," he states.

"Oh, yes. Right," I say. *Keep quiet. Do not inflame the situation – just take the wallet and thank him.*

"Thanks. It's very, um, thoughtful."

"Don't say I don't look after my wife. I only have our best interests at heart. Inside are important documents about visas and my draft Contract of Employment. If you could cast your eye over them before you get back and sign the documents, I can crack on before the Christmas break begins proper."

Yep, he still thinks I am going to go…

I can't believe how brazen he is. Why would I even *want* to look at his Contract of Employment and information on visas, let alone sign forms right now? I haven't said I want to go. And he doesn't get the meaning of this challenge at all.

I take the wallet from him and say nothing further, apart from making my excuses to leave the room so that I can go and tell Evie and Pippa of my imminent departure. As I turn away, I catch sight of his reflection in the window. A smile creeps across his face and he punches the air in triumph. "Mwahahahaa! Houston, we have lift-off!" I hear him crow. I see him send a hurried text.

I add a bottle of wine and corkscrew to my bag – for medicinal purposes.

On the island. Monday, 6pm.

I am here to meditate and ruminate on life and my future. I will sit and *be* and live each day by the rise and fall of the sun and the moon. Installed on the sofa in my onesie, I reach for my novel and turn to page one.

8.15 p.m.

It is impossible to sit quietly. I'm not used to it. My novel remains unread. My mind keeps wandering. I pace around the house, exploring and tidying up.

9.00 p.m.

I try to open my novel to page one.

9.10 p.m.

I pour myself a glass of wine and open my novel to page one.

9.12 p.m.

My mobile pings. The urge to take a sneaky peek at the notification is too great. *He* has played his move on Wordie. *Just one turn*, I plead to my inner critic.

You are supposed to be getting away from screens, Him and your husband and thinking through your predicaments in peace.

That's true, I say, *but this will relax me, and I promise that I will stop after one go.*

I forget the time. Despite the fact that my eyes are heavy with the need to sleep, by midnight I am still thoroughly enjoying myself, engaged as I am in a thrilling battle of words with *Him*. It's only when the battery dies that I stop. Putting my mobile on charge, I climb wearily into bed, swearing that I will not play tomorrow.

Tuesday, midday.

I am in crisis. A Wordie addict.

Every time I make an attempt to pick up my novel, watch TV or think about Geoff and important stuff about my future, I have an all-consuming craving to play Wordie against Him. I can't bring myself to stop.

Amy Richards – switch it off.

I open my novel to page one, but the words bounce around

the page. My mind is too active. I can't stop thinking about Him and longing to stay connected to Him through Wordie all day.

Flicking aimlessly through TV channels, I unintentionally drink the entire bottle of wine. It's for medicinal purposes, and this is one time where I need drugs.

5.00 p.m.
I hunt out another bottle of wine from the kitchen cupboards. One more glass should do the trick…

9.30 p.m.
Absolutely hammered, I can no longer be bothered to fight against the allure of Him and the app. We play avidly for hours. The competition is fierce. He keeps making me laugh with quirky texts.

"I shall not text nor telephone you though, although I think you'd like me to," I slur to myself. "Tomorrow, mobile of mine, you shall be in my bag and I shall be released from your baaad influence."

Hey,
Jason and your mate Becca
are getting hitched.
Fancy being Chief Bridesmaid
to the Best Man?

"*No?*" I exclaim, flabbergasted, to my mobile. And without thinking of the consequences, dial His number.

"Hello, it's me."

"Yes, I know it's you, I can tell."

"Is it true?" I slur drunkenly. "Is she engaged to him?"

"Amy, you're pissed."

"Yesh, yesh. I have had a leetle wine for medicinal purposes only. How did this all come about?"

I hear peals of laughter down the line. "I knew that would be a sure-fire way to get you to call me."

I grin, flattered by his cheekiness. "You are so bad! What do you mean?" I simper.

"Well, you were a bit reserved at your charity do, and so I wasn't sure if you'd had second thoughts about us. And what was all that about in the café when you asked me to tell you something about myself that you could dislike? I've wanted to get you alone for ages, but it's never been the right time."

My heart is thumping so hard that I could scream. My head is crammed full of things I want to say. The impulse to confess to the inner conflict that has been consuming me for months is gut-wrenchingly powerful. I want to blame him for leading me into temptation and beg him for release from my torment so that I may return to *normal*, the way I was before that fateful February day at the doctors. In drink, however, I am desperate to disclose that the very thought of him exerts potent physical and psychological influence over me, and I want him to come clean, stop the flirting and admit that he feels the same way about me. "I need to tell you someshing," I slur. "It's important, *very* important, about you and me."

"What, Amy? You're not bailing on me, are you? I've told everyone now. Fuck knows what your friends and family must think about you and me hooking up, 'cos I'm getting shitloads of grief off my mates. They think you're a bored wife who's getting her kicks by grooming me."

"Sorry? What have you been saying about us and to whom?"

In a puff of smoke, my heart is no longer pounding with lust but with fear and disgust.

"Nothing, really."

"Well, you must have said something?" I reply tersely. "You just said that everyone thinks I'm grooming you. Have you told them about when you and I... you know?"

"Fuck, Amy. It's only banter. Chill out, and I'll speak to you when you're sober."

"Right. I was going to tell you something really personal, but I'm not now," I grump.

"It's not every day that a bloke my age gets involved with someone like you. I don't know that many middle-aged women with a husband and family who are spending a year escaping everyday life and running around having mad adventures, do you? I told them because it's good craic and because when they see us together discussing your challenges, I don't want them to think we're an item."

It is when I hear those words that I instinctively know that it is time. Fear of damage to my reputation, of being mocked for being a cougar and of losing everything that I thought I wanted in life is the motivation I have been searching for.

I hang up on him, delete him from my list of contacts, switch off my mobile and fling it into the bottom of my bag.

Wednesday, 9.00 p.m.
I wake feeling calm. The rest of the day slips gently by. I read my novel in bed and watch wall-to-wall TV. I do not fidget. I do not channel-hop. I am still and able to reflect and focus objectively on everything I have learned from the past year and look ahead to the future.

Thursday, 11.59 p.m.
Back home, I wait for everyone to retire for the night before I go through my weekly ritual of unseen challenge selection for the last time. I want to do this alone. This is the final time I will feel trepidation, nervous anticipation and delight or despair as I take in what's in store for me. My eyes fill with tears as I scoop out the one remaining slip of paper from the Bowl of Chance and Opportunity and hold it to my chest.

Let this, the last, be a good one.

DO THE THING YOU FEAR MOST, AND THE DEATH OF FEAR IS CERTAIN.

I chew on my finger. I chew and chomp and gnaw because I know what this challenge is telling me to do. It's what I dread the most… It's cursed me all my life. It's to be true to myself. "Amy Richards," I whisper aloud. "My nemesis… I will overcome… I will not let it define me any longer. It's time to be completely honest with myself and Geoff. It's time to stop list-making and lying and procrastinating. I have to let Geoff know how I *truly* feel."

Week Three. Friday.

When Geoff comes home from work, I'm making papier mâché in the garage. "Whatever your views about my year of challenges, will you take part in my Closing Ceremony?" I ask him. "Here's my torch." I wave my masterpiece triumphantly.

"I was there at the start, and I will be there at the end," he replies.

"Thanks." I look at him levelly. "I know you've found it tough at times, as have we all, but I strongly believe that it has been an important journey for both of us, and if I don't capitalise on what I have learned over the year, it will all have been for nothing. You must understand that?"

Geoff stands there silently.

"What's the point if on January the first I allow my life to go back to what it was, Geoff? I don't want things to be as they were."

"So what are you saying, Amy?" His eyes spark with displeasure.

"I'm saying that I want to be honest and upfront, stop hiding what I really think and feel because you won't like it, stop forcing myself to do things I really don't want to do and stop saying I'm okay when I'm not, just to please you. I just want to become the person I really am."

"If you're trying to tell me you've become bi-curious, then that's fine. I'm sure Mel and Chris know some good lesbo clubs where we're going – ha!"

"No, I didn't mean that," I sigh, struggling for the right words. "This is serious. You want me to stop avoiding issues, and so I'm trying to be true to myself and tell you what's going on in my head. It's taken this long for me to realise that this year has a clear-cut theme. It's been about giving myself space to analyse the web of my life and my destiny – the web that I've spent the past fifty years crafting. It's only now that I think I'm finally ready to rip it apart and re-design it. I have felt repressed and I crave change, personal growth and happiness."

Geoff stares at me blankly. "But we are moving abroad so that you can do *just that*," he replies. "You'll have a fresh start in a *new* country, in a *new* house, with *new* friends and a *new* career! Amy, I don't understand what you're *getting* at here. I have tried to give you everything you have ever wanted, and I have *never* asked for much in return. And now you say that you feel... what was it? Repressed?"

"Yes!" I shout. "Repressed, frustrated, restrained, stifled, in a rut, a minion. I want to release my inner being and remove the millstone from around my neck."

Geoff looks thoughtful. "Happiness comes to *you,* not you to *it,* and nobody's life is great all the time. I don't understand why people think that they are *entitled* to do *whatever* in the personal pursuit of happiness at the expense of others. Your life's what you made it, Amy," he says calmly. "You can't replay it, so just lighten up, enjoy the ride and look on the bright side. You're lucky. I don't get why you're angry and dissatisfied when you have so *much* and others have so little. It's plain selfish. Think of the *consequences,* Amy. Think carefully before you decide to sacrifice everything we've worked for, harm our family, ruin our finances and damage our *reputation* – all because you've decided it's time to go bohemian and be *true to yourself.*" His tone has turned sarcastic. "Next you'll be telling me you're going to run off with a penniless toy boy, live in a yurt and go tee-total. You're living in fantasy land and need to see that GP. Urgently."

His mobile vibrates. As he pulls it from the back pocket of his jeans, a small pink envelope falls to the floor. He does not notice. "Ah," he mutters under his breath. "I've got to go out. Something's come up. We'll continue this later. But remember, Amy – your life is what you've made it."

"You're wrong," I shout after him. "Life's what I make it and…"

"Not now, Amy. Ring the GP."

The front door slams.

I slide onto the carpet and put my head in my hands. I wonder if he is right. What if I do what I think I should and it's the wrong thing? His words have reminded me of what Pete said about his wife when she left him. I'm not like she was, am I? Selfish? Escaping one life I don't like for another that might suit me better?

I don't want to put anyone at risk. I don't want to appear shallow. I'm not young any more. I know I have responsibilities. I *know* I made vows and decisions of my own free will; I know that the time for making random choices and decisions by swiping left or right without a care has passed and that I should be happy with my lot. Moving away *could* be a new beginning for us.

My inner critic severely reprimands me.

Stop avoiding the issue and playing into his hands. He's trying to push your buttons again. You've spent your entire life making calculated choices and decisions. They have served you well, but nothing remains constant, and your growing dissatisfaction is a clear indication that change is required. You have made many sacrifices, and you are wondering if they were all worth it. If you do not listen to your heart and the messages that this year has brought, then you will have willingly signed up to the fact that your future will always be your husband's future, with all that this brings.

"I don't want my future to be *his* future. I did once, I admit it. I was happy to live his life, but we have reached a new chapter. I want my future to be mine."

Then be true to yourself, Amy Richards. What's the worst that can happen?

I remember the pink envelope lying by the table leg. I pick it up to hand to Geoff later and notice that it is addressed to me. I recognise the handwriting as Cate's. The postmark is dated as two weeks ago. Why hasn't he given it to me?

I tear it open and a small photo falls out. It's quite dark and grainy, but I can just make out Geoff. He is standing, dressed only in his underpants, between two women. They are wearing masks that completely cover their faces and tight white crop tops emblazoned with the logo *'Jx2=OH!'*. I flip over the photo to see one word and a sad face.

Sorry :(

Wednesday, 7.00 p.m.

Geoff symbolically hands me my Closing Ceremony torch outside Daisy Hill Academy and beams proudly for the crowd. I take it from him, avoiding all eye contact, and turn my back to him, holding my torch aloft. There's a quick cheer of support as I link my arm in Bea's, ready for the off. The haunting melody *So Long, Old Friend* accompanies us as we walk the first half-mile to where Cate is waiting for us.

The torch is carried by my friends along the moonlit streets, past Adriano's and Tea and Tranquility to our cul-de-sac and into my kitchen – the place where it all began back in January. A mock-up Olympic cauldron, filled with red, yellow and orange tissue to resemble flames, sits on the kitchen table. Evie solemnly hands the torch to Pippa, who looks ashen. "This poem is for Mum," she says in a wobbly voice.

> *"Thought this year would be scary,*
> *You'd be on the sherry.*
> *We were so wary,*
> *At these challenges aplenty.*
> *Didn't know what they meanty* (ha ha).
>
> *Now the pot's almost empty.*
>
> *We'll miss all the drama,*
> *The weekly palaver.*
>
> *Hope you've found your karma.*
>
> *Learn, grow and go forth,*
> *Set your courth (like course,* she whispers).
>
> *Be brave, bold and true,*
> *Do what you have to do.*
> *Don't chuck what you've learned down the loo.*
> *Or drink life away on Pinot Grigiooo."*

She smiles as everyone claps and cheers. I nod to Geoff, who turns off the kitchen light. Evie switches on the tea lights in the cauldron. "The cauldron marking the passing of Mum's year is lit," she announces solemnly.

"Please raise your glasses," proclaims Geoff. "Amy Richards. Your year of Challenge and Adventure is almost over. I think you've enjoyed it, unlike some of us, ha! Perhaps now we can have peace and return to some sense of *normality*," he snorts, waggling his Pointy Finger at me.

I visualise wave after wave of lightning bolts firing deep into my soul, and I read the coded message behind his words. *What has become of you? Return to the fold. Resist the teachings of the Bowl of Chance and Opportunity. Do as I say, and all will be well.*

"So, what's *your* idea of normality?" I ask coldly.

"I get my wife back, there's an end to your immoral behaviour and indoctrination by this lot – and once we've moved, we'll be free from these nonsensical escapades," he replies.

There's a gasp from Claire, and my blood pressure spikes. The hypocrite! Who is he to preach to me when I've got evidence in my pocket that proves he's a liar and a cheat? All this talk about *morality* and *normality*.

"I find it amusing that you refer to my challenges as *escapades*," I reply. "It looks like you've been enjoying a few of your own this year." I fling the photo under his nose. "I'd like to know what's *normal* and *moral* about *that*? And seeing that you're such an expert on taking responsibility for one's *actions* and looking before one leaps, so to speak, I'd welcome an explanation of what's going *on?*"

Geoff bursts into peals of laughter. "That was a lads' night out prank. You surely don't believe that I would be so stupid as to jeopardise my reputation and sabotage my career prospects around *here,* do you? Surely this is not the time or place to discuss it, darling? Let's not spoil this special night. Raise your glasses to Amy having survived her fiftieth year. Cheers!"

As everyone toasts me, a multitude of thoughts go through my head. Have I jumped to the wrong conclusions? Why would Cate have done such a thing? Why did Geoff conceal the envelope from me?

Cate drags me into the hallway, where The Girls are waiting. "Amy, I'm so sorry. Somebody sent it to me, and I felt you needed to see it. We are your friends, and we don't want to see you hurt. We're truly sorry if Geoff is telling the truth. Claire said we shouldn't tell you and that it might do more damage." She begins to cry.

"*Calm down*, everyone," snaps Bea. "Amy, you know your

husband is partial to a bit of porn. It's no big deal, and it's not as if he was pictured shagging them. I'm proud of you for being true to yourself at last and standing up to him – although it might have been better to have picked a better moment, pet! Throw the picture away, but if I were you, I'd keep an eye on him."

"Why, Bea?"

"Do you love him, Amy?"

"I think so… I don't know…"

"The choice is yours, pet," she smiles. "You know the score. Be true to yourself, and when the time is right, you'll do what's right for you. Just do one thing for me." She leans forward and whispers into my ear. "Look on the Mon-Keys' website, and read up about the benefits of *Jx2=OH!*."

"What?"

"Just do it. And Amy…"

"Yes?"

"Do it soon."

* * *

"Is she fine, darling?" asks Mrs Mon-Key.

"Yes, thankfully," replies Bea. "This has got to stop, though."

"Yes, I suppose I should tighten security at our events even further," broods Mrs Mon-Key. "Social media is such a curse at times. If it got out that our clientèle were in danger of being named and shamed, it would ruin us."

"No! I meant that Amy's husband has to see sense and stop. He's always had a bit of a roving eye, and now he's playing with fire."

"Ah. But that is not *my* concern, Bea, darling. Geoff is a consenting adult, and it is not for us to judge what he does and why. We are there to provide a service and amusement for the community. I do feel for Amy – she's gorgeous – and I sincerely hope that everything works out for them. I draw comfort from the fact that *Jx2=OH!* have convinced him that he should go away to try and cure himself. Sad, though. I've become *very* fond of him since I recruited him at that blueberry-eating challenge. Now, it's late, and I must go. Busy night tomorrow. Toodle-oo – and try not to fret, Bea. I'm just glad one of her friends is aware, just in case, you know. It is best that they go."

Thursday, 8.00 p.m.
I log onto the Mon-Keys' website, as Bea instructed. The link to *Jx2=OH!* is in the Members Only area, and as I've not paid an annual subscription, I'm denied access. I try to recall who might be able to help me. Becca? She was at the Swinging challenge with me... Mr Steele? He was definitely there – he was with my sister. I'm sure she'd assist. I send Jess a text.

Week Four. Saturday 17th December, 2.00 p.m.

Week Four. Saturday 17th December, 2.00 p.m.
It's my official week off from challenges.

"Good thing, too," pants Geoff as we lug a six-foot Douglas Fir through the lounge and carefully position it in the corner of the room. "There," he declares, standing back to admire our efforts. "Right. You girls decorate the tree, and then Mum and I need to talk in peace. HR is pestering me for a start date, and I've promised that I'll have all the paperwork done and dusted by the time I go back. I do hope you used that *retreating* challenge of yours to digest everything I gave you? You haven't said anything, and there's a bunch of stuff to do." He turns to us, grinning. "We'll get Christmas over, and then it's *bye bye, Britain.*" He leaves the room oblivious to the storm clouds gathering.

"He's told me about Australia. You haven't said anything to him, have you, Mum?" scolds Pippa. "How can you wimp out and let him talk you round into doing exactly what he wants again? Hasn't this year taught you anything? Read your challenge diary. They were each chosen for a reason, Mum. Bea said they were 'catalysts for change'. She said she wanted to open your eyes – but they are still tightly *shut*."

"Please. It's Christmas, darling. Let's try to enjoy ourselves. I'm challenge-free, you're on holiday from school and Santa should be visiting very soon. We'd better make some mince pies for the reindeer," I smile.

"God, that's such a cop-out," she replies angrily. "Dad's right. Now you're using Christmas as an excuse to avoid stuff again. The longer you avoid issues, the more difficult it will be, Mum. It's obvious to *everyone* that being with Dad is making you unhappy. And you being unhappy is making *us* unhappy; so admit it to yourself, have the conversation with him, and let him go and emigrate. Loads of my friends' parents have split up and in the beginning, it's tough, but things improve – and from what I see, everyone's happier."

"Stop that right NOW!" I yell, slamming my fist into the sofa. "You and Dad are piling on the pressure, thinking you know it all and what's best for me. However, *neither* of you know what the hell you're talking about. You don't know what's best for me, *and* I'm not *avoiding anything*." I catch my breath and slump onto the carpet, emotionally exhausted. "I'm sorry. I just want us to enjoy Christmas. Nobody is going to control me," I beseech. "Please. Come and sit down, both of you, and take a choccy from the tin."

I pass the tin around.

"Listen," I say gently. "Way back in January – feels like light years ago now, doesn't it? – I never dreamed for one moment that I'd be in the situation I am in now. But that's what's happened. It's easy to be a bystander, advising and passing judgement based on what you see and hear. I can assure you both that my eyes are most definitely wide open now. Here, take another choccy. But I am the one who must live with the *consequences* of the decisions I make, so I will decide what to do without outside influence. Do you understand?"

Pippa nods.

"I honestly do respect what you both say and think and how you feel. However, on this one, you do not know the half of it. You *think* you know what I should do, but you are too young to understand the *complexities* of the situation. Let's try to have a fantastic Christmas – and promise me that you will stop trying to force my hand before I am ready. I swear that I have all our interests at heart, but this is a matter for me and your father. I'm sorry. That's how it is."

My daughters fly upstairs in floods of tears. I let them go, overwhelmed by intense sadness and guilt at what I am putting them through. I try to compose myself by looking out of the rain-streaked window pane at the place we call home and at the two carrion crows flying overhead. My eyes vacantly follow their flight path and I am filled with a sense of foreboding.

I absentmindedly reach for my mobile, my comfort blanket, to check for messages or Wordie app activity – anything to lift my mood, to relax me and to take my mind off things for a short while.

> Aymeee!
> I know you're avoiding me.
> Didn't mean to be an arse.
> I'll treat you to a mince pie.
> The 27th? Deal?

I burst out laughing at his cheek. When I deleted Him, I forgot to block him. The rush of emotion that floods through me spurs me into action. I can't quite believe just how glad I am to have him back in my life. We agree to meet at Bromley's department store.

Week Five. Boxing Day.

Jess phones.

"Happy Crimbo. Just a quickie. We're off skiing. Not that Adam Anthony wants to go. We're gagging to get on the slopes, but he's just not interested, and Stanley's going ballistic again. If I could leave him with you, I would. Fancy having your nephew for a few days? He loved it the last time. It was so lovely to see him bonding with his uncle."

"Did you get my text?" I ask, ignoring her request.

"I can't help, I'm afraid. I'm not a member of Mrs Mon-Key's establishment. Too bloody expensive for me."

"But have you been there? I'm sure my hairdresser Becca said she saw you when we went, as part of one of my challenges?" I lie.

"I have made a guest appearance once or twice, so it's possible she might have seen me. Why do you need to speak to a member? In my experience, most members prefer other methods of communication, ha ha."

"You can't help me, then?" I sigh, ignoring her crassness.

"Sorry, hon. A bientôt."

I refresh the Mon-Keys' website, willing it to provide me with inspiration. The *What's On* section has been updated with information on the many artists appearing over the coming year, accompanied by thumbnail images of the performers. I hungrily scan the list for *Jx2=OH!* – the act is on every Saturday night and has five-star reviews, but the accompanying blurb isn't helpful.

It is the thumbnail, however, that makes me blanch. *Oh, Mrs Mon-Key! What a breach of security!* I think as I stare at the image of my smiling husband spanking... I enlarge the image of the woman's buttock to be absolutely sure. That tattoo is of Daisy Hill Academy's coat of arms, and that could only belong to one person. Josie Jamieson. The Josie Jamieson who was in the pub with Geoff on the night I was dressed as a man. The Josie Jamieson, ex chair of governors, who was dancing provocatively with Geoff and Jess at my charity night.

I sit on my bed, feeling numb. Geoff's been frequenting Mrs

Mon-Key's club and doing rather more than her accounts. He's indulging in *God knows what* with J – Josie – and another J.

I pull out the photo that I have kept hidden under the mattress and examine it for clues. My body trembles with disgust as I recognise the delicate filigree bangle I bought from Dubrovnik for Jess's thirtieth birthday, adorning the wrist of the other half of *Jx2=OH!*...

Bloody hypocrites. All that talk about me, when they have all been cheating and lying. Golfing pal 'Jay' must be Josie Jamieson or Jess. One of them gave Geoff the antibiotics. Were they to treat an STI? And that photo wasn't Geoff at a work do at all. It was at Mrs Mon-Key's, wasn't it? So much for Jess's 'guest appearances'. Her job in the social care sector, 'spreading joy and happiness' is as one half of the sex act *Jx2=OH!*. Mrs Harmer was right all along. All that stuff about Blossom drop, betrayal and treachery has come true. God knows what other skeletons are hiding in the cupboard.

What's the number one thing you really do not want to do when you've just discovered that your husband is having an affair with not one, but two women, and that one of them is your sister? You *definitely* don't want to sleep with him in his bed.

I've always wondered how I'd be if I discovered something this terrible. On TV and in films, the aggrieved party often goes into some kind of psychological meltdown, rages or finds solace in a sharp implement.

I, however, am completely calm. No finger-chewing. No wine-drinking. No kitchen-pacing. Maybe I'm in shock? I don't know. I've never been in this position before. Perhaps it's because they have inadvertently given me the perfect excuse to leave my marriage with my reputation intact. Oh, the *irony*.

So, what next? I wonder if Pete felt similarly when he found out about his wife's cheating, and what he did first. I Skype him for advice.

"Without trust, you have nothing. You told me that yourself,

Pete, and until now, I had never distrusted my man. Jess, my so-called sister, used to joke about him playing away, but I have never had reason to doubt him on that count. In fact," I laugh, "he's the last person I could envisage *ever* having an affair. He's *uber*-concerned about what people think of him, his standing in the community and his *status,* and if he was having a fling, why would he be so excited about emigrating?

"Okay, he's sexist, crass and unthinking, not to mention controlling, selfish and self-centred. Plus he thinks he can fix me by convincing himself I need pills and medical intervention… He's never been deceitful though – until now."

Pete nods, his eyes unwavering. "For what it's worth, my advice is to *do* something, even if you decide to do nothing for a few days. Keep busy. When the time is right, you will know what to do – and I do believe that you will do the right thing, Amy baby. Do you have anything to take your mind off this?"

"Yes, this," I reply, waving my fifty-first challenge slip at the camera. It reads:

IN JANUARY, YOU EMBARKED ON A JOURNEY OF SELF-DISCOVERY.

YOUR AMBITION WAS TO EXPERIMENT, EXPERIENCE AND GROW.

50 CHALLENGES ON, IT IS TIME TO REFLECT AND COMPLETE YOUR FINAL CHALLENGE.

WHAT HAVE YOU LEARNED?

SHARE YOUR NEWLY ACQUIRED KNOWLEDGE AND WISDOM.

**REFLECT ON THE
WARMTH AND HAPPINESS
YOU HAVE FOUND AND
SPREAD AROUND.**

**AND MOURN THE PAST –
SHOULD YOU NEED TO.
MAKE THE DECISIONS
YOU NEED TO MAKE.**

**DON'T LET ALL THIS HAVE
BEEN FOR NOTHING.**

"So, crack on with that and sit tight, Amy baby. What's the worst that can happen?"

27ᵗʰ December, 8.00 a.m.
I know what I want to say, but I can't get it down on paper. Translating my notes and what's swilling around my head into something that people are going to find unputdownable is impossibly hard. Rejected attempts litter the floor, and I'm slowly becoming more frustrated. *At least I'm seeing Him today*, I sigh, as I scribble furiously, read back what I've written and rip it up for the umpteenth time. *Claire said I was smart enough to nail this on my own, but I don't think I can do it without help.*

Geoff marches into the kitchen. "You're up early, Amy? Most industrious." He peers over my shoulder at what I am doing. "Ah, the infamous fifty-first challenge. So, what tasty morsels have you got in store for us, Amy? I'm dying to read this blockbuster – especially the bits about *Him*."

I stiffen. Our eyes meet. Mine emit horror. His signal amusement and triumph.

"You think your friends really care about you, Amy? Only

one of your friends has your best interests at heart, and I am *really* grateful to her for the tip-offs. The others, well, they have used you as their source of entertainment. You've been something to spice up their mundane lives. They've been playing with you, don't you *see?* They don't care about you. They are caught up in the spirit of the game and busy betting on how it will end. Then they will dump you and move on to something more interesting. Such is the shallow nature of man." He admires his physique in the reflection of the oven. "Hey, I'm one *sexy* beast," he preens.

"I don't know what you've been told, but there is absolutely nothing going on and…"

"I'm okay with it, Amy. I'm a modern man. It's no big deal. This year of yours has been good after all. From frigid-fanny in January to come-and-get-it-cougar. Just hope you've kept it discreet. We don't want anything to jeopardise the good name of Brand Richards, do we? How about a spot of role-play tonight? Just thinking about it is making me horny." He leers at my chest.

"Who's been feeding you such garbage?" I whisper. "Whatever you think's going on between Him and me is a figment of your imagination. I can't believe that somebody has done such a vile thing and you've lapped it up. You're unhinged. It's you who needs help, not me."

I'm frozen to the spot. What does he know, exactly? Only Claire knows anything significant. I blink hard. She has always been close to Geoff. They've been friends since long before she introduced him to me, and I've never suspected anything untoward. Why would I? She's been double-crossing me all year, probably. They've had tons of opportunities to talk and trade information about me. And that red tote bag I helped Geoff to choose for his PA. That wasn't a present from Bob at all. It was a reward for grassing on me. Why would she do such a thing to one of her closest friends? I trusted her.

I have to be sure. "Was it Claire?" I ask, panic-stricken.

"Who knows?" he goads. "Shall we call her and find out?" He reaches for his mobile. "Ah, it's in the car. Shame. "

My mobile pings.

"Sexting with Luster-boy, eh?" smirks Geoff. "See you later for some hot lurving... 'gorgeous babe?'"

I let out a huge sigh of relief as I hear his car reversing out of the drive and look to see who has texted me. If it's from Claire, that bloody snake in the grass...

It's from Him.

I'm sooo sorry. I can't meet you today.

"*No!*" I shout at my phone. "Don't you turn on me too. You have no idea how infuriated I am with you. You make me smile. When I feel miserable, you lift my spirits. You are my anti-depressant, and I can't write without your help. I was so looking forward to seeing you again. I'll start to forget what I want to say if I leave it too long. You don't get away with it that easily," I mutter, blind with rage. "You're the one who has been encouraging me to get on with it all year."

I text back.

I have a rough first draft
but I have writer's block.
May I post you what I have?

Send me your manuscript
and I'll take a look.

He gives me his full address, including his postcode.

10.30 a.m.

The document is bulky. I have it weighed at the post office and am politely informed that it will cost a fortune to send, especially as I am insistent that it should be signed for. I can't afford for it to get lost.

> It's expensive to post,
> so I will drop it through your door shortly.
> Hope you don't mind!
> Happy reading! :)

As I pull up outside his house, my mood changes. Now that I'm staring at where he *actually lives*, I feel decidedly uncomfortable. I have goose bumps and am gripped by the desire to run. I don't want to be here. It doesn't feel right.

Amy Richards, just do it quickly.

My nerves are jangling as I stuff the bulging envelope through his letter box. "I don't know if it'll fit," I mutter. "It's got to go, there isn't any other way," I say to myself firmly as I push and wriggle and *squeeze* the envelope through the narrow gap.

I hear it plop onto the doormat, and I heave a sigh of relief.

Later that afternoon.
> Your delivery has arrived.
> I look forward to reading it.

The thought of Him reading my work turns my stomach. What if he thinks it's total crap?

9.00 p.m.

"Mum, I think these are yours? This one is about the blueberry challenge." Evie is holding a pile of papers.

"Here, let me see."

I go into slow mo as I realise that I have inadvertently forgotten to include six important chapters of my work. The version he has is incomplete. *How can I have done that? It's so unprofessional. What will he think? These chapters contain key material, and we can't have any kind of meaningful discussion without them.*

I am so mad at myself for my total lack of organisation that I fire off a text without thinking:

> Are you in or are you out?
> Can I drop round some of the
> manuscript that I forgot to
> include when I posted it to you?
> It is important that you have a
> complete version – it won't
> make any sense otherwise.

9.30 p.m.
He has not replied. I am frustrated.

10.00 p.m.
Nothing. I am climbing the walls.

10.30 p.m.
Sod it.

> Haven't heard from you.
> I am passing your house in
> around half an hour
> and will post the missing pages
> through your letter box.
> If you would like to open your door
> and say hello, that would be lovely,
> No pressure. Amy

> I've had friends round.
> I am drunk.

My house is a tip
and not in a fit state
to receive visitors.

I'm not bothered what
state your house is in.
I only want to give you these pages.
I am going to come round
and post them anyway.
It's up to you if you say hi
or not.

I'll meet you in my front garden.
You can give them to me there.

I casually tell Geoff that I am popping out to see a friend and will be back in about an hour. It's a pitch-black night, and as I drive through his village, I become disorientated. Angry courage spurs me on. I haven't got time to mess about looking for his place. I have to get this to him and get home. I call him on my hands-free. He answers on the second ring.

"Hi, it's me."

"I know."

"I'm turning into your road but I can't remember which is your house. Can you look out for me?"

It is only when I see him waiting for me in his front garden and park up that the purposeful, determined woman instantly dissolves into a nervous, gawky teenager. I get out of my car and walk over to where he's standing. Amazing! For once, his t-shirt isn't scruffy and jeans aren't grubby. He looks *presentable*.

"Hello," I say abruptly, taking an envelope from my bag and ripping it open. "Sorry for being so unorganised. Let me explain what's here and where it fits with everything else you have and then I'll go."

"Go on. Show me." He flashes me an unreadable look as he puts a bottle of vodka to his lips and takes a long drink.

Anxiety is replaced with eagerness and enthusiasm as I take out my papers. It begins to drizzle. Raindrops splash onto my work, smudging the print. "Hell. Trust it to rain now, I laugh easily. They're getting soggy. Do you have a table where I can lay these out?"

"Come in."

He leads me into his and Jason's clean yet untidy lounge. I note a copy of *How to Train Your Dragon* sitting on top of the TV. "That's how this all began," I smile, pointing at the book.

"Yeah," he chuckles, taking another swig.

I start to lay out my work on the table. He snatches up the first chapter, sits in an armchair and begins reading. I stand by the table watching him for his reaction to my writing. He laughs aloud. Wow! This is fascinating. He is laughing at my writing. Intrigued and flattered, I sit on the arm of his chair.

"Where are you up to?" I ask.

He ignores me and continues reading and laughing.

"Where are you up to?" I repeat.

His sporadic peals of laughter are infectious and I begin to laugh with him. I playfully lean across and punch him on his arm.

"Oh, this is unbearable," I giggle, leaning across him to get a better look at what is so riveting. "What's so funny?"

He steals a swift sidelong glance in my direction. I note it in my peripheral vision, but before I can do anything, he grabs me. In one fluid movement, I float from the arm of the chair into his arms and onto his lap.

His mouth finds mine, his tongue wraps itself around mine and he devours me with urgency, passion and need. I know I should resist and withdraw, yet I don't. I don't want to, for if I do, I will regret it forever. I want to let go, to turn my fantasies into reality and allow emotions that have been pent up for so long to be set wild and free.

He takes my manuscript from my hands and throws it aside. As it falls to the ground, I hear the papers scatter. "My papers," I whisper to him wickedly...

Cornflower-blue eyes smile deep into my soul. His mouth searches out mine again, his hands rhythmically stroking my hair, my face and my neck before raw lust overwhelms him and he grabs violently at my t-shirt, my bra straps, my bare skin, his mouth never leaving mine...

1.00 a.m.

Tiptoeing across the lounge, I catch a glimpse of my reflection in the mirror above the mantelpiece. I don't stop to look. I can already see what I need to see. I close the front door quietly behind me and I do not look back. I am emotionally freed.

Back in my car, I check my mobile for messages. Three missed calls, two voicemails and five texts – all from Bea. I call her back. "Where the hell have you been, pet? No, don't answer that. Just get yourself round to number nine, Worcester Drive, right now. What's your ETA?"

"About ten minutes. Why? That's..."

"Just put your foot down and get here as soon as you can. You can't miss her house. I'll meet you at the end of the road at number one."

Bea hangs up. *Why is she ordering me to drive to Josie Jamieson's house at this time of night?* I wonder as I set off.

Bea's right. It's impossible to miss Josie's mansion. It stands out like a flashing Belisha beacon. Her front garden is festooned with Christmas lights and packed with boozed-up revellers.

I park up outside number one as instructed and wait. A gnarled tree branch stabs me roughly in the small of my back and almost gives me a heart attack. I spin around to see where it's coming from, lose my balance and topple backwards into a box hedge.

"Over here, pet. Behind the hedge you are sitting in," hisses Bea, crouching behind a low stone wall.

"You've not gone into flipping labour, have you?" I ask, alarmed, brushing myself off.

"No," she laughs. "We need to be *quiet* and *quick*. What's the charge like on your phone?"

"It's almost fully charged. Why?"

"Turn it onto video recording mode, follow me and *prepare yourself*," Bea whispers. "And put this on."

She hands me a black glitter eye-mask, a pair of black satin elbow-length gloves and a black-and-white-striped convict-style hat.

"Why are we dressed as prisoners?" I ask. "You sure you should be walking about in those thigh-length stiletto boots? They *are* sexy, though."

Bea is unable to hide her exasperation. "It's a *cops* and *robbers* party. We need to avoid detection so take my hand and try to appear pissed – shouldn't be too difficult for *you*. Is your camera ready? Now, would you please *mute* yourself for a minute or so and come *on*."

"We're not going into her house, are we?" I splutter.

Bea takes the lead, and we sway unsteadily through the front door and down the hallway. We stop by the downstairs toilet. The floor is vibrating with the pulsating beat of rock music, the air is thick with cigarette smoke, and the smell of weed, puke and scented joss sticks takes me back to forgotten student parties. There are people everywhere, dancing, talking, slumped in corners and making out.

"We are going into this room. Keep quiet and calm and press record on your phone."

I hear the urgency in Bea's voice. "I will record it too, just in case."

She does not give me time to respond. She opens the door, pulls me inside and pushes me up against the wall beside her.

"Let your eyes adjust to the darkness and press record," she breathes.

And then I see. I see an audience and I see Geoff, Josie and Jess. Geoff is standing on a chair, his hands handcuffed behind his back. He is masked and stark naked, except for a pair of black-and-white-striped socks. A rope hanging from a meat hook in the ceiling is tied around his neck, and he is groaning in ecstasy as Josie and Jess whip him. The logo *Jx2=OH!* is stamped across their chests.

"Come on, then!" Josie shouts, taking a swig from a bottle of wine. "Last time for you to have a big fat Oh with your two J's before you leave us for the land of Oz, you bastard!"

Bea drives me back to her place. She says I will be too shocked to take the wheel, let alone go home alone, but I'm not. The events of this month, culminating in what I have experienced tonight, have brought me release and closure.

As we pass the familiar, the streets and shops and places I know so well, I sniff my arm and smile. It still smells of Him. *Thank you*, I think to myself, *for helping me to rediscover who I really am and who I want to be. Whether you ever read the draft of my writing or help me with it is unimportant. I don't know if I will ever see or talk to you again, but I can guarantee that Amy Parker will complete her fifty-first challenge.*

I reread my text conversation with him one last time. Then I delete it and him from my mobile. This time, I remember to block him. It's time to turn the tide and embrace the unfamiliar – a fresh start on my terms. Life courses through my veins as I consider the possibilities and opportunities. What I plan to do feels right. Very right.

"Well, pet?" sighs Bea, handing me a glass of Pinot Grigio and playing nervously with her hands. "I hope I did the right thing. When you asked us to choose your challenges, mine weren't thought up at random. They were my way of giving you good counsel. I've known about Geoff's demons for a long time, but if I'd confronted you with any of it, even three months ago, you wouldn't have listened. Despite the mounting evidence week on week, you've been hell-bent on brushing your anger, frustration and tears under the carpet and trying to fix things your way.

"Your challenges became a kind of light relief – a distraction from the underlying issues. I did try to reach you – dropping hints to you and Pippa."

"Like about the Butterfly Effect? I remember you talking about it the day after your fortieth, and Pippa mentioned it to me recently. I meant to look it up but I never did."

"I was concerned that you'd end up offloading everything in writing, producing some insignificant blog and seamlessly returning to the life you really wanted to ditch. Your Pippa's a smart kid. We worked together to try to get through to you."

"I heard everything you both said, yet I convinced myself that it was never the right time to go for it. I desperately tried to shield Pippa and Evie from everything. I've only ever wanted to do the right thing, Bea. I thought that Geoff loved me..."

"Yeah, pet," she says sardonically. "He loves you when you clean and cook and make his meals. He *adores* you when you go on his walks, and he *worships* you when you give him exactly want he wants without question. He can't love the new you because he doesn't understand, and he never will. What do you want to do?" she sighs. "You might not want to tell Claire anything yet; Bob and your husband being best mates and all that."

I give a half-laugh. "Claire? She's the last person I want to talk to right now."

"She'll mither you both to work at your marriage and seek spiritual guidance, but you can handle her. Your friendship might change, though, if Bob puts pressure on her not to see you."

I realise that Bea has no idea what Claire has done and decide to remain silent. She doesn't need to know the real reason why Claire and I can never be friends again. I rummage in my handbag for my mobile.

"Now, show me how to upload this video I took and post it on as many social media sites as we can – and give me the contact details of the solicitor you used for your divorce. Then, I need to transfer all the money in our online bank accounts into my savings account and pop home to remove some key documents from the files before the shit hits the fan."

My eyes sparkle. "Are you with me?"

Bea grins and hugs me hard. "Amy Richards. Have *you* come a long way. Mrs Harmer's predictions were bloody accurate. I found love, a baby's on the way – and as for you, you're wide awake."

"It's Amy *Parker* to you," I laugh. "Yeah. That story about the sick tomato plant was a reference to *Jx2=OH!*, and I'm finally getting rid of the Mr *Rhizoctonia solani* fungus – aka Mr Richards. I still don't get why the tarot reader thinks I have a son, though?" I keep quiet about the references she made to 'cancer' Claire and Him.

"Any regrets, pet? What will you do next?"

Thoughts of Claire, Geoff, Jess, my children, Him, my challenges and the past year flash before my eyes. "Bea," I smile, raising my glass. "My marriage is over, and our Girls' nights out at Adriano's are no more – but it's time for new beginnings, and the future is ours to make of what we will. You'll have to wait and see what Amy does next. I always thought that this week would mark the end of my journey, but it's only just begun. And d'you know what? *Je ne regrette absobloodylutely rien.* Come on, where's your laptop? I've a lot to do, and this video needs to go viral."